W9-BBP-497

Ethiopian Stories

Other titles in
The Northeastern Library of Black Literature
edited by Richard Yarborough

ETHIOPIAN STORIES

George S. Schuyler

*Compiled and Edited
with an Introduction by
Robert A. Hill*

SIENA COLLEGE LIBRARY

Northeastern University Press
Boston

Northeastern University Press

Copyright 1994 by Northeastern University Press and The Regents of the
University of California

All rights reserved. Except for the quotation of short passages for the purposes
of criticism and review, no part of this book may be reproduced in any form or
by any means, electronic or mechanical, including photocopying, recording, or
any information storage and retrieval system now known or to be invented,
without written permission of the publisher.

Library of Congress Cataloging-in-Publication Data

Schuyler, George Samuel, 1895–
    Ethiopian stories / by George S. Schuyler; compiled and edited by
Robert A. Hill.
        p. cm. — (The Northeastern library of Black literature)
    Includes bibliographical references.
    ISBN 1-55553-204-7 (cloth bound)
    1. Ethiopia—Fiction.   I. Hill, Robert A., 1943– .   II. Title.
III. Series.
PS3537.C76A6   1995
813'.52—dc20   94-34294
                                                              CIP

Composed in Meridien by Coghill Composition, Richmond, Virginia. Printed and
bound by The Maple Press, York, Pennsylvania. The paper is Sebago Antique, an
acid-free sheet.

MANUFACTURED IN THE UNITED STATES OF AMERICA
98 97 96 95 94   5 4 3 2 1

Contents

PS
3537
,C76
A6
1994

◇◇◇ George S. Schuyler

Born in Providence, R.I., 1895. Soon afterward my parents moved to Syracuse, New York, where I obtained my only formal education. My father was a chef and boasted that nobody in his family had been a slave in 150 years. My mother was also a cook and her grandmother, it was said, had been a Madagascar princess brought to New Jersey (Red Bank) and apprenticed to a Dutch farmer until she was 25 years old. She was never a slave in the legal sense of the word.

In 1912 I quit high school in Syracuse and joined the United States Army. From July 1912 to July 1915 and again from November 1915 to October 1917, I served as private and corporal in the 25th Infantry, stationed in Seattle, Washington, and Schofield Barracks, Territory of Hawaii. Between the two enlistments I worked for a couple of weeks as public chauffeur in Honolulu, and then got a job on a freight boat, visiting China, Japan, Guam and the Philippines.

I was commissioned a First Lieutenant of Infantry at Fort Des Moines, Iowa, in October 1917, serving until December 1918. In August 1919, I obtained a temporary Civil Service appointment in the U.S. Quartermaster Corps and became chief clerk in the Executive Office of the Atlantic Branch United States Disciplinary Barracks, Governors Island, New York City, receiving incoming military convicts and recording their property. Seven months later I lost this job in the general discharge of government clerks. For the next three years I worked successively as porter in a drug store, laborer, machine-tender in a brass foundry, collector for a printing shop, sweeper in a piano factory, dishwasher in a couple of Broadway hash emporiums, house cleaner, building laborer, hod carrier, stevedore and track walker. For a time I took to the road as a hobo.

I joined the editorial staff of *The Messenger,* a radical Negro monthly magazine, in February 1923, contributing a monthly page of satire and humor and occasional articles. In November 1924, I began writing a weekly column "Views and Reviews" for the Pittsburgh *Courier,* a weekly Negro newspaper, which has appeared regularly since then. From November 1925 to July 1926, I visited about 200 cities and towns, mainly in eleven Southern States, writing about the Negro communities for the Pittsburgh *Courier*. In December 1926, I rejoined *The Messenger*, becoming its Managing Editor. The magazine died from lack of funds in August 1928, and in September I went to Chicago, to become Editor of the Illustrated Feature Section, a magazine insert of moron fodder going to forty Negro weeklies. The following January I resigned in order to save what intelligence I possess and confined myself to writing for the Pittsburgh *Courier* and doing some free-lance work.

I have had magazine articles published by *The World Tomorrow, The Nation, The Debunker,* the *New Masses* and *The American Mercury.* An essay "Our Greatest Gift to America" appears in the Modern Library publication *Anthology of American Negro Literature.* Haldeman-Julius has published a Blue Book written by me, entitled *Racial Inter-Marriage in the United States.* My first novel *Black-No-More,* a satire on the American Colorphobia, is published by The Macaulay Company. I live in New York City.

George S. Schuyler,
"Some Unsweet Truths About Race Prejudice,"
in Samuel D. Schmalhausen, ed.,
Behold America!
(New York: Farrar & Rinehart, 1931)

Ethiopian Stories

❖❖❖Introduction

Addis Ababa
Across the headlines all year long.
Ethiopia—
Tragi-song for the news reels . . .

Addis Ababa
In headlines all year long.
Ethiopia—tragi-song.

> —*Langston Hughes*
> *"Broadcast on Ethiopia"*

"There is not a Negro with other than ice water trickling through his arteries," observed George S. Schuyler, the renowned journalist and author of the pair of novellas making up *Ethiopian Stories*, "who is not anxious to do something to help Ethiopia in her hour of extremity, who is not burning to strike through her a blow at white imperialism and aggression." Written at the start of fascist Italy's invasion of the ancient independent kingdom of Ethiopia, Schuyler's comment vividly underscores the intensity of the racially patriotic feeling that the Italo-Ethiopian War of 1935–36 aroused among African-Americans. "It would be a major catastrophe for the darker peoples of the world," Schuyler argued, "if Ethiopia should be defeated and subjugated by the Italians. This is the opinion of every intelligent colored person in the world today, and for once the view of the majority is correct."[1]

Schuyler's *Ethiopian Stories* collects and reprints together two novellas that demonstrate his imaginative ability to describe for a popular audience the deep psychological and ideological investment that African-Americans had in the outcome of Ethiopia's heroic struggle against the Italian invaders. From a literary point of view, it validates the powerful connection linking the "major themes of the Black literature from Africa, America, and the Caribbean . . . to the[ir] social and historic contexts," but, according to Elisabeth Mudimbe-Boyi, "does not necessarily diminish all the value of the literary works that actualize them." Indeed, as I shall attempt to show in this introduction, Schuyler's *Ethiopian Stories* belongs to the genre of literary Pan-Africanism that entails, in the words of Mudimbe-Boyi, "a literary history, textual analysis, and com-

1

mentaries that, thus, can keep alive these contexts and topical works in different times and contexts."[2]

Originally published as serials, these stories represent only a small part of the large body of writing Schuyler produced for the *Courier* that helped to make that newspaper "the most influential black newspaper in the country," with a circulation that would reach a quarter million. His newspaper obligation included the weekly *Courier* opinion column ("Views and Reviews"), which is assessed to have been "one of the most popular and controversial offerings in black American journalism."[3] In addition, he wrote the *Courier*'s weekly editorials and also produced several lengthy investigative features, some of which are now considered classics of 1930s African-American journalism.[4] Schuyler's production of serial fiction for the *Courier* became so prolific that he was obliged to write under various pseudonyms.[5] "I use a nom de plume for every other story in order to avoid monotony," Schuyler explained.[6]

The first of the two novellas comprising *Ethiopian Stories* was written while Schuyler was working on assignment in Mississippi for the *Courier* to increase circulation by recruiting newspaper agents throughout the Deep South. While carrying out this task, Schuyler continued to fulfill his regular journalistic obligations as columnist and chief editorial writer for the newspaper, and kept producing installments for his Ethiopian serial as well. "I am grinding out material by the yard and the pound," he confided by letter to his wife, Josephine, in November 1935.[7]

Schuyler's serial fiction thus forms an important, if ancillary, part of his overall journalistic and creative output during the Depression era. It explains why, unlike so many writers who, in the words of Langston Hughes, went "rolling down the hill toward the Works Projects Administration,"[8] during the Depression, Schuyler managed to be entirely self-supporting throughout the thirties.

Africa was the subject of a distinct subset of the stories comprising Schuyler's pulp fiction. Published over a six-year period in the *Courier*, Schuyler's African tales not only represent a fascinating combination of fiction and realism; they also, despite their origin as pulp fiction, offer a unique addition to the body of African-American creative literature.

The first in the series of Schuyler's African novellas was "Devil Town: An Enthralling Story of Tropical Africa" (June–July 1933). It tells of the near-fatal escapade of a white missionary couple who enter, despite the opposition of an African witch doctor, the mysterious "Devil Town" situated in Liberia's Ganda country. This was followed by "Golden Gods: A Story of Love, Intrigue and Adventure in African Jungles" (December 1933–February 1934), in which a dying African gives to an African-American, Gail Reddick, a map to a secret city as well as two golden statues. Along the way, Reddick is joined by a female missionary; together, the women succeed in overcoming the wiles of Africans and a German trader. The third novella in the sequence was "The Beast of Bradhurst Avenue: A Gripping Tale of Adventure in the Heart of Harlem" (March–May 1934). It recounts the discovery of the headless bodies of a princess of a "cannibalistic" African society and another black woman; the consequent search for the killer results in the discovery and capture of a German scientist experimenting with transplanting the brains of black women into dogs. The fourth serial novella was "Strange Valley" (August–November 1934). It tells the story of Dr. Cranfield, an African-American who rules over a remote, mountain-encircled valley in Africa where he and a group of African-American revolutionists plan and plot the liberation of Africa. "The people have been ready," affirms Dr. Cranfield's chief assistant, Atwater, at the end of the story, "ready to throw the white man out of Africa," to which he adds: "It is for the love of liberty that we are here."[9]

Schuyler translates this theme of African liberation into his fifth African story, "The Ethiopian Murder Mystery" (October 1935–February 1936). Featured here as the first half of *Ethiopian Stories,* "The Ethiopian Murder Mystery" deals with the murder of an Ethiopian prince in his apartment in the fashionable Finchley Arms building in the Sugar Hill section of Harlem. Prince Haile Destu is found with a knife in his back and one finger severed. Suspicion initially points to Mme. Helene Custis, a socially prominent Harlem matron and hairdresser, but then shifts to Crissina Van Dyke, daughter of a prominent Harlem undertaker. When the web of circumstantial evidence tightens around her, she is placed under arrest.

Crissina's father, Philip Van Dyke, hires an attorney, but at this point her case is taken over by her friend and admirer, Roger Bates, a young journalist who is determined to exonerate her. In the course of his private investigation, Bates learns that a mysterious foreign Negro, Ali Sabra, who associated with foreign white men and a white woman, had given up his apartment on the same floor as the Ethiopian prince's just

3

two days before the murder. Ultimately, the trail leads to the discovery of Italian secret agents.

Working on a hunch, Bates turns to a man who has close contact with Ethiopians: Oscar Holcombe, chairman of the Harlem-based Help Ethiopia League. By a variety of ingenious maneuvers, Bates eventually discovers that the murder of the Ethiopian was related to the work of a mysterious Professor Tankkard, who was helping the Ethiopians develop a lethal secret weapon. The story ends with the Ethiopians pursuing the goal of defending their independence at all costs.

"The Ethiopian Murder Mystery" contains a number of subtle auto-biographical resonances that attest to the story's personal significance for Schuyler. The story opens with old Grandma Hassaltine, who, occu-pying her usual seat at the window, witnesses strange happenings in the apartment across the courtyard. She may have been modeled on Schuyler's own grandmother, who was an especially formative influence during his childhood—"a sage, crusty, and industrious matriarch," Schuyler describes her in his autobiography, "the repository of all knowledge, it seemed, and a mine of folklore."[10]

In an unpublished autobiographical memoir, Schuyler adopted the name of "Cornelius Van Dyke," using the same family name that he gives to Crissina, the heroine of "The Ethiopian Murder Mystery."[11] The Schuyler/Van Dyke family is described in the memoir as descended "from a family that had been liberated by its Dutch masters over a hun-dred years before and prided itself on being thrifty, law-abiding, well-dressed and hospitable. . . . The family was proud of its Dutch name and what it meant in eastern New York where the patroons held sway; and it was proud of its position as exemplars of middle-class respectability." This description fits with the image of the black aristocracy of New York, who "took special pride in their Dutch blood and Dutch names," and who, according to the African-American journalist John E. Bruce, writ-ing in 1899 from Albany, New York, constituted "the present crop of darky 'vans,' " an allusion to the prominent families of Van Vrankens, Van Dykes, and others with Dutch family names.[12]

Schuyler's description, in "The Ethiopian Murder Mystery," of the fictional Philip Van Dyke as a man of prominence—"a distinguished-looking old mulatto"—shows a close resemblance to members of his own family circle. Speaking of his own family, Schuyler noted, "It was no mystery how the Van Dykes lived so well. They had aristocratic tastes

4

and were willing to indulge them." As a youth, Schuyler remembers, he "had the Van Dyke desire to be distinguished but not conspicuous," having had instilled in him from childhood "the Van Dyke abjuration: Be Somebody." This latter description accords with the image of Crissina Van Dyke and her European training, intellectual prowess, and personal fearlessness.

"The Ethiopian Murder Mystery" was followed by Schuyler's extraordinary two-part serial describing the international revolutionary conspiracy of the black mastermind Dr. Henry Belsidus. Tremendously popular with *Courier* readers, "The Black Internationale: The Story of Black Genius Against the World" (November 1936–July 1937) and "Black Empire: An Imaginative Story of a Great New Civilization in Modern Africa" (October 1937–April 1938) involve a young Harlem newspaper reporter who is recruited to be the private secretary of the amazing Dr. Belsidus, a brilliant and ruthless black physician who heads up a secret international organization dedicated to the overthrow of racism in America and European imperialism in Africa. Following a black-led invasion of Africa, Dr. Belsidus founds a revolutionary new society on the African continent that also achieves the military power to defeat Europe's attempt at reconquest. Reissued recently in book form under the combined title of *Black Empire* (Northeastern University Press, 1992), "The Black Internationale" and "Black Empire" have been described, with their combination of "action-packed adventure with futuristic technology," as constituting "an Afrocentrist's dream."[13]

Schuyler's eighth and final African story was "Revolt in Ethiopia: A Tale of Black Insurrection Against Italian Imperialism" (July 1938–January 1939). It appears as the second of the two serials comprising *Ethiopian Stories*. The story begins with Dick Welland, a young African-American millionaire on a world tour with his comic sidekick, Bill Sifton. While crossing the Mediterranean aboard a French steamer, Dick becomes involved in an altercation with Ras Resta Gusa, "Duke of Dessaye," when he comes to the rescue of the beautiful Princess Ettara Zunda. Dick becomes drawn into the princess's mission to obtain a secret treasure to use in purchasing arms for the revolt against the Italians. After a series of adventures, they finally reach the sacred Mount Abra Destum in Ethiopia. After obtaining the hidden jewels, which have been stockpiled in a secret subterranean treasury, the protagonists are captured by the Italians, aided by the renegade Duke of Dessaye. They are

5

finally rescued by Ethiopian patriots, who exterminate their Italian captors.

The literary significance of Schuyler's collection of African novellas is twofold. First, for all the heady talk about Africa that abounded during the Harlem Renaissance, precious little fiction was produced on the subject of Africa. (Schuyler was not very sympathetic to the Harlem Renaissance, dubbing it "The Negro Art Hokum.")[14] Second, Africa represented for Schuyler an agent of change, to which he viewed African-Americans as tied in a common opposition to imperialist domination and the myths of white supremacy and black inferiority. Schuyler's novellas actively involve Africans, and African interests drive the plots.

Such an approach is quite different from how Africa is represented in the rest of the literature of the Harlem Renaissance, in which, as Elisabeth Mudimbe-Boyi notes, Africa assumes mainly symbolic form—"the symbol of a lost paradise, the expression of the wish to find it again . . . a mythical place, a dream that replaces the inaccessible 'American Dream,' a dream that allows an escape from the harsh realities of life in a society in which one is a stranger to others and to oneself."[15] It was this didactic purpose informing Schuyler's stories that explains why Africa is not so much celebrated as engaged, not as an abstraction but as a concrete expression of cultural and political realities.

There are only two exceptions to the almost total void that exists concerning African themes in the fiction of the Harlem Renaissance. The first was the Jamaican-born Claude McKay's second novel, *Banjo* (New York: Harper and Brothers, 1929). *Banjo* bears on the theme of Africa's cultural renewal, but from afar. Built around the experiences of the Haitian-born Ray, one of the characters of McKay's first work, *Home to Harlem,* the novel is set in Europe rather than New York. The protagonist, who criticizes along the way the actions and philosophy of African-Americans, leaves Europe at the end of the novel and heads off to Africa. (In McKay's first novel, *Home to Harlem* [New York: Harper and Brothers, 1928], Africa is symbolically represented by a Harlem cabaret with the name of "Cabaret Congo." It is the place where the hero of the novel, Jack, a black soldier returning from France at the end of World War I, pauses to reexperience the cultural ethos of Harlem.)

The second Harlem Renaissance novel dealing with Africa was Rudolph Fisher's *The Conjure-Man Dies: A Mystery Tale of Dark Harlem* (New York: Covici-Friede, 1932). (Fisher's first novel, *The Walls of Jericho* [New

6

York: Knopf, 1928], was a satire on Harlem life and its caste and class divisions, which mirrored those between blacks and whites.) *The Conjure-Man Dies,* Fisher's second novel, is generally acknowledged as the first African-American detective novel. It relates the experiences of a transplanted African conjure-man, N'Gana Frimbo, a Harvard graduate and psychic by profession, who is sought out by various Harlemites wishing "to find out things."[16] He is murdered, but his supposed corpse comes to life and helps to trap the murderer.

In a review, Schuyler called *The Conjure-Man Dies* "one of the most astounding tales of its kind which has come off the press in a long time. . . . The story contains all the elements of a good mystery story," he noted, "horror, suspense, thrills, and a gruesomeness in some parts that makes the reader shudder." Schuyler was greatly taken by the young doctor in the story, John Archer, and his discussions of such topics as medicine, psychology, philosophy, and African culture with the strange character of the African conjure-man, Frimbo:

> Many people are suspected of having killed Frimbo, who[,] later developments show, comes alive and aids in the efforts to track down his own murderer. In several instances, we are given glimpses of the curious, but brilliant mind of Frimbo. Conversing with Dr. Archer, he said once, "The profoundest mysteries are those things which we blandly accept without question."[17]

Fisher, a Howard University medical graduate, was employed as a roentgenologist with the New York City Health Department from 1930 until his death at age 37. The young author died in 1934 on the day after Christmas, a victim of intestinal cancer caused by radiation research. Rudolph Fisher's passing represented a severe loss to African-American literature, compounded by the death just four days prior of Wallace Thurman, whose satirical novels, *The Blacker the Berry* (New York: Macaulay, 1929) and *Infants of the Spring* (New York: Macaulay, 1932), mark the epitome of black disenchantment with the Harlem literary movement and the social fawning that it encouraged.[18]

Schuyler seems to have been engaged in a creative dialogue with the work of both Fisher and Thurman. In his celebrated satire, *Black No More, Being an Account of the Strange and Wonderful Workings of Science in the Land of the Free, A.D. 1933–1940* (New York: Macaulay, 1931; reprint, Boston: Northeastern University Press, 1989), Schuyler offers a stinging indictment, along the lines of Fisher and Thurman, of race improvement champions and the fallacies and fraudulence of American colorphobia. The plot of *Black No More* revolves around the picaresque adventures of the young Harlemite Max Disher ("tall, dapper and smooth coffee-brown"). After undergoing the scientific treatment of a brilliant physician, Dr. Junius Crookman, whereby Negroes can be changed into whites, Disher becomes metamorphosed and changes his name to "Matthew Fisher." In this role he eventually becomes the manager of the Ku Klux Klan–like white supremacist Knights of Nordica and marries the daughter of its leader, who had once rejected him in a Harlem nightclub when he was still a Negro.

Throughout the story, which is a burlesque of the dishonesty and hypocrisy engendered by American racial attitudes, Schuyler manages to satirize many of the leading figures and institutions in both black and white America, most of whom are easily recognizable. The Max Disher–Matthew Fisher character, the only one spared Schuyler's ridicule, appears to be a thinly disguised, if friendly, satire on Rudolph Fisher, counterpoising the "good breeding, sophistication, refinement and gentle cynicism to which he had become accustomed . . . in New York's Black Belt" against the "hard, materialistic, grasping, and inbred" quality of white society. Schuyler's burlesque also partakes of the satires of Rudolph Fisher and Wallace Thurman in puncturing the pride of whites and debunking the myth of white omniscience, at the same time exposing the distortion that such pride and such myths impose upon the values and behavior of blacks.

When he fell ill in 1934, Fisher was actually working on a dramatization of *The Conjure-Man Dies*. The story appears to have supplied Schuyler with the idea for "The Beast of Bradhurst Avenue," a mystery story about a series of gruesome beheadings in Harlem, which he published in the *Courier* in weekly installments from March through May 1934. Schuyler's "The Beast of Bradhurst Avenue" is so full of allusions to *The Conjure-Man Dies,* particularly to the latter's discussion of blood transfusion, the differences between human and animal blood, and how to distinguish different kinds of human blood, that it must be considered a sort of literary acknowledgment by Schuyler of his debt to the ailing Fisher.

The novella starts out with the discovery of the headless body of a young black woman in a sack dumped on Bradhurst Avenue, a principal Harlem thoroughfare. The baffling mystery is assigned to Detective Sergeant Walter Crummel, first-class Harlem sleuth. (The name seems an obvious reference to the nineteenth-century African-American sage and divine, Alexander Crummel, about whom Schuyler learned from his mother as a child.)[19] Shortly afterward, the African Princess Mbula is kidnapped. The trail leads to Ronald Dane, a young white man, who is found bound and gagged in Mbula's apartment. Ronald weaves for the police a strange tale of his and Mbula's interracial love and of their being followed through Europe by members of the "cannibalistic" Guro tribe, which is ruled by the princess's father.

Detective Crummel and his men next carry out a raid on an African religious ceremony that is in progress in the basement of the apartment house. During their interrogation of the participants, the janitor of the building reports that the headless body of the African princess, like that of the previous victim, has been found in a sack lying in the alley. Several other mysterious murders in the same apartment building follow in quick succession, including that of a Chinese laundryman and his West Indian wife. Searching the janitor's apartment, Crummel arouses the ire of the man's wife by picking up her book on witchcraft. Eventually mollified, she goes into a trance and leads the detective to a storeroom used by the German iceman, Karl, who lives on the ground floor.

Crummel finds his way to the iceman's apartment, where he is attacked and knocked unconscious. After Crummel's assistant finds and revives him, they search the apartment and discover a trapdoor concealed in the floor. The mystery of the murders ultimately unravels when Crummel decides to interrogate a German scientist who lives next door to the iceman. He is Professor Eric Grausmann, who claims that he is in Harlem to pursue his life's work of studying the Negro. Grausmann's experimental goal is to transplant a living human brain into the skull of a dog. This requires the heads of young black women, whose brains, according to the German professor, are the perfect size for his demonic project.

The story ends with a poignant exchange between Crummel and Grausmann. Alternately gruesome and humorous, it underscores the bestiality of the racism—revealed in the regime's inhuman "scientific" experiments—that was then politically ascendant in Nazi Germany:

"What did you do with the skulls?"

"I have them in my bookcase. Look for them. Most of the books are a blind."

"And why did you drain all of the blood from the bodies. What was the idea of that?"

"Karl . . . He was a huge beast . . . a ghoul, an ex-butcher. I saved him from the axe in Germany. He served me faithfully because I gave him human blood. That was the secret of his tremendous strength. . . . He was a great brute . . . a sub-human type, but he served me well."

"Why then did you murder him?"

"He was no more use to me. Self-preservation, you know."

The dying man's face was pale and drawn. He breathed with difficulty. He smiled wryly as the ambulance doctor rushed in.

"It's no use, my good man," he sneered. "You fellows will never drag me through your courts. What are three black women compared to my researches? That is what I hate to see ended."[20]

If Schuyler's first detective mystery bears a literary debt to Rudolph Fisher, it also reveals the more personal influence of Schuyler's grandmother, whom he celebrates in "Black Art" (*American Mercury,* 27 [November 1932]: 335–42). "From her easy chair," Schuyler recalls, "she acquainted me at one time with the mournful history of the Chosen People, the wisdom of Proverbs, and the amazing virility of the patriarchs, while at another time, and perhaps with slightly more enthusiasm, she would regale me with strange and hair-raising tales about ghosts and witches" (p. 335). In an unpublished fictional autobiography of his youth, Schuyler also remembers that his grandmother "was full of stories about ghosts and fairies and hobgoblins."[21]

Raised on the blood-curdling stories of his grandmother, Schuyler also recalls how his mother, a paragon of rationality, "denounced all this talk of witchcraft as nonsense, the product of ignorance and superstition, saying that one had to actually believe in such things in order to be affected." Nothing, however, could shake his grandmother's belief in conjuration or necromancy, and she always retorted with "an impressive list of apt anecdotes in support of them."[22] These tales left Schuyler with "an overwhelming ambition to get some of this inside information."[23]

Evidence of Schuyler's willing suspension of disbelief regarding the paranormal or witchcraft appears in *Ethiopian Stories*. (Schuyler's account in *Black No More* of the process whereby Negroes are changed into

10

whites represents a version of the same conjuring metamorphosis that aimed at achieved a state of invisibility, which ambition, according to his grandmother, "could be easily gratified by going through a midnight ordeal.")[24] It manifests itself in the form of Professor Tankkard's death ray in "The Ethiopian Murder Mystery," and again in the figure of "the mysterious Bishop Truli Handem, the protector of the treasure of Ethiopia" and ruler of the sacred mountain of Abra Destum. Schuyler's deep fascination with the subject comes through in this exchange between Princess Ettara and Dick Welland:

> "Few Ethiopians have seen Bishop Handem or spoken to him. He has lived on this mountain more years than any one knows. Before Menelik he was here. Some say he is hundreds of years old."
> Dick smiled his disbelief.
> "Don't laugh," she said. "The laugh may be on you. Bishop Handem is not like other men. It is said he has never left Abra Destum. Here he lives on goat's milk, wild berries, fruit and blood, with only his most trusted men ever permitted to his presence."
> Dick experienced a strange, exhilarating excitement.

With all his respect for the power of conjuring, Schuyler seems to have opposed a specifically "*Negro* literature" largely as a protest against the self-delusion of intellectuals, rather than against the tradition of African-American culture. As early as 1926, just as the literary aspect of the Harlen Renaissance movement was getting underway, Schuyler, in his "Advice to Budding Literati," warned black writers against becoming seduced by the white taste for the "bizarre, fantastical and outlandish, with a suggestion of the jungle, the plantation or the slum." According to Schuyler, the "predominant characteristic" whites associated with black writing was "naivete[,] as befits simple children just a century or two removed from the so-called uncivilized expanses of the Dark Continent."[25]

Schuyler followed up this initial warning with another essay in 1926 that criticized black writers directly. Entitled "The Negro-Art Hokum,"[26] Schuyler's essay ridiculed the notion of a distinctively Negro art, a view that had been advanced a few months before by Alain Locke in an essay, "The Legacy of the Ancestral Arts," in *The New Negro* (New York: Albert & Charles Boni, 1925). Locke based his argument on the establishment by young Negro artists of a "racial school of art" in America on the ferment that African art had created in modern European art: "There is a vital connection between this new artistic respect for African idiom and the natural ambition of Negro artists for a racial idiom in their art expression."[27]

This argument was essentially an expansion of the position espoused earlier in the book by one of its three white contributors, Albert C. Barnes, art collector and founder of the Barnes Foundation in Merion, Pennsylvania. "That there should have developed a distinctively Negro art in America was natural and inevitable," Barnes declared. "The renascence of Negro art is one of the events of our age which no seeker for beauty can afford to overlook." He claimed that "it is as characteristically Negro as are the primitive African sculptures."[28]

Schuyler, dismissing Locke as "the high priest of the intellectual snobbocracy,"[29] rejected any such notion. "Negro art there has been, is, and will be among the numerous black nations of Africa," he observed in "The Negro-Art Hokum," "but to suggest the possibility of any such development among the ten million colored people in this republic is self-evident foolishness." Comparing the work of a cross section of the greatest black authors, Schuyler argued that "their work shows the impress of nationality rather than race. They all reveal the psychology and culture of their environment—their color is incidental." A devout believer in the teachings of John B. Watson (1878–1958), the American experimental psychologist whose work dominated the study of psychology in the United States during the 1920s and 1930s, and whose theory of behaviorism restricted the study of psychology to codifying the relations between environmental stimuli and human responses, Schuyler could not accept any explanation of art or aesthetics that was not environmentally based.[30] By basing his perspective on the primacy of environmental factors, Schuyler not only redefined the concept of culture in nonracial terms; he also made a novel argument in favor of civic equality based on the concept of culture as a function of shared environment. "It is sheer nonsense to talk about 'racial differences' as between the American black man and the American white man," Schuyler declared. "On this baseless premise," he concluded, "is erected the postulate that he must needs be peculiar; and when he attempts to portray life through the medium of art, it must of necessity be a peculiar art."[31]

Schuyler's rebuttal prompted a powerful rejoinder one week later by the young Langston Hughes ("The Negro Artist and the Racial Mountain," *Nation* [June 23, 1926]: 692–94). Considered Hughes's finest essay, it postulated African-American cultural integrity as the basis of any conception of an authentic African-American art.[32] Taken as a whole, these writings—Locke's *New Negro* essays and the responses by Schuyler and Hughes, along with Du Bois's statements ("Negro Art," *Crisis,* vol. 22 [1921]: 55, and "The Criteria of Negro Art," *Crisis,* vol. 32 [1926]: 296)—form an important collection, serving as the foundation for all subsequent discussion about the nature of African-American cultural production.[33]

As the Harlem literary movement approached its apogee, Schuyler remained steadfastly convinced that it had failed to resolve the basic dilemma obstructing African-American consciousness. "The increasing hullabaloo about race pride on the one hand and the scramble to ape as near as possible the noble Nordic's appearance on the other," he wrote in October 1930, "is an amusing contradiction in Aframerican life." In this connection, blacks merely proved themselves, according to Schuyler, to be "good, 100 percent Americans." The result was that

> Yell as the professional "Race men" may about the beauty of a satiny black skin and Negro features, the ruck of Ethiops pay them little heed. True, an increasing minority of Negroes may yawp eloquently about race patriotism but even they are diligently endeavoring to acquire as many Aryan characteristics as the progress of chemistry will permit.[34]

Schuyler was loath to consider himself part of "the race pride ballyhoo"[35] associated with the Harlem Renaissance literary movement. "My mind was shaped in a certain way, and has pretty much remained the same," he explained at the time of his fortieth birthday in February 1935. "If anything, experience and knowledge have merely served to sharpen those prejudices moulded by my parents, grandparents, aunts, uncles, cousins and near neighbors who have, in the main, passed on to the vale of shades." He readily acknowledged that his views regarding racial identity were at odds with many of his peers:

> Some of the more racially chauvinistic of my Negro friends have occasionally charged that I am not a "Race Man." This is quite true. I have no concern for anything as abstract as a race, whatever a race may be.

13

> . . . As far back as I can remember, I felt no awesome or worshipful attitude toward the brethren of porklike epidermis nor any sense of shame or inferiority concerning the tarbrushed folk with whom I am identified.[36]

The next month, Schuyler expressed scorn for "the gabble about race, than which there is nothing more meaningless."

With the Harlem race riot of March 1935, the terminus of the Harlem Renaissance was reached. "In the very citadel of America's New Negro," Roi Ottley wrote, "crowds went crazy like the remnants of a defeated, abandoned, hungry army."[37] Schuyler expressed his satisfaction that the "Cult of the Negro" and the "day of a [separate] white and Negro standard of literary appraisal" were now "happily past."[38] Schuyler rejoiced that "The Sambo Era has gone. The Coon Age is no more. . . . Eroticism is no longer a 'natural.' "[39] Then, in an obvious allusion to Langston Hughes's essay on "The Negro Artist and the Racial Mountain," Schuyler sardonically declared:

> As the mountain labored and brought forth a mouse, so all of this hullabaloo about the Negro Renaissance in art and literature did stimulate the writing of some literature of importance which will live. The amount, however, is very small, but such as it is, it is meritorious because it is literature and not Negro literature. it is judged by literary and not by racial standards, which is as it should be.[40]

Confronted, however, with the trauma of Italy's conquest of Ethiopia and clear evidence of Europe's diplomatic perfidy, Schuyler underwent a sudden and remarkable political conversion. Abandoning his previous opposition to the concept of racial militancy, he emerged in 1935–36 as one of the most outspoken voices in African-American circles in defending the ideal of racial solidarity in support of Ethiopia. This was a period of great stress for the African-American community, with violent street battles erupting between African-Americans and Italian-Americans during August 1935 in Jersey City, New Jersey, and again in October 1935 in Brooklyn and Harlem. Italian-American street vendors were physically attacked by angry blacks, and black leaders called for a national boycott of Italian-American-owned businesses. At the time of the fall of Addis Ababa, in May 1936, an estimated 400 supporters of Ethiopia battled with police in Harlem following a mass meeting to protest the Italian occupation.

This convulsive time is refracted in Ralph Ellison's *Invisible Man* through the character of "Ras the Destroyer . . . calling for the destruction of everything white in Harlem." Etched against the embattled backdrop of the Italo-Ethiopian crisis, Ellison's street orator symbolizes the depth of patriotic racial feeling that the Ethiopian war stirred among black nationalists in Harlem in the 1930s. The symbolic Ethiopian connection underlying the subplot of "Ras the Exhorter become Ras the Destroyer upon a great black horse" is made explicit in Ellison's description of "a new Ras of a haughty, vulgar dignity, dressed in the costume of an Abyssinian chieftain; a fur cap upon his head, his arm bearing a shield, a cape made of the skin of some wild animal around his shoulders."[41]

Schuyler's ideological shift must be viewed in the context of this heightened racial fervor that swept through the African-American community. The author's change of stance can be seen in "The Ethiopian Murder Mystery," when the male protagonist Roger Bates confides to the heroine, Crissina Van Dyke:

> "Now Criss," he said, a new respect for her in his tone, "you've explained how in your desire to help Ethiopia, you assisted Destu in espionage in Europe, and you've told how you became a valued member of his group, uncovering much information of value relating to the plans of the Italians to invade and conquer Ethiopia. Criss, I'm sure proud of you. It takes brains to elude the Italian secret service as you did and to contribute so much to the disruption of the Fascist plans. That's a real service, and I know you did it for the love of the race."

At the end of the story, when Bates meets and talks with the head of the pro-Ethiopian campaign in Harlem, Schuyler paints a scene drawn directly from the agitated circumstances of the time. "I'm a race man, too, Holcombe," the protagonist tells the head of the pro-Ethiopian campaign. "Perhaps I could help you a lot if you would open up occasionally."

In "Revolt in Ethiopia," Schuyler dramatizes the struggle against the Italian invaders by alluding to several well-known Ethiopian personalities, all readily identifiable to his readers. There are two references to

15

the valiant figure of the Ethiopian emperor Haile Selassie I, Negus Negusti or King of Kings. There are also allusions to the infamous traitor Haile Selassie *Gugsa* of Makalle, the only Ethiopian magnate to collaborate openly with the Italians during their occupation.[42] Married to Haile Selassie's favorite daughter, Princess Zenabe Worq, in 1932, Gugsa is personified in "Revolt in Ethiopia" by the villainous Ras Resta *Gusa*, referred to as "Duke of Dessaye [Dessie] and nephew of Emperor Haile Selassie."

The Ethiopian patriot leader in the story, Dedjasmatch *Yamrou* was based on the real-life Ras *Imru*, Haile Selassie's cousin and confidante to the end. Dedjasmatch is an obvious corruption of *Dejjazmatch*, a military title meaning Commander of the Threshold, roughly equivalent to field commander. A member of the ruling house of Shoa, Ras Imru was brought up in Harar with Haile Selassie, who, upon accession to the throne, appointed Ras Imru governor of Gojjam. In May 1935, the Emperor named him regent. Ras Imru surrendered to the invading Italian army in December 1935, after his troop column was halted by mustard gas bombs dropped by Italian planes. The effect of the mustard gas upon the Ethiopians was devastating. "It was a terrifying sight," Ras Imru later said. "I myself fled as if death was on my heels."[43]

Schuyler's reference in the novella to *Abra Destum* (a "remote, inaccessible, sacred mountain of Ethiopia, where Ethiopia's treasure lay") might also have been an allusion to *Dabra Damo* ("Mountain of Damo"). Atop this inaccessible, solitary rock located in Ethiopia's northern Tigray province, stands the monastery of Bishop Aragawi, one of nine Syrian monks who came to Ethiopia sometime during the eighth or ninth centuries.[44]

Before the war began in 1935, Schuyler approached the Baltimore *Sun* to propose that the newspaper commission him to cover the events unfolding in Ethiopia. He argued that he had previous African experience as well as military training and knowledge. The newspaper declined his offer, however, on the ground of "excessive cost."[45]

At this juncture, the *Courier* began to promote Schuyler, along with J. A. Rogers, as the "Two Best Informed Men on Ethiopia in U.S.A.!" The newspaper proudly announced in a front-page headline that it had commissioned the two men to write "a series of articles dealing with the life, customs, history, progress, population and fighting strength of Ethiopia, oldest nation of the Eastern Hemisphere,"[46] although the only article by Schuyler published along these lines was a profile that appeared the following week on marriage and divorce laws in Ethiopia.[47]

Rogers's contribution to the *Courier*, however, became one of the newspaper's greatest journalistic successes. Soon after the outbreak of fighting on October 3, 1935, the *Courier* rushed to arrange for Rogers to go to Ethiopia as its special war correspondent. It was "a shrewd journalistic move [that] capitalized on the growing interest in the battle," states Andrew Buni. Rogers had visited Ethiopia in 1930 to report on the coronation of Ethiopian Emperor Haile Selassie, and was personally acquainted with the emperor and several of his important aides. With Rogers reporting from the front, the *Courier* saw its circulation increase by approximately 25,000 "when the Ethiopian coverage hit the newsstands."[48] There was no precedent in the history of African-American newspaper publishing for so large and instantaneous an increase.

During the summer of 1935, African-American sentiment and desire to aid Ethiopia reached such a level of intensity that even *Time* magazine was obliged to take note that "blacks were swarming to enlist to fight for Ethiopia."[49] "There is something at once ludicrous and dramatic about the clamor of Aframericans to do or die for dear old Ethiopia," coolly observed Schuyler, who felt that the fuss was "beginning to partake of that mob flavor that characterized the Garvey movement, the [Harlem] boycott buzzfuzz and the black Communist blather, all now happily dissolved in the sunshine of sanity." Yet after explaining the impracticality of the idea, and suggesting that African-American support should go instead toward raising funds for "an efficient ambulance corps . . . and a fully equipped field hospital," Schuyler found that he, too, was touched by the idea of fighting for Ethiopia:

> And yet there is something dramatically appealing about the idea. As an old soldier, I would certainly like to participate in such an adventure and press a machine-gun trigger on the Italian hordes as they toiled over the Ethiopian terrain. It is one of the few wars in which I could participate with enthusiasm. The others would be a war against England and another conflict between the North and South.

Schuyler thought it possible that individual African-Americans might "get to Ethiopia in some way and take part in the fracas." In the meantime, however, "the bulk of the blackamoors will just let off steam on corners and in barber shops, and that's all."[50]

17

That was where things stood in July 1935. By the middle of the following month, Schuyler was reporting on an interesting piece of intelligence. "All Africa is closely watching the development in East Africa," he announced to readers on August 17. The source of this information was not the daily press but a conversation that he had with a black seaman named Patrick Campbell, second cook on the Elder Dempster freighter S. S. *New Brunswick,* who had recently arrived in New York from West Africa. "He is a man with little or no formal schooling, and yet (or therefore!!) has absolutely sound views on most things, especially the relation of the darker peoples to white imperialism," Schuyler enthused, adding, "I have met no one any better informed." He then reported:

> According to Mr. Campbell, all of the West Coast of Africa and the Dominion of South Africa, where he has touched recently, are greatly excited over what is about to happen to Ethiopia. The white man's stock in Africa is hitting a new low. Not a single development up there in the horn of Africa is unknown to Negroes.[51]

This bit of news concerning the reaction of Africans on the African continent to the looming crisis further convinced Schuyler of the strategic military and political significance of the conflict. The month previously he had written:

> In brief, the Ethiopian-Italian embroglio will very likely be the match that will touch off the world powder keg again, and I am frankly tickled at the prospect. All the great exploiting powers of the world who are squeezing and exploiting the colored brethren in Africa, Asia and America stand to lose everything by another world war. The exploited blacks and browns and yellows stand to gain much. There is no reason then why they should be for peace.[52]

With the new information from Africa that Patrick Campbell provided, Schuyler felt vindicated. "The handwriting is already on the wall," he wrote in August 1935. "White civilization, especially European civilization, is doomed." In terms that bespoke his expectation of a sort of racial Armageddon emerging out of the consequences of Italy's conquest of Ethiopia, Schuyler declared:

18

Another World War will finish Europe and ready it for another Dark Age with Intelligence in the dungeon and Ignorance on the throne. While it is engaged in committing hari-kari, the colored peoples everywhere, in all colonies, will revolt. And without colonies, Europe, which owes her greatness to the exploitation of yellow and brown and black people, cannot exist.

Thus, as an avowed militarist, I look forward with pleasant anticipation to the results of the Italo-Ethiopian embroglio. If I were a Christian, I might even fall down on my knees and pray for a general conflagration.[53]

Schuyler was in Mississippi when the war finally broke out. At dawn on October 3, 1935, 100,000 Italian troops commanded by General de Bono crossed the Eritrean frontier to begin the invasion of Ethiopia. Over the next months, the Italians advanced slowly in the north and south, with the Ethiopians avoiding pitched battles. But then, on November 8, 1935, Tigre, the capital of the traitor Haile Selassie Gugsa, fell to the Italians without a fight. Writing from Mississippi, Schuyler declared:

I have not yet met any Negro who did not want to do something to help Ethiopia. In the most remote parts of rural Mississippi I have found the colored people intensely interested in the present struggle and burning to do their little bit to aid the largest remaining independent colored nation in the world. Here is their opportunity.[54]

Schuyler used his column to urge support for the recently formed Friends of Ethiopia, organized by his friend Dr. Willis N. Huggins (1866–1940). In "The Ethiopian Murder Mystery," the protagonist receives thanks from the leader of the pro-Ethiopian campaign in Harlem for performing a similar service:

"Come this way, Mr. Bates," said the black giant. He led the way through two well-furnished rooms where at least a half dozen young colored women sat at desks doing clerical work. In the third room behind a flat-top mahogany desk sat Oscar Holcombe, a short, dark brown man with graying hair and piercing eyes magnified by spectacles with heavy lenses.

"This is Mr. Bates of the Negro *Courier*," announced the black giant.

"Hello, Bates," greeted Holcombe, rising slightly and shaking hands.

"I think we've met before. That's some good publicity your paper has been giving us. We can see its effect in our receipts. Well, what do you want now?"

An educator and historian who had long fostered support for African causes, particularly anything concerning Ethiopia, Huggins traveled to Geneva in August 1935 as the representative of the Provisional Committee for the Defense of Ethiopia and the International Council of Friends of Ethiopia. On his way back from Geneva, where he presented a petition on behalf of the two groups to the League of Nations, Huggins stopped off in London and there met with Dr. Azadj Workneh Martin, the Ethiopian minister to Great Britain. After receiving certain assurances, Huggins returned to the United States in the fall and founded the Friends of Ethiopia organization in October 1935.[55]

Schuyler gave strong endorsement to Huggins and the Friends of Ethiopia, which group he claimed "wants every Negro community in the United States to organize a local unit of the organization and pledge itself to send as large a monthly contribution as possible to the national office for hospitalization, schools and child welfare in Ethiopia. . . . There is no excuse this time," argued Schuyler, "that any Negro community can offer for not having a branch of the Friends of Ethiopia. . . . It would be a magnificent spectacle if all over the United States, colored people would swell the ranks of this organization promptly and start a stream of currency toward New York. It would not only increase our self-esteem and pleasantly surprise the Ethiopians, but it would tremendously enhance our prestige in the eyes of the white world which usually expects us only to clown, and is seldom disappointed."[56]

Schuyler's column describing the efforts of Dr. Huggins and the Friends of Ethiopia and urging African-Americans to form local units and raise money to aid Ethiopia in her fight against the Italians appears to have caught the attention of the Italian embassy in Washington, D.C. "I learn to my great delight," announced Schuyler, "that Mussolini's agents in the United States are assiduous readers of the *Courier*, which is coming to be one of the largest thorns in their side what with its vigorous pro-Ethiopian policy in cartoons and editorials, and its employment of J. A. Rogers, the distinguished Negro historian, as its war correspondent in Ethiopia." Rogers had learned, Schuyler reported, that "the Fascists are especially fearful . . . lest the colored people in this country rally in great numbers and with large sums to Ethiopia's support and thus further imperil the Italian venture." He urged that "for once in a life-time, Negroes should demonstrate their vaunted solidarity with their brothers across the sea by making an impressive all-Negro financial contribution to Ethiopia immediately in the hour of her great trial." Schuyler then uttered an ominous warning:

> For, make no mistake about it, if Ethiopia loses and is enslaved, the cause of white imperialism will be immeasurably advanced and the cause of black liberation will be hopelessly retarded. The last of free Africa MUST remain free. Through the Friends of Ethiopia we can help to keep it so.[57]

Through the winter, Schuyler continued to use his weekly column to prod African-Americans to give financial support to the Ethiopian cause. "I have done so," he declared, "because I am convinced that the defeat of Ethiopia and its consequent dismemberment will be a very damaging blow to the prestige and aspirations of colored people everywhere."[58] The sense of urgency was heightened by the news that the Ethiopian armies had failed to break through the Italian defenses in the First Battle of the Tembien, the mountain range in Tigre where the Ethiopian armies had been massing. In the Second Battle of the Tembien, at the end of February 1936, the Italians scaled the mountain peaks and drove back the Ethiopian armies.

In his column on February 29, 1936, hoping to stir people to action by an exemplary expression of racial patriotism, Schuyler reproduced verbatim the text of a lengthy letter from a young African-American in Paris, Dr. Charles Diggs. "If Aframericans really care anything about the fate of Ethiopia," Schuyler promised, "this letter should 'send' them." It is possible that this young doctor provided some inspiration for the character of the protagonist Dick Welland in "Revolt in Ethiopia." Dr. Diggs informed Schuyler:

> This aggression has been a whip to the sleeping conscience of Ethiopia and awakened her to the necessities of modern technic and progress. The young group of Ethiopians has been aware of that necessity of progress for the last ten years, but those who have never left the country were naturally slow in understanding and only under these tragic circumstances did they come to the full realization of the power of

modern technic. Thus came the present trend of thought. How can we progress! By bringing technicians in from the outside. True, but where can we get them without bringing political and territorial ambitions in their wake and therefore pretext for aggression? How can we prevent trouble on account of the natives' distrust of the whites?

To these questions I have always told them—the American Negro. But, Mr. Schuyler, one voice and that of a student does not make a profound impression. I shall always remember the surprise on the young men's faces the first time and that I spoke on the American Negro before the Paris branch of the Association of Ethiopian Youth. I, too, was astounded at their ignorance of us. Believe it or not, they were surprised to know that we had thousands of students in the universities, hundreds of professors and professional and technical men in every branch. They thought that we were only the lowest class of workers. I showed them every photograph of the things that we possess, translated every article I could lay my hands on concerning us and they finally began to understand.[59]

In his column that appeared the week after Dr. Diggs's letter, Schuyler chided his readers along the lines of his youthful correspondent: "American Negroes are standing idly by while Ethiopia is being conquered." In what was to form the thematic backdrop of the plot of "Revolt of Ethiopia," Schuyler went on to emphasize the major need of Ethiopia and how African-American funds could help to make a difference:

We know, if we know anything, that Ethiopia is being defeated, if not this year, then next year, because of lack of money and munitions. We know that she can get neither because everywhere she is refused credit by the white governments which, in the final analysis, all stand together. They would be delighted to see her defeated so they could fall upon her like the vultures they are and rend her limb from limb.[60]

Significantly, Dick Welland, the hero of "Revolt in Ethiopia," uses his wealth to aid the Ethiopian princess in her political mission, thereby serving the cause of the Ethiopian people in continuing their liberation struggle.

By the spring of 1936, the Italians had brought into full play their vastly superior air power and had begun the use of poison gas. At this point, the Ethiopians' defenses cracked, making them unable to block the onslaught of the Italian forces.

22

On May 2, 1936, Emperor Haile Selassie surreptitiously left Addis Ababa by train. Three days later, as the emperor was sailing from Djibouti (a French colony on the Red Sea coast) to take up his exile in England, Italian forces occupied Addis Ababa. Ethiopia was formally annexed to Italy on May 9, 1936, at which point the Italian pacification campaign of Ethiopia was begun in earnest. This was the military and political backdrop to the story that occupies Schuyler in "Revolt in Ethiopia."

"We all ought to know what the defeat and dismemberment of Ethiopia will mean not only to all of Africa, but also to all of America," Schuyler declared in restating the case for aid to Ethiopia. "It is one of the few remaining exceptions to imperialist rule." Invoking Ethiopia's special significance for African-Americans, Schuyler observed:

> It stands as a living disproof of the assertions of our detractors that Negroes have always been slaves and are incapable of self-government. When and if it falls, there will be only Liberia and Haiti to hold aloft the banner of racial self-respect. Liberia is powerless while Haiti frets in the shadow of white American imperialism.

Schuyler was able to find some consolation in the conviction expressed by his Paris correspondent. "It seems to me that the letter from young Dr. Diggs in this paper last week states the case with excellent clarity," he declared. "If that letter fails to stir a mighty spiritual and financial rallying to Ethiopia's aid, then Ethiopia will lose her shirt, and we will lose our soul." Winding up his appeal, he exhorted his readers: "What is needed now is greater spiritual and financial backing from the wide masses who will benefit from the effort. [Others], too, will probably come in time, as enlightenment spreads."[61]

Schuyler's *Ethiopian Stories* thus served the need to foster "enlightenment" about Africa among African-Americans. Schuyler knew that ignorance and superstition about Africa were major impediments to the development of black political consciousness. The condition was most insidious in retarding the outlook of the so-called educated class of African-Americans. "The cynic derives a certain grim amusement from observing how effectively 'education' prevents us from thinking intelligently about our forbears and contemporaries in Africa," Schuyler

opined. "I do not believe I am exaggerating when I estimate that a large proportion of our people firmly believe most of the tripe written about Negroes and about Africa, and are convinced that Africans are simple-minded, 'primitive' folk obviously inferior to us in every way because their habits, customs and thought processes vary from ours." He continued:

> I have heard supposedly educated Negroes "defending" the failure of the Africans to become civilized ere the coming of the white man on the ground that the accident of the Sahara Desert kept the Negroes isolated, presumably from the omniscient Nordics.
>
> I have heard Negroes round-shouldered with degrees concluding that, after all, chattel slavery was *not* absolutely evil but rather a blessing in disguise because it brought millions of Negroes into contact with the supposedly civilized white folks whose association helped make the Negro here more "progressive" than the blackamoor elsewhere, etc., etc., *ad nauseam*.

Schuyler went on to explain that "such terms as 'savage,' 'barbaric,' 'primitive,' 'uncivilized,' are merely epithets hurled at those who are different and live elsewhere." He then launched into a vigorous defense of African cultural traits, displaying a sophisticated appreciation of cultural heterogeneity that was rare for his time. "That most people in this civilization should consider him [the African] an inferior, even sub-human type," Schuyler concluded, represented "a triumph of that Nordic propaganda which we misname education."[62]

The ultimate objective of Schuyler's *Ethiopian Stories* was vindication of the goal of African-American "enlightenment" or modernity, coupled with political renewal. The struggle to save Ethiopia's independence had a symbolic meaning that went beyond the actual events in East Africa. Ethiopia became, in effect, a parable not only for Africa but also for the African-American community. "Let Ethiopia's fate be a lesson to all weak nations and groups," Schuyler warned. "Be prepared! Power and force rule the world today as throughout history. Those who have neither are doomed."[63] Writing in a vein that made him sound more like a proponent than a critic of Garvey's African program, Schuyler held up the Africa to come as a model of what African-Americans might aspire to themselves. "There is every natural resource necessary for the founding of a great industrial society in Africa," he declared. In sum, Africa

24

was "a rich land and some time in the near future, native Africans will not only be inhabiting it and doing the work, but will be governing it as well."[64]

The fusion of racial nationalism with modernity was a requirement of Schuyler's credo. The linkage of patriotism with modernism is a significant thread uniting the two halves of *Ethiopian Stories*. When Roger Bates, the Schuyler-like protagonist of "The Ethiopian Murder Mystery," enters the bedroom of Crissina Van Dyke, he proclaims it "a modernistic glory"; he also notices "the little black modernistic clock on the desk" of Madame Helene Custis ("the acknowledged social arbiter of Harlem") and "the colorfully furnished modernistic establishment of Pierre et Cie on Fifth Avenue." While these details reflect Schuyler's perception of a "modern" design aesthetic, they constitute more than a matter of style. They signify an attitude that enthusiastically embraces a dynamic, experimental present unafraid of innovations; it takes them in stride as part of everyday life.

Ethiopian Stories promotes its author's modernist attitude in a series of dialogues spread across the two novellas. At the end of "The Ethiopian Murder Mystery," the leader of the Ethiopian secret agents politely tells the dumbstruck Bates:

> We are secret agents. We come and go about the world without the ordinary formalities. We change our names as often as our shirts. We forge or steal passports as we need them. We are, Meester Bates, a law unto ourselves. Our only allegiance is to Ethiopia. Our only enduring enemy is stupidity.

Another exchange, from "Revolt in Ethiopia," takes place deep inside Abra Destum, the "remote, inaccessible, sacred mountain of Ethiopia, where Ethiopia's treasure lay." The conversation sums up Schuyler's basic message to African-Americans concerning Africa as a whole and Ethiopia in particular:

> The tall leader halted. Dick heard a tap on wood, followed by four short taps. There were answering taps. Gunsa Hernum muttered a few words in Amharic.
> "He's using the communicating telephone," said the Princess.
> "What, a telephone here?" asked Dick, incredulous.

"They are not as backward as you think," she replied, a trace of pride in her tone. "You saw how they killed the Italians, didn't you?"

Ethiopians are thus shown as being thoroughly competent to wage "modern warfare" if given "modern weapons" to fight against their Italian enemies. The interjection of the princess balances her earlier statement:

> "You are an American . . . and you have the dash and adventurousness of all Americans; that pioneering spirit that conquers, that spirit which has made our people in America the most progressive Negroes in the world. Oh, I know America. I spent eight years there."

The princess's earlier statement recognizes African-Americans as a sort of cultural vanguard in the African world; the later conversation alludes to the cultural myopia from which many African-Americans suffer in their relations with Africans. Taken together, these excerpts represent two sides of a complex cultural argument: that the privileged cultural position of African-Americans should not blind them to the infinite adaptability of African culture, which allows it to master modern technology. Being "the most progressive Negroes in the world," Schuyler seems to be warning, does not mean cultural superiority; rather, as the princess intimates, this very progressiveness carries an equal measure of political responsibility.

Schuyler's sensibility is distinctive in combining the logic of modernity with the adaptiveness of African and African-American cultures. These principles are not viewed as antithetical in the way that, as Frank Lentricchia points out, "the interest in the primitive in writers and artists like [Wallace] Stevens, Picasso, T. S. Eliot, and D. H. Lawrence are all code terms for the literary and artistic modernisms whose solidarity consists in the hatred of what sociologists call modernization." This was exactly why Schuyler had repudiated the patronizing white attitude that eroticized African-American cultural production during the Harlem Renaissance. Schuyler had no desire for what Lentricchia called "the modernist's nostalgia for the barbarous," nor was he interested in the modernist desire "for radical reduction to a condition barely human where we would become translated—were it possible—out of the sickness of our modernization and into mediums for vision, mere mediums."[65]

Schuyler neither hates modernity nor feels out of place with it; he does not propose to become antisocial out of some paranoid sense that modernity poses a threat to his individuality. Rather, as these stories exemplify, his modernist desire consists of the wish to confront the threat of imperialism in New York City, the citadel of modernism, and to assist the Ethiopian patriotic resistance in their guerrilla struggle against the Italian occupation. Both novellas are built up through a series of depictions showing the complementarity of modern science and so-called primitive knowledge. "We need first to learn how to care for our bodies," he pointed out in a *Courier* column devoted to diet and health, one of his long-standing interests. "We need to know about food and diets. We need to know the relation between food and health.[66] The issue reappears in "Revolt in Ethiopia" during an exchange between Dick Welland and the princess over the appearance of the Ethiopian patriarch:

> "I wonder how old he is," whispered Dick.
>
> "They say he has always lived," she whispered, keeping her eyes on the ancient. "Before Haile Selassie, before Menelik, before Theodore, he was here. Our records prove it."
>
> "Silly, he couldn't have lived always," Dick objected, his voice still low.
>
> "He's been here an awfully long time," she insisted. "He belongs to the ancient caste of Ethiopian priests who adhere to the primitive diet. Almost all these Abra Destum priests belong to the old caste. They are much older than they appear to be. My father told me all about them. He accompanied Menelik here once when he was a young man."
>
> "What do they eat?" asked Dick, interested.
>
> "Dates, figs, goat's milk, fresh fruit, beef blood," she whispered. "They refuse to eat anything that is not alive. All grains they consider dirt and flour is quite out of the question. Father told me that some of the priests are over 200 years old and still retain their manly vigor."
>
> Dick was disposed to laugh, yet something restrained him. Who could tell? Perhaps these old priests up here four miles in the air and removed from the worries and cares of civilization HAD learned something about longevity unknown to the rest of humanity.

Even though Schuyler does not engage in an experimental, avant-garde style of writing, such as the use of stream-of-consciousness technique, he still maintains a modernist sensibility. If "one characteristic of modernism is its transgression of national and generic boundaries,"[67] then ample evidence of it exists in *Ethiopian Stories*. Over and above their strong current of cultural modernism, Schuyler's narratives also express a kind of literary modernism.

This figures symbolically in the myth of the ring that is used to plot the narrative in both novellas. The mythic meanings attached to the ring in the two stories are clues to the existence of other narratives that are "situated behind the page, identifiable only through 'tags' in the text," creating a modernist stylistic effect in the form of "a submerged commentary . . . that imitates the pressure of the cultural unconscious (in narrativized form) on any individual performance."[68]

The first such allusion comes in "The Ethiopian Murder Mystery," during the interrogation of Mrs. Custis:

> "And now, one more question and then I'll have to be going. Did you ever notice that the prince wore a ring?"
>
> "Why . . . let me see . . . yes, he did. He wore it on the middle finger of his right hand."
>
> "What kind of a ring was it, do you recall? Very valuable?"
>
> "It didn't look very valuable to me. I used to kid him about it. It looked like iron to me. It was black, but there was some sort of peculiar design inlaid in white, something like a Maltese cross. . . ."

The last observation creates an association with the image of the jeweled black falcon that is the mythic symbol of Dashiell Hammett's *The Maltese Falcon* (1930), probably the most famous story in the entire genre of detective fiction. Like Hammett's masterpiece, Schuyler's story consists of "basically a series of brilliant dialogues, set in motion and bolstered by offstage events."[69] According to the involved genealogy presented in *The Maltese Falcon*, the jeweled bird was a form of "rent" or annual tribute for the island of Malta that was paid to Emperor Charles V by the Order of the Hospital of St. John of Jerusalem. As the falcon moves from country to country, it leaves in its path a trail of death and deceit that has many similarities to the plot in Schuyler's tale. The big difference between the two stories, however, is that whereas the bird in Hammett's novel proves to be a worthless fake, the plans sought after in Schuyler's "Ethiopian Murder Mystery" symbolize the means of na-

28

tional survival for Ethiopia. Consequently, Schuyler's Roger Bates personifies a code of loyalty that separates him from Hammett's rootless antihero, Sam Spade.

Schuyler's serial fiction published by the *Courier* was written during the thirties, the golden age of the modern detective novel. It was also a time, according to Lester Dent, "when American literature was endowed with the most effective training ground in all history—the pulp magazine."[70] The enormous literary success and popularity of Hammett's bestseller ("In *Falcon's* first decade and a half the book saw two dozen hard-cover printings in three separate editions")[71] and the allusion to a Maltese symbol in Schuyler's text alert the reader to the possibility of a "submerged commentary" within the latter work.

The second mythic allusion in *Ethiopian Stories* concerns the "King Solomon ring" that is central to the plot of "Revolt in Ethiopia." Schuyler's heroine describes its significance to her African-American interlocutor:

> "For generations the Emperors of Ethiopia have worn a golden ring once said to have been worn by King Solomon. Before Haile Selassie left Addis Ababa and when things looked darkest, he called Bishop Handem, told him of the impending Italian conquest, and gave him half of the King Solomon ring. Menelik's gold is to be given to no one unless they can produce the other half."
>
> "Then the key to the whole situation is the half of the ring of King Solomon," Dick surmised.
>
> "Yes, that is the whole thing. Once we can get into Ethiopia, get that gold and get out, we shall be able to buy everything we need and send it in to our armies."
>
> "Then Ethiopia will be free," he said, half to himself.
>
> "Then Ethiopia will be free," she repeated.

The ancient myth of Solomon and the Queen of Sheba is transposed by Schuyler and linked to the means of ensuring Ethiopia's survival and freedom. The allusions extend further, however, perhaps even to the suggestion of a literary riff on H. Rider Haggard's classic adventure story, *King Solomon's Mines* (1885). The familiar story of three English explorers in search of the fabulous treasures associated with King Solomon's mines stands figuratively behind Schuyler's story of revolt. Schuyler transcends the genre of the adventure story, however, even as he incorporates all the conventional elements of the classic adventure romance—quest, exotic locales, secret treasures, struggle, heroic survival, and, finally, return home. Schuyler subverts the colonialist assumptions of Haggard's famous text, replacing European acquisitiveness and predatory curiosity with something far more awe-inspiring than any European could ever envisage.

According to Ethiopian legend, as inscribed in the thirteenth-century *Kebra Nagast* (roughly translated as "Book of the Glory of Kings"), it is believed that the Ark of the Covenant, which the Old Testament claims to hold the stone tablets of the Ten Commandments, was brought from Jerusalem by the son of Solomon and the Queen of Sheba, Menelik, who returned with it to Axum after spending a year at his father's court in Jerusalem.[72] The princess heroine explains it to Dick Welland while they are standing outside the "blue silk tent in the center of the temple" that was reputed to contain the Ark. When Dick asks, "What's in that tent?" she replies:

> "The true Ark of the Covenant brought from Jerusalem, and other sacred relics. . . . The tent is guarded night and day by a trusted group of four giants who stand immediately inside the doors. They are relieved every four hours by four other guards. It is a lifetime job for those eight men. If they fail, they die."

Shadowed by the mythology of European cultural superiority, African-Americans were here offered an alternative mythology based on the role of Africans in sacred history. By linking the mythic power of the Ark with the political quest of the protagonists, Schuyler transforms an imperialist adventure story into a tale of revolution and historical vindication.

This "transgression of national and generic boundaries" takes place within the sphere of what Alain Locke defined as "race literature," produced and consumed within the "darkened Ghetto of a segregated race life."[73] "As a Negro in the United States," Schuyler acknowledged, "I, and all my fellow Negro journalists, are barred from employment on the staffs of all newspapers and magazines except racial and radical organs."[74] Schuyler's *Ethiopian Stories* form a literary analogue to the "race records" that were one of the most significant features in African-American popular culture during the 1920s and 1930s. In addition to vernacular blues, race records were the medium for dissemination within the African-American community of black popular ballads, ragtime and jazz songs, minstrel and road show songs, and, significantly, sermons, spirituals, and gospel songs produced by sanctified churches, individual Baptist preachers, and black evangelists with techniques that were very similar to those of secular bluesmen.[75]

"Race records were purchased by the culture that produced the music," notes Paul Oliver, the major historian of the phenomenon. "Made by black performers for black audiences, they constitute a significant guide to the traditions that were relevant to that society as well as delineating the contours of a new popular music."[76] The interwar decades witnessed what scholars now regard as the greatest outpouring of African-American vernacular music in the form of thousands of race records, produced and marketed by a proliferation of commercial companies of which Okey Records and Black Swan were merely the best known.[77] The success of race records fueled a demand for black artists that grew rapidly during the twenties and thirties. Mamie Smith's *Crazy Blues*, for example, sold 75,000 copies within the space of one month in 1920.

A reference to the black vernacular tradition appears in "Revolt in Ethiopia" when the protagonist "hear[s] the voice of Bill Sifton inside [Cabin 34] booming out some Rabelaisian stanzas of that underworld Negro classic, 'Bud.' " This refutes the view expressed recently by Mel Watkins, who finds a "near absence of African-American folk humor" in Schuyler's works. Watkins further implies that Schuyler, like Wallace Thurman, "was only faintly concerned with the folksy but richly transcendent humor of the black masses.[78]

The same social and cultural forces that shaped Schuyler's fiction also helped boost the circulation of African-American newspapers to unprecedented heights in the interwar years. Schuyler offered a droll description of the contents of any black newspaper of the period:

> Advertisement after advertisement and sometimes an entire page spread in two colors advises readers to try this or that lotion or salve. From page two onward we find them rubbing shoulders with advertisements of "Lucky Hand," "Black Cat Wishing Rings," "Indian Herbs," "Make Man Tablets," "Lucky Goldstone," rabbits' feet, tonics

and other nostrums for restoring health, wealth and virility, with here and there a large advertisement of such uplifting phonograph "Race Records" as "Selling That Stuff," "I've Got My Hand on That Thing," "It's Tight Like That," "It Feels So Good" and "My Man Rocks Me With One Steady Roll." In between, of course, are accounts of the current crimes, scandals and accomplishments of Aframericans nicely balanced by well-written essays and editorials on the necessity of cultivating pride of race or insisting vehemently and perhaps sadistically on complete justice for everybody.[79]

Despite its numerous contradictions, however, the black newspaper reflected a vibrant intellectual and cultural milieu that sustained Schuyler for most of his professional life. It also provided him with the major outlet for his creative skills as a writer and political thinker. As the leading black journalist of the Depression era, Schuyler was profoundly conscious of the important role that the black newspaper performed in mirroring and molding African-American consciousness as a distinctive part of the American social order.

"The Negro press more than any other single agency," acknowledged Schuyler, "has welded the colored folk into a compact, race-conscious group and thus enabled them to more effectively deal with the problems confronting them. Wherever these newspapers are widely circulated and read, there the group is most advanced. To kill the Negro press is to cut off the Negro's eyes and ears."[80] In 1937, according to Ira F. Lewis, manager of the *Courier*, at least 60 percent of the newspaper's circulation was "in what is called the south and the border states where the race question is quite acute."[81]

If the mobilization of African-Americans in defense of Ethiopia during 1935–36 represents what one commentator describes as "an episode in Pan-Negroism,"[82] George Schuyler's *Ethiopian Stories* might be said to constitute a phase of literary Pan-Africanism. The pro-Ethiopian aid campaign allowed Schuyler to expand upon his imaginative use of African material begun in *Slaves No More: A Story of Liberia* (New York: Brewer, Warren, & Putnam, 1931), a novelistic exposure of forced labor practices in Liberia. But while Schuyler's journalistic reputation rested on his gift for biting satire, his African-related fiction eschews the use of satire for ideological vindication. At the same time, it rejects literary naturalism for romance and the use of sensuous imagery.

Of the two novellas making up *Ethiopian Stories,* the second bears closest resemblance to the vindicationist tradition in African-American literature. Its treatment of the subject of armed liberation, for example, connects it with Martin R. Delany's *Blake; or the Huts of America* and its theme of militant slave revolution. Published serially between 1859 and 1862 in the *Anglo-African Magazine* and the *Weekly Anglo-African,* Delany's novel did not appear in book form until 1970, when it was finally published by Beacon Press. Delany's two-part novel is acknowledged today to be "the most important black novel of this period and, for the social historian, one of the most significant and revealing novels ever written by an Afro-American."[83]

Blake was motivated partly by Delany's need to raise funds for an expedition to Africa to explore the prospects of African-American emigration and partly by his resentment of Harriet Beecher Stowe's *Uncle Tom's Cabin* (1852). Begun in 1852, Delany's novel takes as its protagonist Henrico Blacus (later known as Blake), a black West Indian who is kidnapped and sold into slavery in Louisiana. He escapes and, via a whirlwind tour, spreads his plan for a collective slave rebellion against the Southern slaveholders. "I am for war—war upon the whites," he declares.

In Part II of the novel, the protagonist sails for Cuba, where he emerges as Blake and becomes the leader of a black revolutionary army. With the help of his friend and distant cousin, Placido, a militant Cuban poet, Blake plots the overthrow of the Spanish colonial regime, even as his army prepares to resist the annexation of the island to the United States. Beyond the defense of Cuba's independence, however, Blake envisages that a free black Cuba will assist the overthrow of slavery in the United States. Accordingly, the novel serves, in the words of Floyd J Miller, "as the vehicle for the expression of a racial philosophy [that is] as radical today as it was when originally conceived."[84] Delany's militant racial consciousness, with its advocacy of a black-controlled Cuba and the need for blacks to demonstrate independence and initiative, would later be mirrored in Schuyler's story of the struggle to regain Ethiopia's independence and the need for African-Americans to channel their solidarity with Ethiopia into acquiring not only greater self-esteem but also an enhanced sense of their capacity for independent action and technological competence.

Schuyler's story of revolution also shares a certain similarity with the

Ethiopianist vision expressed in John Buchan's *Prester John*, published in 1910, four years after the famous Zulu Rebellion in Natal. Buchan had served with Lord Milner in South Africa from 1901 to 1903, and the novel draws on his experiences there. The plot revolves around Rev. John Laputa, a South African who is educated in the United States and attempts to overthrow the white establishment upon his return. "His word," reports a white intelligence officer in the novel, "was 'Africa for the Africans,' and his chief point was that the natives had had a great empire in the past, and might have a great empire again. . . . For years there has been plenty of this talk in South Africa, chiefly amongst Christian Kaffirs. It is what they call 'Ethiopianism,' and American negroes are the chief apostles."[85]

"Revolt in Ethiopia" can be seen to possess a certain resemblance also to W. E. B. Du Bois's *Dark Princess* (1928), a work that greatly impressed Schuyler from the moment it was published. "Although I have only reached Page 127," he informed Du Bois, "I couldn't resist the temptation to write and tell you what a masterful piece of work it is. Beside you other contemporary writers hailed as 'great' pale into insignificance. Not only do I think 'Dark Princess' is a fine work from a literature standpoint, but it is also great as a portrayal of the soul of our people."[86] The novel embodies Du Bois's far-reaching vision in the form of the revolutionary "Great Council of the Darker Peoples," which is dedicated to the overthrow of white imperialism throughout the world. Although the book includes representatives of all the dark races, the chief characters are dark-skinned Princess Kautilya of Bwodpur, India, and her African-American lover, Matthew Towns. The two meet in Berlin, where Kautilya is the head of the secret international council and where Matthew Towns has gone after quitting medical school in the United States because of his frustration over its racially discriminatory system.

Kautilya returns with Towns to America and travels incognito to learn about African-Americans and to help interest them in the scheme for an international union of the darker peoples. After a period of separation, during which she has a baby, the two are reunited and married. When a deputation from India arrives and informs her of the death of her kinsman, Kautilya returns home, accompanied by her husband. The novel ends with her installation as ruler of Bwodpur together with her African-American husband, whose acceptance as co-ruler by her people symbolizes the union of the darker peoples of the world.

Like "Revolt in Ethiopia," *Dark Princess* aims to link African-American racial consciousness with the struggle for national independence in Asia and Africa. Beyond the thematic similarity of collective racial unity in opposition to imperialism and racism, the resemblance of the central characters in both works, namely, Princess Kautilya and her African-American consort in *Dark Princess,* and Princess Ettara Zunda and Dick Welland in "Revolt in Ethiopia," is striking.

The literary Pan-Africanism connoted by Schuyler's *Ethiopian Stories* finds an interesting parallel in the writings and activities of two of the remarkable Pan-African figures of the thirties: J. A. Rogers and George Padmore. Rogers was born in 1880 in Negril, Jamaica, and emigrated to the United States in 1906. A completely self-taught historian, Rogers began his lifelong research into the history of Africans in 1915. His first book, *From "Superman" to Man,* was published in Chicago in 1917, the same year that he became an American citizen. He would become best known for two self-published works, *Sex and Race* (3 vols., 1941–44) and *World's Great Men of Color* (2 vols., 1946; reprint, New York: Macmillan, 1972).

Schuyler and Rogers were close personal friends as well as professional colleagues. The pairing of both men became almost automatic in the mind of readers of the *Courier.* "The sending of J. A. Rogers to Ethiopia is the greatest thing ever done by a colored paper," declared one reader in a letter of April 1936, adding, "Mr. George S. Schuyler and Mr. J. A. Rogers are two of the best writers in the United States."[87]

In 1934 Rogers began writing his pictorial "Your History" column for the *Courier,* drawing upon his *100 Amazing Facts About the Negro* (1934), a work that eventually ran into 19 editions by the time of his death in 1966. "It was I who started him researching and writing about Negro historical characters," Schuyler noted, "and gave him the idea for his 100 Amazing Facts About the Negro on which the *Courier*'s 'Your History' feature is based."[88] Rogers's popular column, which ran without interruption until his death, quickly evolved into a steady flow of self-published pamphlets and monographs on Africans and their history that was to occupy him throughout his long and prolific career.

Declaring that Rogers "knows more about Negro history than anybody I know," Schuyler also praised him for having "placed his facts within the financial and intellectual reach of the widest possible audience."[89] In February 1935, when Rogers's *World's Greatest Men and Women of African Descent* was published, Schuyler stated that he thought that "along with the Bible, the dreambook and the numbers chart, [it] should be in every Negro home."[90] Later that same year, "at a time when almost every Negro who can read (and a lot who cannot) is burning with curiosity about Ethiopia and indignation over Italian aggression," Schuyler eagerly welcomed Rogers's pamphlet *The Real Facts about Ethiopia*. Calling Rogers "the great historian," Schuyler concluded his tribute by asserting that "a million of his books in the Black Belt would work wonders on the Aframerican mentality."[91]

The Pan-African quality of Schuyler's thinking at this juncture may have also reflected the influence of George Padmore, the most prominent black Communist before his break with Moscow in 1933. Born Malcolm Nurse in Trinidad, Padmore joined the Communist party in America in 1924. In 1929 he accompanied the black Communist leader James W. Ford to the second congress of the League Against Imperialism in Frankfurt; later that same year he accompanied William Foster to Russia to attend the congress of the Red International of Labor Unions (RILU or Profintern). The latter body placed Padmore in charge of its Negro Trade Union Committee, which had been established in 1928. Padmore was given responsibility for planning the first International Trade Union Conference of Negro Workers (ITUC–NW), which met in Hamburg, Germany, in July 1930. In preparation for the Hamburg meeting, Padmore paid an extensive visit to West Africa in April 1930, in order to recruit African delegates to the conference. Representatives from Nigeria, Gambia, Sierra Leone, Gold Coast, and Cameroon eventually attended. In 1931 Padmore also took over editorship of the *Negro Worker,* the official organ of the ITUC-NW.

Following Hitler's rise to power in 1933, however, the Soviet Union abandoned its policy of anti-imperialism in order to placate Britain and France, the major colonial powers, as a diplomatic counterweight to the growing menace of Nazism and Fascism in Europe. The Soviet rapprochement with the colonial powers signified, in Padmore's view, "a betrayal of the fundamental interests of my people, with which I could not identify myself."[92] In August 1933 he submitted his official resignation to Stalin's Comintern.

In the aftermath of Padmore's falling-out with Moscow, Schuyler published a lengthy denunciation of the practices of the Soviet and

American Communist parties. He also paid tribute to Padmore's accomplishments. "This militant Negro, as guiding spirit of the International Trade Union Committee of Negro Workers and editor at Hamburg and Copenhagen of 'The Negro Worker' was successful in doing what Du Bois with his Pan-African Congresses and Garvey with his ridiculous UNIA failed to do: actually scare the imperialist powers with colonies in Africa and organize groups of black workers there."[93] Padmore soon regrouped, relocating his activities to England. There, in 1936–37, as an outgrowth of the pro-Ethiopian defense campaign, Padmore and a group of West Indians and Africans, among them C. L. R. James, I. T. A. Wallace Johnson, Jomo Kenyatta, and T. Ras Makonnen, established the International African Service Bureau (IASB), which became the international spearhead of the 1930s Pan-African movement. The IASB also laid the groundwork for the formation of the Pan-African Federation, which was responsible for organizing the Fifth Pan-African Congress in Manchester, England, in 1945.[94]

In the meantime, Padmore sent a copy of his resignation letter ("Why I Left the Communist International") to Schuyler. After receiving the letter, Schuyler published a further comment on Padmore's exposure of Moscow's betrayal:

> George Padmore is a brilliant young radical who did good work for the Communists organizing agitation in the African colonies of England, France, Spain, Belgium and Portugal. *The Negro Worker*, edited by him, enjoyed a wide circulation and was feared by the African imperialist exploiters. The Communists in Moscow paid the bills so long as organizing the colonial Negro workers served their purpose. When they began to collaborate with the bourgeois governments of Europe, they agreed to stop the Red agitation in the African colonies. Suddenly and without explanation they closed down Padmore's office.[95]

Two years later, Padmore sent Schuyler a copy of his just published *How Britain Rules Africa* (London: Wishart Books, 1936), which the latter described as "the most informative and engrossing book that has come [my] way in many a moon." Going further, he added:

> "How Britain Rules Africa" is a *tour de force*. . . . I only wish space permitted me to tell more about this truly remarkable work by a fearless young Negro who is so ably informed and who writes so well.[96]

Notwithstanding Schuyler's anticommunism ("The Communist Party is actually a racket"),[97] which arose out of what he saw as the American Communist party's opportunistic takeover of the Scottsboro Boys' case, his writing during this period formed a significant contribution to the literature of 1930s American antifascism, rivaled among African-American writers perhaps only by that of Langston Hughes.[98] Like the broader African-American contribution to the worldwide movement against fascism, this aspect of Schuyler's work still remains to be properly assessed.

In a broader sense, African-American mobilization against the war in Ethiopia in 1935–36 was a contribution to the struggle against fascism, equaled only by the American Left's response to the Spanish Civil War. Indeed, African-American participation in the general antifascist movement reached its apogee in the Abraham Lincoln Brigade that volunteered to fight in the Spanish Civil War, during which black enlistees were reported to have declared: "This ain't Ethiopia, but it'll do."[99]

Commentators have had a lot of difficulty in acknowledging, much less evaluating, the role of African-Americans in the movement against fascism. The difficulty stems from the reality that fascism for black Americans was not something "over there." African-Americans derived a certain amusement, wrote Schuyler, "from the hubbub in this country over fascism and whether or not it can happen here. . . . The simple truth of the matter is that we already have fascism here and have had it for some time, if by fascism one means dictatorial rule in the interest of a privileged class, regimentation, persecution of racial minorities and radicals, etc."[100] As late as 1940, Schuyler was declaring that "our war is not against Hitler in Europe, but against Hitler in America. Our war is not to defend democracy, but to get a democracy we have never had."[101]

African-Americans have always been skeptical about America's professed attachment to democracy. What makes Schuyler's contribution to antifascist thought in America especially noteworthy, however, is his critique of the racial roots of American fascism. Schuyler extended his critique beyond white American racism to the phenomenon of black fascism.

In a remarkable essay entitled "The Negro Flirts With Fascism," which *American Mercury* rejected for publication, Schuyler noted the existence of "a growing belief that the Negro's long fight for manhood rights in America is futile," which caused "the Negro in surprising numbers to embrace a definite program of racial fascism, as fantastic as it is significant." Schuyler pronounced black fascism "on a par with the Aryan lunacy of the Nazis."[102] He included a wide assortment of movements in his condemnation, such as "the 49th Staters, the Garveyites, the Self-Determination-for-the-Black-Belters [Communists] and the more recent distinguished converts to the infantile paralysis of 'voluntary segregation' [Du Bois]."[103] Noting that "like Fascist movements everywhere, this one is using the beaten and impoverished masses to pull the chestnuts out of the fire for the shrewder middle class whose economic opportunities have been seriously limited of late," Schuyler argued that ultimately, it was "the masses who lose out and the few who profit."[104]

Even today, it is little appreciated by scholars just how strong and wide was this tide of "race chauvinism" in the black community during the thirties.[105] The political phenomenon greatly alarmed Schuyler, who believed that it had the potential to become "an adjunct to a national Fascist movement." Racial chauvinists thus represented, in Schuyler's eyes, a grave political risk at a time when fascism was gaining in ascendancy. "The worst enemies of the Negro race in America today," Schuyler declared, "are those Negroes who preach race chauvinism, segregation and ultimate isolation under the euphemism of group economy. If we are to survive, we must in every sense become a part of, must merge with the nation, and if the nation is unwilling then that is a challenge we must meet with all our intelligence, resources and knowledge."[106]

During his tour of the Deep South, in October 1935, Schuyler noted that studying the effects of segregation had "more than ever convinced me of the soundness of my original and frequently reiterated conviction that segregation in any form, either as doctrine or practice, is and shall ever be, pernicious, stultifying, demoralizing and altogether disastrous." The perspective offered by the racial laboratory that was Mississippi strengthened Schuyler in his conviction that what was desirable and necessary for America was "not racial separatism, but racial association; not segregation, but complete social equality in every conceivable sense of the word."[107]

Schuyler often liked to refer to himself as "Ye Olde Cynic," suggesting that he saw himself as a kind of latter-day Diogenes, albeit in black skin, "this tub and lantern chained to him with padlocks . . . doggedly

SIENA COLLEGE LIBRARY

searching for an honest man."[108] Schuyler's *Ethiopian Stories* and his other African fiction contain a succession of imaginary individuals with whom he could identify. These literary creations supplied Schuyler with a sort of sentimental safeguard against disappointment. Even the villains in his stories seem to have provided him with a certain grim amusement.

Like the legendary Diogenes of Sinope, Schuyler made it his mission to "deface the currency," meaning that he, too, sought "to put false coin out of circulation."[109] Schuyler's caustic wit, haughty independence of spirit, whimsical singularity, and contemptuous rejection of convention were expressions of his lifelong struggle with the problem of radical self-sufficiency, dictated by Cynic precepts governing the training of mind and body. It was for this reason that he was always keen to expose the moral laxity of conventional American beliefs held by blacks and whites about each other and about themselves.

Tragically, like the subsequent disrepute into which Diogenes descended, Schuyler also fell into political disfavor in the African-American community during the fifties and sixties, having abandoned his pre-World War II radical stance and taken up with the conservative lobby's attack against the civil rights movement as part of its anticommunist crusade.[110] *Ethiopian Stories* reflects Schuyler's Pan-African political commitment during the 1930s. From the perspective of African-American literary production, Schuyler's novellas represent a vindication of W. E. B. DuBois's famous injunction: "We insist that our Art and Propaganda be one."[111] Even though the original purpose behind their value as propaganda has long ago passed, the ingenious artistry of their creator and the stories themselves reemerge to fascinate and entertain anew.

—Robert A. Hill
University of California, Los Angeles

◆◆◆Notes

1. George S. Schuyler, "Views and Reviews," *Courier*, November 23, 1935. Schuyler's opinion column began publication in 1924 and continued for the next 40 years (Nickieann Fleener, "George S. Schuyler," *Dictionary of Literary Biography*, vol. 29, *American Newspaper Journalists, 1926–1950* [Detroit, MI: Gale Research Company, 1984], pp. 313–22; Norma R. Jones, "George Samuel Schuyler," *Dictionary of Literary Biography*, vol. 51, *Afro-American Writers from the Harlem Renaissance to 1940* [Detroit, MI: Gale Research Company, 1987], pp. 245–52).

2. Elisabeth Mudimbe-Boyi, "Harlem Renaissance and Africa: An Ambiguous Adventure," in V. Y. Mudimbe, ed., *The Surreptitious Speech: Présence Africaine and the Politics of Otherness, 1947–1987* (Chicago: University of Chicago Press, 1992), pp. 174–84.

3. Bruce Kellner, ed., *The Harlem Renaissance: A Historical Dictionary for the Era* (Westport, CT: Greenwood Press, 1984), pp. 284, 366.

4. Fleener, "Schuyler," pp. 315–17.

5. "Samuel I. Brooks" and "Rachel Call" were the two most frequently used pseudonyms. A listing of Schuyler's serial fiction in the *Courier* is contained in the annotated bibliography that accompanies George S. Schuyler, *Black Empire*, compiled and edited by Robert A. Hill and R. Kent Rasmussen (Boston: Northeastern University Press, 1992), pp. 337–44.

6. Schuyler to Prattis, December 5, 1936, P. L. Prattis Papers, Moreland-Spingarn Research Center, Howard University Library, Washington, D.C.

7. Schuyler to Josephine Schuyler, November 9, 1935, George S. Schuyler Papers, 1912–1976, George Arents Research Library for Special Collections, Syracuse University Library, Syracuse, New York, quoted in Robert A. Hill and R. Kent Rasmussen, Afterword, *Black Empire*, p. 265; cf. Nickieann Fleener, " 'Breaking Down Buyer Resistance': Marketing the 1935 Pittsburgh *Courier* to Mississippi Blacks," *Journalism History* (Autumn–Winter 1986): 78–85.

8. Langston Hughes, *The Big Sea* (New York: Knopf, 1940; reprint, New York: Thunder's Mouth Press, ca. 1986), p. 233.

9. "Strange Valley: A Novel of Black and White Americans Marooned in an African Jungle," *Courier*, November 10, 1934. The final statement is a paraphrase of the Liberian national motto "The Love of Liberty Brought Us Here" (Charles Morrow Wilson, *Liberia: Black Africa in Microcosm* [New York: Harper & Row, 1971], p. 58).

10. *Black and Conservative: The Autobiography of George S. Schuyler* (New Rochelle, NY: Arlington House, 1966), p. 5.

11. George S. Schuyler, "Escape" (unpublished manuscript), George S. Schuyler Papers, File 15/3, Schomburg Center for Research in Black Culture, New York Public Library, New York.

12. Ibid., p. 7. Quoted in William B. Gatewood, *Aristocrats of Color: The Black Elite, 1880–1920* (Bloomington, IN: Indiana University Press, 1990), p. 108.

13. Henry Louis Gates, Jr., "A Fragmented Man: George Schuyler and the Claims of Race," *The New York Times Book Review,* September 20, 1992, p. 43.

14. *Nation,* 122 (June 16, 1926): 662–63.

15. Mudimbe-Boyi, "Harlem Renaissance and Africa," p. 179.

16. A valuable personal reminiscence by Fisher's widow is presented in Kevin McGruder, "Jane Ryder Fisher," *Black Scholar,* 23 (Winter/spring 1993): 20–25; see also Eleanor Q. Tignor, "Rudolph Fisher," *Dictionary of Literary Biography,* vol. 51, *Afro-American Writers from the Harlem Renaissance to 1940,* pp. 86–95; and Margaret Perry, ed., *The Short Fiction of Rudolph Fisher* (Westport, CT: Greenwood Press, 1987).

17. George S. Schuyler, [Roseanne Charlton, pseud.], "Book Review," *Courier,* September 24, 1932.

18. Schuyler and Thurman were boarders together in the Harlem apartment of Theophilus Lewis and his wife—a dwelling that would become immortalized as "Niggerati Manor" in Thurman's *Infants of the Spring,* fashioned after the Harlem rooming house where Thurman, Schuyler, and young aspiring playwright Bruce Nugent lived. Thurman assumed Schuyler's job as editorial manager with the *Messenger* after the latter quit and moved to Chicago. In November 1928, Thurman published the only issue of the magazine *Harlem,* containing Schuyler's short story "Woolf," which Schuyler considered to have been "one of my best literary portraits" (Schuyler, *Black and Conservative,* pp. 142, 158, 169; Wallace Thurman, *Infants of the Spring,* foreword by Amrijit Singh [Boston: Northeastern University Press, The Northeastern Library of Black Literature, 1992]).

19. Schuyler, *Black and Conservative,* p. 18.

20. George S. Schuyler, [Samuel I. Brooks, pseud.], "The Beast of Bradhurst Avenue: A Mystery Story," *Courier,* May 19, 1934; cf. Götz Aly, Peter Chroust, and Christian Pross, *Cleansing the Fatherland: Nazi Medicine and Racial Hygiene,* trans. Belinda Cooper, foreword by Michael H. Kater (Baltimore, MD: Johns Hopkins University Press, 1994).

21. Schuyler, ms. "Escape," p. 4.

22. Schuyler, *Black and Conservative,* pp. 20–23; cf. "I have been amazed by it [African witchcraft] myself," "Views and Reviews," *Courier,* March 9, 1935; see also the short story by Schuyler writing as Rachel Call, "Necromancy," ibid., September 2, 1933.

23. George S. Schuyler "Black Art," *American Mercury,* 27 (November 1932): 339.

24. Ibid., p. 339.

25. George S. Schuyler, "Shafts and Darts," *Messenger,* 8 (January 1926): 9.

26. *Nation,* 122 (June 16, 1926): 662–63, reprinted in Gerald Early, ed., *Speech and Power: The African-American Essay and Its Cultural Content, from Polemics to Pulpit,* vol. 2 (Hopewell, NJ: The Ecco Press, 1993), pp. 85–87.

27. Alain Locke, ed., *The New Negro* (1925; reprint, New York: Atheneum, 1992), pp. 262, 267.

28. Ibid., pp. 19, 21.

29. Quoted in Arnold Rampersad, Introduction, in Locke, *The New Negro*, p. xix.

30. Watson's major works were *Behavior: An Introduction to Comparative Psychology* (New York: Holt, 1914) and *Psychology from the Standpoint of a Behaviorist* (1919). His popular works include *Behaviorism* (New York: Norton, 1925; rev. ed., Chicago: University of Chicago Press, 1930, 1959) and *The Battle of Behaviorism: An Exposition and an Exposure* (London: K. Paul, 1928). Schuyler adopted the precepts of Watson's *Psychological Care of Infant and Child* (1928; reprint, New York: Ayer, 1972) in the raising of his daughter, Phillippa, who would turn out to be one of the child prodigies of the thirties (*Black and Conservative*, pp. 125, 251–53; cf. Kathryn Talalay, "Philippa Schuyler (1931–1967)," in Jessie Carney Smith, ed., *Notable Black American Women* (Detroit: Gale Research, 1992), pp. 983–87.

31. Schuyler, "The Negro-Art Hokum," p. 87.

32. Cf. Arnold Rampersad, *The Life of Langston Hughes* (New York: Oxford University Press, 1986), vol. 1, p. 130. Hughes's essay is reprinted in Early, *Speech and Power*, pp. 88–91.

33. Theodore O. Mason, Jr., "African-American Theory and Criticism—Harlem Renaissance to the Black Arts Movement," in Michael Groden and Martin Kreiswirth, eds., *The Johns Hopkins Guide to Literary Theory & Criticism* (Baltimore: The Johns Hopkins University Press, 1994), pp. 9–15.

34. George S. Schuyler, "A Negro Looks at Negroes," *The Debunker and The American Parade* (October 1930): 27. The issue of beauty standards was a consistent concern for Schuyler. In "The Ethiopian Murder Mystery," it shows up in the form of "the beautiful hair dressing parlor of Madame [Helene] Custis," and the descriptions of the "smell of frying hair" and the picture of female attendants "garbed like Madame Custis . . . busily changing the hair and complexion. . . ." In *Black No More*, the character of Mme. Sisseretta Blandish, with her brisk business in hair straighteners and bleaching creams, was based on the famous Madame C. J. Walker; Helene Custis in "The Ethiopian Murder Mystery" was a burlesque of the white cosmetics manufacturer, Helene Curtis.

35. Schuyler, "A Negro Looks at Negroes," p. 33.

36. "Views and Reviews," *Courier*, February 23, 1935.

37. Roi Ottley and William J. Weatherby, eds., *The Negro in New York: An Informal Social History, 1626–1940* (New York: Praeger, 1969), p. 275; cf. E. Franklin Frazier, "Negro Harlem: An Ecological Study," *American Journal of Sociology*, 43 (July 1937): 72–88; and Cheryl Lynn Greenberg, *"Or Does it Explode?": Black Harlem in the Great Depression* (New York: Oxford University Press, 1991), pp. 3–6, 136–37. The Harlem riot of March 1935 supplied the historical and imaginative backdrop for the violent climax of Ralph Ellison's *Invisible Man* (New York: Random House, 1952).

38. "Views and Reviews," *Courier*, March 23, 1935.

39. "Views and Reviews," *Courier*, January 4, 1936; compare Elisabeth Mudimbe-Boyi's statement: "The image of Harlem (as it comes across throughout the writings, poems, and novels of the period) is that of a place of night pleasures, of a change of scenery for souls in search of 'primitivism' " ("Harlem Renaissance and Africa," p. 180). Langston Hughes, in his autobiography, recalls that Harlem was the place "where now the strangers were given the best ringside tables to sit and stare at the Negro customers—like amusing animals in the zoo" (*The Big Sea*, p. 225).

40. "Views and Reviews," *Courier*, January 4, 1936. Schuyler would have probably concurred with Wallace Thurman's derisive assessment that a state of "emotional hangover" was the only fitting epitaph (*Infants of the Spring* [New York: Macaulay, 1932], p. 187).

41. Elizabeth L. Normandy, "African-Americans and the U.S. Response to the Italian Invasion of Ethiopia, 1935–36" (paper presented to the 35th annual meeting of the African Studies Association, November 21, 1992, Seattle, Washington), pp. 13–14; William R. Scott, *The Sons of Sheba's Race: African-Americans and the Italo-Ethiopian War, 1935–1941* (Bloomington: Indiana University Press, 1993), pp. 136–46, 154; Joseph E. Harris, *African-American Reactions to War in Ethiopia, 1936–1941* (Baton Rouge: Louisiana State University Press, 1994), pp. 97–98; Ellison, *Invisible Man*, pp. 485, 556.

42. Anthony Mockler, *Haile Selassie's War: The Italian-Ethiopian Campaign, 1935–1941* (New York: Random House, 1984), pp. 391–92.

43. Ibid., pp. 81, 392; for a succinct description of the Ethiopian patriotic resistance, cf. Alberto Sbacchi, "Ethiopian Opposition to Italian Rule, 1936–1940," *Ethiopian Review*, vol. 4, No. 5 (May 1994): 37–51.

44. Yonas Admassu, African Studies Center, UCLA, to Robert A. Hill, personal communication, February 21, 1993. Schuyler's use of *Abra* appears to be a distortion of the Ethiopian *dabr*, meaning mountain. In Ethiopia, churches and monasteries are customarily built on top of mountains to indicate the hierarchy in the social and religious structure of the community; by extension, *Dabra* has come to mean church or monastery. The word *amba* also means "flat-topped mountain" (Mockler, *Haile Selassie's War*, glossary, p. xix). The author wishes to acknowledge and express his deep appreciation to Yonas Admassu for sharing his knowledge of Ethiopian culture and history.

45. Wm. E. Moore (managing editor, *The Sun*, Baltimore, MD) to Schuyler, July 5, 1935, George S. Schuyler Papers, Box 1, Arents Research Library. The rejection left Schuyler free to join in the campaign that was rapidly building in the African-American community. On July 21, 1935, Schuyler spoke on the topic "Imperialism in Africa: Is Abyssinia next?" as part of a day-long symposium, "Imperialism in Africa," sponsored by the Father Divine movement. In September he addressed a rally organized by the Communist-led Hands Off Ethiopia Committee.

46. *Courier*, July 27, 1935.

47. George S. Schuyler, "Marriage and Divorce Laws Most Advanced in World," *Courier*, August 3, 1935.

48. *Courier*, October 26, 1935; Andrew Buni, *Robert L. Vann of The Pittsburgh Courier: Politics and Black Journalism* (Pittsburgh: University of Pittsburgh Press, 1974), pp. 245–46. The highlight of Rogers's outstanding reporting from Ethiopia was his exclusive interview with Emperor Haile Selassie, published in the Pittsburgh *Courier*, March 7, 1936. According to figures cited by Buni, circulation of the *Courier* "shot up by twenty-five thousand for the single issue that carried the interview" (p. 247). The Ethiopian emperor, in his interview with Rogers, declared: "The devotion of the Afro-Americans to our cause has touched me and my people profoundly. In the New Ethiopia the colored Americans will find their place" (ibid.).

49. " 'God Help Africa!' " *Time*, July 29, 1935. For a description of African-Americans volunteering for Ethiopian service, see Scott, *The Sons of Sheba's Race*, pp. 62–68, 136–38, 171, 247 n. 1.

50. "Views and Reviews," *Courier*, July 27, 1935.

51. "Views and Reviews," *Courier*, August 17, 1935. In an editorial entitled "White Imperialism Trembles," Schuyler wrote: "White imperialism trembles at the thought of an Ethiopian victory, which, setting an example to the other dark peoples, might well precipitate a great conflagration" (*Courier*, February 29, 1936).

52. "Views and Reviews," *Courier*, July 27, 1935.

53. "Views and Reviews," *Courier*, August 17, 1935.

54. "Views and Reviews," *Courier*, November 23, 1935.

55. Quoted in Normandy, "African-Americans and the U.S. Response to the Italian Invasion of Ethiopia," p. 13. For a biographical sketch of Huggins, see Robert A. Hill, ed., *The Marcus Garvey and Universal Negro Improvement Association Papers*, vol. 7 (Berkeley and Los Angeles: University of California Press, 1990), pp. 777–78.

56. "Views and Reviews," *Courier*, November 30, 1935.

57. "Views and Reviews," *Courier*, December 7, 1935.

58. "Views and Reviews," *Courier*, February 29, 1936.

59. Ibid. Throughout the 1930s, Schuyler was a strong advocate of the training of African-American youth in science and technology: "It has always seemed to me that more Negroes should be active in the exact sciences such as engineering, chemistry, physics, geology, etc. . . . This is the age of technics and the key man is the technical scientist. Without him we should promptly return to a seventeenth-century economy. . . . Let young Negroes prepare themselves for new places and new responsibilities in this new world, and let old Negroes, parents, friends and well-wishers, furnish the scholarships and backing which even genius requires" ("New Job Frontiers for Negro Youth," *Crisis*, 43 [November 1936]: 328–29).

45

60. "Views and Reviews," *Courier,* March 7, 1936.

61. Ibid.

62. "Views and Reviews," *Courier,* September 25, 1937.

63. "Ethiopia On the Spot," editorial, *Courier,* February 23, 1935.

64. "Views and Reviews," *Courier,* August 17, 1935.

65. Frank Lentricchia, "In Place of an Afterword—Someone Reading," p. 329, in Frank Lentricchia and Thomas McLaughlin, eds., *Critical Terms for Literary Study* (Chicago: University of Chicago Press, 1990); cf. Houston A. Baker, *Modernism and the Harlem Renaissance* (Chicago: University of Chicago Press, 1987); and James L. de Jongh, *Vicious Modernism: Black Harlem and the Literary Imagination* (New York: Cambridge University Press, 1990).

66. "Views and Reviews," *Courier,* September 13, 1934. Three years later, he wrote: "It happens that I have been long interested in nutrition and try to keep abreast of the latest findings in this newest field of knowledge. I have also indulged in extensive and prolonged experimentation. . . . It is a sad reflection on the human intellect to see supposedly educated people who want to live long and free of illness continuing to poison their systems with devitalized food when they know better. Most people can see no connection whatever between illness and faulty diet. Yet this is common knowledge to cows and leopards" ("Views and Reviews," *Courier,* July 10, 1937).

67. Vicki Mahaffey, "Modernist Theory and Criticism," in *The Johns Hopkins Guide to Literary Theory & Criticism,* p. 512.

68. Ibid., p. 514.

69. William F. Nolan, *Dashiell Hammett: A Casebook* (Santa Barbara, CA: McNally & Loftin, Publishers, 1969), p. 58.

70. Quoted in Philip Durham, Introduction, in Nolan, *Dashiell Hammett,* p. xiv.

71. Nolan, *Dashiell Hammett,* p. 65.

72. E. A. Wallace Budge, *The Queen of Sheba and Her Only Son Menelik: Being the 'Book of the Glory of Kings' (Kebra Nagast)* (London: Oxford University Press, 1932); cf. Graham Hancock, *The Sign and the Seal: The Quest for the Lost Ark of the Covenant* (New York: Touchstone Books/Simon & Schuster, 1992).

73. Rampersad, Foreword, *The New Negro,* p. xxvi.

74. George S. Schuyler, "It Has Happened Here" (unpublished manuscript), p. 2, George S. Schuyler Papers, Schomburg Center for Research in Black Culture.

75. Paul Oliver, *Songsters and Saints: Vocal Traditions on Race Records* (New York: Cambridge University Press, 1984).

76. Ibid., p. 15. "At the outset of the twenties," Kellner writes, "songs truly Negro in origin—spirituals and blues—were little known to whites and publicly shunned by blacks. . . . As for the blues, frankly erotic and nothing that respectable, middle-class cultured 'colored people' wanted to disclose, they were usually performed in all-black theaters for all-black audiences or in the dozens of cabarets in Harlem where three-piece bands pounded out rhythms for singers

like Bessie Smith. Less celebrated performers are only now beginning to be discovered through new releases of long-forgotten recordings from black record companies like Black Swan Phonograph Corporation (originally, Harry H. Pace) that flourished in the twenties" (*Harlem Renaissance,* pp. xix–xx).

77. Kellner, *Harlem Renaissance,* pp. 39, 151–53, 165–66, 277. The Black Swan Phonograph Corporation was sold in 1924 to the Paramount Company, which continued to issue the Black Swan catalog for years afterward. "Each of these enterprises provided entertainment that could be viewed or listened to in an all-black setting (whether in a theatre or at home) where the distorting shadow of white interpretation was not a significant influence" (Mel Watkins, *On the Real Side: Laughing, Lying, and Signifying—The Underground Tradition of African-American Humor* [New York: Simon & Schuster, 1994], p. 329).

78. Watkins, *On the Real Side,* pp. 415–16.

79. Schuyler, "A Negro Looks at Negroes," p. 30.

80. "Views and Reviews," *Courier,* December 14, 1935.

81. Ira F. Lewis (manager, *Courier*) to Schuyler, October 19, 1937, George S. Schuyler Papers, George Arents Research Library.

82. Robert G. Weisbord, "Black Americans and the Italian-Ethiopian Crisis: An Episode in Pan-Negroism," *The Historian,* 34 (February 1972): 237–38.

83. Floyd J. Miller, Introduction, *Blake; or The Huts of America: A Novel by Martin R. Delany* (Boston: Beacon Press, 1970), p. xii.

84. Ibid., pp. xxii–xxiii. "In *Blake* Delany expresses a militancy which was rare for his time and which would not gain popularity until the 1960s" (Carol P. Marsh-Lockett, "Martin Robinson Delany," *Dictionary of Literary Biography,* vol. 50, *Afro-American Writers Before the Harlem Renaissance,* p. 77).

85. John Buchan, *Prester John* (New York: Doran, 1910); cf. George Shepperson, "Ethiopianism and African Nationalism," *Phylon,* vol. 14 (1953): 9–18.

86. *The Correspondence of W. E. B. Du Bois,* ed. Herbert Aptheker (Amherst: University of Massachusetts Press, 1973), vol. 1, p. 382. Schuyler wrote a brief review of the book that was published in the syndicated *Illustrated Features Section* (November 1928).

87. Isiah Samuel, Jr., Gloster, Miss., to the editor, *Courier,* April 25, 1936.

88. Schuyler to Ira F. Lewis, February 16, 1936, George S. Schuyler Papers, Box 1, George Arents Research Library. Schuyler was responding to the *Courier's* request for him to organize and manage a national lecture tour of the United States for Rogers upon the latter's triumphal return from Ethiopia (Ira F. Lewis to Schuyler, February 11, 1936, ibid.).

89. "Views and Reviews," *Courier,* September 29, 1934. In his special obituary of Rogers, Schuyler observed: "He reached more Negroes with this information than any other writer of his time. . . . His passing is a real loss to historiography" (*Courier,* April 9, 1966). In 1936, Rogers explained that the vindicationist writing of "Negro history" was necessitated "only because there is a white history." He

declared: "In Ancient Egypt, Assyria and India there was no 'Negro' history because there had never been a 'white' one. And the day is coming when there will be no need for Negro history. The information that we who are working in this field have dug out will be blended, we hope, with 'white' history, making neither 'white' history nor 'black' history, but only 'human history' " (*Courier,* November 21, 1936); cf. W. B. Turner, "J. A. Rogers: Portrait of an Afro-American Historian," *Black Scholar* (January–February 1975): 32–39; and Valerie Sandoval, "The Bran of History: An Historiographic Account of the Work of J. A. Rogers," Schomburg Center for Research in Black Culture (Spring 1978): 5–7, 16–19.

90. "Views and Reviews," *Courier,* February 16, 1935.

91. "Views and Reviews," *Courier,* October 12, 1935.

92. Quoted in Robert A. Hill, "George Padmore," in Bernard K. Johnpoll and Harvey Klehr, eds., *Biographical Dictionary of the American Left* (Westport, CT: Greenwood Press, 1986), pp. 306–7; cf. James R. Hooker, *Black Revolutionary: George Padmore's Path from Communism to Pan-Africanism* (London: Pall Mall, 1967); "The Negro American Press and Africa in the Nineteen Thirties," *Canadian Journal of African Studies* (March 1967): 43–50; and "Some Early Efforts at Trans-Atlantic Unity: Africa for Afro-Americans: Padmore and the Black Press," *Radical America* 2 (1968): 14–19.

93. "The Communist Jonah," editorial, *Courier,* June 23, 1934. In May 1932 Padmore had sent Schuyler a copy of his *Life and Struggles of Negro Toilers* (London: RILU Magazine, 1931), stating that it reflected "the results of my last African trip." Padmore went on to inform Schuyler about his underground political organizing in Liberia. In addition to being the first outsider to attempt to form a trade union in Liberia among the Kru "boys" on coastal ships, Padmore also claimed to have "brought out 2 boys—products of Liberia College—in 1932 and trained them in Hamburg in the principle of the labour movement & sent them back to help their folks."

94. Immanuel Geiss, *The Pan-African Movement,* trans. Ann Keep (New York: Africana Publishing Co., 1974), pp. 350–63, 385–410.

95. "Views and Reviews," *Courier,* August 25, 1934; see also George Padmore, "Padmore Answers to Heywood's Slanders: Charge of Being Imperialist Agent Denied," *Courier,* September 22, 1934.

96. "Views and Reviews," *Courier,* July 18, 1936; see also George S. Schuyler, "Hitlerism Without Hitler" (review of Norman Leys's *The Colour Bar in East Africa* [London: Hogarth Press, 1941]), *Crisis,* vol. 48 (December 1941): 384, 389.

97. "Views and Reviews," *Courier,* August 25, 1934.

98. Faith Berry, ed., *Good Morning Revolution: Uncollected Social Protest Writings by Langston Hughes* (New York: Lawrence Hill & Company, 1973).

99. Danny Duncan Collum, ed., *African Americans in the Spanish Civil War: "This ain't Ethiopia, but it'll do"* (New York: G. K. Hall, 1992). For an evaluation of the African-American role in the struggle against fascism, see Cedric Robinson,

"Fascism and the Intersections of Capitalism and Racialism and Historical Consciousness," *Humanities in Society*, 6 (Fall 1983): 325–50; and "The African Diaspora and the Italo-Ethiopian Crisis," *Race & Class*, 27 (1985): 51–65.

100. Schuyler, "It Has Happened Here," p. 1; "Of course, Fascism would be nothing new to American Negroes. So far as they are concerned, it already dominates the lives of the overwhelming majority of colored folk. They are everywhere socially ostracized, economically penalized, publicly discriminated against, and segregated. Most of them are disfranchised. In education, religion, hospitalization and burial they find themselves a people apart" ("Views and Reviews," *Courier*, October 17, 1936).

101. "Views and Reviews," *Courier*, December 21, 1940.

102. George S. Schuyler, "The Negro Flirts with Fascism" (unpublished manuscript), George S. Schuyler Papers, file 8/11, Schomburg Center for Research in Black Culture; see also " 'U.S. Fascists Are Chiselers,' " *St. Louis American*, May 5, 1934; "Schuyler Will Talk on Harlem Fascism," New York *Amsterdam News*, October 20, 1934; and "Views and Reviews," *Courier*, April 21, September 15, and December 1, 1934. In Ralph Ellison's *Invisible Man*, the character of Ras the Exhorter, who is "absolutely against any collaboration between blacks and whites" (p. 391), and his "gang of racist thugs" (p. 421) express one aspect of the phenomenon that Schuyler describes

103. "Views and Reviews," *Courier*, November 6, 1937. Schuyler directed his comments against Claude McKay for his article "Labor Steps Out in Harlem" (*Nation*, October 16, 1937). A spirited two-part rejoinder by Claude McKay was published in the *Courier*, November 27 and December 4, 1937.

104. Schuyler, ms., "The Negro Flirts With Fascism," p. 7.

105. "The proliferation of nationalist ideologies and organizations that reached a climax during the 1920s was followed by a thirty-year period in which nationalism as a significant theme in black thought was virtually nonexistent." (John H. Bracey, Jr., August Meier, and Elliott Rudwick, eds., *Black Nationalism in America* [Indianapolis: Bobbs-Merrill, 1970], p. xlv). The editors attribute the "temporary demise of nationalism" to the economic and political "effects of the Depression," although this was precisely what, in Schuyler's view, produced the heightened "race chauvinism" of the 1930s.

106. "Views and Reviews," *Courier*, May 23, 1937. Schuyler criticized the lack of "a clear-visioned leadership able to speak the language of the masses, yet with sufficient backbone not to yield to the bogus philosophy of the black Fascists" (ibid., July 24, 1937). For all his stinging criticisms of American communism, Schuyler believed that "Of the two evils, Fascism and Communism, both of which [spawn] regimentation and denial of personal liberty, Communism is preferable by long odds for Negroes" (ibid., October 17, 1936).

107. "Views and Reviews," *Courier*, October 26, 1935.

108. "Views and Reviews," *Courier*, October 17, 1936; ibid., November 10, 1934, and October 20, 1934.

109. Farrand Sayre, *The Greek Cynics* (Baltimore, MD: J. H. Furst Company, 1948), pp. 55–56; cf. Ragnar Hoeistad, *Cynic Hero and Cynic King: Studies in the Cynic Conception of Man* (Uppsala: n.p., 1948).

110. Schuyler's shift to the political right is described in *Black and Conservative,* pp. 253 ff.

111. "Negro Art," *Crisis,* vol. 22 (1921): 55. Nick Aaron Ford dates the origin of "the Negro's literary awakening" following World War I to the founding by Du Bois of the *Crisis* in 1910, and describes it as "the first Negro monthly magazine dedicated to literary propaganda in behalf of the race" ("The Negro Author's Use of Propaganda in Imaginative Literature" [Ph.D. diss., University of Iowa, 1945], p. ii; cf. also Abby Arthur Johnson and Ronald Maberry Johnson, *Propaganda and Aesthetics: The Literary Politics of Afro-American Magazines in the Twentieth Century* [Amherst: University of Massachusetts Press, 1979], pp. 31–48). According to Du Bois, "All Art is propaganda and ever must be, despite the wailing of the purists" (Du Bois, "The Criteria of Negro Art," *Crisis,* vol. 32 [1926]: 296).

THE

ETHIOPIAN

MURDER

MYSTERY

A Story of Love and International Intrigue

George S. Schuyler

◇◇◇Chapter 1

New Yorkers mind their business because they have so much business to mind. What goes on in the next apartment is the concern of its occupants—if they are not too loud. That's why none of those tenants who dwelt on the central court of the Finchley Arms, a very swank Sugar Hill apartment house, paid any attention to the loud, quarreling voices in Apartment 4-A, nor to the heavy thud that was swallowed by sinister silence. No one, that is, except old Grandma Hassaltine.

It was she who telephoned Spring 3100 and brought a squad car scrambling up the street with siren shrieking. Grandma Hassaltine spent most of her time in a big easy chair just behind the lace curtains that screened her daughter's apartment from the eyes of nearby neighbors. She was too old to have any business of her own, so she sat and watched the windows across the court to see what happened. She often saw plenty. And heard more.

"I couldn't see in the apartment," she told Big Jim Williston in quavering voice, delighted to be for once, the center of attention, "cause the shades were down, but there was a man's voice and a woman's voice. They talked quiet at first and I couldn't hardly hear them even though the window was open. But pretty soon they got loud. I could hear them but I didn't understand them. All I ever heard clearly was the man saying: 'You must take me for a damn fool.' "

"Then what happened?"

"Well, this man, he came to the window a minute afterward and lifted the shade. I'd seen him before over there. He was a dark brown man, with sharp features, a lot of frizzy hair and about middlin' size."

"Did you see the woman?" Williston asked. He and the white detective leaned forward for the old lady's answer.

"I did and I didn't."

"What do you mean 'you did and you didn't?' " growled the giant Negro, disappointment written in his strong face.

"Well," she replied nervously, waving her handkerchief and looking hastily from one to the other of the officers, "she was walking out of my view when he lifted the shade. All I saw was a lower part of her dress. It was a green dress."

"Then what happened?"

"He said something to her that I didn't understand because he talked

53

kind of funny, like a foreigner. Then the light went out and I heard a yell, like somebody was hurt, and a loud sound like something falling. Then the light went on but the shade had been pulled down. So I thought I'd better call the police."

This little gnarled brown woman sat back in the over-stuffed chair triumphantly.

"Great stuff, Grandma," Big Jim said. "You've been a lot of help."

"Can I go now?"

"Yeah. We'll call you again when we need you."

A big colored policeman escorted Grandma Hassaltine back to her apartment, a few doors down the corridor in the other wing.

"Just another killing," Detective Sullivan remarked in a bored tone, driving his brick-red hands into his trouser pockets as he and Lieutenant Williston went back into the living room of the apartment. "Some guy just put that knife in him. He must have been two-timing her."

"I'm not so sure, Pat." Williston was frowning, trying to figure out something as yet vague and nebulous. "This is not as cut and dried as you may think. Look at that knife."

They both glanced down at the sprawling body of the dead Negro, the huge knife that had killed him protruding from his back. The middle finger of his right hand had been completely severed and was missing.

"The light was cut off," Williston continued, "then he got it. The woman was nowhere near him then or old Mrs. Hassaltine would have seen her. If she was the only person in the apartment with him, she must have turned off the light, and that light switch is twelve feet from the window. She must have moved fast to get over there and fork him like that. We want to get prints of that window shade, the cigarette butts, the electric light button, the door knob and any other place you can think of, but especially off that knife."

"Okay."

"Did you find anything we can use?"

"Only the green lady's handkerchief." The big Irishman took an envelope out of his coat pocket and handed it to his superior. The colored Lieutenant regarded it for a moment then lifted the envelope to his nose and smelled the wisp of cloth that nestled within.

"Humm! Mighty sweet-smelling stuff, and a mighty sweet fuss there's going to be about this killing."

"Why? Don't we have a dozen like this a week?"

"Not like this, Pat. This guy here is an Ethiopian, Prince Haile Destu, according to the Ethiopian Consul, and a big shot in his country. Washington may want to horn in on this."

"What's he doin' playing around over here? I thought those guys were getting ready to go to the mat with the wops over there."

Big Jim Williston smiled slightly and looked around the room of death. "I told you this thing wasn't cut and dried. Well, as soon as the medical examiner and that bunch gets through, we can go to work. And the first thing we got to do is to find that woman in the green dress."

"That's a tough job," said Sullivan, removing his hands from his pocket and scratching his red head, "what with all the dames with green dresses. But she must've been a big broad to drive that bread knife clean through that guy. What a wallop!"

The medical examiners came, did their work and departed with the last mortal remains of Haile Destu. His death was marked down as murder at the hands of persons unknown. The New York dailies gave the murder headlines. The various news services flashed the intelligence to the ends of the earth. Washington gave the royal visitor a becoming funeral and the body was prepared for the long journey back to Addis Ababa. The Negro weeklies carried photographs and were filled with conjectures concerning Destu's death. In a few days it was all completely forgotten by nine-tenths of the public.

But Lieutenant Williston hadn't forgotten, nor had the New York Police Department, nor had the Department of Justice. Every move Prince Haile Destu had made since his arrival two months before in the United States had been checked as near as possible. And yet there was no clue to the identity or whereabouts of his murderer.

Pat Sullivan loped into the Negro lieutenant's office, three days after the murder, and sat down dejectedly. Williston looked up.

"Well, anything new?"

"Nothing. I talked to that doorman again, but it's no use. He went off at twelve to get his supper and locked the front door. Nobody could get in without a key. He still says there were a lot of dames, white and colored, came to see this Destu fellow, but none came with him that night."

"Yes, I know. We've been all over that before. That doorman can't help us any. Well, I'm going to take a long chance. Just a hunch but it's all I've got to go on."

55

"He rose, put on his gray slouch hat, jammed a big black cigar in his mouth and strode out into the October sunshine. Every colored woman who had been acquainted with Prince Destu had a good alibi, he recalled, except one. Madame Helene Custis alone was unable to satisfactorily explain where she was at 12:30 A.M. on the night of the murder.

Williston swung off the bus on upper Seventh Avenue and walked into the beautiful hairdressing parlor of Madame Custis, the social dictator of Harlem and a power politically. He'd have to be careful.

A woman in her mid-thirties, plump and with smooth dark brown skin, she was wearing a two-toned lavender smock and working on a woolly head when he entered. The smell of frying hair assailed his nostrils. Several fashionably dressed colored women were sitting about waiting their turn. Four girls garbed like Madame Custis were busily changing the hair and complexion of as many customers.

Madame Custis peered out of her booth. Her eyes grew cold when she saw Williston and her face hardened. He noticed that. He would remember it. But when she spoke her silvery tones did not betray the emotion her changed expression indicated.

"Come right on in, Lieutenant. Have a seat. I'll be with you in a minute. As soon as I finish with this lady."

Williston sat down. When fifteen minutes had elapsed, Madame Custis finished with her customer.

"Come right back here, Lieutenant," she called from her little rear office. "I know what you want."

Chapter 11

Williston slumped down in a dainty lavender chair in the little office and lit another cigar, eyeing the brown matron. "So you know what I want, eh?"

"Yes," she said. Her brown face and her tone were alike serious. "You want to talk to me again about the prince, I suppose. Well, I don't know anything about it. I told you that before."

"You knew him well, didn't you?"

"Yes, I did." She hesitated for a minute and he thought he detected just a slight glint of fear in her shrewd black eyes. "I met him when he first arrived."

"And you gave a party for him, didn't you?"

"Yes, but I often give parties for prominent people."

"And you went out cabareting with him, too, didn't you?"

"Once or twice."

"And you visited his apartment, too, didn't you?"

"Once or twice, I guess, but I told you all that before."

"Isn't it a fact that you visited the prince's apartment more than once or twice, Mrs. Custis? Isn't it a fact that you went there the night he was found murdered?"

Williston was guessing now, fishing. He watched closely the effect of his question. He thought he detected again that glint of fear.

"No, I didn't," she snapped angrily, like some cornered animal. "I was nowhere near his place."

"Then where were you?" he inquired softly, almost purring, like a great black leopard about to spring, his deep-set eyes seeing through her.

"Why I . . . I told you before, didn't I?" She was uneasy under his calm, doubting gaze.

He shifted his black cigar to the other side of his mouth, a slight, incredulous smile playing for an instant on the other side of his face.

"Yes, I remember what you told me, Mrs. Custis. You're one of the best known women in Harlem. After a hard day in your shop, you went for a walk around twelve o'clock and at twelve-thirty, the time of the murder, you were somewhere on Seventh Avenue between 120th and 125th Street, just rolling along on your poor tired feet, passing hundreds of people on the way, and yet you can't tell me a single person you met or nodded to in a walk of nearly a mile. It is possible, Mrs. Custis, but frankly, we don't believe it."

She bristled immediately, her face a little drawn, and flared angrily. "Well, whether you believe me or not, that's the way it was and you can't make any more out of it."

He smiled, that same incredulous smile. His gaze swept the little office and rested on her purse lying on the desk. With one easy, sweeping motion he leaned over, took it up, opened it before her startled eyes, extracted a little lacy blue handkerchief and removing his cigar from his lips, held the bit of cloth to his nostrils.

"What's the idea?" she asked, puzzled, frowning at him.

He said nothing but reached in his outside coat pocket and took out an envelope. Opening it he extracted a little green silk handkerchief. A broad smile wreathed his strong face.

"This green handkerchief doesn't belong to you, does it?" His tone was insinuating.

"Why, no, I . . . I never saw it before. Where did you get it?" There was just a suggestion of panic in her eyes.

"That's strange, Mrs. Custis. Very strange," he drawled. "Smell them." He handed both handkerchiefs to her. She held first one and then the other to her nose. "The same perfume, isn't it?"

"Why, yes . . . I believe so. They smell alike . . . but . . . well, what of it?" She regarded him curiously, as though trying to read his meaning.

"It's just strange, that's all," he said softly. "Both handkerchiefs, as you say, have the same perfume. The blue one belongs to you, Mrs. Custis. The green one was found in the kitchen of Prince Destu's apartment a few minutes after he was found murdered!"

She straightened up, her face ashen, fear in her eyes, her lower lip trembling slightly. She opened her mouth to speak but no words came.

"Looks bad, doesn't it?" he drawled.

"But it's not mine!" she cried. "You can't connect me with this terrible thing. I wasn't there, I tell you!"

"All right," he snapped, "where were you? You see this looks bad. This is no ordinary perfume, Mrs. Custis. We've found out about that. It's expensive. Only a few women buy it. We've found that out, too. Nobody knows about this coincidence, but if I should call it to the attention of the district attorney, he could make it very unpleasant for you, and I don't think that alibi you are depending on could satisfy. I don't believe you had anything to do with the murder, but I advise you to come clean. It's up to you."

She considered this suggestion thoughtfully, frowning and biting her lip.

He laid the blue handkerchief on his knee, took an empty envelope out of his inside coat pocket and placed the handkerchief inside it. He placed the green handkerchief inside its envelope and put both carefully in his outer pocket. All the time the same enigmatic smile played about his mouth; that smile that tormented her, conjuring the doubt that shone in her eyes.

"Perhaps if you told the truth, Mrs. Custis, this wouldn't look so incriminating."

"But other people use perfume, too," she evaded stubbornly.

"Very true. Very true, Mrs. Custis, but circumstantial evidence is often better than direct evidence. Suppose you be truthful now and tell me where you were at twelve-thirty the night Prince Destu was killed. Otherwise I'll have to take you downtown." He sat back and watched the effect of his threat.

The little black modernistic clock on the desk ticked loudly in the silence. Each little tick seemed a tocsin of impending doom. Fright and panic registered in her eyes. Publicity, suspicion, disgrace, rumor—all these she saw stalking ahead of her—she, the acknowledged social arbiter of Harlem.

"I'm waiting," he reminded. And then more sternly, "But I'll not wait long. This is serious business, do you understand? You can either talk here or talk downtown. I'm giving you a break."

With an obvious effort she looked up from her neatly manicured fingers into his face. Her lips parted, and closed. Then she almost whispered her reply.

"It's true. I lied, but I didn't have anything to do with it. I . . . I wasn't walking on Seventh Avenue like I said."

"Well, where were you, then?" he leaned forward eagerly for her reply.

"I . . . I went up there . . . to the Finchley Arms. I wanted to see him. We had been rather . . . rather close. You understand? But he had been avoiding me of late, I thought. He was a very fascinating man, the most fascinating I've ever met. When he first came we saw a lot of each other, then, we didn't. I wanted to talk with him to see what was the matter."

"Well, what happened?" His tone was briskly inquisitorial. His black cigar was cold in his full lips.

"The front door was locked. The doorman was gone somewhere. I rang the Prince's bell but got no answer. I knew he was up there."

"How did you know that?"

"There's a space between the Finchley Arms and the house next door. You can stand on the sidewalk and look into the court and see his window on the fourth floor."

"You've watched there before, eh?"

"Yes," she breathed. "He . . . he'd been avoiding me for some time. I had been trying to see him for two weeks or more." A faint flush deepened the brown of her cheeks, and her gaze dropped again to her manicured fingernails. "So, I tried to stand there and see what I could see, but the kitchen curtain was down. I went across the street and sat on the bench against the Colonial Park fence, to wait, I don't know what for. Perhaps I thought he might come out with some women. He . . . he was very . . . er . . . popular with the women, being a prince . . . and everything."

"Did anyone come out?"

"Yes, in about ten minutes. A tall slender woman hurried out of the front door, came to the curb and hailed a passing taxicab. She was dressed in a fluffy dress and a wide-brimmed hat." Her voice trembled a bit, perhaps with jealousy, and she laced her fingers in and out nervously. "I saw her plainly when the door of the taxi opened and the inside light flashed on for an instant. I was excited, mad. I felt sure she had come from his place. I knew she had been playing up to him."

"What color was her dress?" he asked casually, as if it were a matter of no great importance.

"Pale green."

"You say you saw her plainly. Who was it?"

"Crissina Van Dyke."

"You mean the undertaker's daughter; the one who just came back from France this summer?"

"Yes," she murmured in low but emphatic tone. "I'd swear it."

"Why didn't you tell us that before, Mrs. Custis."

"I . . . I was afraid to involve myself. Besides, there are a lot of apartments in the Finchley Arms. I couldn't be sure she had come from his apartment. I don't like her, but . . . well, I wouldn't mix her up in anything like this unless I was sure. I still can't believe she could do a thing like that."

"What did you do then?"

"Well," she hesitated, a look of shame coming over her countenance. "I hailed another cab . . . and, I followed her."

"What for?"

"I wanted to be sure it was Crissina. It was. She got out at her house on 139th Street. I saw her again when the cab door opened to let her out. Then I went home."

"In the same cab?"

"Yes."

"What kind of a cab was it?"

"A cream-colored Radio cab."

"You'd recognize the driver again?"

"I think so."

"Thanks, Mrs. Custis. Don't worry. And don't talk to anyone else."

◇◇◇Chapter III

Williston rose leisurely and turned to go. Madame Custis was relieved. Confession is always good for the soul. The little office seemed bigger and brighter to her. In the late afternoon of life, perhaps she was to be excused for becoming infatuated with a young man, and a prince at that.

The big detective paused at the door and turned back, an inquisitive expression on his face.

"Oh, by the way, Mrs. Custis, where do you buy your perfume?"

"At Pierre's, the French perfumer, on Fifth Avenue."

"Where else can it be bought?"

"Nowhere else, I don't think. Not in New York. I've tried."

"Pretty expensive, eh?"

"Yes, it comes straight from Paris. I think Pierre makes it in his Paris establishment."

"Humm. Well, thanks, Mrs. Custis. And now, one more question and then I'll have to be going. Did you ever notice that the prince wore a ring?"

"Why . . . let me see . . . yes, he did. He wore it on the middle finger of his right hand."

"What kind of a ring was it, do you recall? Very valuable?"

"It didn't look very valuable to me. I used to kid him about it. It looked like iron to me. It was black, but there was some sort of peculiar design inlaid in white, something like a Maltese cross. It couldn't have been worth more than a nickel except as a curio or memento. Why? What about it?"

"Oh, I was just curious about it, Mrs. Custis. . . . Now, remember, not a word of all this to anyone. It will be much better for you until I can completely check your story."

"But I've told you the God's truth," she protested resentfully.

"I don't doubt it, Mrs. Custis, but the police must be sure."

He walked out of the shop and hastened to a police telephone nearby and called the Inspector's office.

"Get me a complete check-up on all Radio cab drivers for the night of August 15th at midnight. I want to find out who picked up a well-dressed, dark colored woman about 12:10 or 12:15 and followed another cab containing a very light colored woman in a pale green dress. . . . Yes, I think we're beginning to get somewhere. . . . And say, put a tail on Crissina Van Dyke, at 445 West 139th street. Tall, slender, high yellow, dresses swell and talks with a slight French accent from living so long abroad. . . . Yes, that's right . . . I want to know everywhere she goes, everybody she meets and everybody that calls on her. Okeh!"

A half hour later Jim Williston strolled into the expensively and colorfully furnished modernistic establishment of Pierre et Cie on Fifth Avenue in the fifties.

A wasp-waisted young man in morning coat and striped trousers with rouged cheeks and darkened eyelashes fluttered up and inquired of the detective his business.

"I'm from the Police Department," Williston bluntly announced, showing his badge. "I want to find out something about your perfumes. Are you the manager?"

"I am so-o sor-ry, M'sieu, bu-ut the maneeger I am not. He ees out now."

"Well, you know all about these perfumes, don't you?"

"Oh, yes, of a certainty, M'sieu. That ees my, what you call, beezness."

62

Williston took the two envelopes containing the blue and green hand-kerchiefs out of his pocket.

"Smell them," he ordered, "and see if they're not the same odor."

The young Frenchman sniffed delicately each flimsy handkerchief. His penciled eyebrows arched and a smile of recognition swept over his face.

"Ah!" he sighed. "It is Elegante, ze ver-ry best."

"You people sell it?"

"Pierre he MAKE Elegante. Eet iss hee's greatest creation, M'sieu, and ver-ry, ver-ry expensive."

"Get me a bottle."

The young man fluttered across the room to a little case in the corner and came back with a small bottle not any larger than a demitasse cup. Williston took out the pointed glass stopper and smelled the perfume.

"Yes, that's it, all right. How much does this stuff cost a bottle?"

"Twenty-three dollars and feefty cents."

Williston gave a low whistle and handed the bottle back with a gingerly gesture.

"You don't sell much of that, do you?"

"Oh, no! Jost ze ver-ry few, M'sieu, purchase such delightful perfume. Ver-ry few."

"Do you keep a record of your purchasers?"

"Of a certainty."

"Well, I want you to find out for me who has bought that Elegante perfume since the first of the year. How long will that take? This is important. We've got to work fast."

"We can have it for you thees afternoon, M'sieu. I shall tell ze maneeger."

"That's too long, son. Get your bookkeeper to get the names now. I'll wait."

The detective sat down in a pink upholstered lounge chair, pulled out a black cigar, lit it and blew a great column of smoke toward the cream-colored ceiling. The young Frenchman eyed him with consternation and then hastened back into the office to carry out his orders. He was anxious to get rid of this officer. Suppose some wealthy patrons should come in and find a big Negro sitting down there!

At the end of a half hour the young man fluttered back with a sheet of paper, on which were typed several names and addresses of the purchasers of Elegante in the past eight months. There were fifty purchasers listed in all. Of these, twenty were residents of other cities. Of the remaining thirty, a round half dozen were men. Williston smiled when he saw the names.

He studied the twenty-four remaining names carefully. Four he recognized immediately. They were Madame Helene Custis, the hairdresser; Crissina Van Dyke, the socialite of Harlem; Mom Johnson, who ran the strange, shuttered house on 134th Street where well-to-do Nordics came furtively after nightfall; and Percival Prentiss, the well known Harlem hairdresser, sometimes known as the Faggot Queen.

The others were white women: Katherine Lathrop, wife of the prominent banker, Julius Lathrop; Elizabeth Dinwiddie, the actress, and others almost as famous. He pursed his lips and half closed his eyes thoughtfully. Yes, things were developing.

"Well," remarked Detective Pat Sullivan the next morning when they were all sitting around in the Inspector's office, "it looks like that Van Dyke dame, eh, Jim?"

"Sure does," replied the Negro, "but we haven't got the strongest case in the world."

"I don't know," Inspector Rogan chimed in. "She knew the guy and went around with him, didn't she? She was seen coming out of the apartment house where he was croaked, just about the time when it happened. She was in a hurry. She was wearing a pale green dress. That's the kind of dress the old lady said the woman in the prince's flat was wearing. A handkerchief, a green handkerchief, mind you, was left behind. It had perfume on it that only thirty people in New York owned. Most of them either weren't in town or we can dismiss them. The point is that this Van Dyke dame's name is on the list as a purchaser of that perfume not two weeks before the murder. Looks like a pretty good case to me, Jim. You've been doing good work—using your head. That's what I like. When do you think you ought to make the pinch?"

"I'll go a little slow, Chief," said Big Jim. "Let's keep the tail on her and find out everything we can. I got a hunch there's probably more than one person involved in this thing. There are some points that don't fit, you know. According to the taxi driver, it was not yet twelve-thirty when the Van Dyke woman came out of the Finchley Arms. And Mrs. Custis said the same thing. Yet we know the killing occurred at 12:30 or close to it."

"The old lady might have been mistaken in the time," the Inspector suggested.

"No, her telephone call came exactly at 12:32 and she swears it was right after she heard the thud of Destu's body."

"Well, anyhow," growled Inspector Rogan, "we'll have that Van Dyke gal down for a talk. I think she's guilty as hell."

◇◇◇Chapter IV

A rakish black touring car jerked to a stop in front of the forbidding police building. Jim Williston opened the door and helped Crissina Van Dyke to the sidewalk. She was pale this morning, much paler than her usual color. A tiny dab of rouge on each smooth light yellow cheek but emphasized the sallowness of her countenance. She looked up at the two green globes on each side of the door and perceptibly shuddered. Tall, slender, smartly dressed and with the poise of a princess, she braced herself for the ordeal that she knew was to come. Jim Williston took her arm and together they entered the ominous portals.

Several high police officials sat around the plain office that smelled of cigar smoke. An electric fan on a filing cabinet in one corner whirred away. An officer brought a chair for her and placed it close to Inspector Rogan's desk. That official rose and greeted Crissina courteously. She sat down, her heart pounding and waited for the inspector to begin.

"Miss Van Dyke," he began, "you knew Prince Haile Destu, didn't you."

"Yes, I knew him," she murmured. "We were good friends."

"Where did you first meet him?"

"In Paris, about six months ago."

"And you came to the United States with him on the *Il de France?*"

"Yes, I did."

"Just what were your relations with him?"

"Well . . . ," she hesitated a moment and looked up appealingly as if it were sacrilege to ask the question or to answer, "We were close friends."

"You went around quite a bit with him, didn't you?"

"Yes, a little."

"He visited your home frequently, didn't he?"

"Quite a bit, Inspector."

"And you visited his apartment at the Finchley Arms, didn't you?"

"Why . . . Y-yes, I . . . I did, once in a while."

"Once in a while, eh?"

"Yes, not very often."

"How often, Miss Van Dyke?"

"Oh, I can't remember exactly. I suppose once or twice a week."

"Did you ever meet anyone else there?"

"Yes, he gave two or three cocktail parties for prominent people."

"But sometimes you went there and he was alone, eh?"

"Yes." The answer came almost as a whisper as the color mounted in her cheeks and her gaze dropped to the red leather purse in her hands.

"Did you ever stay there very late?"

There was a long pause as the beautiful young woman looked helplessly about the circle of grim men.

"Once or twice, I guess," she answered finally.

"You visited his apartment the night he was murdered, didn't you?" It was Jim Williston who broke in with that stern leading question.

Crissina blanched. The spots of rouge again stood out startlingly as the natural color drained from her cheeks.

"Yes," she whispered, wilting with the admission. Then she added hastily, "But he was all right when I left him."

"Was the doorman on duty when you went there?" asked the inspector, resuming the questioning after a significant glance at Williston.

"N . . no, he wasn't."

"Well, then," cut in Williston, a note of triumph in his voice, "how did you get in?"

"I rang Haile's bell and talked to him on the communicating telephone, and he pressed the buzzer and let me in."

"So you didn't have a key to Destu's apartment?" queried the inspector.

"No."

"How long did you stay?"

"About ten minutes."

"Short stay, eh? What did you want to see him about?"

"Well," she began slowly, as though the confession was costing her a great effort, "I . . . I went to warn him."

"Warn him about what?"

"Well, you know he was on a secret mission for the Ethiopian government. I knew all about it. I had worked with him in Paris and Geneva. Lately I felt he had been playing around a little too much with people of whom I was suspicious."

"Suspicious or jealous?" Williston cut in again.

Her coral pink lips parted, then sealed tight, and her deep sunken black eyes snapped. Inspector Rogan was watching her closely.

"So it was both, eh?" suggested Rogan, leaning slightly forward. "Who was the woman? Was it Mrs. Helene Custis?"

Crissina smiled disdainfully, her pretty lips curling. "No!" she answered curtly, "it was some white woman."

"A white woman!" echoed the inspector, his shaggy black eyebrows lifting. The other officers leaned forward expectantly. "Who was she? What's her name?"

For some reason that she could not explain to herself, Crissina was pleased at the consternation the information wrought. Whenever their women were involved with black men they became agitated. She could not suppress a smile.

"I'm not acquainted with her. I saw them together at the theatre one night and a few days before he died my father said he saw them flash by him on Riverside Drive in an expensive limousine. He had always more or less taken my advice, so I went to his apartment that night to warn him to be careful in view of his important mission."

Jim Williston rose, approached the desk and stood over her. Rogan pursed his lips and nodded permission for the Negro to take up the quizzing.

"And you had words with him, didn't you?" the Negro challenged.

"Yes, he didn't like what I said and he accused me of meddling in his business."

"Didn't he say: 'You must take me for a damn fool'?"

She started and paled. For the first time she seemed to completely lose her poise. She gripped her red purse desperately as if for support and comfort.

"Yes," she whispered, "he did. But how did you know that?"

"We know a whole lot more than you think we do, Miss Van Dyke. What did you do then?"

"Well, I decided not to say any more about it, seeing that he was angry, so I said good-night and went right out."

67

"Then," continued Williston, "you hailed a taxicab and drove home, didn't you?"

"Why, yes, I did." She looked about at the skeptical countenances of the white officers and the leer on the face of the Negro detective, and her heart sank. Panic possessed her. The tentacles of suspicion were closing fatally about her, slowly, inexorably.

"That's the God's truth," she cried. "I—I—I didn't know he was dead until next morning. When I left him he was all right, except that he was angry with me for interfering with his—er—pleasure."

"And you didn't meet anyone in the elevator or the corridors when you left?" asked Inspector Rogan suddenly.

"No, I didn't see anyone."

"What time was it when you got home?" continued Williston.

"Well, I don't know exactly but I hadn't been there long before the hall clock sounded the half hour. So I guess it must have been around twelve-thirty."

"Whom did you meet when you got home? Your father?"

"No, Dad was asleep. There is no one else lives with us."

"By the way, Miss Van Dyke," Rogan cut in, "you were dressed in pale green with a wide-brimmed summer hat that evening, weren't you?"

"Why, yes, I believe I was."

"And of course you had shoes and handkerchief to match it, didn't you?" His voice was soft and purring, like a lion toying with a mouse.

"Yes, I did." She was plainly puzzled by the line of questioning.

"Is this your handkerchief?" Jim Williston asked casually, taking the wisp of cloth out of its envelope and handing it to her.

The octoroon regarded the handkerchief closely. "Yes," she admitted slowly, "it looks like mine although I wouldn't swear it."

"Smell it," he orderd. "Isn't that the Elegante perfume you use?"

"Yes, I use that perfume."

"Then, Miss Van Dyke," Inspector Rogan announced, "we'll have to serve this warrant for your arrest for the murder of Prince Haile Destu."

"Harlem Society Woman Charged With African Prince's Murder" . . . "Police Arrest Harlem Negress in Prince's Murder" . . . "Pretty Octoroon Charged With Ethiopian Death" . . . "Police Say Harlem Girl Killed African Prince."

These and other screaming headlines blazoned from ten thousand news-stands. The news flashed across the continent and the oceans. Reporters besieged the Van Dyke residence.

No one was admitted. The shades were drawn. A big black policeman had been detailed to keep curiosity seekers moving. The prominence of the Van Dykes and of the murdered man, the hint of a love affair between Crissina and Haile Destu and the enormous bail under which she had been released, all centered the attention of the nation upon the case.

Attorney William Grassety, who was forty-five, famous and resembled a brown bulldog with graying hair, lolled in an overstuffed chair, eyes half closed as he sucked complacently on an enormous and odorous pipe. Former assistant attorney general of New York State and the highest-priced lawyer in Harlem, he had been retained by Philip Van Dyke to defend his daughter.

Van Dyke, a distinguished looking old mulatto, spare and nervous, smoothed back his almost-white hair again and again, as he alternately puffed a long Russian cigarette and knocked the ashes into the receiver at his elbow. On the large sofa nearby sat Crissina, pale and drawn, her lips grimly sealed, and close to her a long, gangling young black fellow, smartly dressed, who talked fast, chewed gum and held the attention of the others.

"Criss is in a tough spot, all right," he was remarking for the nth time, "but we're going to get her out of it. These bulls haven't found out everything. I know Williston. Smart guy, and all that, but he hasn't got all the brains. There's a flaw somewhere and I'm going to find it. I . . ."

"You're going to find it?" Attorney Grassety smiled indulgently, peering at the youngster from under his bushy black eyebrows.

"You're certainly picking out a job for yourself, Bates. Don't you know I've gone over every single clue? We'll get Miss Van Dyke out of this, all right, at least I hope so, but it's not going to be easy. Of course, to you newspaper fellows, almost anything seems possible, but we lawyers have to be practical and face the facts."

"But she's innocent," exploded Roger Bates. "She didn't do it."

"Of course, my boy, of course," boomed the lawyer, "but believing it and proving it is another thing. As you put it, she is in a tough spot. Jim Williston has dug up enough circumstantial evidence to convict a dozen people."

"Oh, there must be some way out," young Bates objected.

"Well, consider the evidence, my boy," Grassety continued impressively. "A man is murdered in his apartment. A woman in a pale green dress is seen in the room with him just a moment or so before his death. The only clue is a pale green handkerchief saturated with an unusual and expensive perfume. Of the 24 women in New York who purchased this perfume since January, according to Williston, Crissina is the only one who is definitely placed by her own admission in the apartment of the man a few minutes before he was murdered. She has admitted to the police that the green handkerchief belongs to her. She has admitted that she and the prince quarreled. She has admitted that they were very intimate friends and that she came to warn him about some other woman, a white woman."

"Of course," he continued, "I know Crissina is innocent, but the point is that all this police evidence will seem to be conclusive to the average jury."

"Yes," Bates objected, "but why should she cut off the fellow's finger. Nobody's thought of that, have they? And couldn't some one else have got to Destu's apartment after Criss left? They didn't have to come from outside the house, did they? Couldn't they have come from some other apartment? And why should we dismiss everybody else that bought that perfume just because Criss admitted that the green handkerchief might belong to her?"

Crissina's face softened into a slight smile of gratitude as the dynamic young man so vigorously championed her cause. Of all her friends he had been the only one to rush promptly to her aid. Good old Roger Bates! It was in times such as these that the true worth of one's friends was revealed. But, of course, she knew it was more than just friendship with Roger Bates. She knew he had idolized her, thrown his heart at her feet a dozen times, and although she liked him better than anyone she knew, she had turned him down because he was an impecunious newspaper man who she had felt had no future. Now he was repaying her indifference with his devotion.

"Bates," said Attorney Grassety slowly, "there may be a whole lot in those exceedingly interesting questions you put."

"There must be," interjected Mr. Van Dyke. "There HAS to be. Grassety, I think you ought to have young Bates to help you in this case. He seems to be so keen and enthusiastic. He's always been a smart boy."

"Thanks, Mister Van Dyke," said Roger, "but I'm in on this case anyway. Any time Criss is in trouble I'm here to help her."

The words moved her deeply. She turned, her eyes damp with sudden tears and touched his hand.

"Oh, Rod!" she exclaimed. The emotion choked her.

Grassety regarded them keenly through a cloud of tobacco smoke that surrounded his bulldog head. They made a nice-looking couple, he thought, he quite black and she almost white, and both handsome. But what would old man Van Dyke say to such a match? There had never been any black folks in his family as far back as could be remembered. But how circumstances change attitudes!

"Now listen Criss," Roger went on, "put on your thinking cap and answer a few questions. First off, how many pale green handkerchiefs do you have?"

"Just one, Rod. I have one for each dress, you know."

"Well, have you worn that pale green dress since then?"

"No, I . . . I just couldn't, Rod. There were too many unpleasant associations. So I just hung it away in the closet."

"All right, we're going up to your room," he announced, springing up and striding toward the stairway.

"Why, what in the world . . . ?" she exclaimed, puzzled.

"Come on!" he commanded. Then to the two men: "We'll be right back."

He preceded her up the broad stairway. She followed in silent wonder. They came to her door. He stepped aside for her to enter. She snapped on the light. The room was a modernistic glory, in black and silver and red. Concealed indirect lights shed a pleasing golden glow over all.

"Gee!" gasped Roger in open-mouthed astonishment. "All the time I've been coming to your house and I've never seen this before."

"Of course not, silly," she laughed, bothered by his enthusiasm and general optimism, "I can't be taking my gentlemen visitors into my boudoir."

"Well, it's sure a swell dump," he complimented slangily. "It must have cost the old man scads of dough. No wonder he is always parking on folks' doorstep when he heard they're low in bed."

"Rod! Aren't you ashamed to fib like that on Dad?"

"Well, I heard," he sang softly, "I only heard. It wasn't told to me, I only heard."

"Rod, you're incorrigible. Now what do you want up here."

"Where do you keep your handkerchiefs?"

"There." She pointed to a drawer.

He walked over, pulled the drawer out and emptied its fluffy contents on the bed. There were handkerchiefs by the score. Laundered and crumpled, white and lavender and blue and pink and red and almost every color of the spectrum. He snorted in disgust, dumped the wisps of cloth back into the drawer and returned it to its place. Then he straightened up, excited once more.

"Your purse!" he cried. "What kind of a purse did you have?"

"Pale green, of course. It's in the next drawer. I haven't used it since that . . . since that night."

Roger Bates snatched out the drawer now keenly on the scent, and fingered among the score or more of purses. They were of all shades and of every material, of almost every size and shape.

In the bottom of the drawer far to the rear he found the pale green purse. He snatched it eagerly and opened it. Inside was a pale green compact and lipstick holder, a package of French cigarettes and to his great satisfaction, a flimsy pale green handkerchief. Hastily he lifted it to his broad nostril and scented its delicate perfume.

"Hooray!" he shouted, dancing around the room and waving the wisp of cloth aloft like a triumphant banner. "This really gets it. Criss, you pretty rascal, I think I'll have you out of this yet."

Rod ambled into the station house, immaculately garbed as usual, a cigarette dangling from his lower lip.

"Hi, Hawkshaw!" he sang at Jim Williston as he strolled into his office and parked on the edge of that worthy's desk.

"What do you want, nuisance?" growled Williston, rearing back in his swivel chair and blowing a cloud of blue smoke from a fat cigar. "Every time I look up nowadays you're hanging around here. What are you looking for now, some time?"

"Ha! That's a laugh," sneered Rod. "Fat chance you'd have pinning anything on me, flatfoot."

"Oh, I don't know about that, kid. Just start something and I'll have you up the river in no time."

"Oh, yeah! You and what other five thousand? If you're so wise, Sherlock, suppose you give me the latest dope on the Prince Destu."

"What! Give you anything for that lying rag you work for? Not a living chance. Besides, why don't you go to the district attorney? He's paid to give out statements. I'm paid to get the goods."

"Another laugh!" Rod cracked, scratching a match on the desk and lighting another cigarette. "The city's throwing money away, then."

"Well," boasted Williston, "you see what I did on that Destu case. I really got the goods on that Van Dyke gal. She's a cinch to get the works. Pretty fast work, eh, Wiseheimer?"

"Ah, that's just a whole lot of guessing. I know all about that. With the State Department at Washington hollering for action, you flatfoots had to nab somebody, and you pick on that fine gal just because she happened to be visiting the guy."

"What's the matter? She your gal, Bates?"

"Well, believe me, Hawkshaw, I got sense enough to know that Crissina Van Dyke didn't murder Destu." Rod spoke earnestly, his bantering manner gone.

"You can't beat evidence, kid," said Williston airily, well satisfied with himself.

Detective Pat Sullivan sauntered in and hailed them.

"Hi, Chief! Hi, Bates! Say, kid, who let you in this place?"

"What is it, a zoo or something? Maybe it is at that, with all you gorillas around," cracked Rod. He was well liked by everyone at the station house. "I'll have to get a card from the Park Commissioner."

The two officers grinned under his banter.

"Hey, what do you think, Pat? This kid's running around here with the notion that we ain't got goods on Crissina Van Dyke."

"Jeez, that's a hot one," the Irishman exclaimed, grinning and shaking his head in mock concern. "Maybe the African guy wasn't croaked at all, at all."

"Maybe not," echoed Williston, and the two officers roared at Rod's expense.

"All right, laugh, you gorillas. But you can't laugh this off." He handed Williston an envelope from his coat pocket.

"What's this?" the Lieutenant growled, straightening up.

"Open it and see, smart feller."

The big Negro opened the envelope while the white officer looked on curiously. Inside was a flimsy pale green handkerchief.

"Smell it, you big goof," ordered Rod. They mechanically obeyed.

"Where'd you get this, Bates?" Williston was all alert now. The hound again on the scent.

"Out of Crissina Van Dyke's pale green purse that she carried the night of Destu's murder and had not used since. Just walked into her room last night, looked in a drawer and found it. Now if I'd been a detective that couldn't have happened, could it?" He leered at the two detectives, enjoying the consternation and discomfiture registered in their faces.

"How do we know this isn't a plant, Bates?" snapped Williston.

"Yeah," added the Irishman, his blue eyes narrowing as their police skill was challenged, "how do we know YOU didn't plant it?"

"You don't know whether it's a plant or not," Rod admitted frankly, "but I know it isn't. See? Miss Van Dyke didn't have but one of these handkerchiefs. She told me that casually before we ever went upstairs. I looked among her handkerchiefs. No two were alike. There was no green one. Then I looked through her purses, found the pale green one and there was this handkerchief. So, flatfeet, if we suppose that the handkerchief you found ISN'T Miss Van Dyke's, then it belongs to somebody else that uses Elegante perfume."

"And you want us to believe that, eh?" sneered Williston, though he was obviously impressed.

"No, Jim, you don't have to believe it. But it's given me something to work on and I'm going to knock this case sky high."

"Go ahead, kid," grinned Williston, "and see how far you get. Maybe you'll find the real murderer." He winked at Sullivan. "Next thing we know he'll be a police inspector."

"Aw, now Loot," jeered Rod in mock sorrow, "I'm sorry you don't think any better of me than that."

"Well, what do you want me to do with this?" asked the black officer, waving the wisp of green coquettishly.

"I'll tell you, Jim. You compare it with that other handkerchief the D.A. has in his safe. They're both alike and both have the same perfume on them. Assuming that there's been no plant, that Miss Van Dyke DID only have one green handkerchief and that this is hers, then who owns this one? Riddle me that, copper!"

Rod sauntered triumphantly out of the office, leaving two thoughtful detectives behind him.

"What do you make of it, Chief?" asked Sullivan.

"That's a pretty smart kid, Pat. And you know I don't sleep any bets, but after all the dame admitted she was in the guy's apartment just before he was croaked. The case against her is good and tight, but we're supposed to make it absolutely certain. I'll have to think over this. It does change things."

Rod hurried to the Finchley Arms Apartments, borrowing a ride from a friendly taxi man. It was an impressive building of yellow brick looming above the fence-crowned retaining wall that separated haughty Edgecombe Avenue from more proletarian Bradhurst. A modish canopy extended on gleaming brass standards from the recessed entrance to the curb. A tall, handsome dark man erect, in plum-colored uniform, trimmed with gold, stood at the door.

"Hi, Frank!" Rod greeted him.

"Hello, Bates. What you up to now? Looking for dirt?"

"Well, you see I know where to come, right up here amongst the dicties. Say, listen Frank, is Ethel Johnson in the office?"

"Yeah, what do you want with her? You know Sam Johnson don't allow no parking in his garage, and I don't mean maybe."

"Always signifying, eh? Naw, I'm not trying to bite Sam, I just want to get some dope for the paper."

"Well, she's got it all." The doorman waved toward the office of the building located in a nearby one-room apartment. Rod went in.

Ethel Johnson was the beautiful and capable secretary of Bennie Moseman, the Semite who owned Harlem's most fashionable apartment house where more than 100 families of the haute monde resided. She beamed as Rod entered.

"What now, Brisbane?"*

"You're always insulting me," Rod returned. "How are you today, sweetheart."

"That's a nice name to call a married lady. I'll have to tell Sam about it."

"Yeah, you would. You always were sadistic. . . . Now I'll tell you what I want to know. Remember the night Prince Destu was knocked off?"

"It seems like I should, brilliant sir," she grinned, shoving her pencil in her hair.

"Well, how many apartments on that side of the house had been recently rented or were vacant?"

"What do you mean by 'recently,' Rod?"

"Oh, say within the past two months."

Mrs. Johnson reached for a file drawer, pulled out several cards and studied them thoughtfully.

"Well, there were no vacancies in that wing at all. But there was a one-room apartment on the same floor rented furnished just two weeks before. Say, what do you want to know all this for? Don't you go putting any lies on this house in that sheet of yours. There's been enough said already."

"Tell me, Ethel," asked Rod, intense now, "who rented that apartment?"

---

*Arthur Brisbane (1864–1936) was the highest paid newspaper editor and writer of his day. Hired in 1897 as managing editor of William Randolph Hearst's *New York Journal,* Brisbane oversaw the newspaper's soaring circulation. He also wrote a widely syndicated column for the newspaper from 1917 until the day of his death—*Ed.*

"You know I'm not supposed to give out information like that, Rod," Mrs. Johnson countered.

"Well, the cops are not supposed to pin a thing like this on an innocent girl like Crissina Van Dyke, either, but they're doing it."

"What makes you so sure she's innocent?"

"Well, I'm just sure, that's all."

"You must be in love with her, Rod." She looked up at him and grinned, knowingly.

"So what?" he challenged. "Come on, give me the dope, will you, kid?"

"What dope?" a familiar voice boomed behind them. Rod whirled around. Behind him in the doorway, hands in his pockets and rolling a fresh cigar around in his mouth, stood Jim Williston.

"Hi, copper!" Rod hailed him, pretending indifference. "What you doing, following me?"

"What dope was it Bates wanted, Mrs. Johnson?" asked Williston, ignoring Rod's gibe.

The secretary looked from one to the other man, her face suddenly grave with concern.

"All right," Williston reminded, his voice a little more stern. "What was it he wanted to know?"

Without any more hesitancy, Mrs. Johnson explained. Rod stood aside, a frown of irritation corrugating his brow.

"So, young Sherlock," sneered Williston, "you think you've picked up something, eh? Well, Mrs. Johnson, let's have the information. It will do no harm to let him know. He's a smart lad. We'll just go up together, Bates, and have a look around. I like your company, you know."

"Well, I can't exactly say that the feeling is mutual, flatfoot."

"Now, now, son, never antagonize the Law," Williston bantered. "All right, Mrs. Johnson . . ."

"It was a fellow named Ali Sibra, some kind of foreign Negro."

"Aha!" Rod exclaimed, leaning forward.

"Is he here now?" asked Williston, eagerly on the scent.

"No, he moved away just two days ago."

"What sort of looking chap was he? Do you remember?"

"Yes, sir. He was tall, black and handsome with bushy hair and features like a Greek god." She spoke with a little more than the necessary enthusiasm.

"Ho! Ho!" chuckled Rod, "the boy must've 'sent' you."

"Oh, shut up, Roger Bates. You're always signifying."

"Did he speak plain English?" Williston pursued.

"No, if he hadn't been black I'd have said he was an Italian."

"Ring for the doorman," Williston commanded.

Frank came in a moment in response to her order given over the house telephone.

"You remember this foreign fellow, Ali Sibra?" asked Williston.

"Sure," Frank grinned in remembrance, "he always tipped swell."

"Who visited him during the time he was here?"

"Not many people while I was on duty, but they were all white. I remember two men and a woman."

"A woman!" cried Williston and Bates in chorus.

"Yes, an ofay gal."

"Describe her?" Williston snapped.

"Well, I can't very well because she wore a veil. But she was tall and looked like she was pretty. She didn't say anything except 'Mr. Sibra, please.' When he called back over the 'phone, he didn't ask who it was but just said 'Send the lady up.' She never did give her name."

"Now the men," Williston queried. "What did they look like, Frank?"

"They came in with this guy Sibra one night and after staying a while, they went back out with him. One of them was tall and looked like a gentleman but a foreigner, I'd say a Spaniard. The other was short and quite dark. Must have been an Italian."

"How long was this before the murder?"

"About a couple of days, if I remember right. The woman came about four or five days before."

"Now the other doorman is Willie Smith, eh?"

"Yes, sir."

"Get him up here right away."

"He's asleep, sir."

"I don't care. Get him up here!"

"I'll telephone him, Mr. Williston," Mrs. Johnson volunteered.

"Why didn't you tell us all this before?" accused the detective, frowning at the doorman.

78

"Nobody asked me. Besides it isn't anything for white people to come here."

"That was a brilliant question, Hawkshaw," jeered Rod, lighting a cigarette and smirking. "No use snapping at this guy because you bulls slept a lead."

Williston glared at him. Then his good humor returned as swiftly. "Well, smart aleck," he inquired, "what do you think about it now?"

"Just like I've always thought. You bulls are barking up the wrong tree. Miss Van Dyke is innocent. Just a victim of circumstances. Now you're getting somewhere. There's something funny about this guy Sibra and his white friends. When you find that guy, Williston, you'll clear up a lot."

"I wouldn't be surprised," the detective agreed. He walked over to the outside telephone and dialed a number. "Hello! This you, Inspector? Yeah. . . . Say, I think I've run into something new on that Destu case. . . . Yeah . . . I want you to send out a call and bring in a tall, black bushy-haired man, with very straight features. A foreigner. He talks with a slight Italian accent. I understand he associates a lot with white people . . ." (aside to Mrs. Johnson:) "About how old was he?"

"About 30 or 35," she answered.

"About 30 or 35. . . . Yeah. He moved away from here two days ago. . . . I'm up here now trying to find something out about him. He moved in here two weeks before the guy croaked. . . . Yeah, we might talk to him."

Willie Smith, a light brown, sleepy-eyed fellow, shuffled into the office rubbing his eyes and grumbling. He recognized Williston, who had questioned him before and nodded to Rod, whom everybody in Harlem knew.

"What do you want?" he asked, addressing the detective.

"You remember this foreign Negro, Ali Sibra, who had the one-room apartment on the south wing of the fourth floor near Prince Destu's?"

"Yes sir, but he moved out day before yesterday."

"Yes, I know. Would you know him if you saw him again?"

"Sure would, the way that guy tipped."

"Did you ever see anybody visit him?"

"Well, lemme see. He didn't have many visitors, but I remember once or twice he came in with white men."

"What did they look like?"

"One was tall and thin. The other guy was short and sort of dark. They looked like Spaniards or Italians."

"Did a white woman ever come to see him?"

"Well, he came in once or twice with a white gal but she always wore a veil so I couldn't be just sure about how she looked."

An idea suddenly flashed in Rod's mind. He leaned forward. Intense. "Listen, Willie, do you remember the night the prince was killed?"

"Sure do, the way the cops grilled me." Willie grinned in recollection.

"Well, think back now," Rod continued. "Did you see this Ali Sibra that night at all? Or did anybody come to see him? Think now!"

Williston nodded his approval of the question, smiling at Rod approvingly.

The sleepy-eyed doorman yawned behind his hand and then furrowed his brow in thought. The others waited almost holding their breaths. For whatever Willie might say would have important bearing on the case.

"Well," he said, after a minute or two, "it seems to me like I do remember."

"Go on, man!" insisted Williston. "This is important."

◇◇◇Chapter VIII

The sleepy-eyed doorman thought carefully, trying to remember the events of the fatal evening.

"Yes," he said finally, "about eight o'clock the prince came in with an old white man . . ."

"You told us that," snapped Williston, impatiently. "The white man left, you said, about 15 minutes later. Is that right?"

"Yes, he left about 15 minutes later. Then in about an hour I remember this fellow Sibra came in with the little dark white man and the white woman."

"You're sure it was the same woman that had been coming to see him?" asked the detective.

"No, sir, I ain't sure. You see she always wore a veil, but she looked like the same woman. Tall and slender like, and dressed outta this world."

"Did you see them leave?"

"No sir, I don't recollect that I did. If they left, they must've left while I was gone to supper between twelve and one 'cause I stayed right on the door, like I told you, I had to with all them bulls and doctors running in and out."

"Did either of these white men or the woman ever stay all night in this fellow Sibra's apartment?" asked Williston.

"Not that I know of, sir."

The detective turned inquiringly to Frank, the other doorman.

"No sir," he answered to the unspoken question, "they never did while I was on duty."

"All right," snapped Williston, "you boys can go."

The two doormen left immediately, glad to get away from the quizzing. Williston addressed Mrs. Johnson.

"Let's take a look at this fellow Sibra's apartment. Has it been cleaned since he left?"

"Yes sir, all apartments except the housekeeping apartments are cleaned every day."

"Who cleans them?"

"The maid, Clara Fuller."

"Get her down here. I want to talk to her. She's a pretty intelligent woman, I recall."

"How would you know?" asked Rod innocently.

Williston glared at him.

"That's all right, Hawkshaw," soothed Rod, chuckling. "No harm meant."

"You're going to keep clowning around until you find yourself over on the Island," the older man threatened with mock seriousness. Then to Mrs. Johnson, "Hurry and get that maid down here."

The secretary rang the apartment in which the maid was working and ordered her to the office. Fully 10 minutes passed before the buxom, smiling Mrs. Fuller put in her appearance, wiping her gleaming black face with her apron. Williston immediately began questioning her.

"Did you clean that Ali Sibra's apartment every day?"

"Yassuh, eve'y day, an' he sho had uh funny smellin' apa'tment."

The statement took every one back. Rod and Williston looked at each other.

"What do you mean?" snapped the detective. "How did it smell?"

"Hit jis smelt funny das all, lak somebody bin smokin' reefuhs er som-pin, but Ah ain nevah seed nuthin'. Ah smelt all tha cigarette butts in the ash trays but none uh dem smelt lak reefuhs. Ah sho looked all ovah dat room but Ah ain't nevah seed none."

Rod leaned forward, his countenance bespeaking the curiosity that filled him.

"Listen," he asked suddenly, while the others turned to hear him, "did this fellow have a trunk?"

"Yassuh, he had uh trunk, all right, uh gr-a-a-t big trunk en uh coupla suitcases."

"What other luggage did he have?" continued the reporter.

"Well, lemme see. Ah rec'lect he had uh li'l squah box kinda boun' wid iron."

"Ever look in his stuff while he was gone?" Rod asked.

Mrs. Fuller glanced at Mrs. Johnson and hesitated to answer. The others smiled knowingly. The secretary nodded encouragement.

"Didn't you just take a little peek around sometimes to see what this funny Negro had?" urged Rod, persuasively.

"Well," replied the maid, looking down at her feet and then grinning sheepishly, "sometimes Ah did sorta look 'round whilst Mistuh Sibra wuz gone."

"Did you ever see what he had in his trunk or his suitcases or the little box?" asked Rod. Williston stood aside smirking at the questions of this amateur.

"Well, sometime he lef' his trunk unlocked, en his suitcases wuz allus unlocked. They wa'n't anythin in 'em 'cept clothes en some papuhs en uh coupla books."

"What kind of books?"

"Laws men, Ah couldn't read 'em. Hit were funny writin', lack uh chicken done stepped in uh inkpot en walked up en down on de pages."

"Um hum, just as I thought," said Rod, more to himself than to the others, "It was probably Arabic."

"What's that?" asked Williston, looking puzzled. "What's Arabic?"

"That's the writing most Mohammedans in the Near East use," Rod explained. Then turning again to the maid, he asked: "How about the little square box bound with iron? Ever see inside that?"

"Nossuh, Ah nevah did. He kep' dat locked up a-l-l de time."

"Was it heavy?"

"Nosuh, hit wa'n't heavy."

"Did there seem to be anything inside it?"

"Yassuh, hit did 'pear tuh have sumpin' in hit, sumpin' dat rattled like."

Rod smiled and settled back, a triumphant look in his eyes.

"Well, you see, smarty," jeered Williston, "you didn't find out anything after all that's worth anything."

"Maybe not," Rod grinned widely, arching his eyebrows knowingly.

"Now Clara," asked the detective, turning to the black woman, "when you cleaned up this fellow's room after he left, did you find anything in it? Think carefully, now!"

"Nossuh, hit was clean as uh whistle. His place allus wuz clean. On'y thing Ah eveh foun' tha' wuz uh bloody handkuhchief one moanin', lak had uh nose bleed."

"What morning was that?" snapped Rod, at once alert.

"Now lemme see," she said, turning her head on one side like an inquisitive chicken. Then suddenly she brightened with returning memory. "Ah know, hit wuz th' moanin' aftuh day foun' dat otha foreign nigguh laid up tha on th' same flo. Ah rec'lects de handkuhchief wuz down in de bottom draw uv his bureau wha he kep his dirty clothes."

"What did you do with it?" asked Williston, taking up the questioning.

"Do wid hit?" echoed the maid. "Ah didn't do nuthin' wid hit. Ah jis leff hit right dar. Hit didn't belong tuh me, en Ah doan nevah tech nuthin' whut don't b'long tuh me. Nossuh!" She shook her head emphatically. The others smiled at her vigorous defense of her honesty.

"Well, that's all," announced Williston. "There's nothing to it, just as I thought, but if we can pick up the guy we might question him. All right, Mrs. Johnson, get your keys and we'll take a look at that room of his."

"Clara will show it to you. She has a skeleton key. I can't leave the office."

"All right, Clara," he ordered, "let's see the apartment. You can come along too, Bates. You're pretty good company. You'll keep me laughing trying to be a detective."

Rod grimaced, winked at the attractive Mrs. Johnson and followed the others to the automatic elevator. They got off at the fourth floor and the maid admitted them to 4-C, the apartment Sibra had occupied. It was one large room with an alcove for cooking curtained off. Simultaneously the two men noticed the peculiar odor of which the maid had spoken.

"Smells like reefers, all right," said Williston. Rod nodded, glancing swiftly about the room.

There was little to see. Just a bed, a bureau, a small table with a radio on it, a tiny bathroom and behind the curtain was a small gas stove, a sink, a closet for dishes and cooking utensils, and a small electric refrigerator. The two windows looked out on the narrow court. A fire escape began at the left-hand window and ran off to the left, evidently serving several apartments. Across the court was the adjoining apartment house from the windows of which Grandma Hassaltine had witnessed the strange happenings that had caused her to telephone the police on the tragic evening.

Rod went quickly to the left-hand window, raised it and stepped out on the fire escape.

"Where you going, Sherlock Holmes?" jeered Williston, biting off the end of a big black cigar. "Don't fall off. You might hurt the pavement."

Rod grinned back at him and disappeared from view. He was back in a moment.

"Do you know," he said with ill-suppressed excitement, "that you can almost see into the apartment Destu had from the end of this fire escape?"

"So what?" sneered Williston.

"So someone could have left this room, crawled along the fire escape, stabbed the prince and returned easily and swiftly."

"And, then I suppose they went back, took the knife out of Destu, hacked off his finger, put the knife back in its hold and left while the old woman was looking at them but didn't see them. I know you're going to make a swell detective." He blew a cloud of blue cigar smoke disdainfully at the ceiling.

"No, they didn't have to do that," continued Rod, very seriously. "I believe I know just how it was done, who did it, and why."

"Well, well, well!" sneered the detective, "Suppose you tell us how it was done, who did it, and why, smart fellow."

Williston was eager enough to hear Rod's version of the murder. Although the evidence against Miss Van Dyke was overwhelming, he hated to believe such a fine, clean girl could be involved in so sordid a tragedy. As a Negro it would have suited him better if Rod's suspicions were confirmed. And yet there was the evidence that placed Miss Van Dyke in the murder apartment almost at the time the crime was committed, evidence based on her own fatal admissions. Moreover, she had been friendly with the prince, friendly enough to warn him against going out with other women, friendly enough to gallivant about Europe with him. Even a fine woman of her type would often murder when it was a matter of love. Many had done so. And yet the leads this young whippersnapper had uncovered were sufficiently disturbing to warrant investigation. Pretending nonchalance, the older man blew a cloud of blue cigar smoke and gazed inquisitively at the newspaperman.

"I said I believe I know just how it was done, who did it, and why," repeated Rod tantalizingly, "but I didn't say that I was going to tell you coppers. I'm not sure yet, but when I am, you'll know it. You cops have got your theory and I've got mine. We'll see who'll get the straight dope."

"Now listen here, you," Williston shouted, disappointed that Rod preferred to keep what he knew or thought to himself. "We can stop you from interfering with the law if we want to. You're just getting a little too smart around here."

"Go on and stop me," Rod jeered, tossing a cigarette out of his package into the air and catching it neatly in his mouth, "and see what I write about this case. This thing is full of dynamite, copper, and if you're as smart as they all say you are, you'll play along with me. You can't lose and you may win. Think it over, Jim."

With that last flip, Rod sauntered out of the room and disdaining the elevator, raced down the three flights of stairs to the lobby, and with a nod to Frank Smollens, the doorman, he hurried out to the curb and hailed a cab which shot him straight down Edgecombe Avenue to 139th Street.

That quiet, spotless, tree-lined thoroughfare lined with stately brown and yellow facades of expensive residences of the wealthier Harlem Negroes was almost deserted at that hour of the afternoon. The shades were drawn at the regal Van Dyke home. Rod dismissed the cab, leaped up the stone steps two at a time and leaned against the bell button.

There was no sound within. He rang again and again. Finally he heard an upstairs window cautiously raised. Glancing up quickly he saw the Van Dykes' maid, Lorena.

"Go on 'way from here," she shouted down. "They ain't nobody at home."

"It's Roger Bates, Lorena. Let me in. I know Miss Van Dyke is there. I must see her. It's very important."

"Well," the girl grumbled, "they told me not to let anybody in here a-a-tall, but I guess you're different. I'll ask Miss Crissina."

She disappeared, lowering the window. Rod waited, impatient as usual of any delay, dragging nervously on a cigarette, straightening his necktie. At last the front door was unlocked and the maid admitted him.

"Where's Miss Van Dyke?"

"She's in the upstairs parlor. She says to come up."

He raced up the broad, curving staircase and into the parlor, his spirits soaring at the prospect of being once again with her. His heart skipped a beat and his breath stopped when he saw her.

She was reclining on a pea-green chaise lounge, dressed in a feathery pink negligee, so much effected by ladies of the better class. One high-heeled pink mule had fallen from her tiny pale foot with its manicured and stained toes, her strikingly beautiful face revealed some of the strain through which she had gone. She smiled pleasantly through her troubles as Rod entered.

"God, but you 'send' me!" he gasped in admiration. "Criss, I guess you're the most beautiful woman in the world."

"Oh, Rod! Why don't you stop your kidding?" but a pink flush crept up toward her brown hair.

"I'm not kidding, Criss," he said earnestly, sitting in a nearby chair, "and you know it. I've never been kidding where you're concerned. When I say I worship you, I'm speaking gospel."

"All right, have your way then," she said, smiling to cover her confusion. "Well, have you found out anything more that will keep your princess from going far up the river, young man?"

"You think I haven't?" he Harlemed. "Say, I've been busy. The State of New York will never get you, gal. I want you for myself."

"Oh, stop your foolishness, Rod. What have you found out?"

"Give your Uncle Rod a kiss and he'll tell you?" he flipped, but in his eyes, so deep and dark, she saw a worshipful plea.

"Tell me first," she bargained, "and if the news is good news, I'll consider this unseemly request. Otherwise, nothing doing."

"Tough, eh?" he mocked, though there was a trace of disappointment in his tone. "Well, I have nerve enough to take one, slim princess, but I know you'll be glad to give it when you hear what I have to say."

"Oh, for Lord's sake, Rod," she cried, "out with it! You don't realize what a strain I've been under or you wouldn't clown so much."

In great detail then, he told her what had happened that morning. She listened attentively.

"Now there you are," he concluded triumphantly. "When we can get hold of this Ali Sibra, I think we'll be pretty close to the murderer."

"I believe so, too, Rod." There was hope in her words and gratitude in her eyes. "That really lifted me."

"Well, do I get the kiss?"

She laughed her assent, revealing a perfect set of pearly teeth between coral pink lips. He approached her reverently, almost half afraid, and touched his large full lips to her small thin ones. His chocolate-colored fingers held her pale petal-like cheeks. Her eyes closed to avoid the burning intensity of his. Suddenly she pushed him gently but firmly away.

"Time out for breathing, Rod! My, you ought to be in pictures!"

"I could do that forever," he confessed earnestly, fixing his intense gaze upon her charms.

"I'll bet you could," she agreed.

They exchanged a few pleasantries and then Rod returned to the case.

"Now what do you make of all this, Criss. You'd known Prince Destu for six months here and abroad. Didn't you know anything about his mission? Didn't he ever tell you why he was coming to the States?"

"Well, the truth of the matter is, Rod," she said slowly, "that I know a great deal about his mission but I was sworn to secrecy in Paris."

"But your life is at stake now, Criss."

"I know, but that's not supposed to make any difference. In this business one is supposed to keep one's mouth, Rod. Otherwise it may mean death sure enough. Don't you understand?"

"No, I don't understand, Criss." Rod frowned in irritation. I'd think you'd tell me what you know. How else can I help you? If you can tell me anything about these people, don't you see how much it'll mean?"

87

She regarded his well-manicured nails thoughtfully and bit her lower lip as she frowned and closed her eyes. He knew some strange struggle was going on within her.

"Were you in love with him?" he asked, his expression hardening.

There was a long interval of silence. Then she lifted her eyes to his.

"I liked him," she replied. "Perhaps I was fascinated by him. He was a great prince, a well-educated, brilliant man, a clever diplomat and the hair to a prosperous kingdom in Ethiopia. I did not love him but I derived pleasure from his charming company. Soon I found myself helping him in his efforts to help Ethiopia. I was sworn to secrecy. Naturally I could not divulge what I knew to the police. It has little, if any, bearing on the crime."

"But now that you may die for this crime," asked Rod, "will you tell me so I can save your life?"

"Yes," she almost whispered, "I'll tell you Rod, but no one else."

◇◇◇Chapter X

Big, florid Inspector Rogan listened attentively, his head cocked on one side as Jim Williston talked. Occasionally he frowned darkly.

"Well," he observed when the Negro lieutenant had concluded, "this thing is getting a little too complicated for me, Jim. I thought we had the goods on this Van Dyke woman, and I still think we've got a pretty good case against her. Yet, that handkerchief story sounds pretty straight and the sudden moving of that Sibra fellow is worth looking into. I put out a call for him like you said. If he's in town the Missing Persons' Bureau will find him."

He leaned over a crude pencil drawing on his desk and studied it for a moment or two, scratching the side of his large nose the while.

"Whether anybody reached the prince's window by way of the fire escape or not," he declared, pointing, "it could have been done. And the maid says there was a bloody handkerchief in Sibra's laundry the morning after the murder, eh? Humph! That could mean something or nothing. I'd like to talk to that fellow."

"Yes, Inspector," added Jim, rearing back in his chair and chewing on the end of a black cigar, "and there's something more needs explaining."

"What's that, Jim?"

"Smith, the doorman who was on duty that night, says that about nine-fifteen this Sibra guy came in with the little dark white man and the tall veiled white woman, but they didn't leave while he was on duty, or he didn't see them leave. Neither he nor the other doorman, Smollens, ever knew either of Sibra's white visitors to stay all night in his apartment. In the first place, it's only a one-room apartment and there wouldn't be room enough unless they all slept in the same bed."

"Well, you can't never tell about them foreigners," the inspector observed, grimacing. "Anyhow, I'll be glad to get hold of that Sibra and have a talk with him. He can clear up a whole lot. So far, we have nothing that changes the situation regarding the Van Dyke woman. She admits she was in the prince's apartment just before he was croaked and she admits they quarreled. That's enough for a conviction."

"But I sort of doubt she's really guilty, Inspector," said Jim Williston soberly. "Yet there's nothing we've got yet that will shake the district attorney's case."

"It's in the bag," Inspector Rogan observed with conviction.

* * *

Speaking with her customary fire and intensity, Crissina told her secret to Roger Bates. The young black man sat forward in his chair listening eagerly as her story unfolded and feasting his eyes upon her pale yellow beauty. Finally her voice fell and she was finished.

"Now Criss," he said, a new respect for her in his tone, "you've explained how in your desire to help Ethiopia, you assisted Destu in espionage in Europe, and you've told how you became a valued member of his group, uncovering much information of value relating to the plans of the Italians to invade and conquer Ethiopia. Criss, I'm sure proud of you. It takes brains to elude the Italian secret service as you did and to contribute so much to the disruption of the Fascist plans. That's a real service, and I know you did it for the love of the race. But there are some things I'd like to know in a little more detail. For instance, did you know the nature of Destu's mission to the United States?"

"No, Rod, I didn't. You see I was just an operative or agent. I did as I was told. In London the head of the Ethiopian espionage was Martin, the Ethiopian minister. In Geneva it was Hawariate. In Paris it was Sooma. In Rome it was Dr. Wanza. Now don't ever whisper a word of this, Rod. You know I wouldn't tell you if I didn't . . . er . . . trust you implicitly."

"Humph!" Rod snorted, "I thought you were going to say if you didn't love me."

"Oh, Rod!" she protested in mock annoyance, but the color swept up her cheeks, her eyes fell and she smiled. She recovered her poise with an effort, avoiding his burning gaze. "Well, to return to the story. These four men directed the European espionage of the Ethiopian government. Under them were many operatives. I was merely one of them. It just happened that I was a close friend of Prince Destu. As I told you, it was he who got me into the works."

"And you weren't in love with him?"

"No, silly! Will you never stop talking about love? You must be crazy, Roger Bates."

"Yes, crazy about you," he confessed, unashamed.

"Well, to go on, Destu was sent to Paris for training in espionage under Sooma, a clever old man who served under Menelik. And as I've told you, we worked together in London, Rome, Geneva and Berlin before we came to the States. Destu was sent here to head up the work in this country. In addition to keeping track of Italian war purchases here and getting over favorable Ethiopian propaganda, he was supposed to arrange credits if possible. He looked to me for advice, and I gave it to him freely, but I did no real espionage work for Ethiopia here. I visited his apartment several times, of course. But Destu was necessarily close-mouthed and kept the details of his business to himself."

"Did you ever have any words with him? I mean did you quarrel?"

"Only once, the night he was murdered."

"What was that about?"

"Oh, it was about a woman, but you understand that I had no personal interest in the matter," she added hurriedly, noticing the gloomy look that came over his countenance. "It was merely that I knew his weakness. He was an admirable fellow in every other way but he was crazy about women. He hadn't been here long before he had an affair with Helene Custis and got her all crazy about him. Well, that was all right so far as I was concerned, but when he began going around with that white woman, I felt it was time to intervene. It wasn't because she was a white woman but because I was suspicious that she might be an Italian agent. When I saw them at the theatre together one night, I thought I recognized her as a woman I had seen abroad on one or two occasions in Rome and Geneva. Then when father saw them driving together on Riverside Drive, I was more than ever convinced that Prince Destu should be careful."

"Did you get a good look at her, Criss?"

"No, not close. You see, we were sitting on opposite sides of the orchestra pit, and they left before the play ended. When the lights went on after the last act, I looked for them and they were gone. That aroused my suspicion, too. I think she must have recognized me and then got him to leave on some pretense or other."

"Did you try to find out anything about her?"

"Of course, but I wasn't successful. All I learned was that they had been seen several places together. Well, I went to him on that fateful night to warn him against this woman. I really had nothing on her. It was merely a hunch. But he got mad and we had a few hot words. I left after about ten minutes and went home. The next morning I read that he had been murdered." Her voice lowered in sorrow as she thought of the tragedy.

"One more thing, Criss. Why did Prince Destu wear the iron ring inlaid with an ivory cross on his middle finger? Did it have any significance?"

"I think so, but I'm not sure. I asked him about it once but he froze up, so I never mentioned it again. But here's something significant. I noticed that both Sooma and Wanza wore them also. I don't know about Martin and Hawariate. Sooma's and Wanza's rings were exactly like that of Destu."

"Did you ever see Destu take it off?"

"No, he couldn't get it off. It was either welded on his finger or it had been placed below the joint when he was quite young. We've been bathing together at Deauville and other watering places and I never saw him even attempting to take it off."

"Well, what did you think about it?"

"I was curious, of course. I thought it might be the insignia of some Ethiopian secret society."

"Could it have had anything to do with espionage?"

"Perhaps. I thought of that when Destu froze up when I asked about it."

Rod's brow furrowed in thought as he lit another cigarette and rose to go. She watched the play of his mobile features. Suddenly he swooped down and kissed her full on the lips and with a mischievous "good-bye," scampered down the stairs. She ran lightly after him, her pink negligee billowing behind.

"You cad!" she yelled after him. "You might have asked for that. Where are you going?"

"I take what I want, young lady," he mocked from the door. "I'm going out to find our mysterious white lady now. I think I've got a good hunch."

◆◆◆ **Chapter XI**

Rod strode east to Seventh Avenue. Although close to six o'clock there was no suggestion of dusk. He made his way easily through the crowds of sauntering colored folk to the Renaissance. He'd get a drink and a sandwich before following his hunch. He nailed two or three cronies as he made his way to the bar. He ordered a Manhattan and proceeded to lose himself in the mazes of speculation.

"Well, it's just too bad for your girl friend, kid," jeered a familiar voice at his elbow.

He turned quickly. Jim Williston was standing close by, a fresh black cigar tilted at a jaunty angle in one corner of his mouth and a drink of liquor in his fist.

"What do you mean, Loot?"

"What's the matter? Don't you read the papers? Look at that!" The detective thrust a 7-star edition of an evening paper under his nose. A headline fairly shouted at him from the printed page.

NEGRO FOUND MURDERED
IN 'LITTLE ITALY'
Man Sought by Police
Stabbed to Death on Tenement Roof

A foreign Negro in his early thirties was found stabbed to death late this afternoon on the roof of a tenement house on Second Avenue in the heart of Harlem's Italian settlement. The man, later identified by the police as Ali Sibra, was being sought for questioning in connection with the recent murder of Prince Haile Destu. The body, still warm, was discovered by Mrs. Enrico Castellone, a tenant of the apartment house who went to the roof to hang up some clothes.

According to the Medical Examiner, the Negro had been dead but a short while. The knife that caused his death was firmly imbedded in his back. No fingerprints were found on the weapon, indicating that the murderer wore gloves. Police identified Sibra from descriptions given by employees of an Edgecombe Avenue apartment house where he formerly lived.

Police attached considerable significance to the fact that Sibra was murdered less than three hours after a call was sent out over the radio to bring him in for questioning. They believe that he must have possessed valuable information bearing on the Destu murder which someone did not want divulged.

There was much more to it but Rod could read no further. He felt a little faint within. He had attached so much importance to the capture and questioning of Sibra. And now the man was dead. Another opportunity to vindicate Crissina was gone.

"Well," observed the sleuth, "that makes things a little tougher for Miss Van Dyke. Sibra might have told us something but they've shut him up."

"But you can try to find those two Spaniards or Italians that hung out with him, can't you? They probably had a lot to do with this killing. They must be around the neighborhood somewhere." Rod spoke excitedly.

"Keep your shirt on, kid," mocked Williston, removing his cigar to sip his whiskey. "We've thought of all that. But it's hard to find two wops in a town where there's a million of them, you know. Besides we've got no good description. All we know is that one was tall and gentlemanly and the other was short and quite dark. That description could fit millions of wops."

"But he must have been living in the vicinity, maybe in that very apartment house. He must have had baggage or something." Rod was grasping at straws now. He saw the lieutenant's lip curl.

"Guess you think we don't know our business, eh?" jeered Williston. "Say, we've been in every apartment in that house and the adjoining houses. Everybody says they never seen this guy before. You know how it is, you can never get anything outta them wops."

"But if he was killed on the roof he must have gone up there with someone, either of his own free will or because he was forced to go. If they didn't live in the house, why should they care whether he was murdered on the roof or in the basement?"

"You're asking me?" sneered Williston. "You must think I was there when he was croaked."

"Wait a minute," cried Rod suddenly, ignoring Williston's thrust, "I've got it! Did you hunt for that little square box bound with iron? That's so unusual. I don't think many people would have one. I'll bet you'll find it in one of those apartments or in the basement. Even if there's nothing much in it, it'll prove that Sibra was wherever it is found."

"Yeah, if we find it," added the detective. "Well, that's worth looking into. I'll call up the inspector."

Suiting action to words, he drained his glass, sat it down with a bang and walked over to the telephone booth.

Rod, left to his own thoughts for a moment, idly trimmed his fingernails with the pocket knife on his gold watch chain and pondered over the turn things had taken. He had believed Ali Sibra could tell much, but now Ali Sibra was dead. Who could have killed him? And why?

"Well," Williston informed him, sauntering back to the bar, "the inspector thinks that tip's worth following. He's having the three houses searched."

"Three houses?" echoed Rod, somewhat surprised.

"Sure, dummy. The house the guy was croaked on top of and the house on each side. How do we know which house he came out of?"

"That's right. You guys DO know something, don't you?"

"We wouldn't have any jobs, kid, if we didn't know something. We ain't so dumb as you newspaper guys think."

"No," Rod couldn't help from adding, "you're dumber."

Williston took it good-naturedly, as he did all Rod's quips.

"One thing's certain, kid," was the detective's parting shot as he turned to go, "you'd better find out something new pretty quick or that high yallah of yours is a gone goose."

Rod felt lost. Just a few minutes before he had been in high spirits. Everything had seemed so hopeful. Now the outlook was dark indeed. IF he could find the woman who had visited Sibra. IF he could find the woman with whom Prince Destu had been keeping company. IF he could find the two men who had visited Sibra. IF he could find the old white man with whom the Ethiopian had entered the Finchley Arms at 8 o'clock on that fateful evening. All "ifs," nothing more. Not a single clue to go on. Absolutely nothing. A stone wall which seemingly could not be surmounted.

He was halfway through his ham and egg sandwich when a thought suddenly struck him with the force of a projectile. Somebody must have seen Ali Sibra move. At least the doorman. Frank Smollens was on days. Frank would know. . . .

Rod gulped down the remains of his sandwich, took the last swallow of beer and bolted out of the door like one possessed. At the curb he hailed a cab, yelling, "Finchley Arms." He fumed impatiently as the taxi careened around corners and sped up Sugar Hill. It crunched to a stop in front of the deluxe apartment hotel. He noted that Willie Smith was on duty.

"Where's Frank?"

"Down in the room. Why?" inquired the doorman. But Rod was already down the stairs and into the basement.

The other doorman opened his room door and admitted the excited reporter.

"What's up, Rod?"

"You were on duty the day that guy Sibra moved away from here, weren't you, Frank?"

"Yeah, why?"

"Did you help him down with his baggage?"

"Sure I did."

"Well, try to think hard now, what kind of cab did he leave in?"

"One of them Radio cabs, I think."

"Was the driver colored or white?"

"Colored, I believe."

"Are you sure, Frank. This is important."

"Yes, I'm sure the driver was colored because I've seen the fellow."

"Then you could identify him?"

"Sure, I've seen him lots of times up and down the Avenue. You know we see them all some time or other at this house."

"Describe that driver for me, will you?"

"Well, he's a short, brownskin fellow, kinda sharp-faced. Gotta coupla gold teeth. Always gotta cigar stuffed in his mouth."

"Good!" Rod cried triumphantly. "Now we're getting somewhere."

It is not difficult to find a short, brownskin man with a sharp face and two gold teeth, especially when you know what firm he works for. The foreman of the taxicab garage was obliging. When the chauffeur came on duty at a little before eight o'clock, the foreman pointed him out. Rod lost no time in getting to him.

"You're Sam Hogans, aren't you?"

"Sure. What of it?" the chauffeur eyed Rod suspiciously.

"Well, a friend of mine, a foreign-looking Negro with bushy hair, got you to move him away from the Finchley Arms a few days ago. He had a big trunk, two suitcases and a small square box bound with iron. Do you remember? I've gotta get in touch with him."

The hatchet-faced chauffeur pondered for a moment, looking up at the ceiling and scratching his head. He seemed to be having difficulty projecting his mind back. Rod's heart sank. This was the last hope.

"Well," the man said finally, "it looks like I do remember uh fella like that. Lemme see. . . ." His voice trailed off as he struggled to recall. Then he brightened. "Sure! I remember him. I had a time fastening that damn big trunk on my rack."

"Good!" exclaimed Rod, elated at the turn things were taking. "Now where did you take him?"

"Well, as near as I kin figger, it was over around 116th Street and Second Avenue. I know when we gits there uh little wop comes out an' helps th' guy in the house with his duds. I helped 'em with th' trunk."

"Could you show me the house? I'll pay the fare down there all right," Rod added quickly.

"Jump in. I'll do th' best I kin."

Straight down 7th Avenue to 116th Street they sped and then turned toward the East River. At Second Avenue the chauffeur turned south, driving slowly, peering at the grim tenements. He had rolled a couple of blocks when he suddenly stopped.

"That's the place," he announced.

It was just another six-story tenement like hundreds of others in the neighborhood. Across the street from it, Rod noticed with a start, were the three adjoining apartment houses. On the roof of the center one, Ali Sibra had been found dead with a knife in his back. There was a policeman stationed at the door.

"Wait for me," Rod ordered. He jumped out, went to the corner drug store and called up Williston.

"What do you want, kid?" grumbled the older man over the wire.

"Say, I'm down here in front of that house where Sibra was croaked today," Rod announced, "and I've found out that he moved from the Finchley Arms to the house across the street. I've got the chauffeur here who moved him and his stuff down. How soon can you get down here?"

"In about ten minutes," snapped Williston. "Hold everything."

Rod bought a couple of good cigars and sauntered leisurely back to the taxicab. He could see Hogan was beginning to get restless. The chauffeur was reassured by his return and took one of the cigars gratefully. Rod lit the other and sat back in the corner of the cab to await the coming of Williston.

He did not have long to wait. Down the street came two black touring cars, each with its complement of detectives. The Negro lieutenant was first on the sidewalk. He strode over to the cab.

"Good work, Bates. Now where is that house? Over there, eh? All right boys. Go right through from the basement to the roof. Look for that square box bound in iron."

"Is that th' law?" queried the chauffeur, a little disturbed.

"Sure. That fellow is Lt. Jim Williston. I just called him. The fellow you moved down here the other day was found killed on the roof across the street this afternoon."

"So you're a dick, too," sneered the other.

"No, I'm just a newspaper reporter trying to get a beautiful woman out of a peck of trouble. Oh, nobody's going to bother you. Don't worry."

Williston sauntered up, asked the chauffeur a few questions and then let him proceed on his hacking after Rod had paid and tipped him.

A blast from a police whistle penetrated the babble of Italian all about them. Lt. Williston looked up. A white detective was beckoning from the doorway.

"Come on, kid," said the older man. "Something must be doing."

The two men hurried across the street to the tenement.

"What's up, Ryan? Found anything?"

"Second floor, front, sir," the detective answered.

Rod and Williston ran up the stairs and entered the apartment on the second floor. A fat, greasy Italian matron was arguing with a large red-faced detective.

97

"What did you find, Kelly?"

The red-faced detective swept his large hands in the direction of an adjoining bedchamber."All of his stuff's in there, sir."

They walked into the room. The bed was neatly spread. There were the trunk, the two suitcases and the small iron-bound box.

"Open 'em up," ordered Williston.

Neither the suitcases nor the trunk was locked. There was only clothing in them. The peculiar lock on the box required some time to negotiate but finally it, too, yielded. At last the lid was flung back. All came closer. Resting on velvet inside was an Arabian water pipe. Nothing more.

The men looked at each other in disappointment and disgust. "Come on," growled Williston, and led the way to the parlor. Rod lingered behind, took the water pipe out and smelled the bowl. As he suspected, there was the peculiar odor of which the maid at the Finchley Arms had complained.

In the other room the detectives were finding out from the now thoroughly frightened Italian woman when her roomer came, who came with him, what he did and other pertinent information. It was a routine matter. They knew some of it already. He had been there five days. His room had been engaged by a tall, nice-looking man who said he came from Venice and spoke cultured Italian. Ali Sibra, she said, talked good Italian but with a foreign accent. He had said he was from the colonies, having been a government clerk at Massawa before being sent to school in Italy.

"Did a short fellow come here to see him?" Williston asked.

"Ah, si Signor. Every day the little man he came."

"Did a good-looking, tall white woman ever come here to see him?"

"No lady came, signor. Always eet was men, the same two men. One beeg man, another small man."

Williston lit one of his black cigars and let the blue smoke curl about his hat brim. "Well, now the job is to get hold of those two wops."

"Think they'll come back here?" asked Rod.

"Maybe. You never can tell what a guy'll do, you know. I'll park a man in here for a couple of days and see what happens."

Rod felt and looked depressed. The case seemed no farther along than before. It was getting more complicated. Ali Sibra had been killed in the same way that Prince Haile Destu had been murdered. In each case the knife used had been buried in the back up to the hilt and was absolutely without fingerprints.

If, as it appeared, the same person had committed both crimes, that would eliminate Ali Sibra from suspicion as Prince Destu's slayer. Who then had slain the Ethiopian? Why had Ali Sibra been spared until today when the police call went out to round him up? No enemy would have been able to persuade the Eritrean to go to the roof across the street. Therefore, it must have been someone in whom he had trust. It was evident both Sibra and his white associates were Italians. Had they fallen out among themselves or had panic seized the whites, and thinking Sibra might have let information get to the police, they had killed him? But what had they all been doing to make them fear the police?

These and another score of questions raced around inside Rod's head.

He left Williston and the other officers as soon as he could pull away, and hurried to the street. As he strode up toward 116th Street, his fertile mind played with another idea which had intrigued him from the start. It was his trump card. He felt in his inside pocket for the piece of paper Attorney Grassety had given him and noted a name and address marked some days before with red ink. It was a gamble, he concluded, but he'd try anything now.

◈◈◈ **Chapter XIII**

Rod boarded a Lexington–Lenox Avenue surface car and sat down to think as it trundled along. Crosstown to Lenox Avenue, then up through the heart of Harlem, pausing for traffic lights and occasional passengers.

He sat there, the piece of paper gripped in his hand, looking absently into space, pondering his next step. Should he attempt it or shouldn't he? Just how should he go about it? He had marked one name on the list he held in his hand. He had marked it several days before because it seemed the most logical.

"Last stop. 245th Street!" the conductor bawled. Rod came back to earth.

If he was right, he mused, as he stood on the corner near the subway kiosk and lit a cigarette, then he would need help. If he was not well enough prepared, they would get away. Yes, he must be prepared. But

Jim Williston was a hardboiled policeman. He would want more to go on that mere suspicion. Yes, he certainly would.

It took Rod several minutes of telephoning before he located the big, bluff detective.

A half hour later the two men met by pre-arrangement at the Big Apple, where, over a couple of cool highballs, they discussed in an undertone the recent development in the case.

"Listen, Williston, I'm on the up and up with you, and I wouldn't give you a bum steer. It's true I like Miss Van Dyke, but I'm willing to follow facts. I want you to be the same way. I don't believe Miss Van Dyke had anything to do with Destu's murder, and I believe you're coming to see the same way I see it."

"Oh, no. Wait a minute, son. Don't get too fast there. Miss Van Dyke's in a tough spot. If her case was to come to trial tomorrow, she'd be good for the chair or at least 20 years. I agree that the croaking of this guy Sibra, right after we sent out a call for him, looks kinds funny. But that don't wipe out the evidence against Miss Van Dyke. We've put her on the spot at almost the very time the Prince got it in the back. She even admits she was there about that time. Boy, we couldn't have a better case." Williston puffed his black cigar contentedly.

"You didn't find the guy's finger anywhere around, did you?"

"No, what of that?"

"Well, a finger ought to be pretty bloody, especially after just being cut off, eh?"

"Yeah, it oughtta."

"Well, both the chauffeur who carried Miss Van Dyke away from the Finchley Arms and Madame Custis have said that she had nothing to her hand except her green purse. The severed finger should have stained the purse a bit, don't you think?"

"Yeah, it oughtta."

"But, there is no stain on the purse she carried nor on the clothing she wore. What then became of the finger missing off Prince Destu's hand?"

"That's a puzzler, all right," Williston admitted. "But finger or no finger, we gotta good case against that broad."

"All right," agreed Rod reluctantly, and taking another tack. "Suppose that ring on Destu's finger was very valuable to somebody, and it must have been, because the murderer went to the trouble of cutting the finger off to get it."

"How do we know the murderer cut it off?" challenged Williston triumphantly. "That's just supposition. We want facts, kid, not a whole lot of theories."

"Don't decry theories, Sherlocko," Rod admonished. "You've always got to have a theory or you won't know what to do. A theory is just merely a plan, like an architect's plan. How could you build a house or a skyscraper without one? Now, my theory is that Miss Van Dyke had nothing to do with the murder. She just called as she said, had a few words with the prince and left. Right afterward, the prince was murdered, his finger cut off and the murderer made his escape."

"All right, smarty, who was the murderer? Let's have his name and we'll look him up?" Williston's tone was jeering.

"I'm getting to that now," said Rod, taking a gulp of his cool liquid. "You admit there was something peculiar about this fellow Sibra who had the apartment right next to Destu's?"

"Yeah, it wasn't quite reg'lar that guy bein' bumped off as soon as we started hunting for him."

"All right. If there was something not quite right about his white companions. How'm I doin'?"

"That's pretty good figurin'," Williston admitted grudgingly.

"Perhaps you'll agree, Williston, that if we could talk to those two Italians and that white woman, who always visited Ali Sibra, they might be able to tell us a whole lot about him and what his racket was."

"Yeah, maybe they could. But they've scrammed somewhere. We haven't been able to tail 'em."

"All right, then, you want them for questioning. I got a hunch where they can be found. I think it's a pretty good hunch. I can't work on it alone because if I bungled they'd get clean away and I might get what Ali Sibra got and what Prince Destu got."

"So what?"

"So, I want you to take a long shot with me, Lieutenant. You are a cop. You can always cover up better than I can and bluster through a mistake."

"What's the proposition?" questioned Williston with the caution of a policeman of long experience.

Rod took out a notebook and wrote a name and address on it. He handed it to the detective, whose brow corrugated in thought as he read it.

"What's the proposition?" he repeated.

"Just this. You have that address completely covered by your men when I telephone to this party. It might be a good idea to have her line tapped. As soon as I call, she'll probably call somebody else. See? We can then gather from her conversation whether or not she has any knowledge of this case. Either that or she'd go out in a hurry. In that event follow her. I'll be willing to bet anything she'll lead you either to these two Italians or to somebody higher up."

"What d'ya mean 'somebody higher up'?" quizzed Williston, suddenly alert.

"That's just my hunch, Lieutenant."

"Well, we ain't got no business playin' other people's hunches," growled the detective.

"I figured out the Ali Sibra angle, didn't I?"

"Yeah, that was pretty good, all right."

"Well, it was just a hunch, too. Go on and try it anyway, Williston. If the thing is a flop, nobody'll ever know."

"Yeah, that's right, kid." Williston brightened at the suggestion. Like all public servitors, he was averse to taking full responsibility without an out.

"Well, will you do it?" Rod leaned forward eagerly.

"Yeah, I guess we can give it a try. But we can't do it right away. That wire-tapping takes time, you know."

"Well, she might be out anyhow," Rod compromised. "Suppose we say six o'clock tomorrow morning. Nobody over there gets up at that hour."

"All right," growled Williston, still uncertain. "Something tells me I hadn't oughtta do this, but I'll take a chance. I'd like to give that Van Dyke broad all the breaks, bad as things look for her."

Rod was jubilant as they parted and it wasn't the Seagram's that was responsible for it. Here was a great gamble and tomorrow morning would either tell everything or nothing.

Rod's alarm clock jangled loudly at five o'clock. He started up wildly from a nightmare in which he was struggling with a thousand blood-thirsty Italians who held Crissina Van Dyke captive.

Noting the time, he hurriedly dressed and, racing down to the side-walk, hailed a gray and silver cab with blue and green lights which was crawling along the asphalt of Seventh Avenue like some great nocturnal bug. It swerved to the curb as if to devour the man.

"Riverside Drive and Eighty-Sixth Street!" he ordered. He leaped inside, slammed the door shut and sank back into the soft cushions.

Down the almost deserted Avenue they sped as the first gray streaks of dawn appeared over Long Island Sound. Then west on 110th Street to the Drive and south to the destination.

"What number?" the chauffeur yelled back.

"Let me off here!" Rod commanded, opening the door. He paid the jehu,* crossed the street and dived into the servants' entrance of a huge apartment house. He hurried back to the superintendent's apartment and tapped at the door. A uniformed policeman admitted him.

"Lieutenant Williston here?"

"Next room. He's waiting for you."

Several men were in the superintendent's dining room, all detectives. On the table sat the dictaphone to which several wires ran. Reclining on the sofa was Jim Williston, clouding the close air of the room with smoke from a black cigar. Leaning in the door leading to the rest of the apartment stood a diminutive West Indian Negro viewing the proceedings with evident disapproval. Rod surmised that he was the superintendent.

"Well, I see everything's all set," said Rod.

"Just waitin' on you, son," growled Williston, "an' after all th' trouble we've taken, there'd better be something to this, an' I don't mean maybe."

"Okeh, Lieutenant. We'll get things going then. The sooner we find

---

*A proverbial name for a swift driver, derived from the story of ninth-century B.C. Israeli king of the same name renowned for the swiftness and bloodiness of his coup and his war against the worship of Baal (2 Kings 9–10; 15:12)—*Ed.*

out, the better." He walked over to the telephone in the corner which was fastened on the wall. "Is this an outside phone?" he asked the superintendent.

"Yes, it is."

"All right then boys. Here goes."

The officers became alert. Rod dialed a number. There was a long wait as the telephone in the apartment somewhere upstairs rang again and again. Rod turned to Williston.

"Are you sure she's there?"

"Certainly, boy. What do you think we are, saps?"

"Well, I wouldn't know," Rod jeered.

The telephone upstairs continued ringing. The sound of its bell came clearly through the dictaphone to which the officer operating it had attached a horn. Williston frowned.

"Wonder what's the matter with that broad?" he growled.

"Probably somebody's croaked her too," a white detective suggested. "Y'never can tell about these wops, y'know."

Suddenly there was an audible click as the receiver upstairs was lifted and a sleepy voice, a woman's voice, vibrant, youthful and English answered.

"O hello' hello' I say, what is it?" The words came clearly from the dictaphone horn.

"Is this Miss Sylvia Ferndon?" asked Rod.

"Yes, quite so. What is it? Who do you want at this unearthly hour?"

"This is a friend, Miss Ferndon," Rod answered, winking at the officer. "I'm calling in reference to our mutual friend who passed away this afternoon."

"What on earth are you talking about?" There was caution in her voice now. "You completely mystify me."

"I'm talking about Ali," said Rod boldly. "I merely wish to say that everyone involved should get away as soon as possible. There has been a leak to the police. I'm afraid they know too much."

"Who are you?" she asked sharply.

"Should I say more," he countered, "when your wires may now be tapped? I'd be a fool. I've warned you. If you are caught it will be your own fault. I've done my duty."

He hung up quickly before she could reply. Williston patted him on the shoulder. "Pretty good, kid," he grudgingly ackowledged.

"Hernando! Hernando!" It was her voice again, this time calling someone in the apartment.

"W'at ees eet? W'at ees eet?" grumbled a man's voice out of the horn.

"Something very strange has happened," she said, her voice betraying excitement. "Some man calling himself a friend just telephoned 'about our mutual friend who passed away this afternoon.' He said everyone involved should get away at once. Then he rang off. What do you make of it?"

"I don't know," replied the man Hernando. "What else did he say?"

"He said there'd been a leak to the police. He must know something, Hernando. You and Guiseppe must have left a clue of some kind," she accused.

"No, no, Sylvia," replied Hernando's voice, sounding a note of outraged pride. "We nevaire make zee meestake. Nevaire! But zair ees something ver' what you call funny about dese business. Dese contry eet ees bad luck to us, Sylvia. Evairy time something he go wrong. Somebody ver' claiver he ees working against us."

"It certainly looks that way. We've been getting nowhere fast. Bostoni is very angry. He told me today we weren't earning our keep. And it's the truth, Hernando. Well, do you think I ought to telephone him and Guiseppe about this strange telephone call?"

"Certainly, Sylvia, and at once. Can we be sure how important eet ees? Certainly, call them. Have them come to breakfast. We can talk much bettair then."

"Not here, Hernando. That man said our wires might be tapped. You can't be sure how much of a line they have on us. Let's meet at Bostoni's."

"Ver' well."

The dictaphone went silent for a moment. Then there was the sound of a number being dialed on the telephone upstairs.

"Can you trace a dialed number?" asked Rod of Williston.

"Sure, it's a cinch. We know what numbers are dialed by the time it takes for the dial to return to the stationary position. Frank's got that down like a book." Williston jerked his thumb toward the officer operating the dictaphone.

"He times it like you'd time a dash man or a horse, with a stop watch."

"That's a new one on me," Rod admitted.

105

"Tell him what number it was," Williston ordered.

"Pennsylvania six nine, nine, eight, one," replied Frank.

"In the Thirties on the West Side," Williston said.

The connection was completed after a long time. A gruff voice at the other end downtown shouted a "Hello."

"Is that you, Luigi?" asked Miss Ferndon's voice from upstairs.

"Yes eetees. W'at you wa'an' these time in de morning, Sylvia? Don't you sleep anymore?"

"It's very important, Luigi. Hernando and I are coming downtown to have breakfast with you. Perhaps in your suite. I don't want to say anymore. We'll bring Guiseppe."

"Ver' well, eef eet ees eemportant. Come down at nine."

The man hung up. "He says for us to come down at nine," they heard Sylvia tell the man Hernando. "Good," he replied. "Now call Guiseppe."

A number was dialed. Frank timed it. Harlem seven naught, naught, naught, nine. "That's in East Harlem," murmured Williston.

"Hello! hello! Let me speak to Mr. Moroni, please. . . . Well, awaken him. This is important." Sylvia's voice was insistent.

There was a long wait. Finally a man's voice answered sleepily.

"Guiseppe, this is Sylvia. Breakfast with Bostoni at nine. Understand? Very important."

"Yes, Mees Ferndon, I understand." He hung up.

"Well," the officers downstairs heard her say to the man Hernando, "that's settled. Now I'll see if I can't get a little more sleep."

"I guess that's about all, Lieutenant," observed the operator.

"What do you make of it?" asked Rod, turning to the detective.

"They know something about this guy Sibra, all right," admitted Williston. "I'll send a couple of men to pick up this guy Guiseppe Moroni and this fellow Bostoni, who seems to be the big shot. We'll go upstairs right now and talk to this dame and the man, Hernando."

"Don't be a sap!" sneered Rod. "You'll spoil everything if you bother these people now."

"What do you mean?"

"Simply that we don't know enough yet," rod explained. "We've made some pretty good guesses but that's about all. We still don't know who killed the prince nor Ali Sibra for that matter. These white people were Sibra's pals, but if they deny knowledge of the killing and claim they were just friends of his, we haven't a leg to stand on."

"One of these guys," protested Williston, "either the one upstairs she called Hernando or the Guiseppe Moroni she just telephoned, met Sibra when he moved down into Little Italy. We can prove that."

"Yes, my dear Lieutenant," continued Rod with sarcastic patience, "but that doesn't prove that they murdered him. Consider this woman upstairs. She was one of those who purchased that Elegante perfume that was on the green handkerchief that was found in Destu's apartment the night he was murdered."

"How do you know?"

"Nothing simpler. I just used a process of elimination, Lieutenant. She seemed the most likely of the two possible suspects and I took a long chance. I've been vindicated. Not only was she Ali Sibra's friend but she was Prince Destu's friend, also. She was in the apartment that night when Destu was murdered."

"But Miss Van Dyke admitted there was no one in there when she called," Williston objected.

"She didn't SEE anyone, Lieutenant, and there's the point. She was there only a few minutes. Miss Ferndon was there when Crissina came to see the Prince, but she stayed in the kitchen. Remember the green handkerchief was found in the kitchen."

"Yes, I get it, boy, I get it," exclaimed the officer enthusiastically. "You figure that when the Van Dyke dame goes out, the other dame comes out of the kitchen. She's hot because the colored girl has been warning the prince against her. She leaves her handkerchief in the kitchen by mistake. All right, in the meantime the prince has lifted the window shade to let some more air in the apartment. He's kinda hot, too, with two dames on his hands . . . As the Van Dyke dame goes out the old lady across the way just sees the tail of her skirt. When the prince speaks again it is to this Ferndon dame. Now either she's leaving or else she switches out the light so nobody across the court can see her in the prince's apartment, she being a white woman. Right after that the prince gets it in the back with that knife. Why, it looks open and shut to me. Let's go up and buzz them two."

"No, there's where you're wrong, Williston," Rod objected. "The way you've figured things out is pretty good, but we've got to find a motive so the case will stick in court. People don't go around murdering folks for no reason at all. Let's get some more information before closing these people's mouths."

"Just what do you mean, young fellow?"

"Be smart, copper. Don't disturb them now. We'll have the four of them together at nine o'clock in this Luigi Bostoni's suite downtown, won't we?"

"Sure, but . . ."

"Well, the smart thing to do is to get down there, get a wire in Bostoni's room by nine o'clock so we can listen in. Then we'll get a raft of information that even the third degree couldn't otherwise get for us. When we've found out all we can, we can walk in and arrest them."

Williston glanced at the white officers. They nodded their approval. "All right, Frank, get your stuff together and we'll go down to the Belgrade Hotel. It's not going to be easy to get a wire in that guy's room without him knowing it, is it, Frank?"

"Can't tell, Lieutenant. It all depends. We'll do our best."

It was eight-thirty when Lieutenant Williston and Roger Bates came out of the Horn and Hardart Restaurant in front of the Belgrade Hotel and sauntered across the street into the lobby. An officious flunky almost ran up to see what these two Negroes wanted. The Belgrade was an exclusive hote, hence no Negroes were wanted loitering around. Because of the civil rights law, they could not be barred, but they could be discouraged.

"Want something?" asked the flunky.

Williston said nothing. He merely threw back his coat and revealed his badge, pinned on his suspenders. The flunky backed away in confusion. The detective smiled sardonically at the reporter.

The two sat down. In a moment a plain-clothes officer bustled over.

"We made it," he confided sotto voce.

"Yeah? Have any trouble?"

"A little. Some guy had the room next to Bostoni's suite and we wanted it. So we told a lie about the pipes leaking in the room overhead and he'd have to get out. They gave him a better room. Then we went into Bostoni's room to fix the pipes, as we told him. Me and Frank had on dirty overalls and an armload of tools."

"What did he say?"

"He raised hell. Said he had company coming to breakfast. We told him we'd be through and cleaned up by that time. Then we started hammering and raising Cain around there until he stamped out of the place until we got through. That was just what we wanted. We made a perfect plant."

"Is he back there now?"

"Ycah, he's there."

"All right, we'd better be getting up there."

"Suppose they shouldn't come?" asked Rod. "Suppose they got cold feet or had a hunch something was off?"

"I'm knowing everything this crowd does from now on," boasted Williston, dragging on his cigar and blowing a column of smoke toward the distant ceiling. "There'll be somebody on their trail all the time. If they don't show up here, I'll have them arrested."

"Okeh, Hawkshaw. Let's get going."

"No, I'll wait a minute. I wanna see this mob when it comes in."

Minutes passed. The two men lolled in the heavily upholstered red chairs watching the great main entrance, scrutinizing everyone who entered the lobby.

"You oughtta make a pretty good cop," Williston observed. "You've been using your noodle on this job."

"Somebody had to," Rod retorted. "You guys weren't getting anywhere. You see, the trouble with you bluecoats is that you're hunting for convictions instead of solutions. You knew that Miss Van Dyke could be convicted on the evidence, so you were satisfied."

"No, kid, I wasn't exactly satisfied. I wouldn't have given you the breaks I did if I had been satisfied. But you have to accept what evidence you have until better is found. A good cop always finds as much evidence as he can. Of course with us, it's just business. With you it's love. Otherwise you would not care. You never did in the past, did you?"

Rod grinned sheepishly as Williston made his point. He started to reply when the detective's hand gripped his knee.

"This is them!" he announced ungrammatically, nodding toward the entrance.

A tall man who looked as distinguished as a Spanish don entered with an equally tall and slender blonde woman clad in a pink summery dress with white hat, gloves and shoes. She was startlingly beautiful.

"I'll bet they're the ones," Rod agreed. "She tallies with all of the descriptions."

"Except that she hasn't got a veil on," corrected the detective.

"Well, thank God for that. It's a crime to hide a face like that."

The couple strolled past where the two Negroes were sitting. The woman turned her cold blue eyes in their direction as she passed. One saw in them steel and the reflection of icebergs. There was just a quiver of surprise in them as she saw the colored men. Then she swept on to the elevator.

"Let's get going," said Williston, rising.

"The little fellow hasn't come yet."

"He'll be along. Besides, we can't afford to miss anything these people have to say."

Rod and Williston rode up on the same elevator with the couple. The older man stopped to talk to Detective Sullivan, who was loitering near one of the hall windows. Rod walked along slowly. He knew Williston was giving the couple a chance to get into Bostoni's suite.

As soon as the Ferndon woman and her escort closed the door behind them, Williston, Sullivan and Rod rushed into the room next door.

All preparations had been made when the two detectives and Rod sat down around the table to listen to the conversation in the other room. An Italian detective was there to translate anything said in that language.

"Well, now what ees eet?" they heard a man's voice, whom Sullivan recognized as Bostoni's, ask.

"Things are getting rather warm I'd say," answered the woman.

"How so, Sylvia?"

"Well, Luigi, first we lose out on the plans just when we imagined we practically had them in our grasp. Then, Sibra is killed. And now this morning some mysterious person calls up around six o'clock saying he's a mutual friend of Ali's and that everyone involved should get away at once. He said there'd been a leak to the police and that our wires might be tapped."

"Humph!" grunted Bostoni. "Why should ze police be concerned with us? Sibra, he was a ver' valuable man, but we deed not keel heem. Eet ees a meestery to us, too, thees murder."

"Do you think they did it?" the woman asked.

"Why should they? He knew ver' leetle."

"Like us," they heard the man Hernando say. "I hate to lose out like this when we have the theeng almost in our hands."

"You haven't found Tankkard, eh?" asked Bostoni.

"No," replied Hernando. "We do not see heem after he leave Destu's apartment that night. Ah, eef we could only find heem. Then we could do sometheeng."

"And Guiseppe," continued Bostoni, "where is he?"

"He's coming," said Sylvia Ferndon. "I telephoned him. He'll be along soon."

"Well," sighed Bostoni heavily, "eet seems we have been outwitted. Cartoni he veel be ver' angry because ve have failed, ve must find Tankkard. Ve mus' get those plans. Ve must find vether ze thing has been shipped an' on what boat, an' vere eet ees to be landed. Cartoni he veel accept no less."

"Ve have done all ve could do," protested Hernando.

"Ve mus' do more, I tell you," snapped Bostoni, "an' do it queekly.

We know almost nothing about dese invention. Eet may breeng disaster upon our armies. Ve mus' find Tankkard at once."

"Hernando and Guiseppe are the only ones who've seen this fellow Tankkard," said the Ferndon woman.

"Ali Sibra saw him oftener and closer than ve deed," Hernando remarked, "but poor Ali he ees dead."

"Ees zair any connection?" asked Bostoni shrewdly.

"Who can tell?" sighed Hernando.

For an hour throughout the meal the conversation in the other room continued with every word recorded beyond its walls. Nothing more of importance was heard until Sylvia Ferndon murmured wistfully near the end of the meal that "Destu was such a sweet fellow."

"Why do you like dese black men so much, Seelvia?" bantered Bostoni. "Everyvair you have some black lover. In Paris, in Venice, in Rome, eet vaas the same. Vat ees dair about zese black men zat fascinates women like you?"

"Ah, Luigi," she sighed, "you can never understand. They're just different, that's all."

Rod and Lieutenant Williston in the next room looked significantly at each other. A slight flush crept up the cheeks of Detective Sullivan.

The telephone rang. Bostoni answered.

"Yes, eet ees . . . Vat? . . . Yes! . . . My God! . . . All right!"

"What is it, Luigi?" the woman asked. "Anything wrong?"

"Guiseppe ees dead. Murdered!"

"What! Where?"

"Stabbed in the back an hour ago. Under ze Second Avenue El. He nevair had a chance."

"Zat ees terrible," cried Hernando, agitation in his tone. "He was probably about to take ze El down here."

"We've got to be careful, Luigi," said the woman, "or they'll wipe us all out."

"We must get zem first," the chief declared grimly. "I'll tell ze others. Hernando, you hunt for Tankkard."

In a moment the woman and Hernando left.

"Stay here and get everything," Frank commanded Lieutenant Williston. Then turning to Rod and Sullivan, he said, "It's got me beat. We don't seem to be getting anywhere. Who is this Tankkard and what plans had he got? What about this invention they're so excited over?

Who croaked Ali Sibra if they didn't? And why was he rubbed out? Why was this Guiseppe Moroni killed?"

"That's a puzzler, all right, Lieutenant," the Irishman admitted. "All that gab was Greek to me. But I know one thing: this guy Bostoni is gittin' ready to wipe out somebody, an' he must know where they are if he's gonna wipe 'em out."

"Good noodle work," declared Williston. "Now get out after this Ferndon woman and that big wop and let me know from time to time what's going on. I want to know everything they do. Take McCarthy with you. Don't let them get out of your sight."

The two detectives dashed out. "Jones," said Williston, turning to another detective, "keep your eye on this Bostoni. He may lead us to something good. I've gotto take a look at this Moroni guy. Want to go along, Bates?"

"No, I've got to get uptown. I'm working, you know," Rod replied.

What he did not say was that he was bursting with suppressed excitement. He was beginning to see light in the case.

Rod dashed uptown in the Eighth Avenue subway, got off at 125th Street and boarded a crosstown car to Fifth Avenue. Walking north for a couple of blocks, he entered a stately apartment house. Looking over the mail boxes in the hallway he pressed a button over the name "Oscar Holcombe." In a moment the door buzzed and he entered the ornate foyer. Proceeding to the automatic elevator, he opened the door, closed it behind him and pressed a button. The lift rose to the sixth floor.

An eye regarded him through the peephole for a moment after he rang and then the door was opened to admit him, and a tall black man with a flashing eye stood aside.

"I'm Bates of *The Courier*," he introduced himself.

"Yes, I know," snapped the black man. "What do you want?"

"I want to see Mr. Holcombe."

"What about?" quizzed the giant, barring the way down the hall.

"It is most important. I must speak to him alone."

"What is it about?" persisted the man. "I must know."

"Well, tell him it is about Bostoni. He should understand." Rod was fishing but he had evidently used the proper bait.

"Come this way, Mr. Bates," said the black giant. He led the way through two well-furnished rooms where at least a half dozen young colored women sat at desks doing clerical work. In the third room behind a flat-top mahogany desk sat Oscar Holcombe, a short, dark brown man with graying hair and piercing eyes magnified by spectacles with heavy lenses.

"This is Mr. Bates of the Negro *Courier*," announced the black giant.

"Hello, Bates," greeted Holcombe, rising slightly and shaking hands. "I think we've met before. That's some good publicity your paper has been giving us. We can see its effect in our receipts. Well, what do you want now?"

"As chairman of the Help Ethiopia League," Rod began, "you are probably acquainted with whoever is representing Ethiopia in this country."

"You mean the Ethiopian Consul?"

"No, I do not mean the Ethiopian Consul, Mr. Holcombe." Rod smiled mysteriously and was gratified to note Mr. Holcombe's eyebrows elevate slightly. "I mean people more powerful than he."

"Well, go on," urged Holcombe, smiling slightly in turn, but admitting nothing. Rod was convinced from that that there WAS another representative.

"I just merely came by to tell you, Holcombe, that Bostoni is planning to 'get' somebody who has interfered with his plans. That's all I have to say except that whoever is going to be 'got' will need lots of protection. The Italians are desperate."

"Where did you get that?" snapped Holcombe, leaning forward, a heavy frown on his face.

"I got it," said Rod. "Never mind how I got it. I'm a newspaper man. It's my business to get inside dope. I'm a race man, too, Holcombe. Perhaps I could help you a lot if you would open up occasionally."

"What do you mean?" asked Holcombe, his eyes narrowing shrewdly.

"I mean this, Holcombe," said Rod, lowering his voice. "I'm probably the most valuable man in the country to you people. I have seen all of the principal Italian agents. I can recognize them easily any time. I doubt that you know all of them. Unless you do, the plans are not safe. Italy will learn them. They'll find Tankkard, and then . . ."

Rod eyed the little graying Negro shrewdly while he was speaking. At the mention of Tankkard, Holcombe's eyes rounded in surprise and then a slight smile played about his full lips. That spurred Rod on to a gamble.

"Of course I know you think he's safely hidden away," Rod continued, "but the Italians are very resourceful. You'll find that out soon enough."

Holcombe's eyes narrowed and he regarded the young man keenly.

"What do you know about Tankkard?" he snapped.

"More than you think I do, old man. I also know that the Italians are going to make it hot for somebody. Did you hear the latest?"

"What is it?"

"A certain Italian, one Guiseppe Moroni, was found with a knife in his back under the Second Avenue Elevated a little while ago. Too bad about Guiseppe. Were you acquainted with him?"

"No, never heard of him," Holcombe replied, his face expressionless.

"Well, I just thought I'd let you know that the Italians are pretty hot about it." Rod remarked airily. "Guess I'll be going now. I've given you the dope."

He rose and walked toward the door. Holcombe sat motionless.

"I advise you, Holcombe," Rod threw over his shoulder, "to notify the right people that the Italians have sent out the word to get them."

"Thanks. Come again, Bates. Always glad to have you. I'll remember what you told me." There was a slight note of mockery in his voice as he smiled enigmatically.

The tall black man ushered him out of the busy apartment.

Rod strode to the elevator grinning with satisfaction.

The mortal remains of Guiseppe Moroni were on the slab at the morgue. Lieutenant Williston had easily established identification. Both doormen of the Finchley Arms had recognized him as one of the white men who frequently had visited Ali Sibra. The hatchet-faced chauffeur with gold teeth who had driven Sibra to the rooming house in Little

Italy recognized the Italian as the man who had met the cab. The frightened Italian rooming house proprietress recognized him as the man who had come every day to see Sibra. Several people at the East Harlem address where Guiseppe lived also recognized him.

What puzzled Williston was how he had been fatally stabbed in broad daylight with hundreds of people all about him and yet his assailant had not been observed.

"That's what gets me," he confessed to Rod that night as they were refreshing themselves at the Old Colony with a brace of Old Fashion cocktails.

"You say the knife was driven deep in his back?" asked Rod.

"Right up to the hilt."

"No fingerprints?"

"Not a one that we could find."

"Significant, isn't it?"

"What do you mean?"

"Well, there weren't any fingerprints on the knife that killed Prince Destu, either. Nor there weren't any on the knife you found sticking in Ali Sibra's back. In neither case was an assailant seen. In the case of both Sibra and Moroni, the stabbing was done in broad daylight. Only Prince Destu was killed at night."

"That's right, boy. We're up against a pretty wise bunch, if you ask me."

"There'll be a break soon I'm sure." Rod spoke with confidence.

"How do you know?"

"You've got Bostoni, Sylvia Ferndon and Hernando Donatelli tailed, haven't you?"

"Sure, we're keeping track of every move. The guy Hernando is hunting for that Tankkard."

"I don't think they'll find him," said Rod, calmly. "But all we've got to do is sit tight."

"You don't think he's dead, too?"

"No, Tankkard is far more valuable alive than dead. He is the key to the whole situation now."

"How do you figure that out?" Williston lowered his drink and regarded the youth narrowly.

"If it hadn't been for Tankkard, there would have been not a single killing," said Rod.

116

The two men rose to go. The waiter came up with his bill on a tray. Rod fumbled industriously through his pockets. Williston grinned knowingly.

"All right, all right!" he laughed. "I'll take the rap. Don't whip yourself to death trying to find the dough. I know you're broke."

Rod grinned sheepishly as the officer paid the bill. "I'm broke all right. I've gotta get some more dough from Bill Grassety."

"Yeah, I know," scoffed Williston. 'I've heard that one before, too. Why don't you get some cash from old man Van Dyke? He's got oodles of jack. You've done some good work. You should at least get a century."

"If I get Crissina out of this, I'll be satisfied."

"Well, maybe she ain't guilty," Williston admitted slowly, then added ominously, "but the evidence is all against her, kid. After all, she admits she was in the guy's room just before he was croaked. Until you can definitely pin the killing on someone else, we'll have to hold her."

"I'll do it, all right, Williston, and it won't be long now. What I want you to do is to keep somebody watching those Italians."

"Don't worry. They'll never be out of sight. . . . Give me a ring in the morning."

The two men parted. Lieutenant Williston strolled up toward Seventh Avenue. Rod boarded the Lenox Avenue street car. At 145th Street he changed to a crosstown car and rode up to Edgecombe Avenue, where he got off. He walked north on Edgecombe Avenue which crowns the escarpment rising haughtily and sharply above the level dreariness of Harlem, and entered the towering Briarcliff Apartments, next door to the Finchley Arms.

Scorning the ancient elevator, he walked up the seven flights of stairs to the roof. He unhooked the penthouse door and stepped out. Below him on all sides lay the glittering lights of Harlem and Washington Heights. On the roof were only mysterious shadows thrown by chimneys, dumb waiter shafts and clothes drying. The night noises of the city rose to greet him from below.

He walked over to the side opposite the Finchley Arms. That exclusive apartment house was a story lower than the Briarcliff, but only a few feet separated them.

He stepped on the fire escape and with catlike tread descended until he was slightly above but opposite the windows of the apartment that had once been occupied by Prince Haile Destu. It was no longer vacant.

Sashes were raised because the night was warm. Inside a pretty young woman moved about. On the floor below him, he knew, dwelt old lady Hassaltine, the State's important witness whose testimony might help send Crissina to the chair. She always sat at her window. He didn't want her to see him in this uncompromising position. So he retraced his steps to the roof. He was satisfied with what he had seen.

He opened the penthouse door, hooked it and prepared to descend. The staircase was dark up there. He struck a match to light his way down to the top floor.

"Put out that match!" came a grating command, and something hard was jabbed into each side of him. "Now get going and don't squawk or it'll be just too bad."

◈◈◈Chapter XVIII

"Make one move and we'll drill you. Understand?" one of his captors snarled, punching Rod in the side with an automatic pistol.

"Now get down them stairs and don't waste time."

Rod noticed that his captors were unmasked when they got down to the top floor where there were lights. They were stern-visaged blacks of a type with which he had become familiar in covering the police courts.

Downstairs and out of the Briarcliff Apartments they went. The men pushed him toward a long black limousine. He opened the rear door and stepped in. The two men jumped in behind him and one sat on each side. The chauffeur, who had been slumped down in the front seat, now straightened up. The car sped off. The curtains were jerked down.

Rod soon lost track of which way they were going, but judged they were going down the express highway because there were soon no stops for traffic. "Say, what's the idea?" he asked once. "You keep your trap shut!" one of his captors growled, so he lapsed into silence.

At last the car stopped. Rod was hurried out and into a loft building. It seemed to be somewhere near South Ferry because the smell of the sea was in the air. He was directed toward the elevator with the warning that "One peep outta you, kid, and we'll drop yuh."

The old elevator rattled up two, four, six, ten, fifteen stories. At the sixteenth floor it stopped. Down the corridor the three men, Rod and his captors, proceeded until they came to an office door lettered "Oriental

Importing Company." One of the men tapped at the door lightly. It was immediately thrown open by a powerful Negro whose manner and movements reminded Rod of a black leopard he had once seen at the Bronx Park zoo. The man eyed them from cruel little yellow eyes and then standing aside permitted them to enter an outer office, motioning to chairs. Then he went to the door of an inner office, tapped and entered. Rod and his captors sat down on a bench. In a moment he returned. He motioned to the trio to enter the inner office.

"Go on in, Bates," growled one of the men. Rod obeyed.

This inner office was more richly furnished than the outer one. Everything the well-appointed office should have was there. Thick rugs, an electric water cooler, filing cases, several comfortable chairs and a huge glass-topped mahogany desk, at which a stately, sharp-featured dark brown man with bush hair sat gazing grimly at the young man as he entered. At the side of the desk sat an elderly white man.

"Ah, Meester Bates, I believe," said the brown man. "We are so sorry to bother you, my friend, but you know too much, Meester Bates, so we must hold you for a while. Not long, though."

"Say, what's the idea?" Rod exploded. Then he suddenly stopped and gazed at the brown man's hand in amazement. For on the middle finger of that hand was an iron ring with a white cross on it. He looked up at the man. His gaze met a smiling countenance.

"Yes, Meester Bates. This is the same sort of ring Prince Destu wore the night he was killed. I see you recognize it. And I know you are bursting with curiosity. Aren't you?"

"Quite right, Meester Bates. I am Sadiu Mattchu. You have never seen me before. I have seen you often. I have been interested in your activities, Meester Bates. This is Meester Tankkard about whom you are so curious. He has rendered a great service to Ethiopia."

The elderly white man bowed.

"Now, Meester Bates," Sadiu Mattchu continued, but more ominously, "just how much have you found out about the death of Prince Destu? As his countryman I am naturally interested."

Rod hesitated. It was all a matter of guess work, hunches, and suspicions with him, but he decided to take a long chance.

"I should think you'd ought to be interested, since it was you that had him killed."

The man's eyes opened wide. He regained his composure with great difficulty. His soothing voice belied the dangerous gleam in his eyes when he spoke.

"So you think I, an Ethiopian, had a prince of my own country killed."

"Yes," continued Rod, sure he was on the right track, "you had Prince Destu killed because you believed he was about to betray his country by turning over the plans of Tankkard's invention to Sylvia Ferndon, the Italians' agent. You must have suspected him all along, knowing his weaknesses. You knew that Ali Sibra was undermining his health and lowering his moral resistance with hashish. You had Sibra killed because Prince Destu might have told him too much. You had Guiseppe killed because he, too, knew a great deal. If you have not already had him killed your next victim will be Hernando Donatelli. Or perhaps Luigi Bostoni. Or maybe even Sylvia Ferndon. These people have helped disgrace Ethiopian royalty. You swore revenge, and you've made good, Mattchu."

Rod watched the play of emotions on the dark face and knew that he had guessed right. When he had finished the Ethiopian was trying to smile away his evident surprise.

"I said you knew too much, Meester Bates," he remarked. "That's why we brought you here, and will keep you here until we are on our way back to our country. We admire your perspicacity, Meester Bates, but it is dangerous to our interests to have you abroad. So we shall keep you here. But tell me how you found out so much? I am curious. Sit down, my friend, sit down. Here, have a cigarette. . . . Now tell me how you learned so much."

"Well, I was sure Crissina Van Dyke didn't do it. I was doubly sure when I found out about Ali Sibra. I thought the Italians did it then, but I changed my mind when Ali Sibra and Guiseppe Moroni were killed in the same manner as Prince Destu. I knew a man must have done it. Tonight I found out how the three were knifed without any telltale fingerprints being left."

"And how was it done, my friend?"

"One of your men is an expert knife thrower who does his work with gloves on. He descended the fire escape on the Briarcliff Apartments until he was just slightly above Destu's window. When the Prince opened the window, that gave your man his chance. That's how it happened that Destu was stabbed in the back. Moroni and Sibra were also slain from a distance. The penetration of the knife to the hilt revealed that it was hurled from a considerable distance. Well, how far off am I, Mattchu?"

"You are doing fine," congratulated the Ethiopian. "I am glad to give you the satisfaction of knowing you are correct."

"And yet," accused Rod, "you would permit an innocent girl to be convicted for a crime of which she is ignorant and not raise a finger to save her."

"Not so fast, Meester Bates, not so fast. It is for Meess Van Dyke's sake that I am going to tell you the truth now."

"But who will believe me? Everybody knows Crissina and I are sweethearts. I have no proof of all these things," complained Rod.

"That is why I have Meester Tankkard here to listen also. He will support your word. It is true that I had Destu and the others killed. Destu was a sensualist. He permitted himself to get involved with that white woman. He let Ali Sibra debauch him with hashish, a habit of which we thought he had been cured. These people came to dominate him. He knew too much to be left alive. He had to die. You saw my bodyguard in the outer office? He is your expert knife thrower. But he will not be punished, Meester Bates; he will be rewarded by his emperior. Tonight we leave, Meester Bates, Sadja and I. How we leave will be our business. We shall carry with us the complete plans for setting up and using Professor Tankkard's death ray which will annihilate the Italians who have invaded our country. The most important part of these plans he turned over to Destu that night.

"The woman was in the Prince's apartment to get them. The others were waiting in Sibra's apartment. My man Sadja was on the opposite fire escape. Another man was in the corridor outside the apartment. The Ferndon woman went to Destu's apartment. Shortly afterward Miss Van Dyke came, staying but a short while and leaving after a quarrel. While she was there the Ferndon woman hid in the kitchen. While Destu and Miss Van Dyke were quarreling my man in the corridor slipped in with his skeleton key and hid in the alcove. Destu, warm with his argument with Miss Van Dyke, raised the window. Sadja threw the knife, my other man turned out the lights. The Ferndon woman, panic stricken, rushed from the apartment. My man promptly got the plans. Then he stopped to get Destu's ring which is very valuable to us Ethiopians in the espionage and diplomatic service as a means of unfailing identification. By the time the police arrived my men were well away."

The Ethiopian fell silent, regarding with amusement Rod's outraged expression which the callous recital had induced.

"This is war, my friend," Mattchu apologized. "Ethiopia is fighting for her life. We cannot be squeamish. Italian bombs have killed thousands of defenseless women and children. What are the deaths of a few men like Sibra, Moroni, Donatelli and Bostoni compared to them?"

"But you haven't attended to Donatelli and Bostoni," Rod chided.

"You err, Meester Bates. This afternoon Meester Holcombe he conveyed to me the information you so kindly gave. When those two gentlemen came here earlier this evening looking for me, I was prepared. They will be found tomorrow, Meester Bates, in the courtyard sixteen floors below. By that time Sadja and I we shall be oh! so far away! . . . And now, Meester Bates, I must take Sadja and return to Ethiopia. Our mission is ended. Professor Tankkard, who has been staying with me a little while, will remain with you. The men who brought you here will see that you do not leave. I wouldn't antagonize them if I were you. In two days you will be free to tell what you know and free Miss Van Dyke. That's fair, isn't it?"

"But how will you get away, Mattchu? Murder is an extraditable crime anywhere. The American government will demand your return."

The Ethiopian smiled, rose and walked toward the door, pausing to place a friendly hand on Rod's shoulder. "Return?" he echoed. "But Meester Bates, there is no record that we are HERE. We are secret agents. We come and go about the world without the ordinary formalities. We change our names as often as our shirts. We forge or steal passports as we need them. We are, Meester Bates, a law unto ourselves. Our only allegiance is to Ethiopia. Our only enduring enemy is stupidity. Well, make yourself comfortable. Goodbye, Professor Tankkard. It has been so good knowing you."

He opened the door, walked out and closed it behind him. In the outer office they heard him say, "Come Sadja, we mustn't miss our plane."

The End

REVOLT

IN

ETHIOPIA

A Tale of Black Insurrection Against Italian Imperialism

George S. Schuyler,
writing as Rachel Call

The warning bell sounded. Late visitors streamed down the gangplank to join the crowd at the Marseilles quay, and the *S.S. Metallic* was nosed gently on its way by a pair of sturdy little tugs.

Dick Welland leaned over the rail and waved at the two blonde little French girls who had made his stay in the wicked seaport so interesting. He sighed pleasantly, as the big white steamer got under way, and lit a cigarette with his silver monogrammed lighter.

It had been a pleasant interlude in his leisurely journey around the world. A year ago, he recalled for the hundredth time, he had been cursing his luck. Then, he was a red cap in Chicago, two years out of Fisk University and no prospects. Now he was wealthy, a man of the world, young, handsome and with nothing to do but enjoy himself in the gay spots of the globe.

The answer was oil. It had never meant anything in his life until nine months before. Then his Uncle Jefferson Welland had conveniently joined his ancestors and, being childless, had willed his immensely valuable oil lands around Kilgore, Tex., to his favorite nephew. Three months ago he had left America behind.

Dick sighed again at the thought of his good fortune. What glorious times there were in the offing for him! There was Alexandria and Cairo coming up. Gorgeous nights with sloe-eyed girls under the tropic moon. He would see all the places he had read and dreamed about. Yes, he was one American Negro with money who did not intend to waste his time in prejudice-ridden America. Not a chance in the world.

The crowd at the quay had dwindled to a white spot by this time. He turned leisurely from the rail and made his way down to his stateroom to unpack, take a shower and go for a turn abut the deck before dinner.

Before Cabin 34 he paused smilingly as he heard the voice of Bill Sifton inside booming out some Rabelaisian stanzas of that underworld Negro classic, "Bud." He pushed open the door to find the comical-looking little bowlegged fellow busily going about his chores.

"You're pretty happy after that stop in Marseilles, eh, Bill?"

"Yes sir. That sure is some town. Yes sir. They sure is a whole lots o' pretty wimmin in that town. And boss, they knows they stuff."

"But they're not like those browns in Harlem, are they?"

"Well," Bill paused and displayed a wide expanse of pearly teeth, "I don't know, boss. They are and they ain't."

"What do you mean: they are and they ain't?"

"Well, I tell you, Mister Welland. I'm used to them wimmins in New York and Chicago. They're all right, and all that, but after Paris and Marseilles, I kinda figure these French wimmins has really got something."

"Bill, I think you just naturally like white women. I noticed how you got around in London and Brussels and Copenhagen. Why half the time I couldn't find you."

The valet chuckled. "Well, boss, you wasn't so easy to find yourself."

They both laughed. They were more like companions than master and servant. Big Dick Welland preferred it that way. Hadn't he come up from the very bottom himself? But for Uncle Jefferson would he not be still lugging leather in Chicago? Besides, Bill Sifton was one of those rare Negro servants who never forgets that he is an employee and did not presume upon his master's good nature.

After his shower, Dick surveyed his six feet of slender, smooth bronzeness in the long mirror on the bathroom door, and then dressed lazily for dinner. When he finally strolled out on the deck in his carefully hand-tailored tuxedo, he was a sight to make any woman look twice. He had not shone in football and track for nothing.

He had made one turn of the deck and was lighting his second cigarette when his attention was arrested by the sight of a tall slender olive-skinned girl in an expensive coral pink dinner gown talking animatedly with a short bearded brown man with wide-brimmed black hat, a long black cape, baggy white trousers and sharp-pointed patent leather shoes. The contrast between the two was so marked that he could not refrain from watching them closely. Only a few feet away, they were so engrossed in their conversation that they did not notice him staring.

The young woman fairly breathed aristocracy. Her finely chiseled head with its carefully coiffured mound of black crinkly hair surmounted a slender, beautifully turned neck. Her skin was flawless, her eyes clear, black, and flashing. The man, by contrast, was shifty-eyed with marks of dissipation and self-indulgence on his face. There was something foppish and yet shrewd about him. He reminded Dick of a snake. Dick greatly disliked snakes. And for no reason whatsoever he decided that he did not like the little brown man in the black cloak.

126

"No, and let that be final," Dick heard her say. She sounded like an American.

"But why?" the man pleaded, spreading his hands apart. "What have I done? Why do you dismiss me in this manner? Am I a mere nobody? Don't I deserve consideration? Why are you so coldly obdurate? I don't think it's fair, Ettara. There are not many left who can give you the proper station in life, you know."

"Well," she said, with finality, "I told you I didn't want to discuss it anymore. I said No, and I mean that, Resta."

"Is there someone else?" The little man's voice hardened.

"It would be none of your business if there were," she snapped. "Now go away and don't bother me anymore."

She turned and strode athletically past Dick, her exotic perfume titillating his nostrils. The little brown man followed her and grasped her arm.

"Listen to me, Ettara," he cried. "You can't dismiss me in this way. I deserve better. . . ."

"Let go of me," she demanded, trying to shake off his grasp. There was positive loathing in her voice.

"I won't," he growled, "until you come to your senses."

It was none of Dick's business but he couldn't stand it any longer.

"Get away from the lady," he commanded, grabbing the little fellow by the collar of his cape and spinning him around. "Didn't you hear what she said?"

The man she had called Resta quailed before the giant American. Then, regaining some of his courage, he shouted, "You mind your own business, fellow."

"That's what I'm doing, buddy," was Dick's ominous retort.

"Well, clear out, then, or . . ."

"Or what?" asked Dick, all tense now.

The handsome fellow stood transfixed by the melodrama.

"I'll teach you something," fumed Resta, reaching into his cloak.

Dick saw the movement. His ham-like right fist shot out and lifted the man in the cape fully a foot off the ground. He sprawled on the deck like a wet rag.

Dick turned on his heel as he saw several passengers and stewards running toward the scene. The girl was looking at him, a combination of curiosity and admiration.

127

"Shall we stroll along?" he asked, nodding significantly at the approaching crowd.

"Sure," she replied, just like an American.

"I guess I shouldn't have butted in like that," he apologized, somewhat weakly. "But he looked like he wanted to start something, so I thought I'd beat him to it."

"It's quite all right," she said. Her voice was pleasant, refined, rather deep. It had lost the sharpened [edge] of a minute ago. "He had it coming to him."

"Who is he? A friend?"

She smiled and the corners of her mouth bent downward. She seemed to hesitate before she spoke and her face clouded as an unpleasant thought flitted across her mind.

"I guess he's not to be blamed," she replied. "He's in love, or says he is, with me. He is Ras Resta Gusa, Duke of Dessaye, nephew of Emperor Haile Selassie, and, alas, my cousin."

Dick forgot himself and whistled softly. He looked at her now with added curiosity. So she was Haile Selassie's niece? He figuratively kicked himself for butting into a family affair.

"I . . . I'm terribly sorry . . ." he began.

"Don't be. You did me a favor. I loathe him, the little swine."

This outbrust emboldened Dick to dig further.

"My name's Dick Welland," he announced. "I'm an American." Then he waited expectantly, just a little breathlessly, for with each moment he told himself more emphatically that here was the most desirable woman he'd ever seen.

"I am Princess Ettara Zunda," she said quietly, adding: "although titles mean very little these days. We've lost everything to the Italians, you know." Her voice hardened.

"And may I have the privilege of the Princess Zunda's company at dinner?" he asked, holding his breath for the shock of her refusal. He was not prepared for her enigmatic reply.

"I'll do it, of course," she said, "but if you're smart, you won't!"

"What do you mean?" He looked at her quizzically, noting the slightly ominous tone.

"You seem like an intelligent fellow," she replied. "It shouldn't be hard for you to understand the circumstances after having knocked down the Duke of Dessaye."

"Why? Is he so dangerous?"

"More than you imagine, Mr. Welland."

"He doesn't look very dangerous to me. What, is he your fiancé?"

"No, but he has been annoying me with his attentions for a long time. He says he's in love with me."

"And how about you?" He watched her face closely and saw her eyes narrow and her expressions harden.

"I am in love with no one," she said. "There is no time for love with so much to be done. I have no time for romance, Mr. Welland. I hope you don't try to start any. You look like the kind that would."

He started guiltily. He had been thinking what a delectable morsel the Princess Ettara would be, and making a lightning calculation as to the time it would take to reach the stage he desired. Now it seemed his hopes were dashed.

"Are you a man hater?"

"No, on the contrary, I like men," glancing frankly at him, "especially your type."

"Thank you," he said, smiling and bowing low in mock gratitude.

"But," she continued, "there is work to do, work of importance. One cannot permit love to interfere with such work."

They entered the lift and descended to the dining salon. Passengers already seated looked up as they entered. They did make a striking couple. The table steward bore down upon them, towel on arm, beaming. As they were seated, the wine steward, with his jangling keys, hovered close by.

"Just what work is it?" he said, picking up the thread of conversation, "that you cannot permit love to interfere with?"

"Ethiopia," she said, almost fiercely, "Ethiopia is enslaved. Ethiopia must be freed."

"Sounds like a pretty big order to me. It looks like Mussolini has just about liquidated the Ethiopian opposition."

"That's not true," she snapped. "You've been reading the white press. The Ethiopian opposition has not been liquidated. We are fighting on bravely, and we shall win."

"You seem confident."

"I am confident. I shall see the day when the Emperor shall again sit in state in Addis Ababa." Her big black eyes flashed.

"And I suppose your friend, Ras Resta Gusa, will also be there in state."

The steward came with the hors d'oeuvres. The little French orchestra was playing a Chopin waltz. And through the windows the golden Mediterranean moon was rolling across the horizon. The *S.S. Metallic* swam like a swan across the pond-like surface. At tables, all around them, ladies and gentlemen in sub-tropical evening dress were dining. Dick Welland sighed softly with satisfaction and looked across at the olive-skinned beauty whose flashing smile was an ecstatic prayer.

Who was she, he wondered, and on what mission was she engaged? She might not be a princess. There were all sorts of strange people traveling up and down the Mediterranean. Well, at any rate, she was the most attractive woman on the boat, he concluded, after glancing around the dining salon.

Suddenly she stiffened and stared past him. The color drained from her cheeks. He turned in alarm. The diners rose as if by command. Coming down the short staircase from the elevator, holding on to the wrought-iron balustrade, and staggering as he walked weakly forward, was a huge black man with bushy hair. Blood trickled from cuts on each side of his face and from between his fingers, where one hand clutched his abdomen.

"John!" screamed the princess. She fought her way like a tigress to his side with Dick close behind her.

The big, black man muttered something to her, thrust in her hand a blood-stained wad of paper, then pitched forward.

The salon was in pandemonium. Stewards rushed forward and bore the Negro to the hospital, with the princess and Dick following. One glance at the surgeon's face told the story. The bushy-haired man was quite dead.

Princess Ettara stood rooted to the spot, her face like that of a person hypnotized, impassive but not thinking, though Dick could see that she was thinking hard.

130

"Shall I see you to your cabin?" he asked, softly, touching her arm.

"Have you got a gun?" she asked with surprising clamness.

"Why, yes . . . but . . ." he stammered. "Well as a matter of fact, I have two."

"Good. Now take me back to the dining salon. As soon as we get there, you leave and get both of your guns. We may need them."

"What's the idea?" He was suddenly cautious. After all, this wasn't his business. He didn't want to get mixed up in anything that did not concern him. It was getting pretty serious.

"Afraid?" she challenged, a suggestion of a sneer on her haughty countenance.

"No," he replied slowly, "I'm not afraid of anything, but you might at least tell me something more about what I'm getting into. Who was that man? Why was he killed? Why do you want guns?"

"Perhaps I do owe you some explanation," she said, softening. "But please let us get back to the salon quickly. When you return with the guns, I shall tell you who that man was."

They made their way to the lift and descended again to the dining salon. Calm had been restored, but the great buzz of conversation indicated the tenseness still remaining. They felt a hundred pair of eyes focused on them as they descended the short flight of steps at the foot of which a man had just died. Stewards had cleaned up the blood thoroughly but Dick could still see it in his mind's eye.

After a short interval, he excused himself and hurried to his cabin. His valet was out. He hastily rummaged through the bag where he had stuffed his black .32 automatic pistol. The gun was not there. Vexed, he went through all the other bags in turn with the same result. Frowning and apprehensive, he turned to the drawers in the bureau to get the German .38 blue steel automatic target pistol he had seen Bill place there when unpacking the bags. The gun was not there.

Alarmed and grim, Dick hurried down to Bill's cabin in second class.

He was about to knock when he heard voices within. He recognized Bill's voice, but not the other. He knocked.

"Who's that?" Bill shouted.

Dick announced himself and the door was reluctantly opened. Bll seemed annoyed. He did not stand aside so his master could enter.

"Do you want me, Mister Welland?" he asked, hiding his irritation behind a bland smile. Dick was not fooled. He beckoned him to come out in the companionway.

"Who's that in there with you, Bill?"

"It's . . . well, it's a gal." Bill grinned sheepishly.

"Where did you meet her? Working fast, aren't you? Needless to ask whether she's white or not, I suppose."

"Well, she ain't black," Bill harlemed. "And boss," he added, "she's a killer, and she's ready."

"All right, go ahead and do your stuff. But tell me, where are my guns? That's what I came down here for."

"That thirty-two is in that black bag and the thirty-eight is in the bureau drawer," said Bill, relieved that he would not be called away.

"Now the hell of it is, Bill, that they're not there. I've looked in everything. They're gone."

"Gone? Why . . . why . . . Chief, they was there a little while ago. After you left I stayed on until I'd fixed everything up, and I saw both them guns."

"How long ago did you leave?"

"About a half hour. I went right down to the salon to get a drink and right away I met this chick. She speaks to me, in English, too, only like a foreigner speaks it; we have a drink, and then I begin talking business. She savvies everything, and we go to my cabin. Just when I'm sharpening up everything you knock at the door."

"I'm sorry, Bill, but I had to find out about those guns. There's something funny going on around this boat. Be careful. A Negro was killed tonight. Died right in the first-class dining salon, and now my guns have been stolen."

"A man killed?" the little fellow's eyes widened. "Who done it?"

"Nobody knows. He was in first class, en route to Djibouti, like a number of colored people on board. Now Bill, you have that nickel-plated revolver of yours, haven't you?"

"Yes sir, shall I get it?"

"Yes, and I'll go in with you. I want to see this girl."

Bill's face fell. Dick laughed. "Oh, I'll just stay a minute," he reassured him. "Don't introduce me."

They entered the cabin. Sitting nonchalantly in the one easy chair, one shapely silken-clad leg carelessly crossed over the other and a long Egyptian cigarette drooping from the corner of her small carmined mouth, was a stunning girl in her twenties, a Mediterranean type who might have come from any of a dozen lands. She lifted her long, black lashes and lazily regarded Dick. The first thing he noticed about her attractive clothes was that they were well made of expensive material. Her shoes were not the sort one gets in cheap stores. Her hair was as attractively done as the coiffeur of a movie actress. She had an expensive bracelet on her shapely left arm.

Bill handed him the "owl head" revolver and Dick made his exit. All the way back to the salon he thought about the woman in Bill's cabin. Obviously she was out of Bill's class. She did not have the appearance of an ordinary prostitute. Why had she gone to Bill's cabin with such alacrity? The warning of Princess Ettara when she accepted his dinner engagement, the murder of the man John, the theft of his two guns, and now this exotic white girl. What did it all mean? What was the connection?

◇◇◇Chapter 3

The princess looked up gravely as he came to the table and sat down.

"Did you get the guns?" she asked, arching her long, thin eyebrows.

"Someone beat me to them," he said, resuming his seat.

"You mean they were stolen?" Her eyes showed alarm.

"Exactly. They've disappeared without a trace. Someone evidently entered right after my valet left."

She bit her lip slightly and frowned down into her dish. Dick watched her carefully.

"Well," she said, resignedly, "we'll certainly need a gun on this boat." She was plainly worried.

"Why didn't you bring one?" he asked.

"I did, but I didn't carry it around with me and so I just know that it is gone by this time, especially after what happened to John."

"That was the man who was killed?"

"Yes, he was my most trusted servant." Her voice caught a little as she spoke, and he thought he detected the trace of a tear on her long lashes.

"Why should they kill him?" asked Dick. "Besides, whom do you suspicion as the killer?"

"Oh, I don't know. We have so many enemies. There's no telling."

"Do you think the same people stole my guns?"

"Obviously. They thought you were with me. They wanted us to be unarmed. I'm quite sure they rifled my cabin before they attacked John."

"We might go down and see," he suggested.

"Yes," she said, smiling, "and get shot in the first companionway. They know we're unarmed."

"But I've got a gun."

"I thought you said your guns were stolen," she complained, though obviously relieved.

"They were stolen, but I borrowed my valet's pistol." Then he told her about the attractive brunette in Bill's cabin. Her eyes brightened with concern.

"Yes, they suspect we're working together," she murmured, half to herself.

"But what is it all about?" he insisted. "Why should they kill your servant and steal my guns? What is your game anyway, Princess, that they consider it so important?"

He felt her withdraw within her shell and an almost pleading look came into her eyes.

"Please don't ask me," she begged, "I just cannot tell you. I dare not. But I need your help, desperately. I'm all alone now with no one to help me except you."

"Me? Well, I must say that I'm not eager to get involved too deeply in anything so dangerous, Princess. I'd like to help you, but after all I'm just on a pleasure trip, and I've never been interested in politics."

"You don't wish to see Ethiopia free?" she challenged, her eyes flashing. "You do not wish to see the Italians beaten and driven out? You are unsympathetic with the aspirations of black men?" Her face was flushed with excitement. Her voice was cold and accusing. She half rose from her chair.

Now that she seemed definitely angered with him, he became alarmed and his first impulse was to mollify the beautiful creature.

"Of course I want to see all colored people free," he replied soothingly, "and I'd like nothing better than to see the Italians beaten and driven out of your country."

"Then why do you say you are not interested in politics? That is poli-

134

tics, and it is dangerous politics. I, a woman, am willing to risk my life. Why should you hesitate?"

"Now, Princess, don't get melodramatic. After all, this isn't my funeral. I didn't come on this trip to fight any wars, and I'm eager to live a lot longer and enjoy myself. Of course I'm sympathetic with the Ethiopians but frankly I can't see how they can win, so why waste time?"

"They can win" she almost hissed. "They've already penned the Italians in the cities and towns. In the countryside black men control. They can drive out the invaders if supplied with arms and ammunition."

He smiled indulgently. "Yes, but how are they going to get them?"

She looked at him a long time, studying him, weighing him. When she spoke it was with careful deliberation.

"You are an American," she began, "and you have the dash and adventurousness of all Americans; that pioneering spirit that conquers, that spirit which has made our people in America the most progressive Negroes in the world. Oh, I know America. I spent eight years there."

He exclaimed in surprise. Sure, that explained her almost American-accented English.

"I graduated from Howard University in 1935," she went on. "It was just before the beginning of the end. I have been in the thick of things ever since. Although a woman, I have rendered great services to my country. Now I am about to render a greater service. You must not breathe this to a soul or it will mean my very life, but I am on a mission now that will make it possible for our eager millions to have arms in their hands and [drive] the Italians to the sea. I must succeed. You understand, I must not fail. I am surrounded by enemies here and everywhere. I don't know how many. I need help. They have killed my John. Now I am alone. Won't you help me?"

It was hard to refuse such a plea. And yet Dick Welland did not relish interrupting his leisurely trip around the world to become involved in what appeared to him to be a dangerous and losing cause in which he might easily lose his life. He still had a clear picture of John Danillo staggering down the steps into the dining salon with his blood marking his progress. He did not want that to be his fate.

He hesitated and his brow knitted in perplexity. She was watching him closely, with rising impatience.

"Very well," she snapped, reading his thoughts, "go your way and

135

enjoy yourself while a brave nation bleeds to death. I shall do my duty. Oh, I could have luxury and pleasure, too. I have money, plenty of money. But I refuse to have it stand between me and what is right."

She rose, and before he could speak, she swept away toward the lift. He hurried after her as if something important were leaving his life, resolved now to tell her that he would help her. She reached the elevator much before him, hurried in, and evidently told the operator to make haste because the door closed almost in Dick's face and the car ascended. Undaunted, he raced up the stairs just in time to see her disappearing into her cabin.

Women were so impetuous, he growled to himself, shielding his apprehension. Then at that precise moment he took swift and honest stock of his thoughts and confessed that he was in love with the Princess Ettara Zunda. It was foolish, of course, to get mixed up in the Italo-Ethiopian mess, he told himself. How could she possibly put arms into the hands of the Ethiopians? Even when they had arms, he recalled, they had been unable to stem the tide of invasion. What hope was there to do so now? It would require millions of dollars, and how would the arms be transported from Europe to Ethiopia? Was there not already a rapprochement between England and Italy with France willing to make amends? It was utterly silly to think anything concrete could be done to expel the Fascists.

Then he thought of the beautiful princess and his resolution was shaken. Maybe it would be smart to find out a little more about the whole business. He could at least go as far as Djibouti.

All the time he had been standing in one place watching the door of her cabin. Only a few seconds had elapsed since her door slammed shut. He turned to go to his cabin, his thoughts still full of the noble young woman, when he was stopped short by a scream from the direction of her cabin.

He whirled, startled, then sprinted down the carpeted hall to her door. There was no sound within. He called anxiously but there was no reply. He tried the door. To his amazement it opened easily although he could have sworn he heard it click as she slammed it shut.

He pushed the door open. The cabin was in darkness. He called again softly, "Princess." There was no reply. He fumbled for the light switch, his hand moving along the wall.

Suddenly both wrists were seized in a steel-like grip, a revolver muzzle was shoved against the back of his neck and he felt the click of hand-cuffs upon his wrist.

◇◇◇ Chapter 4

When Dick left his cabin, Bill Sifton's enthusiasm for his affair was somewhat dampened, and he became more thoughtful. A man had been murdered and his boss's two pistols had been stolen. Yes, Mr. Welland was right: it would pay to be careful.

Bill didn't have much education, but he harbored a whole lot of common sense. Older than Dick by several years, he felt that he was the younger man's protector as well as his valet. He didn't at all like the looks of things with his boss evidently becoming involved. Bill didn't know anything about the Princess Zunda or Dick's encounter with Ras Resta Gusa, but he had a feeling that he ought to be close to the younger man.

The Mediterranean beauty sensed his preoccupation. She crossed her leg higher and slouched so that the V in her dress collar revealed a great deal more than it had.

"Ze black fellow do not like Donia Gabrelli any more?" she inquired, arching her penciled eyebrows and loosing a sugary smile.

"Yeah," he said, suddenly remembering her presence. "Sho do, honey. Who wouldn't like a killer like you? My! My! My!" He stood back from her and eyed her up and down.

"Stan' up!" he commanded, enthusiastically. And as she obeyed, turning slowly around so he could survey her better, he threw his long, muscular arms about her tiny waist and pulled her fiercely to him.

"Ooh!" she exclaimed. "So ze Americaine do like me a little?"

"Yeah," he murmured, feasting on her rich, full lips.

For a full minute they stood there in the middle of the cabin twined together like two vines, swaying gently to and fro with the motion of the steamer. He looked into her jet black eyes as into twin wells and in their depths saw his own image, along with a great deal more that spurred him to bolder action.

Sighs . . . revelations . . . explorings . . . cries . . . groans and exclamations . . . chiding and laughter . . . shivers . . . and then, exhaustion. . . .

Bill reached over and poured both a stiff drink of Scotch. They smiled

137

delightedly at each other as they drank. Then she sank back into his arms like a white bud surrounded by dark leaves, and again sought his full Negro lips. Bill grinned contentedly. He was no hand for long courtships. He liked quick action. What was the use of wasting time when you knew what you wanted? All foolishness, he always said. She stirred her lithe body and her big bold eyes smiled into his.

Yeah, he told himself, she was really a killer. And she had so much class. Bill wasn't used to much class in women. Most of his associates of the other sex had been what he called "battleships", i.e., women who could work their wiles until midnight and then drink until dawn. This girl was delicate, aristocratic, "classy." He began to speculate about her, now that he had accomplished his end.

"Honey, where is you come from?"

"Come from?" she cooed inquiringly. "What is zis 'come from'?"

"I mean what's your country? Your town?"

"Oh, mia patria?" She hesitated, her eyes half-closed. Then, "I am from Napoli. Do you know where zat ees?"

"Uh huh. Yeah, that's in Italy, ain't it?"

"Oh, yes. Zat ees right. Sometime you come zere, yes? Donia Gabrelli, she weel be glad, so glad to see you, an' be ver' nice to ze black Americaine."

Italian, eh? He remembered what Dick Welland had said: to be careful. Then he dismissed it. He could take care of himself. Italian or no Italian, it was a cinch he was going to have a swell trip.

"An' wat ees your citee?" she asked.

"Well, I've lived all over America," he boasted, "from Boston to San Francisco, but I was born in Memphis, that's in Tennessee, one of our States."

"How interesting zat you have travel so mooch. Maybe you take Donia wiz you to America, no?" Her eyes sparkled childishly.

Where wouldn't he take a gal like that. Then he thought of a whole lot of places where he wasn't allowed even to think of beauties like Donia, let alone going around with them. But there was no use discouraging her. He wanted to see her again.

"Yeah, baby, I'll take you to America," he lied, "any time you feel like going."

"Ah, your master, he moost be reech," she exclaimed insinuatingly.

"Sure he's rich," Bill boasted. "He's about the richest black man in the world. Got plenty of oil wells and real estate. He can have anything he wants."

"Ooh!" she exclaimed, all ears. "Maybe he like me, yes?"

"Well, he likes pretty wimmins," offered Bill, not over-enthusiastic.

"Maybe he go to Ethiopia on hees trip. . . ."

"He might, but he ain't said nuthin' about it."

"Maybe he weez ze preenciss?" she speculated ingratiatingly.

"What princess?" Bill was genuinely curious. Was the Boss really lined up with some Princess already?

"Zee Ethiopian preenciss," Donia explained. "She is ver' beautiful, ver' beautiful. Maybe he like her."

"Mebbe so. Is she goin' to Ethiopia? I'd think she'd be afraid of the Italians."

"I don't know," she said, feigning indifference. "Maybe you will find out, yes, and tell your master? Zen he might go. They would make zee nice couple. She look ver' smart. Maybe she has some mission, eh?" Donia was captivatingly suggestive and insinuating. As she talked she cuddled, and her long, slender hands were never still.

Bill wondered why Donia should be so interested in the beautiful Ethiopian princess. It was so unwomanlike to wish for a match between a rival beauty and an eligible man. This Donia was unusual, he told himself. And the thought kept recurring to him.

When Donia finally left after a sizzling kiss in the doorway, something impelled Bill to follow her. She was evidently in a great hurry. She hastened down the corridor to the staircase and went up to first class. More curious now, Bill kept his eye on her. It was not customary for second-class passengers to go on the first-class decks unless they were secretaries or attendants. Donia did not look like either. She was too classy. Perhaps, mused Bill, she was like lots of white girls who are curious about Negroes and go out of their way to have an experience. Perhaps she didn't even live in second class.

She turned down a companionway. He watched her at a distance. She stopped in front of a cabin door, looked quickly up and down as she knocked, then was suddenly admitted. Bill hurried by the door. It was No. 16. He walked along the companionway until he saw the steward. He had met the steward before when the luggage was brought to the cabin.

"Hey," he hailed. The steward stopped with a smile of recognition.

"Who's that woman in Number Sixteen?" he asked.

"Numbaire Seexteen?" echoed the steward. "Zaire ees no woman een Numbaire Seexteen. Zat ees Don Carlos Navarre, ze great Spanish grandee. Eet is his cabin. He has no ladyee weez him."

Bill thanked him and passed on. What was Donia to this Spaniard? If she was Italian, he wasn't her countryman. She wasn't traveling with him. Was it another affair? If so, she was mighty hard to satisfy. He chuckled and started to go to Dick's cabin.

Just then the door of No. 16 opened. Bill stepped swiftly into a cross corridor and watched. A short-bearded brown man with a wide-brimmed black hat, a long black cape, baggy trousers, and sharp-pointed patent leather shoes emerged from the cabin, looked up and down somewhat furtively, then moved off in the opposite direction from Bill.

In a moment, the door again opened. A squat, square-built man with fierce mustaches and eyebrows and a swarthy skin came out, and no less furtively than the brown man, looked up and down the corridor, then hurried in Bill's direction. Bill hastily took out a cigar and when the man was fairly close, began lighting it, thus shielding his face with his hands. The squat man passed hurriedly on.

Bill frowned thoughtfully. Suspicion was replacing mere curiosity. Something was going on, he felt, and Donia Gabrelli knew a whole lot about it. Without thinking much about it, he found himself following the footsteps of the swarthy squat man. The fellow stopped in front of No. 46, tried a key, then another key, then finally unlocked the door.

Five minutes later a beautiful, tall, slender colored woman hurried down the corridor and entered the same cabin. He heard a scream. Then he saw his boss, Dick Welland, race to the door and disappear within. Bill tossed away his cigar and hurried to follow him.

Bill turned the door knob and pushed. The door was locked. He pressed the button and heard the bell ring within. He was debating with himself about notifying the steward, when the door opened slightly and swiftly, and a second later he was gazing into the muzzle of a .45 automatic pistol.

"Inside!" growled the masked man confronting him. He stepped back to permit Bill to enter. "Put your hands behind you!" the man commanded again in hard cruel tones. Bill obeyed. A moment later the handcuffs clicked and the cold steel gripped his wrist.

The man pushed him into a chair and switched on the light. The suite was in complete disorder. Drawers from the chiffonnier were in the center of the room. Clothing from the closet was strewn every which way. The trunks were open, and with their wrists handcuffed behind them and their ankles securely tied with stout cord, lay the Princess Zunda and Dick Welland. Another masked man was carefully searching Dick's clothing. Bill was promptly searched and ordered to lie down alongside the others.

The two masked men conversed animatedly in Italian, went over the suite carefully once more, apparently without favorable result. Finally they gave it up. While one of the thugs covered them with a pistol Dick thought looked suspiciously like his .38, the other man took off the handcuffs and unbound their ankles. Then, without a word, they disappeared. When Bill looked out the door they were nowhere in sight.

"Well," said Dick, rubbing his ankles, "whatever they were looking for they evidently didn't find it. I wonder what it was."

"Something very valuable," she said. "One of the most valuable objects in the world. I barely saved it."

"What is it? If they'll go to all this trouble to get it certainly must be worth it's weight in diamonds."

"It is," she admitted, quietly. "With it in their hands our cause would be lost and their cause would be won."

"I don't understand, Princess. Don't you think I deserve an explanation after all that has happened?"

He thought that for the first time she looked just a little uncertain and helpless. She looked at him searchingly. She seemed to want to tell him something but couldn't. In that moment all his sense of chivalry was aroused. The girl was in trouble and all alone, as she had said in the dining salon.

"I'm sorry," she said, and her tone did not belie her, "but who can one trust? I asked for your help a few minutes ago and you hesitated. Surely that doesn't merit you receiving any further explanation. Of course I am sorry that you have become in any way involved. . . ." Her voice trailed off.

In that moment Dick made a momentous decision.

"You can count on me, Princess," he declared quitely. "I'll see this thing through, whatever it is, because I like you and want to help you."

"And I need your help, too. This last outrage proves how desperate my enemies are."

"The Italians?"

"Yes, the Italians and certain traitors among our own people."

All this time Bill was standing by waiting for Dick to tell him what to do, but when he heard the word Italian it started a train of thought.

"Say, Chief," he blurted, "I think I got the low down on them guys."

"Yes? How?"

Bill then related how he had followed Donia Gabrelli to the cabin of Don Carlos Navarre; how the dark man with the cape had emerged to be followed by a man who closely resembled one of the men who had just left the princess's suite.

"That dark man with the cape was the Duke of Dessaye," Dick explained.

"And I'll be willing to bet anything, boss, that he's tied up with them Italians, else what would he be doing in the cabin with the Italian girl and that mug that handcuffed us?"

"You're right, Bill. Now you'd better go down and see if they haven't rifled your cabin."

"Yes sir. I bet they been down there at my place, all right, since they know I'm working for you."

Bill went out just as the maid came in responding to the princess's ring and began straightening up things. Dick and the princess talked inconsequentially until she had tidied up and gone. Then, as they sipped highballs, she told him of her mission.

"You have heard of Emperor Menelik, yes?" Her long-lashed black eyes glowed as she talked.

"Of course."

142

"Well, he always believed that the day would come when Ethiopia would again be attacked by Italy. He knew it would cost a vast sum of money for Ethiopia to purchase the wherewithal of modern warfare. So he accumulated gold and precious stones from every part of the empire until he possessed an enormous store of wealth. This he hid away in a secret place guarded by a thousand picked men, warlike priests of the Coptic Church, high on an almost inaccessible peak."

"And just how do you plan to get it?" he asked, smiling.

"There is only one way, and that is to give the Coptic Bishop Truli Handem the sign."

"What sign?"

"I'll tell you."

"I wish you would, and all the rest of it, too."

"Well," she resumed, "for generations the Emperors of Ethiopia have worn a golden ring once said to have been worn by King Solomon. Before Haile Selassie left Addis Ababa and when things looked darkest, he called Bishop Handem, told him of the impending Italian conquest, and gave him half of the King Solomon ring. Menelik's gold is to be given to no one unless they can produce the other half."

"So that's what they're hunting for, eh?"

"Yes, the Italians are desperate. They are deeply in debt as a result of the Ethiopian disaster. No one will lend them any money because they can offer no security, nothing but boasting. The huge sum Menelik stored away would be more than enough for their purpose."

"Then the key to the whole situation is the half of the ring of King Solomon," Dick surmised.

"Yes, that is the whole thing. Once we can get into Ethiopia, get that gold and get out, we shall be able to buy everything we need and send it in to our armies."

"Then Ethiopia will be free," he said, half to himself.

"Then Ethiopia will be free," she repeated.

Suddenly Dick asked, "How did the Italians find out that there WAS such a ring?"

"Traitors!" she snapped with flashing eyes.

"Like Ras Resta Gusa?"

"Particularly Ras Resta Gusa," she continued. "That man has overweening ambitions. He wants to become Emperor and is willing to do anything to have the honor. He is willing to serve any power that will pay his price, and he has absolutely no scruples whatever."

"Then you believe he is responsible for the death of John Danillo because he thought he could get the ring which he knew you were carrying but didn't know where?"

"Yes, but he is not alone. We must find out more about this Don Carlos of Navarre. I want to see him, since it is in his cabin that the conspirers meet."

"But tell me, Princess, how did you manage to hide half the ring so well that those thugs couldn't find it? Where is it?"

"They were completely baffled, were they? Well, after John Danillo handed me the half ring wrapped in a piece of paper, as you probably saw, I knew immediately that they would be after me. I had to think up a good hiding place and I did. They'll never find it there."

◇◇◇ Chapter 6

"Where have you hidden it?" he asked. "Since I'm going along with you, I think I ought to know."

She indulged in a crafty, world-weary smile and looked Dick squarely in the eye for a full minute. "I have it on me," she said quietly. "It isn't necessary to go into details."

"Oh, no. Of course not. I merely wanted to know. After all, it looks like protecting you is going to be a busy job."

"Well I'm not exactly helpless, you know."

"Both of us were a few minutes ago," he reminded her. "That's likely to happen again, but they probably won't bother you any more tonight."

"No, I think not. You'd better go and get some sleep now, Mister . . . er . . . oh, dear . . . I . . . I'm afraid . . ." She looked down and bit her lip, then smiled through her confusion. Dick's heart leaped. She seemed more beautiful now than ever.

"Welland is the name," he said, laughing. "Just think of the canal that connects Lake Erie and Lake Ontario. Dick Welland, it is. But it will be all right if you just call me Dick."

"Maybe I shall," she said, "when I know you a little better."

"And may I have the honor of breakfast with the Princess Zunda?"

"Perhaps," arching her slender beautiful neck. "Call me and see."

Dick went thoughtfully to Cabin 34 and switched on the light. Everything was as he left it. He undressed slowly, his thoughts on the evening's swift course of events. He had certainly got into a mess, he mused. As usual he was being a fool for a woman: getting mixed up with murders and murderers, getting involved in plots and counterplots, committing himself to what seemed a fool's errand and probable death, and all for a woman. But what a woman! There was no denying that her strange exotic beauty captivated him. She was almost American, what with her Howard education and stylish clothes; and yet there was something of another age about her, something of the nameless wisdom of the oldest Christian country in the world, and something, too, of the fanatical zeal for freedom. Fool's errand or not, he told himself, he was in for it and glad of it.

He tossed his underclothing on a chair and posed his fine brown body vainly in front of the long mirror. Then he went into the bathroom and took a quick shower. As he was drying himself, there was [a knock on the] door. He threw on his robe, wondering with a frown who it could be.

He opened the door. His visitor was Ras Resta Gusa, whose dissipated face was wreathed with an apologetic smile.

"Well," said Dick, standing directly in front of the door, "to what am I indebted, Your Highness, for the pleasure of your presence?"

"Ah, my American friend is being sarcastic, is it not so?"

"Nope, I just want to know what you want."

"Ah! Well, it is very little, very little. May I come in, Mr. Welland?"

"Yes, come in." Dick stood aside, watching the Ethiopian closely. "So you know who I am, eh?"

"I presume you are also aware of my identity, Mr. Welland."

"Sure, and the identity of your crowd, too." It was a shot in the dark and Dick knew it. But he remembered what Bill had said. Ras Gusa's little eyes became momentarily larger, then they glinted like a snake's.

"My crowd?" the Ethiopian queried, innocently, lifting his narrow eyebrows. "I do not understand, Mr. Welland."

"Oh, I guess you understand, all right. That crowd in No. 16 is evidently no mystery to you, especially when it comes to entering cabins. I know more about you than you think I do, Ras Gusa. And now, what is it you want?"

The Ethiopian's little eyes smoldered as he listened, then his quick smile came back and, without invitation he seated himself in the best chair in the suite.

"Since you have acquired so much wisdom in your short span of life, Mr. Welland," he said, rather suavely, "perhaps you will also be wise enough to give up this project upon which you are about to embark."

Dick looked guiltily to encounter the other's sneering smile.

"What project?" he asked in a hollow tone.

"You are not good at dissimulation, Mr. Welland," the Ethiopian bantered good-naturedly. "You are surprised that I know this when you have told no one, eh? Well, there are many things that I know which you think are not known."

"Oh, yes?"

"Certainly. And I suggest," here his tone grew slightly harsh, "that you continue on your pleasant world tour and not go where you decided suddenly this evening to go. It is a very unhealthy climate, Mr. Welland. Something might happen to you there."

"What are you talking about?" Dick lamely simulated bewilderment.

"Let us not play," grated Ras Gusa. "Let us understand each other perfectly, Mr. Welland, so there can be no mistake."

"All right, go ahead and talk." Dick, affecting nonchalance, got a cigarette, lit it and returned the monogrammed silver lighter to the chiffonier.

"I do not brook interference in either affairs of the heart or of the State, Mr. Welland. Under the circumstances, I believe it will be advisable for you to continue your world cruise and not attempt to go to Ethiopia. Do I make myself clear?"

"Perfectly. Is that all, Your Highness?"

"That is all I have to say . . . now. What more I shall have to say will depend upon your action, Mr. Welland."

"All right," growled Dick, his anger rising. "Now will you get the hell out of here before I throw you out?"

The Ethiopian rose leisurely, carefully adjusting his long black cape, and with a "Remember" look in his little eyes, bowed himself out. Dick was tempted to give him a boot down the companionway but restrained himself.

Dick was mad and also disturbed. There was no telling how many cutthroats they had on board. And there was no telling how far they might go. He remembered with something of a shudder the quivering form of John Danillo wasting his life's blood on the floor of the dining salon. He locked his door thoughtfully. A moment later he changed his mind and had Bill called.

The little bowlegged fellow was knocking at the door in five minutes. "What's up, boss?"

"I think we're in for it, Bill. The Ethiopian was just here and warned me to leave the princess and Ethiopia alone, and he talked like he meant it."

"That man's talking sense, too, Chief. We better leave these jokers alone and study your own business. That is, unless youse likin' the princess."

"Well, I promised her, and I'm going through with it. But I think you'd better stay here with me tonight. These people are desperate. There's no telling what they might do."

"They ain't gonna do nuthin' here, boss."

"Why, they've already killed one man tonight."

Bill looked worried. The fact was that he didn't want to stay in Dick's cabin that evening. He admitted as much.

"That gal's coming back tonight," he said. "She think's she's gonna pick me, but I'm gonna pick her. That's how come I don' wanna stay up here."

"Bill, you're incorrigible," accused Dick, laughing for the first time. "I might have known a woman was behind your reluctance. Still, I sort of hesitate to go to sleep with such cutthroats on board. They've probably got a key to unlock every cabin."

"You aint' got nuthin' they want," Bill pointed out. "Long's you go on about your business they ain't gonna bother you. But when you go off to Ethiopia with that princess, then's when business is gonna pick up, or my name ain't Bill Sifton."

"You've got something there!" exclaimed Dick. "That gives me an idea. I'll trick the rascals. Boy! It's good to have money."

Galvanized into activity, he rushed to the writing desk, grabbed a pencil and carefully wrote on a sheet of paper while Bill Sifton gaped wonderingly. He rang for the steward, then folded the paper and placed it in an envelope which he sealed with wax and stamped with his signet ring.

"Take this up to the wireless room," he told the steward. "Be very careful that you don't lose it." The man disappeared.

"Now I feel better," he exclaimed, grinning. "I think I'll make that Ras Resta Gusa look more like a monkey than he does."

◇◇◇Chapter 7

The next two days passed uneventfully. Ignoring Ras Resta Gusa's warning, Dick saw much of the princess. Each day they had breakfast, lunch and dinner together. They swam together. They sat side by side in their steamer chairs and watched the smooth Mediterranean pass beneath. And the more Dick saw the princess, the more he thought of her.

But even though Princess Ettara made no effort to conceal her liking [for] Dick, she never permitted their friendship to get out of the realm of the platonic.

"I know exactly how you feel," she said, on the evening of the third day at sea as they strolled along the deck, "and I like you a lot too, Dick, but there's work to be done for Ethiopia. And until that work is finished, I cannot think of anything else."

"I suppose you think more of Ethiopia than anything in the world," he watched her closely out of the corner of his eye and saw her perceptibly pale.

"Ethiopia must come first," she said quietly, composing herself. "It is my country. It needs my help. I intend to help it as much as I possibly can."

"And if you fail. . . ?"

"I shall not fail," she almost whispered with fierce earnestness. Then added, more softly, "You must help me not to fail."

They walked along in silence, he stealing glances at her brown profile, and she feeling a strange contentment.

When they parted to dress for dinner, Dick went on to his cabin. The valet had already laid out his linen and dinner clothes, and was sitting at the table playing solitaire. He rose as Dick entered.

"Hello, Bill. How goes it with the fair Donia Gabrelli?"

"I swear I don't know, Mr. Welland. I ain't been able to contact her since that first night."

"Well, I guess she found out all she wanted to know. And then maybe she found you just a little sad, Bill. You know you're not as young as you used to be."

"She didn't get nuthin' off me. She tried to find out about you and when I wouldn't tell her nuthin' she made herself scarce. I reckon she's upstairs with that Spaniard. That reminds me, boss. I seen . . ."

"You mean 'I saw,' Bill. You must watch your English, my lad."

"Well, I SAW that same guy that came out of that Spaniard's cabin and went to that Ethiopian gal's cabin. . . . I saw him going up to the wireless room today. He stayed there quite a long time. He must have been sending a book. When he came down I figured I'd better see what he was going to do so I followed him, and damn if he didn't go straight to the Spaniard's cabin."

"Yes? Well, did you see anything else?" Dick inquired, idly.

"Yeah, an' this is what seems so funny. I walked around the other side of this Spaniard's cabin as soon as I knew he was out on deck an' looked in the window, an' I'll be dogged if all his stuff wasn't packed up like he was getting off the boat."

"But the boat doesn't dock at Alexandria until day after tomorrow."

"Yeah, that's what makes it so funny. It's almost as funny as you havin' me pack up your stuff. You must gonna get off this heah boat an' swim the rest of the way."

"No, we're going to do better than that, Bill," said Dick, almost whispering in the valet's ear. "You go down and get your things ready and bring them up here."

"Pardon me, boss, but what's the idea?"

"Don't ask questions now, Bill. I think I got a plan to beat this syndicate."

Bill shook his head, a puzzled expression on his face which amused Dick greatly.

After bathing and dressing, Dick went up to the top deck to the captain's cabin. The skipper looked at him curiously as he entered the cabin with its gleaming nautical instruments on display.

"Well, my foolish young man," he said, smiling, "I have everything ready for you when you are ready."

"Good! That's what I came up to find out. A lot depends on this, Captain. I know where your sympathies lie, and I know you'll do everything in your power to help us."

"Yes, yes, my boy. We shall have everything ready at nine."

Dick thanked Captain Dumont and, turning on his heel, returned to the main deck where Princess Ettara had promised to await him. He seated himself on the rail and puffed a cigarette.

Suddenly conscious of some presence, he turned quickly and there, grinning amiably, stood Ras Resta Gusa. The man startled and angered him with his perpetual hypocritical smile.

"How do you do, Meester Welland," he greeted him, bending almost double. "I see you are enjoying your trip."

"I'm doing all right, thanks."

"It strikes me, Meester Welland, that you are doing a little better than all right. But you know, I am sure, that luck has a way of turning."

"So what?"

"Oh, nothing, Meester Welland, nothing at all. I must only say that it is extremely dangerous to be too sure of one's self. Do you not think so? Then, too, Meester Welland, it seems to me that you are entirely forgetting our little conversation the other evening and what I said on that auspicious occasion. I do not speak idly, my friend."

"What are you getting at, fellow?" grated Dick, growing angrier.

"Nothing, Meester Welland, except that if I were you I think I should not embark upon a certain adventure."

"Well, thank God, you're not me," growled Dick. "Now I wish you would excuse yourself. You get in my hair."

"Very well, Meester Welland, I shall gladly retire, but remember that you will regret the step you are about to take. You will see me again, my friend, sooner than you think."

With a sardonic smile and a mock bow, the Ethiopian duke moved gracefully away down the deck. Dick glared after him, a puzzled expression on his face. What did the man mean? What did he know?

Princess Ettara, in [a] clinging sea green silk evening gown that showed her magnificent figure to best advantage, came along then and brought him out of his speculations. Their eyes lit up as they greeted each other, and as they turned and made for the lift to take them down to the dining salon, he whispered.

"I wonder if Ras Gusa knows anything?" he speculated. "He seemed in good spirits with apparently something up his sleeves. But I don't see how he could know. I've not even told Bill. Only the captain knows."

"It is strange," she agreed, "I'VE told no one. He can't possibly know, though."

"Well, if he doesn't he and his gang are in for a surprise. By the time they find out what's happened, we'll be in Ethiopia."

"It's a wonderful scheme," she said, enthusiastically, as they stepped off the lift. "It will solve all our troubles."

Dick glanced at his wrist watch. It was exactly 7 o'clock.

They dined leisurely, as if they were not about to embark upon the most hazardous adventure imaginable. Everything was as it had been for the two previous evenings, except for one thing.

"You've noticed it, too?" she whispered.

"Yes, neither Ras Gusa, Don Carlos Navarre or the two men who dine with the Spaniard are here this evening. Maybe they're not hungry."

"I wonder," she mused, toying with her fork. "Ras Gusa never missed a meal in his life unless he had to."

At 8:30 they rose and sauntered out of the salon to the lift. Once on their deck, Dick hastened to his cabin and the princess to hers. He came out with two suitcases and Bill behind him similarly laden down. They deposited them on the main deck and then hurried to Princess Ettara's cabin to get her things.

Dick noted with satisfaction that there was no moon. He, the princess and Bill stood near the rail as the ladder was slowly lowered. Two sailors ran down it with their six suitcases. From the distance they heard the put-put-put of a marine motor. Bill was big-eyed with curiosity, wondering that he had to be working for a crazy man. At last the launch pulled up alongside the ladder and slowed down to the speed of the steamer. The baggage was thrown aboard. The three passengers descended and willing hands helped them into the bobbing launch.

"Well," said Dick, as they sped away in the darkness, "we've shaken that crowd for good."

"How'd you figure this out, Mister Welland," asked Bill, as they sped through the night. "And where is we going?"

"You mean, 'where *are* we going,' Bill," jested Dick. "Well, you'll see in a moment." Then he lowered his voice so that the two men manning the big launch could not hear.

"You remember the night the Ethiopian came to my cabin?" he whispered.

"Sho do."

"Well, I realized then that we were in danger from that crowd and the faster we got off that steamer the better. So I sent a wireless to a friend in Marseilles asking him to charter this launch and a seaplane. The plane is off there a couple of miles or so, I guess, waiting for us. This fellow will be able to pick him up with his searchlight in a little while."

"Then what?" asked Bill.

"We land at Alexandria where we'll take a chartered plane to Beni Shengui."

"Where's that, Chief?"

The Princess Ettara spoke up: "That's an Ethiopian town right on the Sudanese boundary," she explained. "The Italians have made practically no headway in subduing that section of my country. We can easily get donkeys there and make the overland trip to our destination."

Bill scratched his head thoughtfully. "Pardon me, Princess, but did you say them Eyetalians is all over the place."

"Not in that section, Bill."

"But they's in that part what you call destination, ain't they?"

"Well, yes, I suppose they are around there."

"An' ain't they shooting' colored folks what comes in that country?"

"If they catch them I suppose they do."

"Um humph. I just knowed it was somethin' like that. I know I ain't never gonna see Lenox Avenue no mo'."

"Don't be silly, Bill," Dick interrupted. "There aren't enough soldiers in the Italian army to police a big country like Ethiopia. By traveling at night with competent guides we'll probably never see an Italian."

"Well, if we don't," murmured Bill, "it won't hurt me none."

There was silence now except for the put-put-put of the launch riding the mild sea. They were going at great speed and already the lighted portholes of the *S.S. Metallic* seemed like pin points of light in the darkness.

"How much farther?" Dick shouted to the man at the wheel.

"Pretty soon. Pretty soon," came the sharply accented reply.

It was true. Two or three minutes later they saw a tiny red and green light bobbing on the surface. One of the men swung the big searchlight over in that direction. They could easily discern a big flying boat floating majestically.

In a few seconds they were slowing down alongside the float. In a minute they were being helped up the little ladder into the spacious cabin, their baggage coming up behind them.

"This is wonderful," she exclaimed, admiration and satisfaction in her tone and manner.

"I think we arranged it nicely myself," he agreed.

"You mean you arranged it," she corrected. "I don't think I would ever have thought of this. It was dangerous remaining on that ship. That crowd would go to any length to get that ring. But, Dick . . . I . . . I mean, Mr. Welland . . ."

"Go on, call me Dick, please," he begged, "I want you to. After all, we're going to be going through a whole lot together. There's no use being so formal."

"Well," she continued, "I . . . well, this must have cost an awful lot of money."

"Sure it did. Two hundred pounds, to be exact. But that's what money is for. Anytime I go into a thing, Princess . . ."

"You might as well call me Ettara," she interrupted, "since I'm to call you Dick."

"Okeh. Thanks. Well, as I was saying, anytime I go into a thing I look to do it right. It was worth two hundred to get out of that spot."

"You tellin' me!" murmured Bill, almost to himself. Dick and the princess laughed.

The launch sped away. The pilot entered and touched his cap. He was a gangling Englishman with a sandy moustache and pale blue eyes.

"All ready, sir. Shall we shove off for Alexandria?"

"Yes, let's not delay."

"Very good, sir. We shall be there in a little over two hours."

Dick looked at his wrist watch. It was ten after nine. They would be in Alexandria a bit after midnight. By this time tomorrow night they would be in Ethiopia.

The pilot had returned to his cabin. The three great motors roared. The ship turned and taxied across the sea and then lightly took the air and sped eastward.

Dick was in high spirits. He lit one of his favorite Egyptian cigarettes, reclined in his cushioned seat and gazed at the exotic young woman before him through half-closed eyelashes.

"Mister Dick," said Bill, "what's gonna become of our big baggage."

"I've arranged through the purser to have it stored in the company's warehouse in Alexandria until we call for it."

"What about guns? We ain't goin' in that wild country with nuthin' but fists, is we?" There was a note of alarm in Bill's voice as he contemplated the spectacle of three strangers trekking unarmed through the wilds of Ethiopia.

"Guns will be waiting for us in Alexandria, Bill, and ammunition, too. Everything we might need has been wirelessed for. I think we've put over about as complete a job on Ras Gusa and his Italian friends as anyone ever saw. I sure would like to see their faces when they find out that we've flown the coop."

"I'll feel a lot safer when we actually get in Ethiopia," said the princess, more to herself than to the others. "Those people are no fools. I didn't like it a bit when they didn't show up for dinner for the first time on the trip. Where could they have been? Could they have learned anything about our plans?"

"If they had," Dick broke in, "they would have made some move before we got off. Their non-appearance at dinner was merely a coincidence. Maybe they were in the Spaniard's cabin plotting the next step. You know they could have had their dinner served there."

"Maybe so, but all this seems too easy not to have a catch in it somewhere."

"Don't be so scary, Princess . . . er, I mean, Ettara. We've shaken them clean."

Toward midnight the lights of Alexandria appeared in the distance. A few minutes later they were underneath the plane and shortly afterward the big boat was skimming across the seaplane basin to the airport.

"Well here we are," said Dick, gaily, as they slowed up and the landing launch drew alongside. "We'll be through the customs in no time. I think we'd better take the plane immediately for Beni Shengui. We can catch some sleep on the way. Speed is what you want, isn't it, Prin . . . er, I mean Ettara?"

"We can't go too fast to suit me, Dick. There is so much to be done."

The landing launch pulled up at the dock. Their baggage was handed off first and they followed. There was little or nothing to declare at the customs barrier. Their passports were in order. The official prepared to mechanically stamp the books when another man in uniform, a swarthy Egyptian, hurried in waving a message which he handed to the customs officer who quickly glanced over it and then looked up gravely.

"So!" he exclaimed accusingly, glaring at them. Then to a flunky he shouted, "Open that black valise."

The man hurried to do his bidding. Dick's black valise was opened and its contents dumped unceremoniously on the floor. The customs officer took out a knife and ripped the lining. Several small flat white packets fell out. Dick and Bill watched in stunned amazement and disbelief.

"Why . . . why . . . what's that?" Dick blurted.

"So! You want to know what it is, eh? Well, its heroin, just as we were informed in this wireless message," said the customs officer. "You're all under arrest."

◈◈◈ Chapter 9

For once Dick Welland was stumped. He opened his mouth and closed it, then looked as if for succor first at the two customs officials and then at the princess and Bill.

"Them rascals planted that stuff," blurted the valet. "They musta done it when I went down to my cabin to get my bag."

"I knew they were up to something when they didn't come down to dinner," said the princess. "Ras Gusa has never missed a meal in his life except when he had some devilment afoot."

The customs officials were busy ripping the lining of the other bags. From each one a few of the little white packages tumbled out on the floor.

"Quite a clever idea, my friends," mocked the Egyptian official, "and you almost took us in."

155

"Now wait a minute," said Dick, finding his voice at last, "You've got us all wrong. We didn't spend 200 pounds to charter a plane to take us down into the Sudan just in order to bring in a few packages of narcotics. That would be utterly silly. We didn't even know that the stuff was in our baggage until you found it. Why should I smuggle narcotics? I am a rich man. My papers will show who I am. I do not have to engage in smuggling to earn my living. This lady is a niece of the Emperor of Ethiopia. This man is my valet. Do you think people like us would engage in petty smuggling? That heroin is probably not worth more than 25 or 30 pounds. Why should we jeopardize our whole plans just to bring along that stuff?"

The Egyptian listened indulgently, his head, surmounted by a red fez, turned parrot-like on one side, a twisted smile on his plump brown face.

"It is unfortunate, Meester Welland," he said, "and you have a most ingenious explanation which I personally am disposed to believe, but under the circumstances we shall have to detain your party."

"But how long, man? We've got to be on our way. Every minute counts more than you know. Delay may prove tragic. We have powerful enemies anxious to prevent us from proceeding."

"We cannot permit anyone to pass through the customs who brings narcotics into the country," the Egyptian replied, twirling his little spiked mustaches. "How long it will be before you may proceed or whether you will be permitted to proceed is a matter which is up to my superiors. If they believe your extremely interesting, and I might say incredible, story, you may be able to go this afternoon. Come now, I will show you to our quarters."

Princess Ettara came close to Dick and whispered, "What about the American consul? He can help if he will."

Dick nodded his head vigorously. It was a good idea. He had always been treated considerately by the American consuls even though he was a Negro.

"See here," he said, as they were being led along a corridor. "I must get in touch with the American consul on the telephone. May I?"

The Egyptian pondered the matter for a moment, twirling his little mustaches and regarding Dick through half-closed eyelids.

"Very well. You may. I can see nothing wrong about that. Yussif," calling to his assistant, who had brought the message that detained the party, "get the American Consulate and let Meester Welland talk to them."

Dick was led into a spacious office. He noted that the windows were barred with decorative wrought iron. The dark man picked up the French telephone on the desk and called a number. In a couple of moments he called Dick to the instrument.

"Hello," he called. "Is this the American Consulate?"

A sleepy voice replied in strongly accented English, "Yes, these ees ze Americain consulate. Wat you want, eh?"

"I'm an American citizen, Richard Welland. I must see someone in authority there immediately. It is very important. I have chartered a plane to take me down into the Sudan and now I am being detained by the Egyptian customs officials. Will you tell someone in authority, the consul or the vice-counsul, to come down immediately?"

"Eet ees impossible. Zay are all asleep. Eeet ees after midnight."

"I don't care. This is very important. I must talk with someone in authority immediately. Understand?"

"I weel see, sir."

During the long, seemingly endless wait, Dick drummed his fingers incessantly and fumed within. All his plans were going awry. How had the Italian learned about the seaplane? He was sure the message about the heroin had come from the *S.S. Metallic*. He would ask the dark Egyptian. He turned and looked at the official who was sitting by the window, regarding him closely.

"Say, Yussif, where did that message come from about that heroin?"

"Came from ship," he answered shortly, drawing leisurely upon his cigarette.

"From the *Metallic*?"

"From the *Metallic*, Monsieur."

Yes, the Italians must have stood in with the wireless operator. That was why Bill had seen one of them go into the wireless room and stay so long. In that case, the Italians must know of all his plans. Even now they had probably sent warnings to Ethiopia for the invaders to be on the lookout.

"Hello," came a voice from the telephone at long last. "Who is this and what do you want? I am the vice-consul of the United States here."

"Good! I am Richard Welland. You will find my rating in Dun and

157

Bradstreet. I am making a world tour. Just left Marseilles the other day. On the *S.S. Metallic.*"

"But the *Metallic* is not due in until sometime late today," the official objected.

"That's right. I left her with my party at ten o'clock tonight. I got here just a bit after midnight. I had already wired ahead and chartered a plane to take us down into the Sudan immediately but we have been detained by customs because some packages of heroin were found in our baggage. Now those packages were planted by enemies of Princess Ettara Zunda, my traveling companion, in order to prevent her from returning to Ethiopia and to stop me from being of assistance to her. It stands to reason that I would not spend three thousand dollars in order to smuggle a couple hundred dollars worth of narcotics into the country. I am a man of independent wealth. You can easily check on my credit rating. This heroin was placed in the lining of our baggage while we were at dinner this evening. I anticipate that it will be difficult to get released by the customs unless you can come down and help me. I shall be very grateful. I know it is a whole lot of trouble, but I can't see any other way out."

"All right, Mr. Welland. It's a little irregular but I'll come down and see what I can do. Just hold tight."

What a relief! Dick hung up with a light heart and turned to Yussif, the phlegmatic Egyptian, with a broad smile. The official beckoned to him and pointed down the corridor in the direction the others had gone.

"Will he help?" the Princess asked when at last they were alone together except for Bill.

"He'll be right down. It's the vice-consul. I think everything will be right once he convinces these Egyptians that we are not trying to corrupt the morals, if any, of their country. He seemed quite nice about it, after being roused out of bed at this ungodly hour."

"Does he know you're colored?"

"No, I didn't tell him that, but I let him know I had money."

"Yeah," Bill commented, "that gits 'em every time."

Almost an hour passed. Then the door opened and the swarthy Yussif beckoned to Dick. "American consul see you," he announced, and stood aside for Dick to pass.

The tall young American white man who introduced himself as Derek Sullivan, the vice-consul of the United States at Alexandria, got right down to business as soon as Dick came into the big office.

"Now, Mr. Welland, tell me just what you think we can do for you. This is a serious charge, you understand, bringing narcotics into the country. This official," pointing to the Egyptian with the spike-like mustache, "has no authority to dismiss your case. You will certainly have to at least wait until morning when the chief inspector arrives."

That meant a delay of at least nine hours. It was depressing. But there seemed nothing else to do except wait.

"What do you think are my chances?" asked Dick. "This is a frame-up of the rawest kind, but I realize that it looks bad."

"Yes, frankly it does," Consul Sullivan agreed.

"But there are mitigating circumstances. After all the value of the heroin is very little compared to the sums I have spent and am spending for planes alone," Dick countered. "That should weigh heavily in my favor."

"Yes, it should and I shall be very glad to call it to the chief inspector's attention," said Sullivan. "Meantime I would suggest that you wire for references from your home and your bank. They will come in handy in the morning. The chief inspector is a rather hard man to deal with."

After going over other matters connected with the case, Vice-Consul Sullivan took his departure and Dick went back to the princess.

Promptly at nine-thirty the next morning, Dick was escorted into the presence of Chief Inspector of Customs Tumbridge, an Englishman. No time was lost in getting down to business. After the Egyptian official had made his report, the bluff, red-faced Englishman turned to Dick for his explanation. Dick told him exactly what had happened. Mr. Sullivan was there to speak a good word in Dick's behalf. The inspector listened attentively, puffing a cigarette the while and not appearing to be greatly impressed. It was only when he was shown the answers to Dick's cables and radiograms that he seemed to relent.

"I believe your story, Mr. Welland," he said. "It sounds straight to me. Certainly after the murder of the lady's servant and the rifling of your cabins you had a right to be alarmed. Captain Dumont's confirmation of what happened and your references tip the scales in your favor. At the suggestion of Mr. Sullivan I'm going to let you off with a small fine. But what I want to know now, Mr. Welland, is where you are going on the plane you have chartered?"

Dick sensed danger. He glanced quickly at the American vice-consul, who almost imperceptibly shook his head and frowned. Dick decided that he must conceal his mission.

"The Princess Ettara Zunda wishes to return secretly to her Shoa estates without interference from the Italians. So I am flying her as far as Beni Shengui from whence she will travel overland to her destination."

"Do you plan to enter Ethiopia with her, Mr. Welland?" asked the inspector suavely. Dick glanced quickly at the American vice-consul and again noted his frown.

"Well, I hardly think I would care to enter Ethiopia in the present state of affairs," he evaded, gazing innocently into the inspector's eyes.

"All right, then. We'll confiscate the heroin. The fine will be one hundred pounds," the inspector decreed. "But be very careful in the future."

It was a matter of only a few minutes before Dick had arranged payment. He, the princess and Bill piled into the vice-consul's automobile and were driven to the airport where the plane he had chartered still awaited them. On the way Mr. Sullivan explained why he had frowned during Dick's examination.

"It's a good thing you didn't tell him you were going into Ethiopia with the Princess. He would have sought to prevent you. That's why I signaled to you. Happily you understood. Officially I do not know myself that you are going into Ethiopia or else I would have to advise you against it. The American Government does not encourage citizens to visit that country, nor does the Italian government. We have no representative there. If you get in difficulties with the Italians you will be in hot water sure enough." The vice-consul grinned good-naturedly. Then he added: "Keep your eyes open and make a full report to the nearest American consular or diplomatic officer as soon as you come out. And remember you have no authority from us to enter Ethiopia. It's a good thing you already have an Egyptian visa or you might have trouble getting away from here."

Dick had already arranged with the bank to deliver 1,000 pounds of English money at the airport at the same time that he arranged for the payment of his stiff fine. He had money, equipment, maps, and everything he had ordered all neatly packed away in the big transport plane.

They bade Mr. Sullivan adieu, climbed aboard and gave the British pilot and his assistant the signal to go. It was 10:30 A.M.

The big ship ran for a half mile before taking the air. It leveled off at about 1,000 feet and headed straight south for their destination 1,500 miles away. They were due, barring accident, to arrive at Beni Shengui before dark.

Bill Sifton sat up front, Dick and the Princess farther back. They watched the scenery flash by: the lazy serpentine Nile, bordered by wide greenery interspersed with white villages and towns, while on each side stretched the baking desert.

Dick was in high spirits. They had outwitted the Italians again. Once they landed in Ethiopia and started on their way, there would be little chance of anybody catching up with them.

Neither Dick or the Princess spoke for a long time after the plane started, each being lost in thought. They passed over Cairo at a 200-mile clip; at 11:15 as they lunched they saw the great dam at Assouan, and Dick knew they had covered 500 miles. Khartoum flashed into view at 4:30. Two more hours and they would be at their destination. The big plane came down at the airport there to refuel. They got out and stretched their legs while the petrol was poured into the tanks. Then at 5:00 sharp the plane took off again. They would just about make Beni Shengui before dark.

"Well," said Dick, "we've outsmarted them, Ettara. They've just about reached Alexandria now. Next thing they know we'll have the gold and be out of the country."

"I hope so," she replied, "but we are dealing with very resourceful people, Dick. You must remember there IS such a thing as radio. The Italians probably know exactly where we are going and when we are scheduled to reach there. Have you forgotten that they knew all about our plans to leave the ship and almost prevented us from leaving Alexandria?"

"That's right, but I still think we've outsmarted them."

The Princess just smiled and patted his hand.

At around 5:20 Bill shouted: "Look there!" and pointed to the east.

Flying much higher than their ship but coming straight toward them were three military pursuit planes. Dick focused his binoculars on them. At first he couldn't believe what he saw. Then a second glance convinced him. He handed the glasses to the Princess. After one look she announced, fantastically: "Italians!"

"But they can't fly over British territory," he complained.

"But they ARE flying over British territory," she pointed out, "and they're looking for us."

It seemed that way. The much faster pursuit planes quickly overtook them. They circled around the big transport plane at almost twice its speed and then loafed on its tail. Dick watched them with apprehension. If the Italians landed the same time as their plane, they would be unable to escape. Were they to be captured in the end?

About 6:50 the big plane dipped her nose and made for a collection of huts, alongside a large cleared space. The Italians also descended. It was dusk. They made a landing on the rough field but before the propeller had stopped turning the three Italian planes had landed on each side and in the rear. They were now on soil the Italians claimed. Dick handed a high-powered rifle to the princess and another to Bill. The crews of the Italian planes were already running toward them.

◈◈◈ Chapter 11

The Italians were coming from each side and from the front. The English pilot and his navigator were still in the cabin, perhaps reluctant to come out at this crucial moment. Dick jumped out and stood under the high wing. Bill Sifton stood in the door on one side, the princess in the other. From the line of huts on the edge of the cleared space a crowd of robed natives came running.

The six Italian aviators closed in on the big plane, each one with a big black automatic pistol in his hand.

"Let them have it!" shouted Dick.

The three rifles cracked almost in a volley. The Italian pilot and his observer coming from the front pitched forward, laid low by Dick's and Bill's shots. One of the Italians approaching the princess's side clutched his shoulder with a howl, dropping his pistol in his pain.

The three remaining Italians stopped short in their tracks as their comrades fell. Again, the high-powered rifles cracked. One Latin fell with a hole in his forehead. The other two turned and ran for their planes. Dick and Bill raised their rifles but they were too late. The surging mob of Ethiopians was surrounding the luckless aviators, brandishing weapons of all sorts. There was a moment's melee and then the natives left the bloody bodies of the men they had slain and turned to the big plane.

"Now we're in for it," cried the English pilot, snatching his pistol.

"Wait. I'll take care of this!" said the princess, taking command. She pushed past Bill Sifton, stepped down to the ground and took her place slightly in advance of Dick. The pilot and his navigator busied themselves throwing the equipment of the party on the ground. Their haste was evident. They knew of the hatred of the Ethiopians for all white people.

On came the ragged crowd brandishing knives, swords, spears and modern rifles.

"Put down your rifle," she said to Dick, and laid her own on the ground. He quickly followed suit.

Leading the Ethiopians was a tall, thin black man with a sparse black beard, bushy black hair. Obviously a leader, he was clad in a robe of spotless white and wore a pair of military shoes. A heavy military pistol sagged from a leather belt around his waist. He wore a white helmet. As he approached the wing under which the princess stepped forward, he halted and raised his hand to his followers to do likewise. He stepped forward to meet her.

The princess spoke rapidly in what Dick supposed to be Amharic. The Ethiopian leader bowed low, took her hand and kissed it, then placed it lightly on his forehead.

"Dick, this is Dedjasmatch Yamrou. He is in charge of the Ethiopian patriots in this district," the Princess announced. Then she turned again to the Dedjasmatch.

"Me spik lettle Angleesh," he said haltingly, smiling at Dick.

"That is good. We can all understand each other. Where did you learn English?"

"Long time 'go," he explained, "I go by Angland country one time. Stay big Ethiopian house. See much good," smiling at first at the princess and then at Dick. Then growing stern, he continued, "Whyfore airplane from Italians? Whyfore big plane?" glancing at the two Englishmen who by this time had, with Bill's assistance, moved all the equipment out on the ground. It was almost dark now. The navigator ran to the far end of the clearing with an armful of flares.

"They are all right, Dedjasmatch," said the princess. "They brought us down here. They must leave at once." He nodded his head slowly in agreement. She explained their pursuit by the Italian planes.

"No like no white mens around," he grumbled, as the pilot approached them hurriedly.

"We've got to leave right now or we can't get out at all. As it is we'll have to use flares," the Englishman declared. "We can't stay here overnight, especially after what happened to those Italians."

"Very well," Dick told him. "Leave as soon as you can. I suppose all our stuff is unloaded."

"Yes, sir, quite. Well, we'll be going. Wish you a safe trip." The Englishman turned, climbed into the cabin and spun the propeller. His assitant came running back. The flames outlined the end of the big clearing. The assistant climbed into the pilot's cabin.

"Clear the way over there!" shouted the pilot, pointing to the field that stretched behind the big plane.

Dedjasmatch Yamrou gave a sharp command to his followers who ran and picked up the equipment and left the field behind him, Dick, Bill, and the princess.

The big transport plane turned around. Its lights were switched on. The propeller roared. The plane raced down the bumpy field. Soon its wheels were scarcely touching the ground. Then they left the ground as the big ship approached the line of trees at the end of the clearing. A sharp lift and it roared over the tops of the trees, barely touching them, and was soon but a tiny red light in the distance, then disappeared entirely.

The headquarters of Dedjasmatch Yamrou was a large mud-and-wattle house with a grass roof and a wide veranda. It was a meandering structure of several rooms. One of these was assigned to the princess and a somewhat less pretentious one to Dick and his valet. Tubs of hot water were brought for their refreshment by tall black young women.

In about an hour, Dick and the princess were ready to accept the invitation of their host to dinner. He was dressed in immaculate white robes. The princess had donned a white duck suit and Bill had dug out Dick's expensive Palm Beach suit. The Dedjasmatch favored them with an expansive ivory smile, and rose respectfully as they entered the room.

When they had taken their chairs, he offered grace in a sonorous voice, and then clapped his hands. A servant entered with a great bowl of turtle soup, which he served in smaller bowls placed on each plate. Then came some excellent river fish, followed by giant snails cooked in palm butter thickened with cassava flour. Gourds of cool palm wine were soon emptied and refilled. The pièce de resistance was a great haunch of rare beef, which the Dedjasmatch carved with a huge razor-sharp hunting knife. For dessert there was watermelon, followed by excellent Italian cognac. Dick supplied American cigarettes.

"Well," said Dick, pushing back from the table, "this is the best meal I've had in a long time. How do you do it? I thought you people were at war."

"Much war," said Yamrou, gravely, "but not war here. Italian white man come by one time with black Italian soldier. Ha! Ha! Mebbe fifty man, yes." His laugh was harsh and cruel.

"What happened?"

"Ha! Ha! Ha!" he exploded. "Not fight; we kill. We go by camp when white man sleep. Shoot gun. White man come quick. We kill. Every night we kill somewhere. White man no can sleep soon. We stop trucks, take guns, food, bullet, clothes. Everything we get from white man. Ha! Ha! Ha!"

"I should think they would find you here and send a big expedition after you."

The Ethiopian's eyes narrowed until they gleamed. "Only airplane come, like today. We make space so they land. Then . . ." He rubbed the palms of his long slender hands together and grinned significantly from Dick to the princess and back again.

"So you have enough of everything?"

"No enough. Need bullets. Need machine gun. Need petrol for airplane."

"Then you have airplanes?" Dick showed his astonishment.

"Ha! Ha! Us take much plenty Italian airplane. Three good one us get this day, eh? Can fix up sometime but us get too small petrol."

"Yes, Dedjasmatch," said the princess, "we understand your problem. You have many loyal soldiers but you don't have enough to fight with. We are going to get it for you. Gold will get it for you and we are here to get the gold."

"Gold, Princess!" the commander's eyes widened. "Where? Italian man got gold mine. Ethiopians got no gold. Can't buy gun and bullet with mud."

"We shall get gold, plenty gold," she said, "when we get to Abra Destum."

"Abra Destum!" he repeated the words reverently, crossing himself.

◈◈◈ Chapter 12

Dick thought suddenly of a daring scheme. He turned to the commander.

"See here, Dedjasmatch, how far is it to Abra Destum?"

"Far too much," replied Yamrou. "By foot long, long time. Maybe t'ree week. By donkey maybe smaller. Maybe two weeks. Much hill. Bad country."

"It's hard traveling, Dick," the princess added. "There are no roads to speak of, you know. Nothing but trails. What roads there are we'll have to avoid because the Italians patrol them. Is that not so, Yamrou?"

"Truth!" exclaimed the officer, wagging his leonine head sagely. "Only night time can mans walk on road."

"Just as I thought," said Dick. "Now listen." He drew his chair closer and leaned forward, his eyes sparkling with the enthusiasm of his new idea. "I take it that every day counts. Every day the Ethiopians have less and less arms and munitions. Every day the Italians go deeper into the country and consolidate their gains. So we're working against time. We've got to put arms in these people's hands soon and get them added supplies of munitions or they will never be able to win. Three weeks is too long. Two weeks is too long. Besides we'll be exposed to all kinds of danger on this long journey to Abra Destum."

"Yes," the tall black man nodded his head and stroked his sparse black beard. "Very true. But no can go other way to Abra Destum. It's far too much."

Dick frowned impatiently. "I know it's a long way, over two hundred miles, but why can't we fly there and get it over with in an hour. We have enough gasoline from the three planes to carry us there and on to Djibouti afterward. It's a chance that we'll be taking trying to reach there on donkeys or afoot. Remember Ras Resta Gusa and the Italians will be trying to find us and stop us. It was they who had those Italian pursuit planes follow us. They will send others and next time we may not be so lucky."

166

"Ah!" exclaimed Yamrou, showing his white teeth. "Good plan. Ver' good plan. But where you land on Abra Destum? No field there. All hill 'n' tree. You die there if you land."

"And who's going to fly the plane?" asked the princess. "I can't fly, you can't fly and there's probably nobody here that can fly."

Dick frowned darkly. No, he hadn't thought of that. There they were with planes and gasoline but no pilot.

"I fly," said Yamrou, quietly.

"You?"

"I fly," repeated the officer. "I learn fly in Angland. I fly good."

"Why . . . why . . . why didn't you tell us before?" Dick was so amazed, and also gratified, that he was quite beside himself.

"I tell you now. Before you not ask. Remember, I tell you only need petrol."

"Then you can fly us to Abra Destum tomorrow?"

"Yes. But no can land. No field. If land, we die," he extended his long slender hands and turning his head on one side hunched his shoulders.

"It's our only chance, Ettara." said Dick. "They'll do anything and everything to stop us now. The longer it takes us to carry out our mission, the less chance we have of completing it. They'll stop at nothing. You know how they murdered your servant, how they sent that woman after Bill, how they rifled our cabins, how they learned about our plans from the radio man and then planted that heroin in order to hold us. Those aviators were bent on killing or capturing us if we had not beat them to it. Now we've got to get away from here in a hurry."

"I agree with you, Dick. But what's the sense of taking a plane if we can't land?"

"Those Italians had parachutes," observed Dick, brightening. "Why can't we use them? Then Dedjasmatch can fly over the mountain and we can bail out with our guns and equipment. It will be a cinch."

"Jump out?" the princess perceptibly paled.

"Of course," said Dick, impatiently. "It will be a cinch."

"But I've never jumped with a parachute before," she objected.

"Neither have I, but I'll do it this time. All you have to do is pull the cord and say your prayers," Dick smiled reassuringly.

Dedjasmatch Yamrou glanced at Dick admiringly. "Ver' good!" he exclaimed, nodding his bushy head and showing his snowy teeth. "Ver' ver' good! Many parachutes we have. It is ver' simple."

"Now there you are!" Dick exclaimed triumphantly. "We can leave here right after daybreak and be over Abra Destum a little after sunrise. Can't we, Dedjasmatch?"

"It can be done," the Ethiopian assented. Then, smiling, he said: "Meester Welland. You have what Americaine say 'good head,' yes."

It was still dark when Bill Sifton shook Dick awake. "Come on, boss. It'll soon be crackin' daylight. That Jasmatch fellah's already up an' so's th' princess."

Dick jumped out of the comfortable bed and stretched. It was the first good sleep he had had, free from care, since the night before leaving Marseilles. Every night on the *S.S. Metallic* had been one of suspense and strain. And the confinement at Alexandria had permitted him to sleep only fitfully.

"Where is we goin', boss?" asked Bill, fetching a basin of water and a towel.

"We're flying to the mountains in central Ethiopia, Bill, just as soon as we can get away. Get all that camping equipment: the sleeping bags, the canvas bucket, the canvas water bag, the aluminum pans and knives, forks and spoons, the flashlight and extra batteries, and all the other odds and ends, and pack them securely in one big bundle."

"That'll make a mighty big bundle, sir."

"That's all right. We're going to drop it by parachute. Then we'll jump out after it."

"What 'we'?" cried Bill, suddenly pausing as if frozen. "You ain't fig-gerin' on me jumpin' outta no plane, is you?"

"You shouldn't say 'ain't,' Bill," Dick cautioned, smiling as he hurried through his ablutions and morning shave. "And I've told you so often about saying 'is you.' I'm afraid I'll have to send you back to school, Bill."

"Boss, I ain . . . er . . . well, I'm not kiddin'. Is . . . Are we going to jump out of a plane sure enough?" Bill's eyes were wide.

"That's exactly what we're going to do, Bill. There's no place to land on the mountain with a plane, so we've got to drop over the side with our parachutes."

"S'pose that ol' parachute don't open?"

"Well, Bill, if it doesn't open it will be just too bad. But parachutes usually open."

"Can't I just stay around here until you'all come back?"

"We're not coming back this way, Bill. You'll just have to go along or stay here with the Ethiopians."

"Well, I guess I'll have to go along, boss, but I'd just as soon be walking, if you ask me." Bill shook his head and went grumbling about his work. He hadn't bargained for anything like this when he became Dick's valet.

In a few minutes Bill gathered all the necessary equipment into a huge bundle bound with stout native cord. Dick, the princess and Dedjasmatch Yamrou were standing by one of the small pursuit planes. The Ethiopian commander had on one of the dead Italians' flying helmets, as did the princess and Dick. Another was handed to Bill when he put down his bundle. It was still dark but toward the east there was the first gray intimation of daybreak.

"Now, we're going to be closely packed in there," said Dick. "There are four of us and three is a big crowd for a plane this size."

"And where are we going to put that huge bundle?" asked the princess. "We'll be lucky to find room for the rifles in that plane when we all get in there."

"On top," grunted Yamrou. Bill caught the idea immediately. With little difficulty they fastened the bundle securely to the top of the cabin behind the pilot's hood. Meanwhile some of Yamrou's men had placed flares at the end of the field.

Dick got in first, the princess followed and then Bill. What with their parachute[s] and the rifles they were packed like sardines. A native whirled the propeller. The engine explosions echoed over the hills. Yamrou turned the plane and ran down the field. The machine lifted easily, hopped the line of trees bordering the field and turned due east toward Abra Destum, remote, inaccessible, sacred mountain of Ethiopia, where Ethiopia's treasure lay.

The little plane labored manfully with the heavy load, rising ever higher and higher over miles of primeval forests from which here and there curled a lazy column of smoke. It was rough going. The plane bucked and lurched as they hit air pockets over the rugged mountains.

Thoughts flashed through Dick's brain as they approached nearer and nearer their destination. There were scores of unanswered questions. Suppose they DID get to the place where the treasure was buried, would it be turned over to them? And if it were placed in their hands, how would they ever get it to Djibouti or anywhere else? There was just one chance in a hundred of getting out of this. Had he been a fool to come on such a mission?

He looked up to find the princess's eyes studying him with a softness and confidence which made his doubts of his wisdom flee faster than the plane carrying him to his new adventures.

Bill Sifton, terrified and hanging on to the bundle of equipment, tied midway between the two seats, was ashen gray. Yamrou, imperturbably, drove the plane higher and higher toward cloud-capped peaks they were rapidly approaching. The going became even rougher than it had been. Yamrou signaled that they were up 10,000 feet.

Now they were approaching the great mass of rock which Dick guessed to be Abra Destum. Its summit, just a few hundred yards below them, was wreathed in the clouds. Here the forest was replaced by dwarfed trees and scraggly bushes. It was an utter wilderness with no human in sight. On each side the great mass of rock fell away almost perpendicularly to an awful depth. Dick wondered how anyone had ever been able to climb it, let alone bring treasure up there.

Yamrou circled the summit and dropped several smoke bombs. Then he looked significantly at Dick and signaled him to jump. With some difficulty he got out of the narrow seat. For a moment he looked at the awful desolation below him and his heart sank. But there could be no turning back now.

He pulled himself all the way out of the seat and, closing his eyes, dived overboard. When he knew he was clear, he pulled the cord, waiting with curious calm for one hurtling toward the earth. Then a great pull and his speed slackened. He breathed easy again. The parachute had opened.

Dick floated lazily to the mountain, remembering Yamrou's instructions on the manipulation of parachute cords to keep from being dragged. He soon untangled himself and stretched thankfully. He looked up and saw both the princess and Bill floating down. Then Dedjasmatch now leaned out and cut the cords binding the big bundle to the top of the plane, attached to it a parachute and let it float down. Then firing a blast from his machine gun that echoed and reechoed around the mountain, he turned the nose of his plane toward Beni Shengui and was soon but a speck on the horizon.

It was a desolate world in which they found themselves here on the backbone of creation. A few scrub oaks and weeds divided the place between them. The hot sun was driving away the mist now. They could see for scores of miles in every direction. The mountain seemed to stand as king amid a kingdom of mountains, rising like the hump of a camel with awful precipices on every side, their bottoms lost in great growths of giant trees. There was no trace of a trail of any kind.

"Well," said Dick to his valet, "I see you made it all right."

"Yeah, I made it all right," said Bill, "but I know I ain't gonna be the same no more if I live to be a hundred, I never was so scared."

"So was I," Dick acknowledged.

"And I," admitted the princess. Then she looked around her. "Dick," she said, "we've got to get going and try to get in contact with our soldiers and have them carry us to Bishop Handem."

"I've been hunting for a trail but I can't see any. Why, we can't get off this mountain." Dick frowned and looked about him.

"We don't have to worry now, Dick," she reassured him. "They saw Yamrou's signals. I'm sure they will be along shortly. There's evidently a secret way to get up here."

"Now that we're here," said Dick, "it does look as if a plane COULD land here without much trouble. All we need do is cut a few dozen of these scrub oaks in order to make a runway. We could get a run here of at least a thousand feet. Perhaps we can get out by plane!"

Dick's spirits rose as he thought of the possibilities. No matter how much gold there was, Yamrou could fly it out in a couple of trips. He told the princess about it as Bill unfastened the bundle and divided the equipment into two packs.

"It's possible," she agreed. "It's just possible that we can do it. but

171

first we've got to get the gold. It will not be any too easy. Bishop Handem will be very cautious, I'm sure."

"Does he know you?"

"Of course not. He may know of me. Few Ethiopians have seen Bishop Handem or spoken to him. He has lived on this mountain more years than any one knows. Before Menelik he was here. Some say he is hundreds of years old."

Dick smiled his disbelief.

"Don't laugh," she said. "The laugh may be on you. Bishop Handem is not like other men. It is said he has never left Abra Destum. Here he lives on goat's milk, wild berries, fruit and blood, with only his most trusted men ever admitted to his presence."

"Has the Emperor ever met him?"

"It is the law that the Emperor must come once a year at least, and bring treasure. This is the first year in our history that an Emperor has not been able to do so. Bishop Handem knows why."

"But you have no message from the Emperor to give the bishop, have you?"

"I have the ring. The bishop will know that it would not be sent except for one purpose and by a person trusted by the Emperor."

"Where are you keeping it?"

"It's in a safe place," the princess smiled. "I don't want you to know, Dick, because we might get in some difficult position and you might indicate in some way your knowledge of where it is."

"Okeh. I can hold my curiosity in leash."

Bill brought the princess and Dick their rifles and ammunition and then dropped Dick's pack down in front of him.

"Well, we're all ready, boss. Where do we go from here?"

"We don't go, Bill. We just wait here until somebody comes from below to lead us off this mountain before all three of us break our necks." Dick laughed at the puzzled expression on his valet's face.

"Suppose don't nobody come?" asked Bill, scratching his head. "What we do then?"

Dick's jovial reply was drowned by a roar of motors overhead. The three looked skyward. A squadron of six bombing planes was bearing down rapidly from the East. Their markings were Italian.

"Lie down flat," Dick yelled. The princess and Bill obeyed with alacrity. But already it was too late. The planes circled over them. Men tumbled over the sides and floated to earth on each side of the little party. They were Italians, all right.

Bill raised his rifle to shoot.

"Don't!" cried Dick, holding down the muzzle of his gun. "It's no use. They've got us. There are too many of them."

Disappointment, chagrin and tears revealed themselves in Princess Ettara's face. Her hand sought Dick's. It trembled as it gripped his.

At least a dozen soldiers were approaching from as many directions with rifles at the ready.

❖❖❖ Chapter 14

Dick dropped his rifle and lifted his hand high above his head. Bill and the princess did likewise. The Italian soldiers, sturdy fellows in shorts and shirt sleeves with deeply bronzed arms and faces, hustled them together. A squat, square-built man with swarthy skin, and fierce mustaches and eyebrows, pushed through the circle of soldiers. Like them, he wore a khaki shirt, but otherwise he was dressed in civilian clothes: long khaki trousers, a white helmet, and mosquito boots. He eyed the three captives.

There was something vaguely familiar about the man. Dick tried to remember where he had seen him. Then Bill Sifton murmured out of the corner of his mouth: "Of the ship. One o' the Eyetalians. I seen him comin' outta that Spaniard's cabin and go into the Princess's cabin. That's th' guy all right."

The Italian, evidently in charge of the detachment, turned to the soldiers and snapped out a command in his language. Three of the twelve soldiers dropped their guns and began searching the prisoners. They removed each garment, searching it carefully, until all three stood nude.

Enraged and helpless, Dick had to stand by with two bayonets at his back while the shocking indignity was visited upon the princess. When they had searched and found nothing, the commander shouted another order. The men now turned to the bundles, searching every article minutely.

Dick new what they were looking for. Princess Ettara, with a bayonet point pressing against her back, was crying convulsively. Brave though she was and hardened to dangerous adventure, the humiliation was too much for a girl of gentle birth.

Dick could stand it no longer. "Give her back her clothes, you swine!" he shouted at the swarthy leader. "Where do people like you come from?" It was the first word he had spoken, being ignorant of Italian, but he was unable to keep silent any longer. He had hardly spoken when the sharp points of the bayonets pierced his bare back. The squat Italian turned with a sneer on his face.

"So," exclaimed the man, a cruel smirk on his brigand's countenance, "I am a swine, eh?" Dick was surprised that he spoke English. Perhaps he WAS the same man Bill had seen on the ship.

"Well, we shall see who is swine?" he added. He spoke to a soldier. The man promptly took the sling off his rifle and handed it to him.

"Now, Meester Welland, we shall see who is swine?" he repeated. "Lie down on your face. Hurry up!" the soldiers prodded Dick again.

"What for?" asked Dick, eyeing the leather sling and then glancing into the maleovolent visage of the Italian. "What's the idea?"

He was pushed violently from behind for an answer. He sprawled forward. Princess Ettara screamed and rushed toward him. The sling in the commander's hand rose, described an arc and descended with a cruel whistle, cutting into her shoulder. The pain was maddening. Blood spurted where the metal of the sling cut into her beautiful smooth skin. She screamed and fell over in a faint across the recumbent form of Dick.

The Italian picked her up and slung her to one side. Willing bayonets pinned Dick to the earth. The rifle sling rose again, and with an ominous whistle, bit deep into the flesh of Dick's back. The pain was excruciating but he only bit his lip to hold back his cries. Again and again the heavy strip of leather lashed Dick's back until it seemed that each time would be the last he could possibly stand. He was dizzy, numb with pain, aching in every muscle. Suddenly the punishment ceased. Bill stood helpless with tears in his eyes, bayonet points stuck in his back.

"Now, Meester Welland," sneered the Italian, "I weel ask you question an' you weel answer truth, eh?"

Dick said nothing.

"Do you hear me, Meester Welland? Or mu' I use ze whip again?"

Dick turned over painfully, his back a patter of red welts from which blood dripped. He sat up and nodded slowly.

"Aha, you are what you say, reasonable now, eh?" grinned the Italian. "Now you weel tell me where ees ze sacred ring?"

"What ring?" asked Dick, fencing for time. There was a chance that the soldiers guarding the treasure somewhere on the mountain might put in their appearance. They must have seen Yamrou's smoke bombs or heard his machine-gun signal.

"Come, come, Meester Welland. Do you tell me or do I resume? Remember, Meester Welland, you are no longer ze wealthy Galahad. You are in Ethiopia and zees ees now white man's country. Understand. You tell me where ees ze ring or you be very sorry."

"I don't know anything about any ring," growled Dick. "I've never seen any ring. What kind of ring is it?"

The Italian eyed him maliciously and gripped the leather sling tighter. "I am not ze fool, Meester Welland. I know all about you. I was wiz you on ze sheep w'en you were, oh, so gallant to zee woman. I know all about ze airplane you hire to leave sheep, even BEFORE you leave, see? I know you fly from Alexandria. I know you help keel Italian fliers. You have been ver' ver' indiscreet, shall we call it? For less than that man have died. Now, you know about these ring. You shall tell me now what you know."

"You didn't find any ring on us, did you?"

"No, you have been ver' clever, Meester Welland. But you know where ees ze ring and that you shall tell me at once."

"I'll tell you nothing, you miserable, detestable blackguard," Dick shouted. "Now go on and do your cowardly worst."

"Ver' brave, Meester Welland. Well said. However, I shall wheep you no more. Perhaps zat woman have ze ring. Yes, I shall see." He turned to the prostrate princess who was just reviving from the cruel blow he had delivered, and touched her with his boot. She started, her eyes distended with terror. He looked down at her beautiful body with lustful approval, then winked at the surrounding soldiers. They all grinned.

"Stand up!" he commanded with a growl.

She slowly obeyed, looking helplessly at Dick, watched carefully by his two guards, and Bill, who was likewise unable to aid her. The Italian came closer.

"I want that ring," he growled. "You have it. Give it up immediately or I'll whip you until you do. Understand?" As he spoke he shook the sling back and forth in front of her face.

"Now see here," cried Dick, "you can't whip a woman. Can't you see she has no ring?"

"Oh, so I cannot wheep a woman, eh? We shall see, Meester Welland," he hissed. "Now, wench, give up that ring."

Princess Ettara's chin tilted and her neck arched proudly with all the noble blood of twenty centuries.

"You swine!" she cried. "Do you think I would give you a ring if I had one? Do you think I would do anything to injure or betray Ethiopia? Do you think for one minute that in order to save my skin I would yield to you? No, a thousand times, NO. If I must die, I shall gladly do so, but I shall tell you nothing."

The Italian's face hardened as he looked at the slim, nude, young princess standing defiant before him, as haughty as though she were addressing the slaves on her former vast estates.

"You weel tell sometheeng when I am finish," he threatened, tightening the sling about his wrist. "I weel wheep you worse than I wheep your lover. I weel wheep you until you weel be ver' glad to talk. I weel teach you smart n——rs a lesson. But before you get zee wheep, zere ees sometheeng else." He walked closer and placed a hairy paw on her delicate shoulder. He surveyed her perfect figure.

"Stop!" she cried, falling back in loathing as she divined his intention. Two soldiers grabbed her while the Italian smirked, his damp lips working with lust. Dick and Bill tried to move toward her but the other soldiers closed in on them.

She screamed piteously as, throwing down the sling, he took her shoulders in his big hairy hands and pulled her to one side as she struggled against him, her tiny fists beating against his gorilla-like chest. Her screams echoed over the mountainside and deep valleys beyond, as he pulled her toward a scrub oak.

His face was close to hers as he forced her backward. Her head swam as she fought against him.

"Afterward you weel tell, eh?" he chuckled.

Suddenly, as she was almost forced to the ground, the man straightened up with a look of surprise and pain on his face, turned half way round. Blood gushed from his lips. Then his knees buckled and he fell at her feet.

The two soldiers beside her released her in their fear and amazement as the agent sprawled at their feet, a neat hole in his forehead. They reached to pick him up and then stumbled over his recumbent form and lay silent, little trickles of blood appearing from holes in their heads.

Forgetting Dick and Bill, the other soldiers rushed around like bewildered chickens. One after the other they fell in their tracks as death mysteriously halted them. When fully half of them lay dead, the others threw down their rifles and ran in panic in all directions.

But faster was death. No sound came to disturb the stillness of the summit of Abra Destum, but one by one the Italians perished on the sun-drenched mountain top until not one remained. Dick and Bill looked at each other, wondering, incredulous. These deaths were uncanny, unbelievable. They looked about them, neither saying a word. The princess was not too amazed to hurry into her clothes. The two men followed suit.

Then they heard a whistle. They started in fear, gazing all about the summit of this weird pile of rock which loomed above the surrounding mountain peaks.

"We better git outta this place," yammered Bill, looking around fearfully.

Again came the strange, chilling whistle. Dick looked to the right at a row of stunted oaks about a hundred yards away, unable to believe what he saw. The whole row of trees moved to one side, sliding easily and revealing a long narrow gap in the rock.

Now heads appeared. Woolly heads. Black heads. Then gigantic slender Negroes in dirty khaki appeared to the number of a half dozen, each bearing long rifles. They wore heavy mountain shoes, wrap leggings, khaki shorts and shirts. Leading them was a tall dark brownskin man armed with a wicked-looking .45 calibre pistol.

"Don't move!" the princess cautioned.

The three awaited the arrival of the Negroes who stepped nonchalantly over the bodies of the fallen Italian soldiers. The man with the pistol approached the princess, saluted and spoke to her in a strange tongue as he lifted his hand in salute. After a minute or two of animated conversation, she turned to Dick and his valet.

"Dick, everything is all right at last. This is Gunsa Hernum, chief of Bishop Truli Handem's bodyguard."

She spoke to the tall Negro again. He came forward and shook Dick's hand gravely. Then he pointed toward the narrow trench from which he and his men had just emerged.

"We're to go down there," the princess explained.

Gunsa Hernum stalked into the trench. They followed him. His soldiers brought up the rear. Dick and Bill looked at the dead Italians. The tall Negro, turning, noted their questioning glances and smiled grimly. He spoke to the princess.

"He says the eagles will take care of them," she explained.

The trench was very cleverly contrived: a slot cut in the solid rock of the mountain top. The scrub oaks were planted in a thin patch of earth on two slabs of neatly fitting rock which swung outward and backward, uncovering and covering the narrow trench at will and screening it from view from above.

Gunsa Hernum descended the narrow flight of stone steps that described a spiral deep, deep, deep into the earth. They followed him, feeling their way in the Stygian darkness, the Ethiopian soldiers clumping down behind them. They heard the slabs of rock above move back into place.

It was a long silent descent, rather difficult for Dick and Bill because they had their bundles and the passage was so narrow.

Dick experienced a strange, exhilarating excitement. They were approaching the end of their journey. In a few moments now, he felt sure, they would be in the presence of the strange monarch of the mountain, the mysterious Bishop Truli Handem, the protector of the treasure of Ethiopia.

The tall leader halted. Dick heard a tap on wood, followed by four short taps. There were answering taps. Gunsa Hernum muttered a few words in Amharic.

"He's using the communicating telephone," said the princess.

"What, a telephone here?" asked Dick, incredulous.

"They are not as backward as you think," she replied, a trace of pride in her tone. "You saw how they killed the Italians, didn't you?"

"I saw them die, but I don't know how it was accomplished," Dick confessed.

"That's got me guessin', too," Bill mumbled.

"Their rifles are equipped with Maxim silencers," she explained, "and telescope sights. The silencers are fastened to the muzzles of their rifles, the telescopic sights are fastened to the barrels just ahead of the chamber. Thus equipped the rifles make no sound discernable more than a few feet away, and the telescopes pull the target up close. They heard Yamrou's machine-gun blast and saw the smoke bombs and the plane through one of the bushes and camouflage. But then the Italian squadron came and they stayed down until it went away."

"Well, I wish they'd have come a little sooner," said Dick, ruefully, wincing from the pain of his wounds, "and saved me from that beating."

The sound of sliding bolts ended all conversation. A door opened silently. It was heavy, at least six inches thick, and studded with iron. Beyond was a much wider flight of stairs. As they passed through the doorway, they noticed that on each side of it stood a gigantic Negro in pure white robe edged with gold. The two giants wore rude leather sandals. Each one was holding a shining automatic in his right hand. They saluted Gunsa Hernum as he passed.

Down the stairs they went, stairs lighted by two rude torches that filled the place with acrid smoke. At the bottom of the stairs, the leader gave a command. The second door, wider and higher and thicker than the other, was flung open after much shooting of bolts and bars. Gunsa Hernum marched through. They followed him and found themselves in a chamber about twelve feet square hewn out of solid rock.

There were two doors to this stone chamber lit by four torches. In the ceiling was an air duct. The walls were hung with rich blue and gray striped cloths and on the floor were leopard skin rugs. Along the two side walls were long carved benches.

The leader spoke swiftly to the princess and looked at Bill.

"Your man will have to stay here," she said to Dick. "Only free men and lords may enter the presence of the bishop. Bill is considered a slave by these people."

"Who's a slave?" growled Bill, belligerent.

"Never mind, you stay here," Dick ordered. "I guess they won't eat you."

"Ah wouldn't know," Bill observed, looking at the lean giants surrounding them. "These jokers look mighty hungry."

179

The princess and Dick laughed as he sat down on one of the benches and pulled out a cigarette.

And yet they were far from being at ease. They had survived everything so far, but what would be their reception by the patriarch?

"Are you sure you have that ring?" Dick asked anxiously.

"Yes, I have it. But for a time there I thought I wouldn't."

"Where is it?" Dick was curious. If the Italian agent hadn't been able to find it on her, where could it be?

"Listen, darling. I have it. But I'll show no one until I get in Bishop Handem's presence. Those are the Emperor's orders, dear. Don't feel badly if I carry them out." She looked at him appealingly.

"Of course, sweetheart. I want you to do just as you wish. You know more about this than I do. I was merely curious to know where you could have hidden it so successfully."

"Well," she laughed, "you'll know soon enough."

Gunsa Hernum walked to the second door now. The soldiers accompanying him stood back. They were going no farther. He tapped on the door. It opened slowly, silently on its great hinges sunk into the primordial stone. Their hearts stood still. They gasped at the sight that met their eyes.

⬥⬥⬥ C h a p t e r 1 6

Before them, and not more than ten feet away, was a stone wall, the top of which reached far beyond the limits of the flickering lights from the long torches held by the two black giants who stood on each side of the doorway. The wall curved gently in each direction.

The two giant guards, with their long white robes trimmed with gold, turned to the left. Gunsa Hernum followed them and then the princess and Dick.

The place was as still as death. A musty subterranean odor mingled with the acrid smoke from the torches. Their heels clicked against the solid rock floor of the eight-foot passage.

They walked for all of 60 paces along this wall with its huge stones set in mortar, then the guards halted at a great doorway of oak studded with iron in the design of an eight-pointed cross.

"I wonder what's the idea?" Dick whispered.

"It must be an underground temple," the princess replied in a very low tone. "All our temples have an inner and outer wall. Then comes a big outer court where the public, the deacons and the priests, not engaged in service, congregate. There are four doors, one at each cardinal point of the compass, which lead to this court. Then we should pass to another court which is reached through four more doors placed in the same manner. This should be much larger. . . ."

The thunder of the great iron knocker on the door interrupted further explanation. The door slowly swung open. The guards passed through with their flaming torches. The others followed.

They were in a great cavern, its sides worn by antiquity or chipped smooth by masons. The dome was lost in subterranean blackness, but there was evidently some vent for the egress of the smoke, for, although the circular wall of the 200-foot cavern was lined with giant torch-bearing guards in white robes trimmed with gold, the air in the place was quite clear. The torches gave enough light to make objects easily distinguishable.

On their left stood a great assemblage of black officers in khaki uniforms like that of Gunsa Hernum, several high-born women in gorgeously embroidered white robes, and several youths and girls in their early teens, also garbed in rich costumes. Not a single person was seated.

On the right side stood a golden throne on a low platform. It was overhung by a rich velvet canopy with scalloped edges hung with golden fringe. On each side of the platform stood ranks of richly garbed priests and immediately behind the platform stood a line of high church dignitaries in white and scarlet robes. Each person present wore a silken cord of bright colors from which hung suspended a cross on a tiny silver casket.

Seated on the golden throne was a little shrunken black man with [a] strongly seamed face and sunken eyes that glowed like smoldering coals. His hair was snow white and abundant. His long beard was also white. He sat slightly bent over, as if with the burden of many years, his gnarled and ancient hands gripping the arms of the golden throne.

In the very center of the underground temple stood a square tent-like structure of rich cloth, seemingly heavy blue silk, with a door at each point of the compass.

Gunsa Hernum stretched himself full length on the rock floor at the edge of the long heavy rug that ran to the foot of the regal platform. He kissed the floor three times. Princess Zunda followed his example and Dick did likewise. The old man on the throne waved his wasted hand in a slow motion before him and the three rose and stood respectfully at attention.

Now a high dignitary came from behind the throne and, standing slightly to one side, began to intone a chant that must have been old when Rome flourished. His rich voice reverberated in the huge cavern. Now the other priest brought from the folds of his rich robe an illuminated scroll and read what seemed to Dick to be a prayer. It was lengthy and brought many responses from the priests and nobles.

Then the ranks of priests on each side of the throne moved forward into the space between the platform and the strange tent-like edifice in the center. Dick saw that they bore drums, lutes and rhythmic clicking sistras similar to those he had once read about being borne by the priests of Isis 5,000 years ago. Soon the wild religious music filled the vast room, stirring the blood and quickening the pulse until one wanted to fling oneself into a frenzied dance.

As the music grew wilder, the priests did [a] dance in perfect time as they paced: whirling, stopping, turning, stamping their feet.

It all moved Dick profoundly and made him feel rewarded for venturing on such a risky undertaking. Here was a Negro civilization older than any other except India and China; a civilization that had flourished before Greece and Rome, before Carthage, yes, before Egypt. Here were all the forms, the elaborate ritual, the culture that had made Ethiopia the admiration of the ancient world. Here it survived in spite of Mussolini, in spite of perfidious England, in spite of Ethiopia's desertion by the traitorous League of Nations.

As the weird ancient music finally died and the priests fell back to their places, Dick wept unashamed. What a pity that this civilization should be destroyed by brutal Fascism. No, he resolved anew, it must not die; not if he could prevent it.

The high priest came forward and spoke softly to the old bishop on the throne. The ancient Negro waved his bony hand slowly in assent. Then the high priest turned to the little party by the door and motioned to them to approach the throne.

Gunsa Hernum stepped aside and motioned to Princess Ettara Zunda. She glanced reassuringly at Dick and then walked slowly towards the dais. Dick followed at several paces and the commander of the bodyguard brought up the rear. They stood in a line, the princess a pace in front, before the throne.

The wizened old man seemed no less noble at close quarters. His finely chiseled features were like a cameo. His bushy white hair and his beard were neatly combed. His white silken robes were elaborately embroidered in blue and gold. Most remarkable of all were his eyes. Old, but alert, they seemed to bore right through you.

He waved gracefully to the priest, indicating that the audience could begin. The head priest, a gigantic, leonine man, spoke to Gunsa Hernum. The young commander replied rapidly but respectfully in Amharic, pointing to the ceiling and accompanying his report with graphic pantomime. When he had finished speaking, the high priest turned to the bishop, whom he addressed in Geez, the ancient Ethiopian religious tongue, as Dick learned later from the princess. The bishop nodded his head and spoke a few words in a surprisingly strong and steady, though somewhat high-pitched voice.

Now the high priest turned to Princess Ettara Zunda and said a few words in Amharic. She replied, her voice betraying the emotional stress under which she was laboring. Near the end of her speech, something she said caused an exclamation to rise from the assemblage. The priests looked at each other in surprise and Bishop Truli Handem leaned forward with added interest.

He talked rapidly to the high priest in the ancient ritual language. The statement was communicated to the princess. She smiled and bowed.

"He wants to see the ring," she whispered to Dick. Then she replied to the high priest.

The entire assemblage waited tensely to see the royal token which would release the ancient treasure of Ethiopia into the service of Ethiopia. Bishop Truli betrayed his interest by the greater intensity of his gaze.

Dick was more curious than anyone present. Ever since that night on the Mediterranean when John Danillo had fallen in a pool of blood in the dining salon of the *S.S. Metallic* after handing the Princess the precious bauble, Dick had been wondering where she could possibly be keeping it to have escaped the thorough search by the Italians both on the ship and on the summit of Abra Destum. He made a silent genuflection to her cleverness.

The Princess flashed a triumphant smile at him and slowly lifted her arms.

◇◇◇Chapter 17

The slender hands went swiftly to her head. Her fingers parted the hair on top where it was thickest. You could almost have heard a pebble drop, so quiet was the great cavern.

"Come on, Dick," she whispered. "Help me with this." As he came closer she took his hand in hers and ran his finger through her hair.

He felt a bump, explored it and discovered a broad piece of black adhesive tape fastened to a part of the skull where a square patch of hair had been cut away.

"Pull it off," she commanded.

She winced and exclaimed as he pulled the tape away from the scalp. Then he gasped. Attached to the underside of the tape was a semi-circular band of gold. At one end of it was half of an oval signet bearing the royal coat of arms of the kings of Ethiopia.

She smiled triumphantly at him, a glint of mockery in her eyes, then advanced to the dais and handed the half-ring to the high priest. The gigantic ecclesiastic examined it closely and respectfully, then placed it in the gnarled and outstretched hand of Bishop Truli Handem.

The ancient turned the bauble over in his left palm with the forefinger of his right hand, leaned forward and inspected it closely. Then for the first time the old man looked up and smiled. They were amazed to see that he possessed a fine set of teeth.

"I wonder how old he is," whispered Dick.

"They say he has always lived," she whispered, keeping her eyes on the ancient. "Before Haile Selassie, before Menelik, before Theodore, he was here. Our records prove it."

"Silly, he couldn't have lived always," Dick objected, his voice still low.

"He's been here an awfully long time," she insisted. "He belongs to the ancient caste of Ethiopian priests who adhere to the primitive diet. Almost all these Abra Destum priests belong to the old caste. They are much older than they appear to be. My father told me all about them. He accompanied Menelik here once when he was a young man."

"What do they eat?" asked Dick, interested.

"Dates, figs, goat's milk, fresh fruit, beef blood," she whispered. "They refuse to eat anything that is not alive. All grains they consider dirt and flour is quite out of the question. Father told me that some of the priests are over 200 years old and still retain their manly vigor."

Dick was disposed to laugh, yet something restrained him. Who could tell? Perhaps these old priests up here four miles in the air and removed from the worries and cares of civilization HAD learned something about longevity unknown to the rest of humanity.

But now everyone's attention was directed to Bishop Truli Handem, who still regarded the bauble in his hand with rapt attention. Finally he looked up and spoke to the head priest. That official took the ancient's hand as the old man rose and with slow but steady steps walked to the square blue silk tent in the center of the temple and disappeared through one of the four doors.

A great buzz of whispering followed the bishop's disappearance. Dick and the Princess were the cynosure of all eyes.

"You see," explained the Princess to Dick, "it is extremely unusual, I understand, for Bishop Truli Handem to ever rise in the presence of anyone except his closest aides."

"What's in that tent?"

"The true Ark of the Covenant brought from Jerusalem, and other sacred relics. No one may enter the inner shrine except the very highest officials of the church. I have heard that only Bishop Truli Handem and his high priest are permitted to approach the Ark. The tent is guarded night and day by a trusted group of four giants who stand immediately inside the doors. They are relieved every four hours by four other guards. It is a lifetime job for those eight men. If they fail, they die."

"Do you think the treasure is there?"

"Quite possibly."

"I wonder when we'll get it and be able to get on our way."

"Humph!" she exclaimed. "Who can tell? We can't rush these people. They are skeptical of all outsiders."

"Even a royal princess like yourself?"

"Yes, even of a royal princess. If you had been living two or three hundred years you would be skeptical, too, wouldn't you?" she inquired, smiling.

Now there was a stir in the crowd. The tent door opened and the ancient white bearded man slowly emerged, one of his gnarled old hands held by the high priest. They walked slowly to the throne. The bishop sat down, opened his left hand and looked into it. They could see plainly. There were now two half rings nestling in his palm, identical in size and shape.

The old man took one in each hand, between thumbs and forefingers, then dramatically brought them together until the edges met and the two halves became one ring.

An audible "Ah" came from the onlookers. The old man smiled gently and looked at the Princess Ettara. Then he spoke slowly in Geez to the head priest who towered above his throne and nodded his leonine head understandingly.

The head priest came down off the dais and spoke to her slowly in Amharic, as if to give weight to every word. Dick watched her face in an effort to tell by her expression what effect the words were having. When he had finished he stepped back. The princess spoke a few words, then she stretched herself full length and kissed the floor three times. Taking the cue, Dick did likewise. The ancient bishop waved his wasted hand in slow motion before him. They rose and stood respectfully at attention as they had before.

"It's time to leave," she whispered. "Walk backward slowly until we get to the end of this rug, then bow low and the audience is over."

This was done, and soon they were where they could relax, back near the wall where the black giants in their white robes held the flaming torches aloft.

Now the head priest's voice boomed out. Gunsa Hernum detached himself from the crowd and stood at the head of the rug. He gave the prone salute and then approached the dais. The head priest, even taller than he, spoke to him in low tones, and placed a small leather bag in his hand. Bishop Turli Handem sat motionless like a statue carved out of mahogany or teak. Gunsa Hernum saluted and walked backward to the end of the rug.

He handed the bag to the princess. She beckoned to Dick and the three passed again through the great doorway in the stone wall and found themselves once more in the musty eight-foot-wide passage way, preceded by the two giant guards with their flaming torches.

In a few moments they were back in the 12-foot stone reception chamber hung with blue and gray striped homespun and with the leopard skins strewn on the floor.

As they came through the door Bill Sifton rose from one of the benches with a much relieved look on his face.

"Boss, I'm sure glad to see you," he said, " 'cause this place gives me th' creeps. To tell you th' truth, I don't like these here Africans no more'n them Eyetalians." He rolled his prominent eyes at the giant Ethiopian soldiers sitting on a nearby bench. "When's we gonna git outta this place?"

Dick smiled and turned inquiringly to the princess. "Well, Ettara, you haven't told me yet what the old man's verdict was."

"Are you anxious to know?" she asked archly, teasing him.

"You'd better tell me right away before I die of curiosity."

She sat down on the bench where Bill Sifton had been sitting and Dick sat beside her. Bill stood near, all ears, while Gunsa Hernum leaned against the oaken door. She leaned close.

"Darling," she began, "I know you'll be surprised."

◇◇◇ Chapter 18

"Of course I'll be surprised," he laughed. "I want to be surprised. That's what makes life interesting, isn't it?"

"Well, sometimes. Only I shouldn't like to be surprised again like we were up on the mountain."

Bill Sifton snorted in agreement. "You sho said somethin' then," he muttered.

"Go ahead and surprise me," said Dick.

"Look here," she directed. She opened the small black leather bag very carefully, taking a precautionary glance about. No one was looking. Gunsa Hernum was still leaning against the door frame but talking to one of his soldiers. Dick peered into the open bag and his mouth dropped open. Bill Sifton leaned over his shoulder, took one glance at the contents and gave a low exclamation of excitement and incredulity. The leather bag was almost filled to the brim with precious stones that threw black flames from the torches. Princess Ettara quickly pulled the drawstring and closed the bag.

"God!" cried Dick. "It's a king's ransom!"

187

"It's more than that, Dick. It's salvation for Ethiopia. With these jewels we can keep our men in the field for years, if we can only get safely out of here. . . ." Her voice trailed off in a fearful doubt that showed off in her large black eyes. "Oh, Dick, we've just got to get out safely. We must."

He slipped one arm about her slender waist and drew her gently to him. "Don't worry," he said, "We'll make it. I think we ought to lose no time in getting out of here. What we need now is a good, dependable guide. You'd better speak to Gunsa Hernum about that, so we can probably start early in the morning."

She nodded acquiescence. "Which way should we go out, Dick? By Beni Shengui or by Djibouti? Either way is dangerous now, what with the Italians watching this area."

"Yes, and it's a three-week trip by foot to Beni Shengui, and Lord knows how long it would take us to reach Djibouti."

"We could go through Wallega," she suggested with sudden hopefulness, "and make our way to Kaffa, and from there into Uganda where we'd be safe. From there we could make our way to Nairobi."

"Yes, but think how long it would take," he objected. "We'd be as safe in the Sudan as in Uganda and Kenya, and the facilities for getting out of the Sudan are better. If we can make it to Khartoum, we can easily get a plane to Cairo or Alexandria."

"I guess we'd better try to get out that way, then," she agreed a little wearily, leaning sleepily on his shoulder. The excitement and strain were beginning to tell on her. Dick noticed it.

"You'd better ask Gunsa Hernum where we can stay for the night, whether he can get us a guide and a party of armed men to accompany us, and finally, whether he can get in touch with Dedjasmatch Yamrou. It may be that the Ethiopians have a suitable landing place near here. If so, we can make our way there and in a few hours we'll be in Khartoum."

"All right," she replied. She turned to the tall commander and engaged him in Amharic. They talked with animation for several minutes. Finally she turned again to Dick.

"He says he has a place for us to stay. I think everything else is all right, too. I'll talk to you about it later."

Gunsa Hernum led them through the door through which they had first entered. They climbed the stairs down which they had passed but a short time before. Bill Sifton followed behind, grumbling under the weight of their equipment.

"What did you say, Bill?" asked Dick, amused at the valet's undertone.

"Ah said," repeated Bill defiantly, puffing under his burden, "that Ah'd sho be glad w'en we got shed o' this business. Ah didn't come 'way f'om New York to be runnin' 'round no mountains and jungles."

"Cheer up, old man," Dick said laughing, "it won't be long now."

"Yeah," mumbled Bill, "that's what Ah'm afraid of."

The princess laughed and Dick joined her. They were more than half way up the staircase now. Suddenly the tall commander stopped. His torch revealed a narrow door in the wall, a door they hadn't noticed on their way down. He tapped once, then tapped four times sharply, just as he had done before. There were similar answering taps immediately. The narrow door slid to one side. Gunsa Hernum stepped to one side and gestured them to enter.

The giant sentry on the inside bowed low as the princess passed but continued to hold his torch aloft so that they might see their way. They were in a sort of ante-chamber about eight feet square. A door led to another room. The ante-chamber was bare except for two benches. The commander bade them be seated and then disappeared through the door beyond.

"Well, what did he say?" asked Dick, anxiously.

"He has our quarters all prepared for the night and he will supply us with a competent guide and a squad of soldiers. The nearest landing place for a plane is 25 miles from here across very difficult country. He can supply us with three donkeys."

"Then we ought to be able to make it in one day," Dick exclaimed enthusiastically. Even Bill looked interested in that.

"No, dear, I think it will take longer. We can only travel very slowly, and not at all after 9 o'clock in the morning," she said.

"Why not?"

"The Italian patrol planes are over this area every day. They know about Abra Destum. If it weren't so inaccessible, they'd have attacked it long ago. Gunsa Hernum says that as it is they have outposts surrounding it at a distance of twelve miles. We'll have to get through them somehow."

"We will," declared Dick, thrusting out his chin. "We'll get through if we have to crawl. But tell me, what did he say about getting Dedjasmatch Yamrou?"

"He may be able to get him by short wave but the powerful Italian station at Addis Ababa is always interfering. It's a slim chance, but he's willing to do anything to help us."

The door opened and the grave young commander entered. He spoke to the princess and then stood to one side and beckoned them to enter. The large domed room hewn out of the solid rock was roughly 30 feet square and seemed to have once been a smaller cave which the Ethiopians had enlarged. Gigantic beams shored up one part of the ceiling, probably weaker than the rest. The great room was divided into four compartments, two on each side, by curtains of striped blue and gray cloth, evidently homespun, that hung from ropes stretched across the room. At the far end stood a powerful field radio set, with a table and a large gasoline engine for generating power. It was the first place they had been in the bowels of this mountain where there were electric lights.

The young commander showed them to their compartments, each equipped with a field bed, a small table, a basin and a water filter on a iron stand. Bill threw down the heavy luggage with a sigh of relief.

Gunsa Hernum called to the princess and Dick, and showed them the wireless telephone set. He started the engine. Its reverberations sent strange echoes through the underground. He sat down at the table, put on earphones and was soon busily at work trying to get Dedjasmatch Yamrou at Beni Shengui. They waited silently as he monotonously called the code number. Again and again he tried, every once in a while looking up annoyed.

The princess looked grave. Dick frowned. Unless they got the aid of Dedjasmatch Yamrou, how long it would take them to get back to Europe where they could dispose of the treasure in gems?

Gunsa Hernum continued to work at the dials. At last he disgustedly took off his earphones, hunched his shoulders and looked disconsolately at the princess.

"By George! If he can't get Yamrou we're sunk." Dick frowned darkly.

"He'll get him," she insisted with desperate hope. "He's GOT to get him."

Bill Sifton straightened up from his work, listened, then shook his head dolefully, and bent again over the field stove where he was preparing a meal, grumbling the while.

"Boy," he muttered to himself, "you sho is sunk now. Ah jes knowed we nevah would get outta this place."

"What did you say, Bill!" asked Dick.

"Nuttin', boss. Ah's jes thinkin' Ah sho like to git outta this place."

"Well, don't worry. We'll get out all right."

But Dick wasn't really so sure. Neither, now, was the princess. Gunsa Hernum tried time and again without avail. Finally he looked up and spoke a few disconsolate words in Ahmaric.

"He says it's no use, Dick. He can't get anything."

"Tell him to keep on. We've GOT to get Yamrou. It's our only chance to get out of here. We'll never make it if we have to depend on donkeys. Even if we get by the Italians, it will take us weeks to get to civilization. Tell him to try again. Yamrou's probably the only one that can work the radio at Beni Sengui, and he may not be there right now."

The princess spoke to Gunsa Hernum, insisted that he keep on. He turned indulgently but pessimistically to the dials and tried again.

Minutes went by. Bill Sifton had the meal almost ready. The Eddoes were half boiled and the thick steaks he had carved from the fresh haunch of beef hanging in a cool recess in the cavern were ready for the fire.

"Shall I cook this heah meat, boss? Ah'm gittin' mighty hungry, mahself." He looked longingly at the three thick steaks awaiting the grill.

"I suppose we might as well eat, Ettara," said Dick. "Call your friend over to join us. Bill, you'd better broil a steak for him, too. He can try again after we eat."

Soon the steaks were sizzling over the charcoal fire. Bill went to cut a fourth steak for Gunsa Hernum, but when he returned with it and prepared to put it over the fire, the Ethiopian officer violently objected.

"Wait, Bill," cautioned the princess. "He doesn't want it cooked. He wants to eat it as it is. These people never cook their meat."

"They eats it raw?" asked Bill, incredulously.

"Sure," Dick cut in, "didn't you know that? All these East Africans eat their meat raw."

"Well, they sho kin have it," grumbled Bill, eyeing Gunsa Hernum suspiciously, "but I noticed that fellah down to that other place et HIS meat cooked, only it wasn't cooked enough. Ah don't want no rare meat, mahself. Ah likes mah meat well done."

The meal soon got under way. The Ethiopian cut his meat into narrow strips with his razor-sharp knife, dipped them in a fiery sauce and ate the flesh without batting an eye. There was silence for several minutes as they all did justice to the food.

Suddenly the radio began to crackle and sputter, Gunsa Hernum rose and ran to the dials, twirling them this way and that to get volume.

At once a stentorian voice came from the loud speaker. Gunsa Hernum turned excitedly, showing his magnificent white teeth. He shouted to the princess.

"He's got Yamrou," she cried, jumping from the table.

Dick followed her over to the radio. The Ethiopian officer looked at her and nodded his head. She spoke quickly, breathlessly into the mouthpiece.

"Yamrou? Dedjasmatch Yamrou? . . . Are you there? . . . This is Princess Ettara Zunda speaking from Abra Destum. Can you hear me?"

"This is Yamrou speaking," came the voice in English. "Yes, I hear you. . . . I rejoice that you are safe."

"Listen carefully, Dedjasmatch," she commanded. "We are ready to get back to Europe. Understand? . . . We must have a plane at the landing field about 20 miles from here. Do you know where it is?"

"I know," Yamrou replied. "I come when you say."

"Good! We leave here tonight. Understand? We should be there early tomorrow morning. Watch out for Italians. They are all about us, hunting for us. Be careful!"

"I hear and I obey. Dedjasmatch Yamrou will not fail."

"Very well. That is all."

Gunsa Hernum said a few parting words in Ahmaric and then shut off the radio. The meal was finished in gay humor over Gunsa Hernum's excellent native wine. As they smoked, the Ethiopian described the route they were to follow and what to do in case the Italians put in an appearance.

In a short while he took his departure, promising the princess to return for them in a few hours when it would be completely dark. The three turned in for some much needed rest, after they had anointed their wounds with a healing ligament Gunsa Hernum had ordered for them.

It seemed to Dick that he had scarcely closed his eyes when he felt a hand on his shoulder. He rose quickly to a sitting position, rubbing his eyes. For a moment he forgot where he was. Then he heard Bill's voice.

"That man's heah, Mistah Dick," the valet announced. "We bettah git ready."

Dick hurried into his clothes. Already Bill had packed their things in two bundles. In a few moments the princess emerged from her compartment. Gunsa Hernum was pacing back and forth waiting for them, twirling a giant electric torch in his hand. As they assembled, he spoke to Princess Ettara.

"He says to follow him," she translated.

Dick and Bill shouldered their bundles and rifles and followed her and the Ethiopian officer out of the hospitable quarters where they would have preferred to have slept for many hours more.

Down flight after flight of stone steps, past the big door to the audience chamber, down and ever down until it seemed that they would never stop. What tremendous toil it had required to cut these interminable steps into the virgin rocks! For how many centuries had they been here? Dick wondered.

They continued in silence with Gunsa Hernum's flashlight cutting a hole in the Stygian darkness ahead. Downward, ever downward.

Suddenly the Ethiopian halted. Again they heard the familiar tap on wood. There were taps in reply. Then a great door creaked on its hinges and a draught of cool fresh air came as a welcome relief to the stuffiness of underground. The Ethiopian snapped off his light. They heard the movement of feet, and then sharp commands in a low tone. Someone came to either side of them as they walked out into the open. They could see nothing. There was no moon.

"He's leaving us here," she told Dick. "The soldiers will guide us to the secret airfield. Let's pray that the Italians don't find it first."

"Where did you put the jewels?" asked Dick, anxiously.

"I gave them to Bill to wrap in our things."

"Have you got them, Bill?" Dick turned to his valet.

"Nuthin' diff'rent," replied that worthy. "An' where Ah gottem, Ah reckon no Eyetalian ain't gonna fin' em."

"All right, then. Let's get going. I'll bet we have a tough journey ahead of us."

"Yes, Gunsa Hernum says it is difficult."

The three donkeys were brought up and mounted. A soldier held the bridle of each animal, two walked behind and three walked in front. Gunsa Hernum had warned Princess Ettara that they must maintain absolute quiet because voices carried far in the high altitude.

Alongside vertical cliffs, down precipitous ravines, across rushing streams and then up almost perpendicular ascents the little cavalcade made its way in utter silence through the intense darkness.

Twice they halted to give the animals a rest and a drink, but not for long. Time was valuable. All too soon they began to see the first gray streaks of dawn. With the dramatic suddenness of daybreak in the tropics, the darkness lifted. They were in a country of incredible wildness, like a piece of stiff paper some giant had crumpled in gargantuan hands. To their right was an awesome canyon a half mile deep. The narrow trail, not three feet wide, wound precariously around the towering peaks. Two or three miles ahead and below they saw the flat black lava field.

"That's the airfield!" cried the Princess, breaking the long silence.

As if in reply there came from nowhere a burst of machine-gun fire and bullets ricocheted off the rocks ahead.

◈◈◈Chapter 20

"Down, flat!" cried Dick, falling off his donkey and yanking it with him to the rocky trail with the assistance of the soldier who held the bridles. The others followed suit, crouching behind the beasts, their only protection.

Another stream of bullets tore along the rock wall behind them, sending stones and chips showering down. Dick tried to see from what direction the bullets were coming. He decided that the attack must be coming from the right flank, now their front.

There was barely room behind the three donkeys for the eleven persons whose lives hung in the balance. Each time the machine guns across the way spoke their angry message, the bullets struck lower and lower. Undoubtedly the Italians had the range. To leave the position was to court death; to stay was to make death a certainty. If they could only silence those machines guns!

Desperately Dick studied the far side of the chasm along which they had been crawling like flies, his field glasses barely peering above the fat little belly of his donkey. The others looked to him, awaiting some word of command, their rifles ready to spit back if they could find anything at which to shoot.

Another blast of machine-gun fire, this time a bit lower, and another shower of stones and chips. Bill Sifton ducked low, rolling his eyes comically. The eight Ethiopian soldiers waited stoically. They had been trained to do whatever they were told to do. Instinctively they looked for leadership to Dick. But Dick was as puzzled and uncertain as they.

"We've got to get out of here, darling," said the princess, changing places with a soldier in order to be alongside Dick. They're getting closer and closer. If they aim a little lower, they'll have us."

"But if we get up and try to run for it," Dick objected, "they'll mow us down in a flash. Once we leave there's no protection. The next bend in the trail is at least fifty yards to our rear. And if we run forward we'll have to go over a hundred yards exposed. We won't be able to make it. . . ."

Again the death rattle of lead gouged into the rock wall in their rear. The soldier on Dick's right ducked and grinned. Death had just missed the lot of them again, but by a closer margin. Dick swept the other side of the canyon again with his glasses. It was at least 600 yards away. He could see nothing. Smokeless powder leaves no trace. Having complete command of the trail and apparently its exact range, they could afford to patiently wait until the party should attempt to make a run for safety. It would be playing right into their hands.

He peered to the right and left at the little party lying prone with nothing between them and death except three donkeys that were being held down with difficulty. As he looked there came another hail of bullets, but this time from another angle. Evidently there were several machine-gun nests covering the trail. They were trapped like rats. Perhaps they should have tried to get overland to Kenya or to Djibouti. But even as the thought came he dismissed it with a grimace. No, they had done the best they could. The Italians, hopeful of capturing the rich treasure the princess had obtained from Abra Destum, had probably surrounded the entire area.

If that was so, he thought, brightening, if he could break through here, he might be safe. There were probably not more than two or three machine guns in the nest across the way. If he could only reach the next bend in the trail, perhaps they all might get through.

"Well, boss," yelled Bill, "Wha we go f'om heah? Them jokers ovah tha is gettin' mighty close."

"You mean they ARE getting close, Bill," bantered Dick. "You must be careful of your English."

"Ah ain't got no time foh no English now, boss. These Eyetalians is gettin' too close fo' me. If that last shot had bin jes a lettle lowah we'd all bin in Glory, an' Ah don' mean however. We sho does need some whatchyacallum? Cammyflag?"

"You mean camouflage, Bill," Dick corrected, chuckling at his valet's mispronunciation. Then a sudden idea flashed through his mind. He looked about him and the idea grew to magnificent proportions. "Bill," he shouted, "I think you've got something there."

"Whatcha mean, Boss?" Bill's eyes shone with excitement.

"We can get out of here by using camouflage. Or else we'll have to stay here and get plugged."

"Well, Mr. Welland," interrupted the princess, "will you please tell me where we are to get this camouflage. I'm willing to put it on if you can find it."

"Yeah," added Bill, "an me, too."

"Get our canteens and the big water bottle and pass them over here. Get me that canvas bucket, too," Dick directed.

Bill carried out his instructions, being careful to keep as low as possible. In a few moments Dick had the water bottle and canteens and was pouring water into the canvas pail.

"Now pass me handfuls of dirt," ordered Dick, as he scooped up some of the loose soil from the trail and threw it into the bucket. With the help of Bill, the princess and the nearest soldier, the water in the bucket was soon a soupy mud.

"Now, darling," turning to Princess Ettara, "tell the soldiers to take off those white robes, and be quick about it. Pass each robe over to me."

She told the soldiers what to do, after some initial hesitancy they quickly obeyed. As each robe was passed, Dick plunged it into the bucket

196

of reddish brown mud until it was saturated, then slit it with his knife. The big robes drank up much of the mud but Dick replenished the supply, using all of the water except a pint or so in the water bottle. Then the robes were rubbed in the mud until brown.

"If this doesn't work," he laughed, "we won't need any water."

"What are you going to do, darling?" The Princess was all curious, as were the others.

"Well," he explained, when he had dipped the last garment and the heap of mud-soaked robes were spread out behind them, "Bill's talking about camouflage gave me an idea. They've got this spot covered. If we make a run for it they'll annihilate us. If we stay here, they'll get us anyway. All right, this is the way we leave: These robes are now the same color as the ground, aren't they?"

"Yes, that's right," the princess nodded her head. A sudden burst of machine-gun fire, a little higher this time, made all of them duck.

"If they're the same color as the ground to us," Dick continued, "they're the same color to the Italians. So we're going to fasten these slit robes to the enemies' side of our donkeys with one edge dragging on the ground. Three of us can crouch behind this screen and walk alongside the donkey until we get to the next curve in the trail where we'll probably be out of range."

The princess explained to the Ethiopians who saw the point immediately. Everybody was in gay spirits now. The first donkey was draped with two of the robes.

"You go with two of the soldiers," Dick directed her.

She crouched behind the screen alongside the donkey and called the two soldiers. Slowly they started on the perilous journey of a short hundred yards. Ten yards. Fifteen yards. Twenty yards. There was no sign from the other side of the canyon that the ruse was detected. Forty yards. Now they were half way, moving slowly but surely toward safety. Sixty yards. Now, three-quarters of the way. A little bit more and they would be safe. Dick clenched his teeth until they hurt. Oh, if it would only work, if it would only work!

The first attempt was a success. The donkey, with his mud-colored drape screening the princess, and two of the soldiers rounded the corner of the trail to safety. The others were jubilant.

Again there was a rattle of machine guns across the way. The lead flattened and ricocheted aganst the rock wall. There was a cry and a gurgle as one of the nearly naked Ethiopians rolled over in agony and then lay still, his useless rifle clutched in his hand. One of his comrades calmly took the rifle and the dead man's ammunition. There was no time to be sentimental here.

The loss of one of the men decided Dick on a desperate course.

"Bill," he said, "you go next and take three of the soldiers with you. We've got to get out of here as soon as we can. Another volley like that and we'll all be goners. Four is a whole lot to put behind one donkey but you can crouch two abreast. Make it snappy. I'll follow you at ten or fifteen paces."

"It sho ain't gonna grieve me tuh leave heah," Bill replied, carefully preparing to go.

The donkey was got on his feet, the cloth adjusted and the men put in place. Then the second trip started. Instead of walking the donkey, Bill made it canter along. When the second group got about 15 yards, the third group, under command of Dick, started on its journey with equal speed.

Rat-a-tat-tat-tat! Rat-a-tat-tat-tat! Again the distant machine guns spoke. The fleeing party could hear the lead thudding against the rock and humming as it spun off into space. They had moved none too soon. Looking back they saw the bullets kicking up the dust in the trail where they had been lying but a few moments before. Dick urged both parties forward faster. Soon they came to the bend. It was even sharper than he had supposed, making an acute angle and offering welcome protection from the increasingly accurate fire.

Once out of range, the soldiers were given back their sodden garments to dry as they marched, and the cavalcade again got under way, grateful for the escape from death. Going down hill now, they hastened at accelerated pace, Dick and the princess riding side by side wherever the trail widened into what might have been almost called a road.

"That was a little too close to please me," she observed, smiling wryly.

"I wonder if we can get through. They seem to have been waiting for us there." She looked at him questioningly.

"We're safe so far. What's worrying me is when we get out in the open. If that's the only nest, we'll be too far for them to reach us with their fire. But if they're all over the place it'll be a tough job getting away."

At Dick's suggesting, the princess ordered the soldiers to make all speed down the trail and to the lava field where Dedjasmatch Yamrou was to meet them. In obedience they cantered more briskly down the trail, the little donkeys matching the pace of the lanky warriors. The sun was quite high now and the rugged landscape was clear in all directions. Their descent was away from their destination now. For a half hour they went down, down, down, over rocks, gullies, landslides and little brooks that cut across the trail, until at long last they reached the bottom.

The bed of the stream was almost dry. The trail ran along beside it, meandering up and down but never more than 50 feet above it. They were in a narrow gorge not more than 200 feet across, which widened out as they continued their descent.

Dick was eyeing the sides of the canyon very sharply, his rifle at the ready. The quickest on the trigger in a situation like this was the longest to live. The Ethiopian soldiers were equally alert.

But nothing happened. Finally, ahead of them loomed the opening of the canyon and beyond was the black lava field. The strain and tenseness lessened. For the first time the soldiers began to converse. One big black fellow laughed throatily. Their gait speeded.

"Well, it sho won't be long now," observed Bill. "Ah ain't nevah been in love with no airplane but Ah'm sho gonna be glad tuh see this un. Them Eyetalians shoot too straight foh me."

"Yes, we'll soon be there, Bill," Dick agreed, scanning the skies for the expected plane.

It did seem as though their ruse had shaken off their pursuers. Dick smiled as he thought how puzzled the Italians must be at their sudden disappearance. He looked at Princess Ettara. She was really an ace, he mused. So few women were at once beautiful, smart, healthy and natural in their association with men. She was self-reliant, too. He understood, had long understood, why the Emperor trusted her with so dangerous a mission. Once they got out of this and back to Egypt and

Europe, he planned, they could marry. The thought struck him pleasantly. He whistled softly a popular tune he had heard in Paris.

They were now only a few yards from the great mouth of this canyon; the great mountains fell away on each side. Ahead of them the heat waves played across the black expanse of lava. It was evidently the floor of an ancient volcano, for about six miles across the floor the rugged mountains started again, their summits lost in the few scattering clouds that hung like little balls of cotton in the blue heavens. All about them silence was eloquent.

"Ye-e-s, Mistuh Welland," Bill burst out suddenly, as if there had been no pause in his remarks, "it sho won't be long now!"

Dick's retort was drowned by shouts from either side of them, followed by gruff commands. The little party looked up startled and dismayed, their hearts pounding violently as they gripped their rifles.

It was no use. Dick saw at once. So did the others. At the very opening of the canyon, perching up 50 or 75 feet on either side was a party of Askaris, black Italian soldiers from the coast colonies, numbering altogether about sixty, and under the command of two white officers. Each group had a tripod machine gun in position and covering the little party. To move another step meant instant death. Dick, Bill and the princess threw down their rifles. The Ethiopian soldiers followed suit.

The Italian officers and their Askaris scrambled down the steep sides of the canyon and surrounded the party. The senior officer, a rugged fellow in his thirties, walked up to Dick, looked him up and down. Then he turned to the princess and coolly surveyed her from head to foot.

He addressed her roughly in Italian. She replied haughtily.

"What does he say?" asked Dick.

"He says we are under arrest and will be taken to headquarters. I guess it is the end, darling." Her voice caught.

"Well, we made a good try anyway," he comforted.

"Yeah," mumbled Bill, "but it wa'n't good enough."

The Askaris herded the Ethiopian soldiers together facing the far canyon wall at the direction of the junior officer, a youngster apparently just out of military school. Eight of the Askaris lined up about 50 feet from the doomed men, their service rifles at [the] ready.

A crisp command and the rifle butts moved to right shoulders. Another command and the firing squad sighted down its rifles. A final command and a volley rent the quiet canyon. The Ethiopians toppled over in a grotesque heap. Another sharp command and the Ethiopians' rifles were gathered up. It was all done in a swift, cold, matter-of-fact manner.

"Well," Dick said in hard low tones to the princess, "I see civilization has at last reached Ethiopia. I suppose we'll be next."

"They died so bravely," she sobbed. It was the first time he had seen her so visibly emotional. "Not a murmur for mercy! That is the way I, too, shall die, sweetheart."

"Ah, Princess, but you shall not die," spoke up the elder officer, smiling grimly at their look of surprise that he could speak English. "Oh, no, you shall not die . . . not yet. First, we go to headquarters. There you will find someone who wants to see you!" He laughed wickedly, shouted an order and they moved forward.

◇◇◇ Chapter 22

The cavalcade debouched from the canyon, skirted the ancient lava field, where Dick had thought by this time he would be boarding Yamrou's plane, and continued until they reached a broad stream which ran alongside a small settlement of thatched mud huts. Dick scanned the sky for sight of Yamrou's plane, but all in vain. Only a few hawks and vultures appeared above, speeding toward the narrow canyon where seven Ethiopian warriors lay dead in a heap.

"Something MUST have gone wrong," he whispered to the princess as they jogged along on their donkeys. "It seems strange that Yamrou didn't show up. It's funny, too, that the Italians knew just where we would have to come out of the mountains. How is it they chose THAT particular canyon instead of any others?"

"You think they found out in some way, Dick?" She eyed him reflectively.

"Of course," he insisted. "There's been a leak some way. The only ones who knew the route we were taking were Gunsa Hernum and Dedjasmatch Yamrou. The soldiers knew but if one of them had been a traitor he would have been spared, wouldn't he?"

"It would seem so, darling. But I hate to believe that either Hernum or Yamrou would do a thing like that. It's just impossible in the case of

Hernum. And Yamrou is as loyal as they make them." She was positive and yet she felt misgivings.

"Then you think all this is merely a coincidence?"

"I admit it looks strange, Dick. But I can't believe Hernum and Yamrou would betray us. What motive would they have?"

"Well, that bag of jewels is certainly worth a big fortune or I'm greatly mistaken. Money has changed people's allegiance before, and will probably do so again. Bigger men that Yamrou have betrayed their country for a price. After all, it's easy to say we were captured and the jewels confiscated by the Italians, isn't it?"

"But in that case, why should either of them split with the Italians when they could have had us murdered by their own men and kept all the jewels for themselves?" She looked at him triumphantly as she posed the question.

"Yes, you've got something there," he admitted, admiringly. "Nevertheless I still say it's more than a coincidence."

Now they were entering the small settlement. On the outskirts sat a big Italian bombing plane with two sentries keeping watch over it. There were at least a hundred soldiers loitering about, all black Askaris: gigantic fellows with big fezzes on their heads that made them seen even taller. Evidently this was an important post.

They were hustled through the narrow lanes between the huts until they reached a larger and more pretentious mud-walled house with an expansive sheltered veranda. It had evidently been the chief's house in the recent past, but now three or four white officers lounged in the hammocks, smoking and talking. They straightened up and greeted the senior officer conducting the captives. Dick gathered that they were congratulating him since he bowed his acknowledgment and made some deprecating retort.

Although the shutters were open, the big room into which the three captives were pushed was in semi-darkness. There were straw mats on the floor and in one corner was a folding military cot with its white mosquito bar folded up. Nearby was a water filter on a folding iron stand. In the center of the room at a large field desk sat a tall, slender, almost ascetic-looking man in white from helmet to shoes. To Dick he seemed faintly familiar. The officer who had captured them spoke to the man very respectfully as "Captain Fraschetti."

Bowlegged Bill Sifton had also been studying the man at the desk.

Suddenly he blurted out: "Well, hush mah mouth, if it ain't that Don Carlos Navarre off the ship."

The man looked up quickly with a scowl. Dick recognized him, too. The officer turned around and brusquely ordered quietness. Dick had always suspected that Don Carlos Navarre was an Italian secret agent. Now he knew that he was the notorious Captain Luigi Fraschetti.

Fraschetti eyed them coldly and then gave the officer an order. The latter saluted, turned on his heel and left the room. Minutes passed and he did not return. Dick was tired and wanted to sit down. He knew the princess and Bill did, too.

He turned to Fraschetti. "Can't we have something to sit on?" he asked, somewhat irritably.

The man looked up as coldly as ever, then continued writing.

"Ask him in Italian for a chair," he urged the princess, "I'm tired of standing."

She complied. Fraschetti looked up again, scowling, and snarled out a few words.

"He says to sit on the floor if we are tired," she translated.

Just then the officer returned. With him was a short bearded brown man with a white helmet, cordovan leggings, gleaming patent leather shoes and a neat khaki uniform with a Sam Browne belt. It was the Duke of Dessaye, Ras Resta Gusa.

"Resta!" cried the Princess. "Are you behind this?"

The little brown man turned with a smile and rubbed his short black beard. Then he bowed elaborately to the princess in mock humility.

"This is an unexpected pleasure, Your Grace," he said, displaying his even white teeth. "Who would have thought that we would have met so soon again and under such singlar cirumstances, if I may so characterize this meeting? How small is the world after all! I trust you will be comfortable here, Your Grace. Our accommodations here are extremely meager but the place has a quiet charm and the scenery, as you have probably noticed, is superb. I trust you will be with us for some time."

Then he turned to Dick and stepped back in mock surprise.

"Meester Welland! You here, too? This . . . This is really too much. I am overwhelmed, Meester Welland. So you DID come to Ethiopia after all, regardless of my warning? Ah, you Americans! There's no stopping you, is there? Ah, well. Where there is the will, there is the way. Is that not the way you say it, Meester Welland?" He rocked back on his heels gloating over their predicament, enjoying it to the fullest. Dick sealed his lips. Why talk with this snake? The Duke chuckled.

Suddenly he dropped this mood and turned in a businesslike way to Captain Fraschetti. They conversed for a few moments in Italian but in such low tones that the princess could not understand what they said.

When they finished, Ras Resta Gusa spoke to the offier who had captured them. He in turn shouted an order through the door, and in a few moments three gigantic black soldiers entered, deposited their burdens and retired.

"Please be seated," invited the Duke, seating himself close to Ettara.

Captain Fraschetti remained behind the field desk. The others formed a semi-circle around it. Dick surmised that Ras Resta Gusa would do the interrogating. He was determined to give them no information. Princess Ettara's eyes told the same determination. He knew Bill Sifton wouldn't talk.

"I told you on the steamer," the Duke said to the princess, "that I could give you the proper station in life. I offered you my hand and you spurned it."

"You are a traitor, Resta," she snapped. "I have known for a long time that you were selling out Ethiopia. This proves it beyond doubt. I could never marry a traitor. I wouldn't touch you with a stick, Resta. You're unfit for human association."

His beard bristled and his eyes blazed. He leaned forward like a dog straining at a leash, then he regained control of himself and leaned back nonchalantly.

"A pretty speech, Ettara. Very beautiful. My offer is still open. I am a big man in Ethiopia now, Ettara."

"You are a traitor to Ethiopia," she cried. "I hate traitors."

"Well, as you will. There's no changing a woman's mind, I suppose." He shrugged his shoulders and smiled at Fraschetti. Then continued: "But now we have business before us. Ettara, you went to get part or all of the royal treasure. Since you were hurrying away from Abra Destum, I presume you received the treasure: that the half-ring worked like a charm on the ancient bishop. Very well, we want that treasure, and we're going to have it. Understand?"

"Do you see any treasure on us?" mocked Dick.

"No, I don't Meester Welland. But we shall all be able to see it when you show it to us. Where is it? We have searched your baggage to no avail. Come, come. If you have the treasure, turn it over immediately and we'll let you go on your way."

"And if I don't?"

"Then," said the duke quietly, "I shall be very sorry for you."

◇◇◇ Chapter 23

"What can you do except shoot us?" challenged Dick. "Naturally we expect that."

Ras Resta threw back his head and laughed softly and wickedly.

"It is very funny, very funny," he chuckled.

"What's so funny?"

"Your simplicity, my friend, your amazing simplicity," the duke replied. "Do you think we would shoot you before getting the treasure. Ah, no. You will tell us where is the treasure. Then . . . well, we shall see." He turned to Captain Fraschetti and spoke rapidly in Italian. The Captain replied in austere tones, seemingly weighing each word.

The Princess paled and started. Dick looked quickly from her to the captain. Then he looked at Res Resta Gusa to find that rascal smiling contentedly.

"The captain," the duke explained, "is very, very, impatient, my friends. He does not like delay. He has the impatience of the go-getter, as I believe you Americans call such people. He wants the treasure now. I suggest, my friends, that you tell him at once."

"And if we don't . . . ?" asked Dick.

"Then we have other methods, Meester Welland, that are very, very unpleasant, I assure you."

"I suppose you mean torture."

"Well, I shouldn't use such a crude word, Meester Welland. Suppose we say . . . persuasion. Come now, what shall it be? You can't get out of this, Meester Welland. You're about as securely a prisoner as anyone could be. You got away from us on the ship. You eluded us in Alexandria. You escaped us at Beni Shengui and again on top of Mount Abra Destrum. But now you are in our hands. You won't get away this time,. Meester Welland. No one will save you because no one knows where you are. Not even your friend Dedjasmatch Yamrou who was supposed to meet you at the old lava fields in his stolen Italian airplane."

205

Dick's heart sank. Then they HAD overheard Gunsa Hernum's broadcast to Yamrou! No wonder they had been able to trap them so handily. He frowned, and glanced quickly at the princess. She seemed quite hopeless now.

Captain Fraschetti spoke out roughly to Ras Resta. The duke muttered a reply out of the side of his beard.

"You have one more chance, my friends," said the duke. "And it is the last chance. Where is the treasure you got from the bishop? We cannot fool around any longer."

"To tell you the exact truth, Duke," Dick replied, quite truthfully, "I really don't know."

"And you, dear Princess," Ras Resta turned to the beautiful woman he loved after his fashion.

"I am glad to say, Resta, that I, too, do not know."

"What about you, man." The Duke turned to Bill.

"Ain't nobody tol' me nuthin' 'bout no treasure," replied Bill. "It's the first Ah ever heard tell of it. Whut kinda treasure, big boy?"

"Ah!" flared the Duke, his little black eyes flashing, "you are all lying, lying, lying! Do you think we are fools? We know every move you have made. We want that treasure and we are going to have it." He turned to Captain Fraschetti and they talked rapidly. When he had finished and turned again to the prisoners, Dick knew they were in for it.

The senior officer who had arrested them went to the door and snapped out a command. Six big black soldiers entered under the command of a bigger and blacker noncommissioned officer. The officer spoke rapidly to them. The noncom grinned and saluted. They moved over by the prisoners and stood at attention.

"The officer pointed to the princess and spoke to the noncom. Ettara screamed, "No! No! Oh, Dick! They're going to torture me!"

Dick jumped up, only to face a drawn automatic pistol in the officer's hands. He stood for a moment undecided.

"Don't do anything, Dick," she pleaded. "They'll kill you."

"But they'll . . ." his voice trailed off helplessly.

"Yes, I know, but . . ." she shrugged her shoulders hopelessly.

The officer led the way into an adjoining room. The princess, held firmly by each arm, was dragged in after him. The door slammed shut.

The duke sneered at Dick. "You were very wise, Meester Welland, not to attempt any heroics. It would have been foolhardy. Now, my friend, what we want to know is where is the treasure. Tell us, and the princess will be unmolested, and you and your man can go on your way. Refuse to tell us and we shall proceed with the 'persuasion' of the princess. It will all be well within your hearing."

"You beast!" Dick growled, helpless and impotent. "It would certainly give me pleasure to kill you."

"Undoubtedly, my friend, undoubtedly. But I'm afraid that'll not happen." He spoke softly. Then, turning to Captain Fraschetti, he winked. The Captain yelled toward the closed door to the inner room.

All was silence for a few moments. Then a piercing scream came from the inner room, followed by another and another. Dick jumped from his chair. Immediately two muscular soldiers banged him back into his seat. Captain Fraschetti spoke to the duke. Ras Resta turned to Dick, smiling malevolently.

"Well, Meester Welland, will you tell us now, or shall we continue to persuade' the princess?"

Dick hesitated. He knew he was in a tough spot. He cared more for Princess Ettara than all Ethiopia's or anybody's treasure. What did it matter if they DID lose the treasure, if her life was spared? He had plenty of money. They could go off somewhere and live happily. . . . But could they? Her life was tied up with Ethiopia. She wouldn't want him to betray her people, even to spare her life. . . . And yet a man couldn't sit and listen to the woman he loved enduring the tortures of the damned.

Another agonizing scream came from the adjacent room. It was a long anguished scream that told of tortures unendurable.

"Well, Meester Welland," observed the duke, his manicured fingers interlaced in front of him, "will you tell us what we want to know or shall we continue to 'persuade' the princess?"

As he spoke the screams came again, chilling Dick to the bone. It seemed that if he heard it once more he would go insane. He MUSTN'T hear it again.

"We are waiting, Meester Welland," the duke reminded him looking knowingly at Captain Fraschetti. "Where is the treasure?"

"I swear I don't know," Dick answered, "or I'd tell you."

"You did get treasure, didn't you?" The duke leaned forward, his little eyes glistening.

"Yes . . . yes . . . we did." Dick was thinking fast. He knew that if they hadn't been able to find it in the baggage, Bill had either cleverly concealed it or it had been lost in their haste to escape the Italian machine-gun fire.

"We had it, all right," he continued. "But when we were fired upon we had to run to escape death and in our haste we lost the bag containing the treasure. It bounced out of a donkey's pack and fell into that deep canyon. We couldn't stop to get it. We had to leave it down there, figuring we could come back and hunt for it after we escaped from the Italians. So we're telling the truth when we say we don't know where the treasure is. I don't and neither does Princess Ettara."

Ras Resta Gusa scowled and regarded Dick fiercely as though to see through him to the truth. Then he turned and reported to Captain Fraschetti, who was no less pleased. They conferred together for several minutes, plainly in a dilemma. The fact that they had not found the treasure on the captives lent support to Dick's story. He gathered this and was accordingly enjoying their difficulty.

After considerable talk with his chief, the duke turned again to Dick. He was suddenly no longer perturbed. He stroked his beard deliberately and eyed his captive. Finally he spoke.

"Meester Welland, we are very sorry the treasure was lost. Since you know about where it was lost according to your interesting story, we are going to give you an opportunity to find it. If we cannot find it, Meester Welland . . ." the Duke stopped and smiled devilishly.

"Then I suppose you'll kill us," Dick filled in.

"Perhaps, my friend, but it will be very, very slowly. You will, how do you say it? Die by inches. Ha! Ha! Ha! Ha!" His diabolical cackle filled the room. "Come, Meester Welland. We go now. There is no time like the present. I hope for your sake and her sake, my friend, that you find the bag."

The midday sun was blazing down now, making the baked plain a veritable gridiron. The three captives, minus their baggage, were again mounted on their mules. In front of them rode the senior officer commanding the troops, Captain Fraschetti and the Duke of Dessaye. Alongside and behind them strode black, gigantic Askaris.

They had scarcely started when Dick moved his donkey close to Bill and the princess so that they were riding side by side.

"Darling!" he whispered, leaning close to her. "What did they do to you?"

"Nothing. They just took me though the adjoining room into a room beyond and placed one of those Askaris to watch me."

"You weren't tortured?" Dick was amazed and chagrined.

"No, they never touched me," she insisted.

"That damned Ras Resta tricked me," he growled.

"How is that, darling?"

"Well, after you were taken out of the room they asked me to tell where the treasure was. They couldn't find it in our things. I told them nothing until I heard cries and screams from the adjoining room. I couldn't stand it. So I told . . ."

"Oh, you didn't?" She gasped and paled. She saw all their work gone for naught.

"No, I didn't tell them where it was because I don't know myself. I made up a tale about having lost it when we were attacked by the Askaris' machine-gun troop and having to run for our lives. But that just put us in more hot water because they're now taking us back over the trail to find the treasure. If we don't find it we'll REALLY be in the soup."

Bill snickered and chuckled to himself. The two turned on him.

"And now, Bill," asked Dick, "where in the world IS the stuff?"

"Sshhhh! Quiet, Chief. Ah got hit wha they ain't nevah gonna find it in uh million yeahs. Jes don' ask me 'cause they liable tuh make yuh tell, an' if yuh don' know you cain't."

"But they've searched all our things, Bill. If they couldn't find it, I don't see where you could have put it. There are at least a pint of those gems."

"That's all right, boss. Don't worry. Ah'm lookin' out foh yuh."

"Yes, but what do you think is going to happen when they don't find the jewels? You heard that renegade say we'd die by inches, didn't you?"

"Yeah, Ah heard him," said Bill, nodding wisely. "We bettah cross that bridge when we git to it. Don't worry. Ah knows wha th' stuff is, an' Ah ain't gonna tell."

"Sssshhh!" cautioned the princess. "Here comes Resta."

The Duke of Dessaye was cantering back toward them. He showed his gleaming white teeth in a smile and moved his donkey close.

"I trust Your Grace is enjoying the journey," he remarked, lifting his helmet. "And you, too, Meester Welland." He spoke with the usual irritating mockery in his voice.

There was no reply. The princess drew as far away as she could. The duke's little eyes blazed. He controlled himself with difficulty.

"I think it an excellent idea for you to ignore me now, Your Grace," he almost hissed, "because you will have such a long time to be so very close to me."

"What do you mean?" she flared, her face flushed to the hairline.

"I scarcely think the statement requires elucidation, Your Grace," he mocked. "I am vain enough to believe that I used excellent English. Didn't I, Meester Welland?"

"Now see here, you rat," Dick flared. "Whatever you're going to do to me, do it. But leave her out of it. She doesn't want your game and you know it. Why don't you leave her alone?"

"Ah, you love her, eh?" the duke grinned an enjoyment his cold little eyes did not reveal. "Well, that will make marrying her all the sweeter to me. It will be a glorious wedding, indeed. I shall let you see it, my friend, before you die."

"So that's it, eh?" Dick stormed. "Well, suppose I refuse to take you to the treasure. Since I am going to die anyhow, why should I accommodate you?"

"Now, now, Meester Welland," Ras Resta soothed, "don't get excited. You are usually quite cool, except when someone is getting tortured." The man's eyes twinkled and he chuckled when Dick started as if pin-pricked. "I see Her Grace has informed you that she was untouched. Very clever of me, wasn't it, Meester Welland? One of the native women substituted. It is quite an old trick, quite an old trick. Have you never heard of this in America? . . . Well, I shall see you again . . . soon."

He cantered back to the two Italian officers, his loud throaty laugh echoing back from the high mountains on their left. Dick gritted his teeth grimly and gazed straight ahead.

It was late in the afternoon when they reached again the point on the precipitous trail where they had rounded the shoulder of the mountain behind the camouflaged donkeys to escape the machine-gun fire. There was already nothing left of the dead Ethiopian soldier except a few particles of flesh still sticking to his skeleton. The vultures, scavengers of the tropics, had done their work well.

"Now, my friends," said Ras Resta, coming back to where they were halted with the Askaris all about them, "this is the place. You will go down there and find the jewels and bring them back. Understand? You will be covered by machine guns at all times. Farther up the canyon one of our patrols waits to cut you off in case you should foolishly decide to make a break for it. You already know that we control the mouth of the canyon. Now any peculiar move on your part and these restless young men will be disposed to doubt your motives and shoot. They are very good shots, too. They scarcely ever miss. . . . All right, now. Get going! Over the side!"

The canyon was extremely steep, not quite perpendicular, but so steep that only a few scraggly bushes grew here and there. The soldiers and their officers grinned and jested as the trio made its way slowly down the side. Sometimes they yelled advice in Italian and Somali as the three came to an especially difficult place.

The princess's soft hands were soon scratched and bruised. Perspiration ran down her face in streams as she struggled to maintain her footing. The two men tried to make it easier for her but they could scarcely do better than she. What made it seem even more difficult was the knowledge that there was nothing down there for them to find; that each moment brought nearer the time when they would have to tell their captors they could find nothing. Finally the princess sank down, exhausted.

"I . . . I . . . I'm afraid I'll have to rest," she gasped. "I can't go on."

Dick sprang to her side, wiped her beautiful face with his soiled handkerchief, fanned her with it. She gave him a wan, grateful smile. He looked above to the trail. Captain Fraschetti and the machine gunners were watching them closely.

Bill pretended to keep looking around, going 25 to 50 yards to the right and left. Finally he worked his way back to Dick and the princess.

211

"Guess we betteh go on back now," he suggested.

"What's that?" asked Dick in surprise. "Go back for what? You know what it means, don't you?"

"Ah reckon Ah got uh joker in th' hole," he said, smiling knowingly. "Come on, Meester Welland. You cain't lose with old Bill lookin' out for yuh. Ef Ah don't fool them Eyetalians, it'll s'prise me. Ah really gotta good bet, Chief."

Thus assured, Dick helped the somewhat recovered princess to climb back to the trail. It took a long time and the sun was rather low. When at last willing hands pulled them up on the trail, they were so weary they fell exhausted in the dirt.

"Well," said Ras Resta, grinning sardonically, "did you find them?" Behind him were assembled the Italian officers and the black soldiers.

"We found th' bag," announced Bill, holding up the leather "but somebody musta found it 'fore we did. They ain't nuthin' in it."

Ras Resta Gusa snatched the bag, looked into it, felt into it, then turned it inside out. It was completely empty except for a tiny sliver of diamond caught in the seam.

The man stood nonplussed, at a loss for words, his jaws sagging open. The two Italian officers shot a barrage of questions at him, cursing, apparently threatening. He hunched his shoulders, pleaded almost tearfully in Italian. They were all beaten. They had been so sure of getting the jewels and now someone had got to them before they did.

They presented such a doleful, discouraged picture that Dick could not help laughing. Ras Resta turned on him like an animal.

"Hah! You think it funny, eh? Well we shall show you something REALLY FUNNY, my friend, when we get back to the village."

Glumly the party retraced its steps. The Italians and the Ethiopian were angry and chagrined, in a mood to vent their sadism upon the prisoners. The princess with difficulty concealed her alarm over Ras Resta's threat to force her into marriage with him. Dick was furrowing his brow over the whereabouts of the priceless jewels he had turned over to his valet. Only Bill Sifton seemed unruffled. He rode along contentedly humming a barroom ditty.

The party made good time to the mouth of the canyon, but even before they reached it the sun was almost behind the mountains and the light was rapidly falling. The Italians ordered a faster speed and the black Somalis lengthened their stride.

As they came out of the canyon and turned right toward the village, a droning sound caused all eyes to look upward. Like a sparrow, a lone plane was darting across the sky, high in the air, making for the village. It was so high that it was impossible to distinguish the markings. They watched it as it circled and rapidly descended. It was, they assumed, another plane from the Italian air base. It was flying low now a couple of miles off.

Suddenly there was a gust of smoke followed by a burst of flame and in a moment the sound of an explosion reached them. Now the little plane rose and circled again high above the flames from the bomber near the village. Consternation swept the Italian ranks. At a command they hurried forward on the run as the flames from the village rose high. It was obvious that the little destroyer was not an Italian plane. Could it be Ethiopian? Dick hoped against hope.

Down came the plane again in a dive straight at the village. Smoke and flames were left in its wake and the approaching party could hear the explosion of the incendiary bombs. Before they had come a mile closer the entire village was in flames. Soldiers were running frantically in all directions. The villagers had run off to one side. It was fortunate that they did. Or perhaps it was by design.

At any rate the little plane came down, roaring close to the ground. In the rapidly gathering darkness the approaching party could see its two machine guns spitting flames like geese before a shotgun.

Dick pulled his donkey close to the princess and signaled to Bill.

"It's an Ethiopian. He'll probably turn on this column next. When he starts firing, stay right where you are, take off your hats and wave them. The Italians will scatter. That will make you conspicuous. Understand?"

"Ah gotcha," said Bill.

"You're right, Dick," she agreed. "I'll bet it's Yamrou."

"Ah know 'tis," Bill remarked.

"How do you know?" asked Dick.

Before Bill could reply, what Dick surmised happened. The attack plane swerved from its village target and sped toward the approaching column, flying low. The Italians blew whistles and screamed commands. The soldiers sprang from the road and began to scatter in skirmish formation, but before they could half complete it the little asp was upon them spitting death.

Panic-stricken, no one stopped to fire on the oncomer. Back and forth went the plane spreading death. Dick, Bill and the princess stood absolutely still in the center of the road, an island in the sea of pandemonium.

Now the plane zoomed up a few hundred feet. Down came two red flares. From the mountains on the right came answering shouts. It was now almost dark but Dick and his party could see the hills fairly alive with white-cloaked Ethiopian warriors who had probably been hiding there all the time.

There were yells, shouts and screams as they converged on the Italian soldiers. Around the nearby village, now a sheet of flames, there were scenes of sanguinary conflict as the Italians waged a losing fight against the Ethiopian soldiers and the revolting villagers.

Dick, Bill and the princess continued to wave their helmets. Finally the plane came down about a quarter of a mile from them. Two black pilots jumped out, looked cautiously about, then one of them approached the trio with drawn automatics. He was a tall, thin man with sparse black beard, bushy hair under his helmet and dressed in a khaki uniform splattered with oil. Dick recognized him at once.

"Yamrou!" he yelled. "Here we are with the princess."

He came up and bowed low to the princess.

"Dedjasmatch Yamrou is sorry," he said, "that the princess have trouble. There is spy somewhere tell Italians when you leave Abra Destum. But ever' theeng is good now." He waved his hand in a broad semi-circle to indicate the scene of carnage. From every direction now were coming

214

cries and shots as the little garrison of Italians was slowly being decimated.

Yamrou explained to the princess that he had waited and waited at the rendezvous appointed and wondered why they had not arrived. Then had come an Ethiopian woman from the village with a little note to one of the Ethiopian outposts in the nearby mountains telling of the capture of the party. The outpost commander relayed the news to Yamrou who immediately got into action.

"But who sent the note?" asked Dick. "We didn't."

"Ah did, boss," Bill spoke up.

"You?" chorused Dick and the princess.

"Yeah, Ah tell youh how 'twas. When them Eyetalians got us 'n' took us tuh that village Ah figured we'd need all th' help we could git. So Ah jist wrote, 'Held in village by Eyetalians,' and signed 'Princess Zunda' on a little piece of scrap paper Ah had. When we gits in th' town, Ah gits uh chance tuh whisper tuh one o' them good-lookin' Ethiopian browns an' slip her a piece o' change. All Ah say is 'Dedjasmatch Yamrou' two or three times 'cause Ah don't know her lingo, see? Well, she savvyed all right."

"Splendid, Bill. It saved our lives. There's no telling what would have happened if they'd got us back to that village after not getting the jewels." Dick patted the little fellow on the shoulder.

Dedjasmatch Yamrou pulled out a whistle and blew several blasts upon it. Answering whistles came from the darkness. In a few minutes the Ethiopians began to assemble, coming in by the dozen, by the score, by the company. In an hour almost a thousand were gathered outside the town. Most of them were carrying some article of Italian equipment or uniform, evidence enough that the Italians had been wiped out.

The Ethiopians led by Yamrou now marched to the village. Dick, the princess and Bill rode in front of Dedjasmatch. Only a few smoldering ruins remained but two or three of the most solidly built houses remained intact, though blackened by smoke and flames. In one of these houses Yamrou established headquarters. The alleys were strewn with debris and abandoned equipment and the unburied bodies of Italians and Somalis, some horribly mutilated. On the outskirts of the village stood the blackened skeleton of the giant Italian bomber which had brought Captain Fraschetti and Ras Resta Gusa to this isolated place.

Dick wondered if they had suffered the same fate as the other Italians massacred by the enraged Ethiopians.

When they descended from their donkeys, Bill disappeared with some mumbled excuse while Dick and the princess went into the house with Dedjasmatch Yamrou. The place was in fairly good order except that there were signs aplenty that the Italians left there hurriedly. In the largest room a table was set for a dinner that never came off, and in the adjoining room there was still food on the field stove. Yamrou's servants soon made everything spic and span and went about preparing the evening meal. Yamrou assured Dick and the princess that there was no large force of Italians within a hundred miles. His men had reported to him that the local Italian force had been exterminated as far as they could ascertain.

At this juncture Bill Sifton entered with a big yellow bar of laundry soap in his hand and a broad smile on his face.

"Well, boss," he chortled, "Ah got it."

"Got what?"

"Dem jewels, of course. Ah'm suttinly uh smart joker. Stuff was right wha Ah lef' it when they tole us tuh drop our bundles."

"Well . . . !"

"Well," echoed Bill, beaming and handing Dick the big yellow bar of soap, "heah 'tis."

Dick frowned and turned the laundry soap over in his hands and then looked at Bill with a puzzled expression. Bill snatched back the soap and while the others watched in fascination, he took his knife and cut the long bar through the narrow way from top to bottom. They leaned forward and gasped as he revealed the sparkling treasure of gems in the scooped-out bar.

"W'en you give me them stones," he explained, "Ah figgered we might get in uh jam so Ah put 'em wha I figgered they wouldn't be foun'. Ah knows these Eyetalians an' Ethiopians ain't so strong on bathin'. W'en they searched our stuff they didn't pay no 'tenshun to that soap. Ah come back an' found it right with th' rest of our stuff."

216

Over the dinner table Dick, the princess and Dedjasmatch Yamrou held a little council of war with Bill Sifton listening in. There was obviously no time to be lost. In the first place, there was no assurance that Captain Fraschetti and Ras Resta Gusa had been slain with the others. If not, they might be able to communicate in some way with the Italian head-quarters with the result that a swarm of planes would soon be swooping down upon them. In the next place, Dedjasmatch Yamrou had said that the Ethiopians were on their last legs unless they could get more arms and ammunition, immediately.

"We mus' leave in the morning," declared Yamrou. His gravity gave the impression that it would be dangerous to tarry longer.

"Why not tonight?" asked Dick. "That field out there is quite level. You can put your men around it with torches. We'll leave all our equip-ment here. That will lighten the load. We can get to Beni Shengui in a little over an hour, refuel and be on our way to Khartoum and get there by morning. From there we can take a plane direct to Alexandria, and with luck we should be in Marseilles by evening."

"Oh, if we only could," the princess exclaimed. "Can we do it, Dedjas-match?"

"Ver' dangerous," he said quietly, "but can do."

"All right," said Dick, pushing back his chair, "let's get going. I can't get out of here any too soon."

Once it was decided to go, things began moving with great speed. Dedjasmatch Yamrou bellowed commands and soldiers began running hither and yon getting material for flares. Dick, the princess, Bill, and the tall commander hastened to the little airplane guarded by a squad of soldiers. Yamrou and his co-pilot went over the engine and checked the gasoline and oil. Meantime the soldiers ran to their positions a mile on each side and ignited their flares.

Dedjasmatch Yamrou gave final orders to his second in command. Dick, the princess and Bill clambered in the best they could. The co-pilot stayed behind. The commander took his seat. The engine roared and the propeller whirled. Across the flat lava bed the little plane sped, and less than half way down the lighted square it left the earth and sped west-ward toward Beni Shengui.

It was an hour of extreme discomfort for the four people crowded in the cramped quarters intended for two persons, but it was an hour speeding toward freedom. The moon was shining brightly, for which they all sent up a prayer of thanks. Inconvenienced though they were, they were thrilled by the wild Ethiopian scenery.

At a little before nine o'clock, they sighted the lights of Beni Shengui. Yamrou circled the field, dropped five or six flares and landed neatly with scarcely a jar. They all piled out and stretched their limbs. Yamrou bellowed commands and in a few moments a stream of soldiers each bearing a five-gallon can of gasoline came pouring out of the village. The gas tank was slowly filled as Yamrou's mechanics went carefully over the engine.

It is 450 miles northward as the crow flies from Beni Shengui to Khartoum. While the finishing touches were being put on the plane, the four travelers conferred again. Dick was anxious for Dedjasmatch Yamrou to get the radio station at Khartoum so that arrangements could be made to charter an English plane and have it waiting when they arrived.

"No, no, no!" the Ethiopian objected. "Ver', ver' bad. Italian station pick up. Italian plane shoot us down quick, quick."

"He's right, Dick," added the princess. "It would be foolish to chance it now that we're so close to freedom. So far they don't know where we are. Let's keep them in the dark as long as we can. When we get to Khartoum, we can telephone to Cairo or Alexandria for a plane."

Dedjasmatch Yamrou nodded his bushy head. Dick realized how foolish it would be to run any chance of letting the Italians know where they were, and promptly gave up his idea.

It was a little after ten o'clock when the trusty little plane roared into action again and sped down the field toward the line of flares that marked the end. Something over half way it took the air and just barely skimmed the tall trees that bordered the field.

The occupants were as cramped as ever, although they carried nothing except themselves, a canteen of water and the precious bar of yellow soap. Wedged in the narrow space, they were scarcely able to move, and yet with each mile they breathed more freely, knowing they were that much nearer to safety. The moon was still shining brightly and the swiftly moving scene below them was one of great beauty. Soon after starting they caught sight of the Blue Nile. They kept sight of it until the towers and minarets of Khartoum loomed up straight ahead.

It was almost one o'clock when Dedjasmatch Yamrou circled the airport and made a good landing on the concrete runway. Turbaned black soldiers raced across the field toward them, their bayonets gleaming in the bright moonlight. A white officer followed.

The formalities were soon completed. The trio had nothing to declare and their passports were in order. Dedjasmatch Yamrou was permitted to depart after refueling with the thanks of Dick, the princess and Bill ringing in his ears, and her promise to hasten the needed munitions. Dick inquired about the plane north to Cairo and Alexandria on the regular schedule.

"It leaves at eight o'clock in the morning," the agent said, shortly.

"Is there any way of getting out of here before that time? Isn't it possible to charter a plane?"

"It would cost a small fortune," objected the agent, smiling condescendingly.

"That's not the point," snapped Dick. "The cost doesn't bother us."

"Well, well, I'll see. Just sit down." The agent reached for his telephone, dialed a number. There was a long wait.

The princess sat leaning on Dick's shoulder, half asleep. Bill nodded nearby. It had been a strenuous day. They all needed rest badly.

The agent began talking to someone over the telephone. Finally he looked up, placing his hand over the mouthpiece.

"It will cost you two hundred pounds," he said. "Can you pay it?"

"Of course we can pay it, although that's sort of high, isn't it? We're only twelve hundred miles from Alexandria."

"Well that's what this pilot is charging, and there's no other one in town who can fly one of our big passenger planes. You'll either have to take him or await the regular plane."

"All right," said Dick, after a moment's hesitation, "tell him to come on. We don't want any delay."

A half hour later a small open car drove up with a young couple inside. It was the pilot and his wife.

"I'll have to have my money right now," he said, eyeing Dick and evidently expecting this big Negro to hem and haw.

"Very well. Will you take American Express checks?" Dick fumbled under his shirt, finally opened one of the pockets of his money belt and pulled out a book of the traveler's checks. He borrowed the agent's pen to sign a thousand dollars' worth. Then he called Alexandria about chartering a plane.

219

The pilot watched and listened with widened eyes and growing respect. His young wife kissed him goodbye and drove back home in the car.

It took but a few moments for the husky black mechanic to trundle one of the big passenger planes out of its hangar, fill up its tanks and prepare it for the trip. The three piled in gratefully and sank back in the upholstered chairs.

The English pilot started the engine, turned the plane around and then shot down the runway, northward to the Mediterranean, following the silvery course of the Nile.

It was their first real rest since they had left the cozy subterranean quarters of Gunsa Hernum. The hum of the engine lulled them to sleep. And as the plane hurtled through the moonlit night they were lost in slumber. They had outwitted the Italian Secret Service at last. Or had they?

◈◈◈Chapter 27

When Dick woke up it was already day. A brilliant sun was drenching the Nile Valley, its green fields and its pretty white villages with incandescent light. He glanced at his wrist watch. It was seven o'clock. They had been in the air four hours and should be approaching Cairo. He looked out the window to his right and there, sure enough, far beyond the stately pyramids, were the glistening towers of the ancient capital.

The princess was still asleep, a pretty picture in sepia, her head nodding slightly as the big plane took the air pockets and bumps. Bill Sifton was snoring loudly enough to almost drown out the muffled hum of the powerful engines.

Dick smiled to himself. Yes, they had certainly thrown the Italians completely off the trail. Even if Ras Resta Gusa and Captain Fraschetti had escaped, he reasoned, they could not possibly find their way until daylight and might have to hide several days from the vengeful Ethiopian guerrillas of Dedjasmatch Yamrou. But if they did escape and did get in touch with an Italian outpost, it would be unlikely to have a field radio. And if it did have one they could do no more than tell headquarters at Addis Ababa that their quarry had escaped. Another thing in their favor, thought Dick, was the fact that the Italians, or rather Captain Fraschetti and the duke, very likely believed that the jewels HAD been lost in the deep gorge enroute from Mount Abra Destum to the point where the Italian soldiers waylaid the convoy.

All in all, there was little to worry about. He had been smart enough to telephone American Vice-Consul Derek Sullivan in Alexandria to make arrangements for chartering the plane to France, and doubtless these arrangements would be completed when they landed in Alexandria. If so, no time would be lost and they ought to be in Europe that night, with a good chance that the Italians were completely thrown off the trail.

He glanced across the way. The princess had awakened but there was still sleep in her eyes. He felt he could stand some more sleep himself. So much had happened in the 24 hours since they had left the cozy subterranean quarters of Gunsa Hernum in the bowels of sacred Mount Abra Destum. But a little over 48 hours had elapsed since they had taken off in the little plane piloted by Yamrou for the flight from Beni Sengui to the mountain treasury. And just 72 hours had gone since their chartered plane had left Alexandria with the goodbye of Vice Consul Sullivan ringing in their ears on the quest into the unknown.

Airplanes made such a difference. The same journey by any other available transportation would have taken weeks and weeks. Now it was merely a matter of hours. Who knew where they would be a week hence? He stretched his legs and arms, then looked over to where the princess was trying desperately to remove the ravages of sleep by vigorously massaging her cheeks.

"Want me to do that?" he offered, grinning.

"Oh, you musn't look," she complained with mock seriousness, "until I've finished. It's terrible for a lady to have to be traveling without even a powder puff or rouge."

"You're just as pretty without them."

"Now, don't try to flatter me, Dick. I know I look terrible."

"But you don't, darling. Really," he insisted, slipping into the seat beside her and pressing his left arm about her. "You look beautiful to me under any and all circumstances. May I have one kiss?"

"Well," she held her lips up to him, "just one. Remember, we've got work. . . ." His lips over her lips smothered the rest.

She looked around guiltily to see if Bill was looking. He was, and smiling broadly.

"Bill, I think you're mean. You might at least close one eye."

All three laughed at that.

Cairo was rapidly left behind and in a few minutes they were coming to the great seaport, Alexandria, where for 3,000 years Orient and Occident have met. Soon they were over the city and approaching the airport. Speed slackened. They fastened their safety belts. The plane flew down the field, then banked sharply, straightened out and came back to a perfect stop.

Attendants ran out with portable steps and baggage carts. The three hurried out of the plane. In the little knot of people gathered near the plane, Dick spied Sullivan, the tall, young American vice-consul, who came forward, beaming.

A few minutes later they were driving out to the American Legation for breakfast.

"I've chartered a plane for you," said the young diplomat as they sped down the palm-lined avenue. "It's French. It will take you direct to Antwerp, stopping enroute at Tunis and Marseilles. You should get to your destination late tonight."

"When do we leave?"

"The plane will be ready at eleven o'clock or just as soon as we settle the financial end. It is costing a lot of money."

"That's nothing. The speed is worth it. I trust you haven't mentioned my name. You know the Italians have spies everywhere."

"Yes, I know," Sullivan reassured him. "No names were used. They only know that the plane has been chartered for a wealthy American through the good offices of the consulate. I'll have your draft cashed and pay them in advance before you show up."

It was all done in good order. While they refreshed themselves and had something to eat, Derek Sullivan made all the financial arrangements.

At 10:45 in the morning they jumped into his car again and sped back to the airport. Shortly afterward they boarded the big French transport plane and in a few minutes they were winging their way toward Tunis. They arrived a little after 5 o'clock.

There was a stop of an hour during which they had dinner brought out to the plane while it was refueling and undergoing careful inspection for the long flight across the Mediterranean. Thanks to Derek Sullivan, the American consul in Tunis arranged to have several native police detailed to keep anyone away from the plane.

"Oh, darling," she sighed. "I'll be so relieved. This has been a hard assignment but you have made it easy. I should never have succeeded if it hadn't been for you, Dick."

"So, now I suppose you'll say 'yes' when I ask you to marry."

"Well, just wait until this job is over with, Mr. Welland," she said smiling, the color in her cheeks deepening. "The Emperor comes first, you know."

"You mean Ethiopia comes first."

"Yes, that's what I mean, Ethiopia."

The big plane droned on over the Mediterranean. In a rear seat Bill Sifton slouched, a suspicious bulge in the front of his khaki shirt.

"Well, Bill," said Dick, "I see you're still hanging on to that bar of soap."

"It ain't nevah lef' me, boss, an' hit ain't gonna. We bin through too much to lose this now, 'cause Ah done bin tuh Ethiopia mah las' time. Believe me!"

The happy couple laughed. The motors ahead droned ceaselessly, inviting slumber. Dick dozed off. When he awakened suddenly as the plane took a bump, his watch told him that they should be approaching Marseilles. The glow of its lights loomed over the horizon. Not long afterward they landed. It was nine o'clock.

While the plane took on more petrol, the princess sent a telegraph to the Emperor. It consisted of only one word and was unsigned.

That word was "Success."

◈◈◈Chapter 28

It was almost midnight when their plane set down on the Antwerp air-field and brought their eventful journey to an end. When they had gone through the routine customs and passed beyond the barrier, a distin-guished-looking elderly brown man of medium height stepped up, smil-ing with outstretched arms. With a little scream of delight Princess Zunda fell into his embrace.

"Daddy," she said finally, "this is Mr. Richard Welland who has made it possible for me to carry out this job. Dick, this is my father, Prince Dano Zunda, the Emperor's brother."

The two men shook hands cordially.

"We must go now," said the prince. "My car is waiting without. I just drove in from Paris when I received notice from London that you were on your way. We are having an important conference at midnight."

They got into the big black limousine and Bill sat alongside the giant brown chauffeur. They threaded their way slowly through the giant streets of the Belgian metropolis to the Britannic Hotel. Registration over with, they took the lift to the suite Prince Dano had engaged.

In another hour they were refreshed and dressed in the clothing Prince Dano had procured. The nobleman was seated in the parlor of the suite with a tall, heavy-set blonde white man of Germanic caste features, and a small sharp-eyed man of dark mien who might have been an American or an Egyptian Jew. Prince Dano introduced the first man as a Herr Schnubbel and the second as Monsieur Malo. They were evidently eager to get down to the business at hand. They had waited for nearly an hour.

"Now, Ettara," began the prince, "we are first to get an appraisal of the jewels which Monsieur Malo will make right here. On the basis of this appraisal Herr Schnubbel will grant credits that will enable us to get arms for our men in the field. Herr Schnubbel represents Krupp's and is entirely responsible."

"Krupp's?" echoed Dick, unable to conceal his surprise. "But I thought the Italians and Germans were working together!"

M. Malo, Herr Schnubbel and Prince Dano smiled indulgently.

"You have evidently been reading the newspapers, my friend," snick-ered M. Malo, stroking his tiny beard. "This is business. Whatever the jewels are worth, they can be sold right here in Antwerp tomorrow for

224

gold. This is the world's diamond and jewel capital. Our German friends are very eager to get gold, and for that they are only too glad to exchange such munitions as any purchaser may desire. It is business, my friend."

"Ja," added Herr Schnubbel, "it iss business. And good business, too. Now, the jewels. Let us get down to our proposition."

"Yes, Ettara," added her father, "let's lose no time. These gentlemen have been waiting for almost an hour."

"Very well, father." Princess Ettara opened the large handbag she was carrying and removed the bar of yellow laundry soap. Everyone leaned forward. "Bill," she called, "bring me a knife, a basin of water and a towel."

Bill hurried in with these things. At her further order he cut through the middle of the bar of soap and, picking out the fortune in precious stones, he dropped them into the basin of warm water, washed the soap off them and placed them in the center of the large fleecy bath towel. The princess and the two white men gawked round-eyed at the treasure.

"Priceless! Priceless!" murmured M. Malo, rubbing his hands.

Herr Schnubbel grunted wiht satisfaction, his little protruding eyes glistening with avarice.

"All right, Monsieur Malo," said the prince, "suppose you get to work and appraise them. Every hour counts at this juncture."

The appraiser opened his black leather bag from which he took a powerful electric bulb and a shade, a long wire and a jeweler's eyepiece. Then seating himself at a small table Bill brought, he went to work while the others watched.

Minutes passed. A half hour went by. There was no sound except the occasional scratch of M. Malo's pen as he made notes and placed the individual jewels in separate little envelopes on which he penned a brief note of description and worth. An hour passed. Dick looked at his wrist watch. It was a little after two o'clock. The princess squeezed his hand and they smiled at each other. This was the end of their great adventure. Now they were ready for a greater one.

It seemed as if it had all been something of a dream, that reign of suspicion and intrigue on the *S.S. Metallic,* that wild flight across the Mediterranean, the nightmare in Ethiopia, the flight back and now together and safe here in this staid city of merchants and jewelers.

"Well," said M. Malo at last, looking up from his toil, "it is remarkable. I have never seen a collection like it. The stones are marvelously cut, as good as we can do today, yet some of them must be thousands of years old."

"How much are they worth?" the German blurted out, eager to get to the point.

"Not less than one hundred and fifty million francs," he announced dramatically.

"One hundred and fifty million francs!" echoed Schnubbel, his deep voice betraying his awe.

"That's a million pounds," exclaimed Prince Zunda.

"Five million dollars, to you," said the princess, looking up at Dick.

"That will buy a great deal of butter and gasoline, Herr Schnubbel," reminded the prince. "And now that you have the figures, what can you offer us?"

The German made some hasty calculations on a page of his memorandum book for several moments before he was prepared to speak. Then he was brief and to the point.

"For a million pounds we can give you much. You spoke of one hundred thousand rifles with one hundred fifty rounds apiece. That will cost a million and a half American dollars. You say you want ten bombing planes and twenty fighters. That will cost you seven hundred fifty thousand dollars. Your five hundred machine guns will cost forty pounds apiece or a total of twenty thousand pounds. For your five hundred machine guns you will need at least two thousand rounds apiece, which cost two thousand pounds. This will take up half the value of your jewels. Then, you need field radio sets and medical supplies. You will have almost half of your credit left."

"And how soon can delivery be made, and where?" asked Prince Dano.

"We shall make the deliveries through the Sudan within six weeks."

"But isn't that British territory?" objected Dick.

They all laughed except Princess Ettara. Their cynical peals of mirth somewhat relieved the solemnity of the occasion.

"There will be no difficulty, my friends," said Schnubbel. "It will go down to the Ethiopian boundary as agricultural material bound for Uganda which, of course, it will never reach. Prince Dano and I have done business before. Eh, Prince?"

Prince Dano smiled. He and Herr Schnubbel went to one side to discuss something privately. In a short while the German left an important-looking document with the Ethiopian nobleman, took the jewels and he and Monsieur Malo departed.

Prince Dano discreetly retired to his room. The lovers sank back on the sofa and looked triumphantly at each other. It was all over.

"Well, my dutiful little princess," he said, "now that you have done your little job for Ethiopia, how about giving me a break? Shall we get married tomorrow?"

She squeezed his hand and her eyes sparkled mischieviously.

"Why tomorrow? Why not today? We ought to be able to get enough sleep between now and when the license bureau opens this morning. Don't you think so, darling?"

"And how!" He took her in his arms and held her close.

Just then, the door opened and Bill Sifton came in rubbing his eyes sleepily and yawning.

"If you ain't wantin' me no mo', Ah'm gonna git me some sleep," he complained.

"Ah ain't no English. Ah'm American," growled Bill, going out.

"And now," said the Princess, snuggling closer, "I'm going to be an American, too."

The End